Salmon River Kid

Also in this series by Joseph Dorris

SHEEPEATER: TO CRY FOR A VISION
SOJOURNER OF WARREN'S CAMP

Salmon River Kid

Joseph Dorris

iUniverse LLC
Bloomington

SALMON RIVER KID

iUniverse books may be ordered through booksellers or by contacting:

iUniverse
1663 Liberty Drive
Bloomington, IN 47403
www.iuniverse.com
1-800-Authors (1-800-288-4677)

ISBN: 978-1-4917-2130-8 (sc)
ISBN: 978-1-4917-2132-2 (hc)
ISBN: 978-1-4917-2131-5 (e)

Library of Congress Control Number: 2014901027

Printed in the United States of America.

iUniverse rev. date: 03/05/2014

To the memory of Chuck Borland,
a friend who gave so much to others

Acknowledgments

MANY PEOPLE have inspired and encouraged me to write, and each has had a part in this book as in my others. A special thanks goes to my family—to my wife, Susan, who has always supported my many interests, including my writing, and who offered insight on the foods, dress, and culture of the times; to my sons, Scott and Tim, who accompanied me on numerous backpacking trips, including several to the Idaho Salmon River country; and to my daughter, Krystle, who always encouraged me to continue writing and helps as my assistant. Nothing would have been possible without my family.

As a boy, I grew up in McCall, Idaho, and wrote down the stories some of the pioneers of the region shared with me. Among these individuals were Sam and Jesse (Tim) Williams, Carmel Parks, Ray Beseker, and Dave Spielman. My father, William Dorris, a game warden and bush pilot, took me hunting in this country and related his stories, especially about the Sheepeater Indians. My brothers, George, Mike, Pat, and Bill, who are also bush pilots, have all shared their knowledge of the Salmon River wilderness and accompanied me on many trips as youngsters. My sister, Linda, read the manuscript, giving me valuable suggestions. Montana ranchers Jane Wertheimer and Jim Raths reviewed information on ranching.

Published sources included Johnny Carrey and Cort Conley's *River of No Return*; Sister M. Alfreda Elsensohn's two volumes, *Pioneer Days in Idaho County*; Bill Gulick's *Chief Joseph Country: Land of the Nez Perce*; Cheryl Helmers's *Warren Times,* a compilation of news articles of the Warren region; and Dr. Liping Zhu's *A Chinaman's Chance.* I also used various articles on the Chinese of Warren from part of the Payette National Forest Heritage Program written by Lawrence Kingsbury, Kathleen Prouty, and Sheila Reddy. Technical mining information was based on Leonard S. Austin's *The Fire Assay*, Ronald C. Brown's *Hard-Rock Miners: The Intermountain West*, Frank Crampton's *Deep Enough*,

Will Meyerriecks's *Drills and Mills*, Otis E. Young's *Western Mining*, and the General Mining Act of 1872.

The cover is from my oil painting titled *Snow Whiskers,* and the line drawings are my pen-and-ink sketches.

Author's Notes

As a young teenager, while I was looking for a quartz ledge near Warren's camp (Warren, Idaho), Tim Williams, a longtime prospector, pointed out to me a scarcely visible cabin, nearly crushed by fallen timber. "That's where some of the Chinese lived that placered this hillside." I could see the distinctive cobbles lining the gulch behind the cabin. "Last time I was in that cabin, the dishes were still on the table. I don't know what happened to the Chinese, though." That experience and others sparked within me a longing to learn more about these and the other inhabitants of Warren's camp and the Salmon River country. *Salmon River Kid* is based on some of these long-ago inhabitants' stories.

In 1871, a teenage white boy and a teenage Chinese boy resided in Washington (Warren), Idaho Territory. Among other historical people were Frederick, Susan, and their son, George Shearer, at their ferry (now the Howard Ranch); Fred Burgdorf at his hot springs; Warren Hunt; Charlie and Polly Bemis; Sheriff Sinclair; Dr. C. A. Sears; and R. McLane. Historical vignettes involving these people are accurate, and readers will recognize other historical individuals used in context. The ways in which the fictionalized versions of these individuals interact with Samuel Chambers and his father have, of course, been invented. Life at Warren's camp and along the Salmon River, as represented here, is based on historical accounts of the time.

The raft trip down a portion of the Salmon River is based on the actual river rapids in the sections above Lucile Bar. The Chinese somehow managed to navigate the Salmon on rafts when carrying gold to Lewiston. One account cites several Chinese being held up by highwaymen, but rather than lose their gold to the highwaymen, they cut the straps and allowed the bags of gold to drop into the river.

During the time period of this novel, miners wintered on the bars along the Salmon River and managed to recover enough gold to pay for grub until they were able to return to their richer placers and quartz mines in the mountains. Several of the original families of Warren's left their claims and businesses to homestead on the river at a lower elevation, where they raised gardens and stock.

Ranch life at Slate Creek is based on historical descriptions of the town and accounts of the lives of settlers, some of whom purchased land from the Nez Perce and built businesses to support and supply the mining camps that were scattered throughout the Idaho wilderness.

All geography—the rivers, canyons, lakes, and mountains—is described as it is. Although some of the trails are lost, the routes and ferry crossings described are accurate. What was Elk Creek in 1872 is now named Elkhorn Creek. Meadow Creek is now named Warren Creek. The mines and mills that are depicted and the events surrounding them are historically correct. Bradshaw's mill is based on the first mill to refine silver ores. The Sweet Mary and the O'Riley are fictional but based on similar mines. Most of Warren's buildings have disappeared, but they included the businesses depicted, except for some names like Ma Reynolds's boardinghouse and Hinley's assay building. Little evidence of the Chinese structures remains. The hand-washed windrows of cobbles mark the Chinese placers. The Chinese cemetery remains. The Chinese terrace gardens remain, now overgrown and returning to the land.

Chinese continued moving into Idaho Territory during this novel's setting, eventually widely outnumbering the white miners. Many reworked the old placers. Others supported their countrymen as merchants, packers, saloon keepers, gardeners, and doctors. They brought China with them, including their opium, gambling, and religion. Most never returned to China but drifted away from Warren as the placers became depleted. Ah Kan, the last Chinese person to inhabit Warren, died in 1934.

Polly Bemis, at nineteen years old, is depicted arriving by pack train in the summer of 1872. Kan Dick is based on Ah Kan and Lee Dick, two Chinese doctors who resided in Warren. Sang Yune depicts Ah Toy, a gardener and merchant who tended the Celedon Chinese gardens on the slopes above the South Fork of the Salmon River.

This region is on the western edge of Sheepeater country, and the Sheepeater Indians depicted relate to characters in my first novel, *Sheepeater: To Cry for a Vision*. A forthcoming novel will bring the characters from the three novels together in depiction of the Sheepeater War of 1879.

I have tried to describe the life and times in Warren, Idaho, and along the Salmon River in the early 1870s as it was. Where possible, I have used the language, customs, dress, and practices of the times. For example, the term *Chinaman* simply referred to a person from China and was the proper and acceptable term of the day. Similarly, *Indian* was the common term used to describe Native Americans. The Chinese referred to the whites as "foreign devils" or the "white devil." I have generally avoided derogatory terms, but where used, they are intended to capture the reality of those times and are not used with malice or intent to offend.

I recognize that there may be errors in this depiction of the times of the 1870s and the historical events portrayed. In some cases, available sources are in conflict. Where I could determine the more accurate description, I have done so. However, I accept responsibility for any factual errors and welcome any corrections.

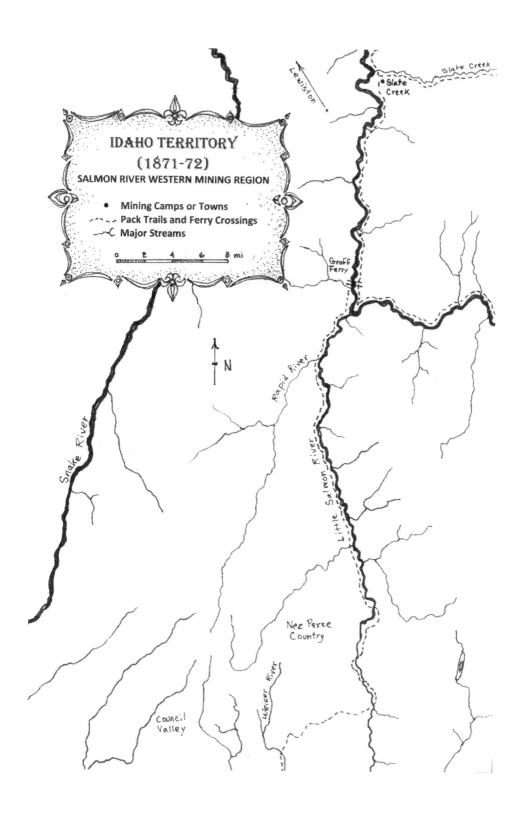

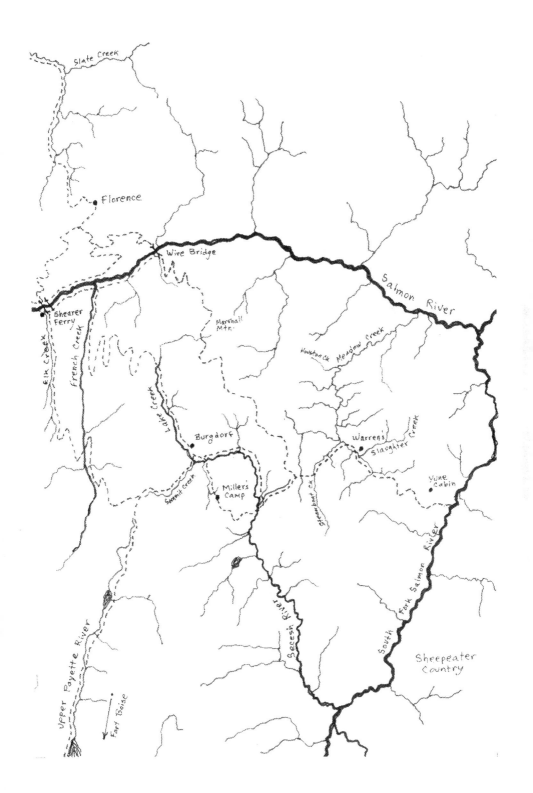

WINTERING

Chapter 1

SAMUEL CHAMBERS CLUCKED to Spooky, his four-year-old black gelding, encouraging him on in the heavily falling snow. The mule, Molly, trudged behind, carrying most of Samuel's and his father's gear. They were leaving Warren's camp and the high country and heading for lower elevation to winter on the Salmon River.

Samuel pulled his short tan frock coat more tightly about himself. He watched ahead to where his father concentrated on keeping his mahogany bay horse, Buster, on the trail, now blanketed in the snow that continued quickly to pile. Their animals were probably the last to be leaving the gold camp. He thought about the hardrock miners who remained behind and would work throughout the winter, and he reflected on the handful of townspeople who would keep Washington's saloons, boardinghouses, and mercantile stores open to support them. Soon the camp would be utterly snowbound—except by snowshoe—for at least six months, isolated from the nearest homestead by about forty-five miles. "At the end of the world," folks often told him.

They had topped Steamboat Summit above Warren's camp and were dropping toward the Secesh River and beyond, toward Fred Burgdorf's hot springs. The thought warmed Samuel. This past spring, his father and he had first visited Burgdorf during a similar snowstorm on their journey in.

He had expected to be headed home to Iowa by now. Such were their dreams. They had come out looking for a lost gold strike that his father's civil war comrade, Kevin O'Riley, had found, but O'Riley had died from a war injury before he could return to Idaho Territory in search of it. And while his father and he had not found it either, there was still a glimmer of hope. Samuel had discovered a good-looking quartz ledge, and the placer near their cabin had showed good gold before the water ran out. Each was reason enough to winter on the Salmon and to attempt another mining season. But Samuel wondered how they would survive the winter. Even if they found a place and had plentiful wild game, they had very little money for grub.

At Burgdorf's hot springs they paused for a swim. It was customary for the miners to do so, and one never knew the next opportunity he would have for a bath.

The hot water quickly eased Samuel's saddle fatigue. He recalled the first time he had bathed here. He had been embarrassingly skinny, and now that he was a couple of months shy of fifteen, people were finally not taking him for thirteen, like that old man Jenkins, who worked for Burgdorf, had. Jenkins had kidded him about girls but then laughed and said it didn't matter because there weren't any in the territory except one downriver at Slate Creek. Samuel's heart caught as he recalled the man's words. Slate Creek might not be far from where they would winter. He glanced down at himself—not as skinny as back then, but still not much of anything else either. Samuel wanted to believe he could finally see himself in his father's appearance—tall with solid shoulders and hands, sandy blond hair, and light blue eyes, although Samuel's eyes were more vivid.

Later, while dining on elk steaks, gravy, and potatoes, Samuel told Fred Burgdorf of their plans to winter on the river.

"Yah, you just spend the vinter there. Spring vill be here in no time. Maybe this year vill be your big year," he exclaimed, his watery blue eyes shining. Burgdorf was somewhat short in stature and solidly built. He had immigrated from Germany and come to Warren's camp in '64 as a placer miner. He had learned of the hot springs from the Chinese and staked a claim. Since then, he had built his place into a way station where he now provided hot meals, baths, and lodging.

Early in the morning, under a wintery blue sky, Charles and Samuel packed their mounts and said farewell.

"Need anything on our way back through next spring?" Charles asked.

"Yah, you just bring me some vhiskey. I'm tinkin' I vill be needing some after all this snow." Burgdorf snapped his suspenders and rocked forward, looking down a bit at Samuel and then back up at Charles as if to make certain neither would forget.

Charles laughed. "Trade you for a meal, then?"

"Yah, I vill."

Resuming their journey, Charles broke trail while Samuel and the mule followed. Samuel glanced around at the snow-blanketed meadows.

The snow lay over a foot deep. In the grip of winter, more than eight feet would accumulate. He wondered how Fred Burgdorf would survive while being isolated all winter.

As if reading his thoughts, his father spoke. "Mr. Burgdorf won't have it so bad. He can snowshoe over to Washington for some doin's, and Mr. Hunt will be bringing in the mail and news all winter."

"Just not any whiskey," Samuel said.

"I 'spect he has plenty," Charles admitted. "Whether or not he has any come spring will depend on how many travelers are through and how bad the snow gets."

The animals pushed through the new-fallen snow, and after a few hours, they reached the freight landing, a high point above the Salmon River where packers rested their stock and transferred supplies and equipment. From there, the narrow China trail, as some referred to it, descended steeply, dropping nearly five thousand feet in elevation over fifteen miles of tortuous switchbacks.

Samuel paused to gaze at the rugged, timber-covered mountains across the Salmon River canyon, now blanketed in white. The snow ended far below, where the timber thinned into grassy open ridges that cascaded downward before fading into purple shadows.

The trail plunged over the ridge, and they quickly descended, traversing steeply downward. Slowly, the snow diminished until the trail emerged as a muddy ribbon clinging to the hillside. Samuel recognized the spot where a passing pack train had nearly swept him from the trail during their trip in. He shivered and gazed down the barren, grassy face toward the ravine below—over a thousand feet—to where he could make out the mule carcass he knew was there.

By evening, they reached the Salmon River and turned downstream toward Frederick and Susan Shearer's cabin. A couple of flickering kerosene lamps swung on the cabin porch, winking in the dark, welcoming them. On their journey in, father and son had struck up a good friendship with the Shearers and their son, George. This was especially the case with Charles, who shared the Southern Uprising as a common bond with George, although they had served on opposite sides.

While Samuel related his adventures, he noticed Mrs. Shearer eyeing him as if looking at someone back from the dead. She had not changed. Similar to Mr. Shearer, she was slender, her face was pleasantly creased, and gray streaked her dark hair. Of course she and the others had heard bits and pieces about Samuel's accident and his encounter with the highwaymen, but his father and he had not visited with the Shearers since they had been through the previous spring.

"It's mighty fine to see you, Samuel," Mrs. Shearer exclaimed, looking him up and down. "I do believe the high country has treated you better than I thought it would. You so remind me of my George when he was your age, before he went off to war—same color of hair and eyes—so handsome."

Samuel felt himself flush. Mrs. Shearer was a lot like Ma Reynolds back in Washington, always fussing over him.

Charles briefly explained their plans. "We're looking for a cabin below here. Raymond Hinley indicated he thought a couple of fellows had started a homestead and had an acceptable winter placer. He said he did some assays for them a few years back."

"I know of a place about four miles west of us. I'm not sure if it's the same as what Mr. Hinley is thinking, but it might do you," Frederick Shearer explained. To Samuel, he appeared older, his hair was thinner, and his face seemed more strained, but his features hid a strength gained through years of rugged life.

"Two men spent a winter there. They might have been ne'er-do-wells. Never did come by our place after they got settled." He shook his head. "I checked it out. It's just a wide spot in the trail. Not enough land for a homestead. Don't know about any placer gold, though it wouldn't surprise me. There's gold up and down this entire river, but it takes more effort than I'm willing to give to get any."

Early in the morning, they led the stock to the ferry landing. The river murmured below—silvery with black shadows, edged in ice. The muted grays of the surrounding rock and hillsides reflected in its waters. The river no longer scared Samuel, not like last spring when it was near flood stage, pounding with whitewater.

Samuel helped lower the ramp and led the horses and mule aboard, where he tied them off. The ferry, a wide deck over two smaller boats, bobbed on the moving water. The animals stamped in nervous protest to its unstable movement. Samuel stroked Spooky's muzzle, talking to him and calming him.

"All set?" George asked, but not awaiting an answer, he took the sweep and angled the bow into the current. He struck up a conversation with Charles as if he had no cares in the world.

The ferryboat shuddered and then began moving across, pushed by the current. Samuel recalled Mr. Shearer's explanation, and he now understood how the current and angle kept them moving across without them slipping downstream and snapping the wire. "Mostly used for safety," Mr. Shearer had explained about the wire.

Samuel peered through the crystal water to the gravel and boulder-strewn bottom, watching for trout. The river was low, and they could have easily swum it with their horses, except their gear would have gotten wet. Some broken ice floated past. He shivered. Had they tried, they wouldn't have survived in the frigid water for long.

Leaving the ferry, they headed west and followed the river downstream. Like liquid night, it flowed silently through gray canyon walls, dismal and bleak. Neither summer light nor autumn color remained. The grass had bleached to muted tones, and the shrubs were naked and bare. The evergreens were dark, almost black. Rock formations stood stark and fractured, etched against the towering walls, and deep shadows filled the canyon.

Ahead, the river swept gently north and then back to the west, entering a section of unbroken cliffs that plummeted steeply into the river. Samuel recognized this as the place where his father and he had first encountered Quinton Dudgin and Ramey Smith and their partner, Clay Bender. Images of Dudgin murdering Bender sent a clammy chill through Samuel. He also recalled their intent to kill him as well since he had witnessed the murder. He now figured Dudgin and Smith were the men who had held up the Chinese pack string a month ago and the same men that his father and Sheriff Sinclair had chased into the canyon. He wasn't much worried. Most likely they were smart enough to leave the country.

He gazed at the sullen river sliding beneath the cliffs and hesitated. His eye caught on a section of sandbar and rock ledge that seemed to have been worked. He peered uphill, up the brushy draw toward a notch above. At one time, it could have been a trail.

"Pa, I think that cabin's here." He turned upward off the trail, forcing Spooky through thickets of elderberry and buckbrush toward a small flat.

They discovered the remains of a cabin nearly hidden from view by heavy brush. A portion of it was dug into the hillside. The cabin roof was largely caved in. Pack rats had moved in and built nests under the puncheon plank floor and the old bed frames. A stove sat in one corner, although the stovepipe was missing. The shutter covering a glassless window had come apart, and they found the door off its hinges in the brush to the side. Blackberry brambles grew thick across the bench. Were it not winter, it would have been excellent cover for rattlesnakes. Samuel shivered. He had almost been killed because of a rattlesnake.

"It ain't a garden spot," Charles said. He kicked at the door. "Guess it'll have to do."

They unloaded their gear, turned the stock loose, and immediately began making repairs.

Later, Samuel returned to the Shearers' and procured a length of stovepipe and some nails. George accompanied him on the return trip and helped them rebuild the roof.

"Might as well have built a new cabin," George said when they finally finished.

"Maybe so," Charles replied. "I'd invite you to stay for a cup of coffee, but we've run out since Washington."

George laughed. "I'd rather offer *you* some. As well as anything else you might need—maybe feed for your stock. There won't be enough grass up this valley." George nodded up the brush-choked creek that trickled down past the cabin toward the river.

"Much obliged. We'll manage for a while."

"If need be, we can winter your stock. We have good pasture. And if the winter gets too severe, we can trail them out to Slate Creek. It rarely gets snow farther downriver. Most of the packers winter there."

Samuel knew his father would not accept George's offer—not if they could manage things on their own.

George turned to go. "Come on upriver anytime you want to visit. Being you're a neighbor, there won't be a fare. Even if you are a Yankee."

"Mighty obliged," Charles replied.

George Shearer had spent much of the war in Union prisons. Nevertheless, Charles and he had put aside their differences. As George had pointed out, "I rarely met a Yankee who was tolerable of the South, let alone one who actually fought in the war." Most of the men who had come west did so to avoid the war.

Father and son stood a moment, watching George ride off. The emptiness and silence of the canyon quickly surrounded them.

"Guess we best get to work, son. We have a mighty big chore ahead of us before the winter clamps down."

They began putting in a store of firewood, which proved scarce. Only spindly, barren trees and briar-choked brush covered the grassy slopes above them. Eventually, they located a pile of driftwood caught on the upstream side of a sandbar along the river and hauled pieces to the cabin to be cut into firewood.

A few days later, a driving storm bringing a mixture of snow and sleet down the canyon revealed that their horses and mule were dangerously exposed. They began building a pole-and-brush shelter near the small creek under which the animals could huddle out of the wind.

Charles tossed more brush onto the shelter. "Maybe we won't get any placer mining in. Maybe all we do is survive the winter and get ready for next season."

"If that's so, I'd better get started hunting and bring in some meat."

"My thoughts exactly."

Their cabin and the bar faced south. This gave them a few hours of winter sun during the day, which somewhat warmed the cabin and hillsides above them. Otherwise, the cabin was in deep shadows or the grip of night. Samuel already felt the bleak, gray days pressing in, and spring seemed an eternity away.

After the storm, the snow evaporated from the exposed slopes, and the weather briefly warmed. Samuel discovered the remnants of a flume and sluice box scattered under the blackberry briars among the boulders where the men before them had been working the bank. Together they repaired the sluice and repositioned it near the excavation. A ditch had already been cut from the small creek across the hillside. They reopened it to bring water through a short wooden flume to the head of the sluice.

They began first by working the old excavation, carrying buckets of sand and gravel to the sluice, tossing out the larger stones, and allowing the water to wash the smaller material through the box. Black sand accumulated behind the cleats, along with a few tiny specks of gold.

The sight of gold sent a surge through Samuel, but he also recognized what he was seeing.

"This is nothing but flour gold—too fine to add up to anything," Charles confirmed.

"I saved about a pound of quicksilver, Pa. We can run the black sand and check." But Samuel knew what the results would be.

"No need. We'd best stockpile it for now, but I'd hate to find out all we've been collecting is ten cents' worth of gold a day."

Samuel nodded. They both knew. "What else are we going to do? It's a long time till spring." He piled the black sand under the blackberry brambles on some discarded boards. Maybe the gold would get better.

Chapter 2

THE TEMPERATURE CONTINUED to drop as the sun slid farther into the southern sky. It was well below freezing at night and frequently remained so throughout the day. A light snow soon covered the ground, and the water along the river's edge froze.

Occasionally, they visited the Shearers, purchasing some food and coffee and helping with chores whenever possible. They did some figuring based on supplies they would need to make it until spring. Unless they found more gold, the gold they had mined in Warren's would not get them through the winter.

Fortunately, game was plentiful, as animals moved out of the high country to escape the deepening winter snows. Mule deer came down into the draw above the cabin, and Samuel shot one whenever needed. Some days he hunted geese or ducks that gathered on the river. The first goose he shot seemed like a feast to them, but now they needed cornbread and beans and anything green to eat.

On the warmer days, father and son continued to try to wash sand from the bar, but after a few minutes, their fingers and hands became numb, and the black sand clumped into frozen chunks.

"I don't know how they did it," Charles said. "Supposedly, they mined these bars all winter."

"Then they must have built fires to thaw the gravel."

"Not enough gold to warrant that kind of work—not here, anyway."

"Maybe they concentrated on digging down to bedrock, and then during spring runoff, they washed what they had dug."

"We could do that," Charles replied. "Nothing much in the upper sand anyway—at least nothing we can see. To blazes, I hope there's some gold in all this." He waved at the growing pile of black sand.

They began clearing off a large area, shoveling the sand to the side, working downward to what they hoped would be gravel and rocks beneath.

Before Thanksgiving, Samuel guessed the temperature was near zero. Snow from the last storm lay in patches in the draws and sheltered areas and crunched underfoot. The peaks above the river were blanketed white. The ice continued to creep outward from shore, seizing the water, until only a few black ribbons flowed free. Steam rose from the few remaining open areas, where a few ducks and geese huddled.

They remained indoors, constantly tending a small fire, trying to keep warm. Although the sun shone, the temperature remained bitter cold.

Samuel helped his father prepare some grouse, which was their contribution to Thanksgiving dinner at the Shearers'. The Shearers said not to bring anything, just to come. His father insisted otherwise. A day ago, Samuel had hiked up the draw behind the cabin until he had reached the spruce trees where he knew grouse liked to roost. He found and killed two.

Later, they attempted baths since neither of them wished to be in a woman's company in his present condition. Thus far, baths had been little more than splashing themselves with cold water. This day they heated some water and filled the tub, soaping and sponging themselves off and rinsing their hair as best they could. They washed their clothes in what water remained and hung them in the corner of the cabin to dry, assisted by a crackling fire to speed the process.

"At least we won't smell like a couple polecats," Charles said, standing next to the stove. "Not so much, anyway."

That night, a frigid chill crept into the cabin and woke Samuel. Shivering, he rose and shoved a couple of pieces of wood into the stove. Frost coated the doorjamb. He quickly crawled back into his bed, pulling his coat over his blankets, his feet still stinging from the cold. He had never experienced temperatures this bitter.

In the morning, steam lifted from the river, and hoar frost dressed the world. Grass blades bent into long, icy sprays. The brush and trees donned tiny frost needles along their lengths.

The two waited until the sun flooded the canyon before taking to the trail. Even then, the sun seemed frozen, scarcely having enough energy to penetrate the haze of golden frost crystals. Buster and Spooky billowed clouds of steam into the air, crunching the soil under their hooves. Samuel thought of Warren's camp, which was much higher and colder and, by now, completely buried in snow. He thought of Mr. Hinley, who would be doing assays all winter. He could picture him near the furnace, pushing at his red hair or adjusting his spectacles. At least he would be warm.

When they reached the ferry, they waited for George to bring over the boat. The river flowed sullen and glassy, reflecting the muted gray winter colors. The ice reached out from the banks. Only the swift current kept it from freezing solid.

The boat crossed with ease, breaking the ice near the landing.

They led the horses aboard and tied them off.

"Here, Samuel. You take the sweep," George called to him.

Samuel gulped but took the rudder. "You sure?"

"I'll help you find the angle." George pushed the rudder against the current. The bow swung away from the landing. "The current's slower this time of year, but it's still there. Feel that?"

"I think so." Samuel could feel the deceptive power of the water beginning to push the boat.

"Hold her steady, and the current will do the rest." He released the rudder.

Samuel held on, fearful at first that the water would push him back, but he discovered he could easily hold the angle by pushing the rudder against the current. Steadily, the ferryboat moved across.

"Back off a bit when we get close to the landing so the bow doesn't strike hard."

Samuel did, managing to bring the boat in with a soft bump. George jumped off and tied it.

They lowered the ramp and let the stock off, turning them out into the pasture. George broke out some hay and threw it down. Buster and Spooky immediately began pulling it apart. "Some Thanksgiving for them as well." George laughed.

"Should have brought Molly," Samuel said. "She's having a hard go of it."

"We'll send some leftovers home for her," George offered.

The dinner was more food than Samuel had seen since Independence Day. The Shearers commented favorably on the grouse his father and he had fixed, but Samuel knew it was no match for the roast chicken and ham Mrs. Shearer had cooked. They had sourdough biscuits with raspberry jam, potatoes with rich gravy, beets, and beans. Then Mrs. Shearer brought in a pumpkin pie, topped with some whipped cream, and buttermilk to wash it down. Somehow, Samuel found room.

He had not said a word.

"Samuel don't talk much, does he?" Frederick Shearer commented, winking.

"Only when he's not eatin' or sleepin'," Charles replied.

Samuel looked up to their laughter. The look in Mrs. Shearer's eyes said it was fine with her.

"This is mighty fine fixin's, Mrs. Shearer," Samuel managed. "Thank you for inviting us."

"Son, you are very welcome." Mrs. Shearer beamed and patted his hand. The other men murmured their belated thanks.

Shortly, the men retired to the sitting room with their pipes and some whiskey. Samuel got up and helped clear the dishes, and Mrs. Shearer began washing them.

"It's sure nice to be here." He took a plate from her and dried it.

"I'm sure glad you're here too," she replied. "It's been a long time since I've had a youngster around, though I swear you've growed like a weed."

"I think it's a good thing President Lincoln declared this time of year to be Thanksgiving," Samuel continued. "God's given us a great abundance in this land, and we *should* be thankful."

"Now where did you hear that about Mr. Lincoln?"

"Eighth grade."

"I knew you were a smart one." She smiled. "My George went to Tuscorara Academy in Pennsylvania. You're going to go somewhere someday. I can tell." She patted his head.

Samuel almost ducked away but let it be. Sometimes it felt good to be fussed over a bit. Briefly he thought of his own mother and his younger sister, Elizabeth, back in Iowa.

"I might go to China someday, but things over there aren't so grand. Most of the Chinese coming here lost their land or are rebels hiding out."

"And who tells you that?"

"Sing Chen. He's a year older than me." Samuel began drying the utensils and putting them in the box where they were stored. "He was born in the year of the dragon. I was born in the year of the snake."

"And how do you know this?" Mrs. Shearer asked, appearing intrigued. She gestured to Samuel to add wood to the fire while she filled the kettle with more water and set it on to heat.

Samuel fit some wood into the burn box and began telling Mrs. Shearer about the Chinese, about the festival of the moon, about being called a foreign devil, and about trying to teach Chen how to read and write.

Mrs. Shearer fixed some tea, and they sat at the table.

Samuel told her of other events since they had come through last spring. He liked talking to her because she listened well. He told her about his hunting accident when he was thrown from Spooky and how Sang Yune helped doctor him and save his life. He told her about selling vegetables with Chen and about the bandits jumping the Chinese pack train. Then he talked about finding the O'Riley.

"Anyone else in Washington about your age?" she asked when he finally finished. "I haven't kept up with the news as much." She smiled. "Any young ladies?"

Samuel blinked. He was getting drowsy, but Mrs. Shearer's question brought him awake. A bit embarrassed, he thought of Miss Lilly, remembering her flashing red hair, hazel eyes, and, curiously, her shapely figure. Her memory tugged at his stomach, reminding him he had promised to visit her. "None really my age. At least none that count." He then remembered the girl at Slate Creek.

"Hey, how far's Slate Creek?"

Mrs. Shearer arched her eyebrows. "A good day, if travelin's good. Thinking of going there?"

"Maybe." Samuel wondered if she knew about the girl but decided not to ask. He doubted his father and he would have reason to go to Slate Creek, being it was that far.

"Do you hear from your family back in Iowa?" Mrs. Shearer continued.

Samuel nodded. He felt a lump in his throat. He knew for certain his ma and little sister, five and a half now, weren't having as fine a Thanksgiving as he was. He knew his grandma wasn't. He knew Uncle Jake and his cousins weren't. They had remained behind at the family farm trying to raise enough food to survive until their return.

"They're doing okay," Samuel managed.

"I figured you two would have gone back by now."

"We can't sell the mine until we prove it up, and … we're just not done." That was the truth, Samuel realized.

She nodded and smiled. Samuel sat for a moment, thinking. His eyes drooped.

"All talked out finally, I see," Mrs. Shearer said quietly. She rose and went to the sitting room. Voices and pipe smoke filtered in. Shortly, she was back and took his cup.

"You're staying here for the night." She tapped Samuel on the shoulder. "Come on. You can have the room you had last time."

The temperature remained frigid through the following week. The Shearers said it was the earliest and worst cold spell they could remember. They feared some of the fruit trees would be winterkilled.

It was all Charles and Samuel could do to keep a small fire going in the cabin and keep warm. The creek beside the cabin froze over. They chopped a hole in the ice in the river through which to draw water and kept another area open for their stock. They also broke out the hay they had cut and mixed it with some feed from the Shearers to help get the stock through. They would buy more feed if necessary, but each purchase cut into their money.

Samuel had borrowed a couple of books and spent much of his time reading. He wondered if Chen was reading the words he knew from the book that Ma Reynolds had given him. Samuel knew Chen. Likely as not, he would have figured out much of the book long before Samuel returned.

Sometimes Samuel read to his father. Sometimes they invented stories to tell. Sometimes they played checkers. At first, they talked about the coming mining season, what they had to do to prove up the O'Riley—and how promising the last two assays had been.

"I thought I could see gold, Pa," Samuel recalled. "Under Mr. Hinley's glass, you could really see it. That's just the start. I know it's going to get better the deeper we go."

They talked about the Sweet Mary—how they were going to drill and blast the two boulders and get to the gravel underneath, how rich the gold would be, and how many nuggets they would be able to pick out of the sluice.

"I hope no one discovers our dig and works it over the winter," Samuel worried.

"It's under snow, son. Besides, they would have to wash it bucket by bucket and melt the ice to have any water," Charles reminded him. "We just have to be the first ones back when the water starts running in the spring."

They talked about how good it would be when the seasons turned, but now each day continued to shorten. The shadows lingered longer and arrived earlier. The canyon remained in darkness most of the day. By four in the afternoon, it was dark, and by five, night.

Soon the stories and the talking and the plans diminished. Soon there was nothing new to plan or discuss. They sat quietly in the darkness of the canyon.

Warren Hunt, the expressman, stopped by the cabin one morning. Samuel remembered him from Independence Day, a tall man with chiseled features who spoke strongly.

"Heard you were here. Didn't know if you might not have a letter for me to carry."

The two were surprised, the thought not having occurred to them, having been isolated from any town.

"I come through about every two weeks. No problem in swinging up here to check. Put a flag near the trail."

They invited him in for a cup of coffee and to share a few minutes.

"Only a minute. I have a schedule."

Usually Hunt stayed with the Shearers and then again with Burgdorf before he reached Washington.

Hunt told them, "It's already making for the worst winter I've seen at Warren's since the strike in '62. Not so much in snow yet, but it's mighty cold."

Samuel hoped for light snow and an early spring.

"Good snow makes for a good placer season, not so much for the quartz mines. They fill with water come spring."

Samuel corrected his thoughts and hoped the snows would be deep.

The cabin was up off the trail and mostly hidden by brush, but Samuel occasionally caught sight of a rider going through if he was paying attention. Sometimes he sat where he could watch through a crack in the door and check the trail. There was no glass window, only an opening with shutters, which they now kept closed in the bitter cold. Light filtered in through a few gaps; otherwise the cabin was dark except for their kerosene lamp they infrequently lit and the glow from the woodstove.

One night he awoke. A spot of moonlight filtered through one of the cracks, illuminating an area on the floor near his head. Frigid air had seeped in along the floor. He rose to put a piece of wood into the stove. He lifted the flap on the edge of the window, looking out at the moonlit landscape, its glow reflecting off the water and ice.

A flaring match lit up a man's face upstream, and a chill washed over Samuel. Two men sat their horses and were looking in his direction.

They milled about for a moment or two. When Samuel was about to wake his father, the men turned and continued upstream and soon passed from sight beyond the trail's bend.

"I wouldn't be too concerned," Charles said the next morning. "It's easy to misjudge where you want to be on trails in this country."

"They were watching the cabin, Pa."

"I'm sure they smelled wood smoke and were considering waking us for a place to warm up and stay the night."

"Doesn't seem to make sense. They had already passed us by."

"Who knows what they were thinking?" Charles's voice had an edge.

Samuel let it drop, but something about the men nagged at him. Later, he noticed hoofprints near their sluice.

One morning at breakfast, his father addressed him. "If I'm figuring right, about fifteen years ago this day, your ma had a rude awakening."

For a brief moment, Samuel wondered to what his father referred. He had lost track of the days. His father had not. This day, he turned fifteen.

"I can't say I have much to give you to mark this day, son. I was hoping by now we'd have a pile of gold and be back home. All I can say is happy birthday."

"Thanks, Pa." Samuel embraced his father.

"When we get somewhere where I can buy you something, I promise, I will."

"Sure." Samuel knew of no place they could go, and they had little money with which to buy anything.

Chapter 3

One morning, Samuel woke to his father packing gear. Outside was pitch-black.

His father watched him awaken. "How about you fry up some bacon, and we'll finish those spuds we got from the Shearers?"

"Where you heading?"

"I'll tell you over breakfast." Charles rolled his blankets and tied them tight. "Make a little extra coffee." He stepped out the door. A cold blast of air swamped the cabin. "I'm bringing the stock up."

Samuel wanted to pull his blankets up tighter and go back to sleep, but he forced himself out of bed. He pulled on his trousers and blue dobby shirt and fixed his suspenders. He stoked the fire and presently had breakfast going, musing that his father did not hold in surprises well.

As his father stepped back in, cold again blasted across the room. "You'll need to pack your bedroll and your other set of clothes."

Now Samuel's curiosity was killing him, but he did not give in just yet to his father's game. He served up the bacon and sliced spuds and poured two cups of hot coffee.

"You and I are going to go have Christmas dinner at Slate Creek."

"We are?" Samuel almost dropped his plate.

"We need to buy some supplies, and I want to talk to folks." He raised his cup to Samuel.

"Whoopee!" Samuel wolfed down the remainder of his breakfast, cleaned and stowed the dishes, and finished throwing his gear together.

As light streaked the sky, they were headed down the trail. The elevation would drop by several hundred feet, enough that there would be no snow. The trip would take a full day, maybe longer if traveling became rough.

Ice covered the trail in places. The horses and mule clattered across, sometimes slipping on the sidehills. Samuel cringed, remembering the thread of a trail ahead that crossed the narrows.

Huge clouds of steam billowed into the air across the river at the Indian hot springs.

"If there was an easy way across, that wouldn't be a bad idea about now." Charles pointed.

Samuel studied the roiling clouds for a while, shivering and watching his own breath. The sun was out, but the temperature had not climbed much. His ears and nose stung. He tried to pull his coat collar across his mouth.

Groff's ferry appeared abandoned. It made sense; no one would be coming down the Little Salmon River, the direction from which his father and he had come last spring. Country in that direction was now locked deep in snow.

After they turned north, they entered country they had never seen. The canyon broadened; the river widened. At every draw, a new stream emptied its additional waters. In places, the side canyons were impossibly steep and were choked by brush and trees. Where there were larger streams, the creek bottoms spread out for short distances, creating small openings in the canyon walls, presenting some level land but not much.

Samuel recognized a Chinese placer camp across the river opposite them, several miles below Groff's ferry. The Chinese had built a low-slung stone hut, its only apparent wood being the beam across the door and the driftwood roof. He wondered how they reached the hut. Groff's was the nearest ferry, but using it would certainly be too costly for the Chinese. Then he noticed the raft sandwiched in the ice near where a couple of Chinese worked rockers.

A couple of black holes appeared cut into the hillside above the men. "Pretty smart," he said.

"What's pretty smart?" Charles turned in his saddle.

"See the holes on the far bank? The Chinese are tunneling in along the old bedrock that used to be the riverbed."

Charles squinted toward where Samuel had indicated. "Yep, it looks like placer gravel. A terrace, I think they call it." Charles clucked at Buster. "They might be pretty smart, but their method is a lot of work."

"And if nuggets are lying on that old bedrock like there's likely to be, then they're doing just fine."

Charles smiled. "Maybe you should check along the river near our cabin for something like that. You might make us rich yet."

Samuel decided he would.

Late in the day, they reached a placer camp at Lucile Bar. Smoke came from a couple of white canvas tents near the river. A few men were wintering, trying to make grub until they could return to richer diggings in the spring.

The creek had been diverted across the hillside above to feed a sluice that ran downslope across the bar. Ice coated the box, and long icicles reached to the ground. A couple of men were at work but paused to say hello as they rode past.

Directly across the river, they saw two more Chinese operations, and they encountered yet another small placer camp downstream after another mile.

"Looks like all the good bars must be down this way, son."

"Looks like they're all taken up as well."

With the early winter darkness, they were still several miles from Slate Creek when they decided to camp for the night. The going had been slow, and ice floes had spread across the trail in numerous places, making it difficult for the horses and mule.

They moved well off the trail near a stream that trickled through blocks of ice and snow.

"At least I don't have to worry about rattlers," commented Samuel.

"Then you haven't heard about them ice rattlers," Charles said. "They're the worst. Look just like frozen sticks. Should you accidentally thaw one, it'll bite you twenty times and then again before you know what happened."

His father said it so casually it took Samuel a brief moment to realize the joke. "Yep, I suppose they're about as bad as those ice rats. Like that one there." Samuel pointed at a rounded cobble. "Look just like rocks until they attack you, eating your eyes out."

Charles stared at Samuel. "We start telling stories like this now, what's it going to be like when we really get cabin fever?"

"Time to go mining?" Samuel quipped.

"I hope so."

Samuel picketed the stock and fed them some of the grain that Molly carried.

His father had gathered wood and had a fire snapping against the cold by the time Samuel returned. Samuel could not help but picture the pieces of wood coming to life, turning into snakes.

They fixed a supper of venison and warmed some biscuits and coffee. Although only about five o'clock, the night was pitch-black. Stars hung like frozen lights in the still, frosty sky.

Pulling their blankets about their shoulders, their breaths rising in the night air, they watched the night sky as the fire burned down to a bed of glowing embers.

"It looks like you can just reach out and grab the stars," Samuel said, sweeping his hand toward the sky. "Never looked like this in Iowa."

"Iowa's different. Sky's not as clear," Charles said. "But they do look sharper than usual. Must be the cold."

Samuel leaned back, staring upward, studying the blazing points of light. "You reckon the night was like this when the angels visited the shepherds?"

"Could be. I've often wondered the same seeing the stars shine like they do this time of the year."

"I can imagine what it must have been like. Night lights up. Angels come swarming about, singing and such. Would have scared the blazes out of me. Sure would have made me a believer."

Charles laughed. "Me as well."

A meteor lit the sky.

"See that?" Samuel pointed. "Maybe they're coming back."

"Might be."

Moments later, another meteor streaked across the sky, brighter and longer, disappearing behind the mountains.

"Might be a meteor shower."

They watched until the night cold became too much to bear but saw no others.

"Come on, son. It'll be a long day tomorrow."

They built up the fire a bit to ward off the plummeting temperature and pulled their blankets about themselves for the night.

Chapter 4

EARLY MORNING, they woke to frost on their bedrolls, their boots frozen. They waited until the sun rose and glistened from the ice- and snow-covered gorge before riding out. In a couple of miles, they reached a broad, grassy bench where a few cattle grazed, steam billowing from their nostrils.

"Must be John Day's ranch," Charles said. "We're nearing Slate Creek."

The river pinched into a narrow canyon, and the trail narrowed as well. In places, men had cut away the rock to widen it. The river spilled a hundred feet below, its black water spitting up bits of white spray where it buckled over the rocks. It then swung sharply west and bent back upon itself, piling in monster swells and whitewater against the far cliffs. Samuel studied them. No human alive could possibly carve a trail across that cliff face. The trail barely clung to this side as it was.

Shortly, the river gorge opened before them into a series of low, grassy benches. Several rough buildings were scattered on a barren plain adjacent to the river—a couple of general stores, a hotel, a blacksmith and livery, and a couple of ranch houses. Numerous whiteface cattle, horses, and mules grazed the hillsides beyond the buildings. They had reached Slate Creek.

"About a dozen families," observed Samuel. "Not exactly a town."

"The only one close enough for us to reach."

The street was empty except for a hitched wagon patiently awaiting its owner, the first wagon Samuel had seen since Fort Boise. There was not a trace of snow, although the temperature was well below freezing.

"Come on, Samuel," Charles said. "We'll stable the stock and take a room in the boardinghouse."

Samuel glanced up, wondering about the cost.

"Either that or we camp out again. Think of it as a Christmas present. That's why we're here. Besides, the animals could use the feed."

Samuel could not believe his ears. They entered Slate Creek House and spoke to Mrs. Wood about a room.

"I got one," she said cheerily, "but anyone else arriving will have to use the barn."

Their room was not fancy—a kerosene lamp on a table with a washbasin and mirror, a large bed, and hooks on the wall to hang clothing. A portrait of George Washington hung on the striped wallpaper. A window peered out toward the river.

"A real bed, Pa." Samuel flopped down. "I could get used to this." He bounced a moment.

"Mrs. Wood will serve dinner at dark. Between now and then, we can get haircuts and a bath," Charles said.

"A real bath this time," Samuel observed.

They had arrived early Christmas Eve morning. After they had cleaned up and got their clothes washed, Charles told Samuel he would be looking up some men about the O'Riley.

Samuel wandered into a store that had red ribbons and bells hanging in the window. A sign said Freedom Post Office. Samuel looked around. Shelves were piled with mining gear and ranching tack, and bins held dried onions and cornmeal. He decided the store was much like Scott Alexander's Mercantile back in Washington.

"Can I help you, son?" The clerk, a man with black hair, appearing to be in his midthirties, came over.

"Just looking for a present for my pa."

"Yup, how about some new pipe tobacco?" The man indicated a canister on the counter.

Samuel liked the aroma. "Probably not. Maybe some socks. My pa's are about plumb wore out."

"Haven't seen you around before."

"Just came in for some civilization and Christmas dinner."

The man nodded. "Well, welcome to Slate Creek ... or Freedom, as some folks are insisting." He showed him where the socks were piled. "Where you coming from to reach civilization, pray tell?"

"We're out of Warren's camp, wintering on the river a few miles down from Shearers' ferry."

"You should have wintered down here out of the snow. Maybe could have got work at one of the ranches."

Samuel glanced at the bleak, grass-covered hills. "It does look like good ranching country. No gold?"

"Nope. Plenty in the bars along the river, but here? Nary a flake. People first thought the slate rock held gold. It didn't. Turned out to be something different than slate anyway. But the name Slate Creek stuck. Some of the rock had some sulphurets and copper and such, but no gold. So after a bunch of holes were punched, they gave up."

"How come everyone's still here then?"

"Slate Creek's now the jumping-off point for the trail to Florence." He pointed northeast toward the mountains. "About thirty miles." Then he shook his head. "Pretty wild town, Florence is. It's better a kid like you is in Washington. I understand a couple decent families summer in Washington at least."

"Yep," Samuel offered. "The Manuels and Osborns have little children." He found a pair of socks. "How much?"

"Four bits. Anything else?"

"I could use a cup of coffee. Maybe sit for a while and stay warm."

The man laughed. "You'd be welcome. The coffee is on me. You can catch me up on the doin's up at Warren's camp."

"Thank you, sir." Samuel took the coffee and handed him his gold pouch.

The man looked up. "No coin?"

Samuel shook his head. "Everyone at Washington insists on dust."

The clerk opened the pouch, took a small pinch, and examined the gold. "You mining this?"

Samuel nodded.

"Pretty good gold. Looks to be about sixteen dollars an ounce."

"That's what I was figuring," Samuel said. Gold was worth twenty dollars an ounce, but he knew native gold was naturally alloyed with silver—more so up at Warren's than on the river.

The clerk weighed out the appropriate amount and added it to a small canister behind the counter. "Reminds me of Florence gold. Now that was somethin'. Gold was everywhere just under the soil. Some folks got as much as seven or eight ounces to a pan."

Samuel almost choked. "Guess we shoulda gone there." That amount of gold in a single pan was impossible. The man had to be funning him.

"Nope, Florence is done. The placers are dried up. There were no quartz ledges to speak of. Just Chinese moving in there now." The clerk wrapped the socks in a square of paper, tied it, and pushed the package toward Samuel. "Warren's camp ... now that's the place to be for long-term prospects. Yup, seems to me they have some paying quartz mines.

That means Washington will stick around for a while. That means Slate Creek might survive as well."

Samuel raised his eyes.

"Freight still comes through here. We're the main supply town this side of Lewiston. Of course, all the freight comes out of Lewiston and goes up to Mount Idaho. From there, some goes across the Milner Trail to Florence, but most of it now comes down White Bird Hill and across to here and then on up to Florence. After Florence, the pack strings drop down and cross the Salmon at the wire bridge and then head on up into Washington. If Florence dries up, it will all just come through here and follow the river—same as the way you came down—and then on up to Washington and some of the other camps up that way."

"Miller's camp?"

"Yup, and some along the Secesh that might be opening up." The clerk took the lid off a jar that held colorful, striped candy sticks. "Have one. It's Christmas."

Samuel could not resist. "Thanks."

"You'll notice most of the pack strings winter here. We got good grass on the hills. Lots of hay. Good climate for growing some vegetables. Now some orchards. Mr. Wood planted apple trees when he got here in '61. He's getting some good fruit now. Yup, I think Slate Creek will stick around. We have a good future."

Samuel tasted his piece of candy—cherry. He savored the sweet flavor. It had been this past summer the last time he had had a piece of candy—from Sing Mann. "Lots of Chinese are moving into Washington as well, but I think you're right. The quartz mines are starting to do okay. Running night and day. Both the Charity and the Rescue mines are running crews all winter. The Chinese don't work the quartz mines; they don't know how. And I think more quartz mines will be found. I even found a ledge."

The man peered at him. "Now that's somethin'." He laughed. "Men look for years without making a strike."

"I thought I was going to be looking for years as well."

"How's the gold?"

"So far, it looks real good," Samuel continued, half wondering if he should share anything more. "The assays went over three ounces of gold and seven ounces of silver."

"Yup, I'd say it's good." The man whistled. "Sixty dollars a ton is good. Even got decent silver. Got any investors?"

"My pa and I aren't sure what we're going to do with it yet," Samuel replied. "We've got it up for sale, but I'd like to work it. I think it's going to get richer, but it takes a lot of gear—drill steel, hammers, powder. We'll have to build a trail and haul out the ore. Pay someone to crush it. All that."

"We've got mining tools here." The clerk gestured toward the overflowing shelves. "I'll be more than happy to grubstake you. 'Course, you have to pay for freighting it in."

"Thank you, sir," Samuel replied, emptying his cup. "I'll tell my pa."

"Keep me in mind if you need an investor." He reached out his hand. "Name's Ralph Clark."

"Samuel Chambers." They shook.

"Thanks for the coffee, Mr. Clark, and Christmas joy to you."

"Christmas joy to you, Samuel."

So this is Slate Creek, Samuel thought as he left the store, cherry candy in his mouth, *a ranching town that exists to support the mining camps.*

His father met him back at their room.

"Got an investor in the O'Riley, if you want," Samuel said.

Charles raised his eyes. "I thought that's what I was doing."

"Did you?"

"Maybe, but you go first."

They talked. Charles mentioned he had met a rancher that had some interest.

Later, they gathered for dinner. They recognized a couple of the miners from Warren's as well as Warren Hunt.

"Is that the Chambers?" Hunt said, almost booming, coming over and sitting. "You guys left your cabin for a bit of civilization?"

"Exactly."

Hunt settled down and began spreading butter on a thick slice of wheat bread.

Charles addressed him. "Anyone in Slate Creek hear anything about the Chinese pack string that was jumped a while back?"

"Nothing more than what you heard. I expect those men are long gone. Like those outlaws Samuel jumped."

One of the men nearby looked up. "You're the kid that jumped them highwaymen?"

Samuel nodded. He was surprised they had heard.

"Heard about the man they killed. You're mighty lucky they kept going," the man added, returning to his meal.

"Doesn't matter," Hunt remarked. "There'll be some more to take their place. Kind of the way it is when gold's involved."

Charles added, "You should know. I hear you've been chased around the country a bit by some."

"More than once. I swear those scallywags can smell whenever a gold shipment is going out, and then they wait for me. Worst time was when Florence just opened up, and I was about the only one carrying out the gold. I had a shipment of well over two hundred pounds of dust to take out to Lewiston."

"Two hundred pounds!" Samuel nearly spit out his spuds; a numbing sensation flooded him. He could not envision two hundred pounds of dust. "That's gotta be … gotta be around forty thousand dollars!" Ralph Clark had not been kidding when he said some men panned out seven or more ounces in a single pan.

Hunt looked at him. "That's about right, Samuel. That's pretty good ciphering, I'd say.

"Anyway, the miners in Florence noticed a couple drifters hanging around, so they gave me a heads-up. I got nervous, so I had a friend take the gold out during the day. I wrapped my saddlebags in a gunnysack and strapped them to his mule. He took it to the next station, where I'd normally be changing horses. I snuck out after dark, picked up my gold, and went straight to Lewiston. Didn't stop for a thing 'cept to change horses."

Hunt eyed Samuel. "You sure you don't want to take up my job? I'm gettin' ready to retire. Coming across Camas Prairie in this snow and then climbing through it up to my ears to Florence and Warren's is about all I can handle anymore."

"Nope." Samuel remembered Hunt asking the same question when he raced Spooky last Independence Day. "I'd rather be finding gold."

Hunt shook his head. "That's called gold fever, Samuel. Anyone ever tell you it gets in the way of a real paying job?"

Christmas morning, Samuel gave his father the socks. "Christmas joy to you, Pa."

"And to you, son. Thanks." He unrolled them. "They feel real nice."

"I know you push it on the socks. Maybe these'll last awhile."

"Here, here's a little something for you." Charles handed him a scarf. "I know you can use this around this time of season."

"Thanks, Pa." Samuel swung it around his neck and was silent a moment. "I wonder how Ma and Elizabeth and everyone are doing."

"They should have received the money we sent. I told her to buy everyone something. I told her some of the gold came from the Sweet Mary, named after her. Maybe that'll take her mind off of all that's been going on."

After breakfast, people cleared the room of the tables and set out all the chairs they could find for Christmas service. Someone had decorated a tree with colored paper and popcorn strands and set it up near a small table with lit candles. Reverend Nathan Earl arrived shortly to a packed room. Several people remained standing. Samuel tried to offer his chair, but they declined.

A woman began playing "O Little Town of Bethlehem" on a badly tuned piano. Samuel joined in, remembering the words he had learned at school. She continued on to "Hark! The Herald Angels Sing," but that one tested his abilities. He croaked a time or two on the high notes and gave it up.

Reverend Earl read the Christmas story. When he came to the part about the shepherds standing watch, Samuel reflected on the stars from a night ago. When he talked about how difficult it must have been for Mary, being young, unmarried, and pregnant—perceived as the worst of all possible moral failings—Samuel found his thoughts on Miss Lilly. How was it some people found love and others never did?

A girl his age with beautiful golden hair and sparkling eyes stepped to the front. She sang the most beautiful "Silent Night" he had ever heard. The congregation was asked to join on the last verse, but Samuel could not. He concentrated on picking out the girl's voice from the others. He shivered. *This is the girl that Jenkins mentioned.* He wished he knew her name. He quickly slicked his hair, wondering if she had noticed him. It did not matter what his father had cautioned before about women. He suddenly knew he was in love—never mind that he had not spoken a single word to her.

Samuel heard no other words of the service until it concluded. He found where the girl was sitting—behind him on the far side of the small room with a man and woman and some younger children.

His heart pounded. He had to say hello, but he could not just walk up and say *hello.* Somehow, he had to meet her.

People lined up, filing past, thanking Reverend Earl. Some congratulated the girl. He caught her name—*Bonnie.* He said it to himself and listened again to make certain before he headed her direction, nearly tripping in trying to get across the room.

He addressed Reverend Earl. "Thank you, Pastor. I haven't heard such good preachin' for a long time." He pumped his hand.

Reverend Earl looked up, a bit puzzled. "Why, thank you, son." He pulled back his hand. "You must be a newcomer."

"Yes, sir." But Samuel avoided adding anything more and continued toward Bonnie. And then he stood in front of her—an angel with startling green eyes and flowing golden hair with a hint of red. His knees felt weak. "Really good job, Bonnie," he blurted. He tried to shake her hand. He saw a flash of puzzlement in her face. "I mean, you sounded—" Samuel felt himself being pushed out of the way.

"Bonnie McCracken, you sung that just beautiful, just beautiful." A huge man who was pushing his tiny wife before him shoved himself in front of Samuel. Others crowded behind, and Bonnie was quickly lost.

Before he could work his way back, she was gone, whisked away. Frantically, Samuel looked around for her—but no Bonnie. Others stood around visiting. Mrs. Wood had the room set back up and brought out coffee and platters piled with cookies and cakes.

Samuel stepped from the hotel and searched the streets. His father came up to him.

"You haven't heard a word I've been saying."

He looked at his father. "That was her, Pa. That was Bonnie. Did you hear her sing? Did you ever hear such a voice so beautiful? Have you ever seen a more beautiful girl?"

"Only one," he said, "and I see some of her in you."

Samuel still had not heard a word; he continued searching the street for Bonnie.

Chapter 5

THE MORNING AFTER CHRISTMAS, Samuel was surprised when his father invited him to take a ride. "I told you about the rancher who's interested in our quartz mine. He's invited us out for further discussion."

"Does he want to buy it?"

"He didn't say that. I told him how it was you who found it. He said he'd like to meet you."

Samuel was taken aback. "He wants to talk to *me*?"

They saddled up, headed north a short distance, and then turned east along Slate Creek, a broadly flowing stream. A modest ranch house appeared amid a copse of cottonwoods. Apart from it stood several outbuildings. A fence surrounded a rather large garden, and an orchard grew at the far end. Cattle and mules were scattered across the hillsides.

When they turned up the track toward the house, a couple of ranch hands rode up.

"Howdy," Charles greeted. He rocked forward in his saddle. "Paying a visit to Mr. Stromback."

"Welcome. They'll be at the house," the older hand, a man with a weathered face and graying hair, replied.

The other man, maybe nineteen or twenty, with dark stubble and a rough face, carefully studied Samuel, making him feel uncomfortable.

"You guys aimin' to stay a piece?" the younger man asked, directing his question more at Samuel than at Charles.

Samuel wanted to ask him what business it was of his.

"A short business visit is all," Charles replied.

The younger man nodded but kept his eyes on Samuel—gray-looking, fidgety eyes.

"Take care, then," the older man replied.

They rode past the men to the low-slung ranch house.

"Pa, it looks like our old home. See, you can see they even have roses by the door—prairie roses."

"How can you tell that? It's winter."

"Dried rosehips."

They dismounted and walked to the door. A short-haired dog, a collie of sorts, came running from around back, its tail wagging.

"Ma used to have them. They were special to her." Samuel remembered how his mother loved the roses.

"Reminds you of our old home, then?" Charles wondered.

"Our old farm." Samuel resolved he would plant his mother some roses when they returned to Iowa and again had a home of their own— just as soon as the O'Riley began producing.

They heard people at the door.

"I remember now," Charles said. "They were yellow."

The dog jumped and whined for attention. Samuel stroked its muzzle.

A man and young boy came out to meet them. They were the man and boy who had been sitting near Bonnie. Samuel's heart began racing. *This is the ranch where Bonnie works.* The man was about his father's age, with flecked blond hair and heavy crow's-feet.

"Hey, Charles," Jon Stromback greeted strongly and shook his hand. "And here be your son, Samuel." He spoke with a slight Swedish accent.

"Yes, sir." Stromback had a solid grip that matched his broad shoulders.

The young boy, seven or eight, muscled his way to the front.

"Here be my son, Josef."

"Howdy, Josef," Samuel greeted him. He reminded him of his younger self, towheaded with light blue eyes and an impish smile. "Fine place you got here. Fine looking dog too."

Josef beamed. "His name's Roundup. He's just good for tellin' us that folks are here. Is all he's good for."

"Welcome in. Meet Mrs. Stromback and the rest of the family."

Samuel's heart nearly stopped. He caught a glimpse of Bonnie standing behind a slightly plump, well-figured woman.

"Welcome, welcome." A wide smile crinkled Mrs. Stromback's face. "I'm Rebecca."

"Pleased to meet you, ma'am." She reminded him of Ma Reynolds and contrasted with his own mother's soft, quiet manner and slender figure.

Two small, blond-haired girls bubbled out. "My daughters, Kerstin and Sophia," Mrs. Stromback introduced. Kerstin curtsied. Sophia ducked behind her mother and peeked out. Samuel strained to see Bonnie. Their eyes met. She glanced away.

"And this is my niece, Bonnie." Mrs. Stromback's greenish eyes sparkled.

Samuel could see where Bonnie got her eyes.

Heart hammering, hoping he would not sound clumsy, he took Bonnie's hand and nodded slightly. "Pleased to meet you, Bonnie."

She laughed. It was laughter of silver. "Pleased to make a proper acquaintance of you as well, Samuel." She curtsied.

"Here be the lad I told you about who found the quartz mine," Stromback declared.

Samuel felt important as they flooded into the dining area. He was reminded of the Shearers' home; however, this was larger, having separate rooms and painted walls.

"You men all have a seat," Mrs. Stromback offered. "Bonnie and I'll get you some coffee." They slipped away into the next room, the two small girls following, and soon returned with steaming cups, Kerstin carefully balancing a plate of shortbread. Josef pulled up a seat beside Samuel, studying him.

"The family wants to hear about your quartz mine, Samuel," Stromback said, surprising him. Although he did not fully know what the visit was about, he had expected the usual: the men would be talking, and the women would be off doing women things.

Feeling all eyes on him, especially Bonnie's, Samuel began. He wondered if he would say things right or if he would come across a bumbling fool. He kept to the basics and tried not to glance at Bonnie too much. She listened intently. She had small dimples that crinkled when she smiled. Her teeth were smooth and incredibly white. Samuel felt embarrassed by his own dingy appearance—by his tattered, badly worn clothes.

"But how'd you know it was gold?" Josef implored, eyes wide.

Samuel forgot where he was in the story. "Oh … Mr. Hinley, he actually showed me in some samples what to look for."

"You have to show me some."

"For sure, someday." Samuel felt relieved to be finished. He did not like all the attention.

"You'll excuse us, Samuel?" Stromback addressed him. "I would meet with your father."

"Come on, children, I have a game to play." Mrs. Stromback suddenly rose and led the two girls off.

"I want to visit with Samuel and Cousin Bonnie," Josef protested.

"You too, Josef," Mrs. Stromback insisted. "You can show Samuel your roping before he goes."

"You betcha." Josef jumped up and traipsed after his mother.

Samuel was surprised to find himself sitting alone with Bonnie, although the two men were in the adjacent room. He felt awkward, uncertain, not knowing what to say.

"It must have been exciting when you found out you had discovered gold," Bonnie said. Her voice was melodic.

"It's a feeling hard to describe," Samuel began. "You work and work every day, checking rock after rock, and then when you find out you actually have some gold ... well, it's hard to explain."

Bonnie laughed quietly. Samuel felt funny. He knew he was in love.

"Tell me about coming from Iowa," she asked, eyes sparkling.

Samuel began talking. And he talked. *They* talked. Samuel had never found anyone who was easier to talk with—except Miss Lilly, he remembered, now embarrassed. He told her of Iowa, his family, placer mining, and the Chinese.

In turn, Bonnie told him about Slate Creek and the ranch. "I came out here three years ago when I was twelve to help my aunt and uncle. My mother died, so my father sent me to live with relatives. Sometimes I visit Uncle Nathan in Lewiston."

"I'm sorry to hear," Samuel managed. He thought of his own mother far away.

"It's a blessing," she quickly replied. "My mother was ill for a very long time."

"Why don't you live with your uncle?" Samuel figured living in a city would have been better for her.

"I could, but I enjoy the ranch very much."

He wanted to ask why she didn't live with her father, but something told him not to. He noticed she talked a good deal about the Strombacks. They had been friendly with the Nez Perce Indians since they had begun the ranch.

Samuel told her of meeting some Nez Perce in the Salmon Meadows last spring and how he admired their appaloosa horses.

"Uncle Jon has two appaloosas," she said quickly, her eyes lighting up. "I do believe they are the most beautiful animals in the world, and they run like the wind. One is almost unaware while riding them."

Samuel's heart quickened. "You like riding?"

"As often as possible. When I have free time, I sometimes ride up into the hills with Uncle Jon and Cousin Josef. It's very beautiful there."

Samuel knew then he was not talking to any ordinary girl. She was at least handy with horses. But her speech and mannerisms were quite proper. "So where did you live before?"

"We lived in Seattle."

"You speak very nicely, and you sing beautifully." Samuel did not know how else to say it.

"My mother was a wonderful teacher. She … she sang and played the piano."

Samuel sensed that Bonnie did not have the heart to say more. "That's very nice," he managed.

"I'm helping Aunt Rebecca teach Josef and the two girls." She shook her head slightly, settling her flowing hair. "The children are so precious. Part of my job is helping care for them."

As if on cue, the two small girls came rushing into the room, bouncing around Bonnie, giggling, their curly hair bouncing, Josef chasing after.

"Here, here, children," Mrs. Stromback said as she came in. "They escaped me," she apologized, looking slightly exasperated. "Come on, you three. I have a story. We can visit the young man later."

The girls reminded Samuel of his sister, Elizabeth. He shook his head, watching them go. "I'm trying to help teach my Chinese friend how to read."

A shadow flashed across Bonnie's face.

"His name is Sing Chen. He's a year older than me. Probably, he saved my life."

She brightened. "You must tell me."

Samuel told her about Chen, but then, sensing some disapproval, he refrained from telling her anything more about the Chinese. That's when he felt his father's and Stromback's presence. He wondered how long they had been standing and listening.

Charles interrupted, "Samuel, Mr. Stromback would like a word with you. Then we'll be on our way. It's a long trip back."

Samuel felt crushed. He wanted to remain forever and to really get to know Bonnie. He wondered at this mystery, for surely, Bonnie was something like a mystery.

"Sir?" Samuel addressed Stromback.

"Will be a minute, lad," he said, leading him into the next room. "Besides finding a gold mine, I hear you can handle horses."

So it was not about the quartz ledge after all, Samuel thought. "I've ridden a bit. Helped back in Iowa on the farm—otherwise, that is all."

"We have a good ranch here, Samuel. I've talked to your pa. If you'd like to take a break from mining when the weather warms a bit and spend a few days with me ranching, you'd be welcome."

Samuel could not believe his ears. He wanted to start immediately.

"Your pa speaks proudly of you. When he told me how you kept at it until you found that quartz ledge, I told myself here was a man who has gumption. I hold that quality high."

A warmth flooded Samuel.

"Don't get me wrong. My hands are good, hardworking men. You wouldn't be replacing anyone. I'm just giving you a chance at ranching before the trails open and you can get back to mining. You still have an obligation to your father."

"Yes, sir, I do," Samuel managed. "And to my family back in Iowa."

"Hell, son, let me come out with it. Ain't any men in Slate Creek near Bonnie's age, except our hand, Rex. And though he works for me, I'm not sure he's the best type for Bonnie. Lately, he's been hinting about courting her. I thought maybe if you showed up for a few days, she'd figure out there's others out there who have better heads on their shoulders."

Samuel felt his ears burning. He bit his lip to keep from grinning.

Stromback noticed. "I'm not suggesting a damn thing. You'd have a lot of provin' to do, same as any man. But it might do Bonnie some good to get to know someone new—someone who has some different notions."

"I reckon I'd welcome that very much, sir." Samuel tried to sound businesslike, but his heart pounded in his ears. "When would you like me?"

"I was figuring mid-March," Stromback replied. "That's when we get some of our worst snows. We have packers' stock to watch and feed."

Samuel felt devastated. *March.* "I'd like that, sir." He fought to hide his disappointment. "Wouldn't mind coming by earlier if you reckoned I could be of help sooner." His heart still hammered. He almost wished he had not said it. He did not want to push his luck.

"Could be. I'll send word." He offered his hand, and they shook. "Of course, if you and your pa have reason to come back before then, I'd expect you to visit."

Samuel already wondered how he would get his father to return.

After another quick cup of coffee—too quick for Samuel—they said their farewells, pausing long enough for Josef to show off his roping on a set of steer horns tacked to a log. Samuel wondered where he would get a rope for his own practicing before March. He had never roped a steer in his life.

Back at Slate Creek House, Samuel hardly remembered dinner. All he could think about was Bonnie and returning to Slate Creek to work for Jon Stromback, but then he started thinking about Miss Lilly, and a knot grew and twisted inside his stomach.

Later, as they prepared for bed, Charles addressed him. "I reckon now there's three things that can keep you quiet for more than a minute: eating, sleeping, and a girl."

Samuel caught his glance. He did not know how to respond. He had been wondering if his father remembered what Jenkins had said and had brought him to Slate Creek for more than just Christmas dinner. He thought about Miss Lilly and how he liked her. He hardly knew Bonnie. Maybe it wouldn't work. He hated these new mixed-up feelings.

"I think my father once cautioned me when it comes to women—to not get the cart before the horse," Samuel replied slowly as he pulled up the blankets. "I've managed to do that, but I'm thinking he had other reasons for bringing me to Slate Creek. Right now I'm not sure if I should thank him or cuss him."

Charles sat up from unlacing his boots. "I'm sorry if I've complicated things, son. Maybe Mr. Stromback had other thoughts about why he invited us out, but I sure didn't know about his niece, at least not until I saw the family at services. Then I thought I best be quiet."

"I'm obliged," Samuel quickly said, managing to smile. "I 'spect that was a good idea."

Samuel stared out the window at the darkness enveloping the land, catching the stars glittering above the mountain peaks. He had looked forward to spring, when they could return to Warren's camp and prove up the O'Riley, but now he looked forward a few months to when he would again be able to visit with Bonnie. A warmth settled in his middle, and then a fleeting dread. *What about Miss Lilly?*

Chapter 6

IN MID-JANUARY, a heavy winter storm set in with steady, wind-driven snow—snow that piled up, thick and deep, turning the canyon white and closing the trail. The naked limbs of cottonwoods and willows became icy white fingers. A sheer rock outcrop across the river and a few patches of open water were the only areas outside the cabin that were not white.

Father and son remained in the cabin, briefly leaving it to take care of the stock and to get water or wood. The snow sifted in through the cracks and around the window, piling in lines across the floor and their bedding.

After three days, the wind began to die. Frigid air, well below zero, moved in. The snow became tiny ice particles, pushed freely by the wind, piling in deep drifts. Except for a small section of fast water, the river froze.

Cold seeped into the cabin, chased away only near the stove. They quickly burned the available wood. Samuel made a couple of trips to the driftwood pile. When he stepped into the cold, it bit his nose and ears. His scarf helped but his breath caught in it and froze into icicles. He hitched Molly, steam billowing from her nostrils, to a couple of logs and dragged them to the cabin where he could work on them. In the cold, the wood split easily under the swing of his axe, but his hands and fingers stung and became dangerously clumsy.

They chopped ice to expose the gurgling water underneath for drinking and cooking, but new ice quickly formed.

"Never in my life have I been this cold." His father hovered near the stove. "A few minutes outside is all I can take."

Coffee had been their steady companion. A hot cup warmed their hands and bathed their faces, and it warmed going down. They were nearly out.

"Guess some coffee would have been a better gift than a pair of socks," Samuel observed.

"Now I wouldn't say that. I drink the coffee, it's gone. I wear the socks, I still got 'em."

"Maybe we can borrow some more coffee from the Shearers."

"Try to buy some."

"We can go back to Slate Creek and get some," Samuel suggested. "Plus we have other things we could get."

"I'm guessing you'd like to go back and say hi to that girl again."

"Yep."

In the late afternoon, Mr. Hunt came up to the cabin with two letters. His packhorse trailed behind.

They offered him some coffee. It was their last.

"Can't stay but a minute," he said. "I've been battling drifts all day. Need to get to the Shearers'. Tomorrow I'll see how far up the trail I can get."

Samuel noticed the snowshoes strapped to the extra mount along with the mailbags.

"You go in there all winter?"

"I try to get in every two weeks. Usually the snow is no problem until I get up halfway to the freight landing, then it can be four to six feet deep. The summits will get twenty or more feet."

"Twenty feet!" Samuel found it difficult to believe.

"At least," Hunt corrected. "I snowshoe in from where I hit the deep snow, though I won't go in a blizzard. The mail will just be late." He drank his coffee. "Now there's another job for you, Samuel. If the winter stays bad, you could hire out as a Boston jackass."

"A what?"

Hunt laughed. "When the pack strings can't get in, they take the supplies as far as they can go, usually the freight landing. Then they hire a bunch of men to pack it in over the snow. Freighters call them 'Boston jackasses.'"

"I can see why," murmured Samuel.

"Pay's good—about forty cents a pound. 'Course it takes about a week." Hunt sized him up. "I figure you're about up to carrying fifty pounds. Get yourself twenty dollars."

It sounded good until Samuel considered fifty pounds on his back and struggling on snowshoes for near sixty miles through snow and back.

"It's the only way they get anything until the pack trains can get in in late May or so. I hear grub is already getting tight. There's about fifty whites and about fifty Chinamen snowed in, trying to winter."

"How's everyone doing?" asked Samuel. He was thinking about Scott and Mr. Hinley.

"They're doing good. They did up Christmas just dandy. They had an oyster stew on Christmas Eve with a bit of persuasive drink, lots of singing, even a dance. Now that's something you can't beat up there at Warren's, even in the dead of winter. When ol' Charlie Bemis and Rube Besse take up their violins and Nate Jenkins takes up his banjo, now that's somethin'."

Samuel recalled the men and a couple of others like Peter Beamer, who played the flute and wrote the music. They were hard to beat anywhere in the county. He had danced to their music a time or two at the stag dances, and he would defy anyone to sit still during their playing.

"Much else going on at Washington?" Samuel wanted to know.

"About thirty men are still working around the clock at the Rescue. Though I hear it's headed for shutdown. Another legal issue."

Samuel laughed. The Rescue might have had more gold pulled out of it than any mine in the district, but it was always in litigation. The only men making real money on the Rescue were the lawyers.

"I don't know what the miners will live on if they do shut down," confided Hunt. "It's been a terrible winter up there. Like I said, supplies are already running low."

"What about the other mines? Any good strikes?"

"I know the Hic Jacet, Charity, and Keystone are all operating. The mills are running, and more ore is being stockpiled for milling this coming summer. Seems winter is the best time to be underground. There's no water in the mines."

Samuel remembered that. He also remembered that a deep snowpack was essential for a good placer season, and this winter, it was deep.

Hunt drained his cup. "Thanks for the coffee. If you want a letter going out, I can pick it up in a few days." He headed back out into the blustery, cold day.

Samuel turned to his father. "Washington ain't the only place running low on supplies. We gotta get some more coffee, Pa. I don't want any more parched grain or spruce needle tea."

After Hunt left, they read both letters. One was an elated answer to last autumn's announcement they were coming home. Any money they could send in advance would be a blessing. Everyone was looking forward to their return.

The second was in response to the last letter Samuel wrote when they departed Warren's and explained they would winter on the river.

My Dear Charles and Son, Samuel,

I was so grieved to hear you will not be returning until sometime next spring. We had so hoped to see you by now. The weather has been raw, and we have had bouts of snow and rain; however, we are holding up the best as can be expected. My mother seems not to be faring any better. She talks always about missing Father. I try to have Elizabeth help her with little chores and such, mostly to keep her from dwelling too greatly on Father. I feel if you both were home, she would fare more lively. Especially you, Samuel. She misses you so.

However, I understand, my dear husband and son, your decision to winter. The good Lord has always provided for us, and I feel, as you surely must, that He has in store a buyer for our mine. I will pray you will be able to return to the camp early and finish your work in time for spring planting.

If you should find gold where you winter on the Salmon River, I would ask that you consider this: I know you would agree that I should begin making inquiries on land. In this light, Uncle Jake and I have investigated a parcel of land not too distant from our farm here, and we find it quite suitable for raising crops. If agreeable, and you could send as little as two hundred dollars, we could hold this parcel until your return this spring.

For my son, Samuel. I have cautioned you before about the Chinese. Their beliefs and customs are quite contrary to ours and may easily lead you into severe temptations. I pray you understand and will abide by my cautions. Treat them with human decency when required, but it will serve you better to avoid any associations.

Finally, I must say how joyous it was to receive the money you sent in your last package and letter. You would have taken great satisfaction with the looks of deep appreciation on everyone's faces on Christmas Eve when they received the gifts I was able to purchase. I did spend something additional on Elizabeth for a doll and on Cousin Daniel because he has been such a fine help to Uncle Jake and to me. You would be proud of your cousin, Samuel, for all the assistance he graciously gives.

I shall write later, but must rush to post this. I will pray for an early spring and for your health. God bless you and keep you.

Your loving wife and Samuel's mother,
Mary Chambers

His mother's words made Samuel feel her presence and brought forth images of the cabin they shared on the family farm. His uncle Jake hobbled around on his one leg, having lost his other to a Minié ball, but he managed to keep things going. Samuel knew he belonged in Iowa and should be helping as well.

In Samuel's reply to his mother, he told about meeting Bonnie and Christmas at Slate Creek. He avoided making Christmas sound like too much fun. He told her that he might help on the Strombacks' ranch for a while before returning to Warren's camp. He wrote glowingly about the O'Riley—how he could actually see gold in the rock, and that it would only be a short time before they proved up and sold the mine.

Chapter 7

THE DAYS BEGAN LENGTHENING. A warm chinook evaporated some of the snow along the canyon floor and trail. Samuel and his father began operating the sluice again. The gold remained tiny specks of flour gold. Only occasionally could they scrape out some coarser pieces.

Finally, Samuel amalgamated some of the fines with the small amount of mercury they had. He hoped to be surprised by more gold in the fines than he suspected, but after several hours of panning, he had only a few small, frothy clumps.

"Doesn't appear to be much, Pa."

His father shook his head. "I was afraid of that. We've mostly been wasting our time."

"I say we forget about running any of this and keep digging deeper. Eventually, we gotta hit bedrock."

Samuel also took to hunting and exploring the canyon. Besides the mule deer, bighorn sheep came down the cliffs across the river. Samuel often spotted them in the mornings, particularly where steam rose from a warm seepage and saltlick.

"If it wasn't so rocky over there, I'd try to get Spooky down to where I could get one," Samuel said. "I don't understand why they aren't over here where I could get one."

"Nor do I," Charles said. "I'd welcome something besides venison."

Another day, when Samuel walked upstream along the river, he noticed a bald eagle on the shore pulling apart a salmon carcass. It ripped out chunks of meat, gulped them down, and gazed intently about itself. A second eagle swooped down from a snag, landed nearby, and hopped over toward the salmon. The feeding eagle allowed it to rip out pieces as well, so Samuel figured it was its mate. Both stared intently at Samuel almost as if daring him to try to take their meal.

Shortly, the first bird spread its wings and hopped away to the river's edge, where it pecked at another carcass until it could get a grip. Pulling it from the water, it dragged it across the cobbles, having little trouble in moving the three-foot-long salmon.

Something must have spooked them. They squawked and leaped upward, beating their wings, lifting themselves off the gravel bar in mighty strokes, heading upriver and dipping down as their wings swept back and then rising as they came forward, powerful and majestic. Samuel felt his heart race at their beauty. They turned and winged their way back past him, nearly directly above, crossed the river, and settled in another tall snag.

He was surprised to see a young bighorn ram poke its nose out of the willows and walk to the river for a drink. Several ewes followed.

Samuel laughed to himself. There *were* bighorns this side of the river. The sheep paused and drank awhile. They appeared in no hurry to turn back to the safety of the canyon walls. Instead, they wandered along the riverbank, pulling at the withered grass.

Samuel watched until they began heading back. The land sloped steeply back from the river and swept up toward a barren, rocky ridge. A few pines hugged one side of it. The ridge continued upward and merged with another, more densely forested one. He figured the bighorns might be bedding near the rock outcrops and working their way across the nearby grassy ridges for forage.

Quickly, he made his way back toward the cabin for his rifle. He greeted his father near the sluice.

"Saw some sheep upriver a bit," he said. "I'm going to see if I can get one."

"They on this side?"

"Yes, sir, just above the bend."

"In that case, go ahead. We need the meat." He leaned on his shovel. "Watch your footing. These hillsides can be mighty treacherous."

"Right, I don't need a broken leg."

Samuel retrieved the rifle, checked it, put a couple of rounds in his pocket, and grabbed a length of rope and a piece of biscuit.

Heading back to where he had seen the bighorns, he began a steep traverse up out of the river bottom. A small draw entered just beyond. He traversed back to gain elevation and then back upstream, cutting across the top of the draw, rounding the corner, and checking the next draw below him. He did not see the sheep.

He traversed back again, climbing higher, now reaching the broken rock he had seen from below. He changed direction, heading upstream, cutting beneath the rock outcrops. A broad-leaved plant he did not recognize, its leaves withered to grayish brown, crackled loudly as he brushed them. He climbed to avoid the plants.

At the top of the next draw, there was still no sign of the sheep. He feared they had heard him. He sat for a moment, watching, trying to catch movement. The slopes upriver appeared starkly barren. He gazed downriver, not looking directly to where he thought the animals could be, but trying to catch movement from the corners of his eyes. If the bighorns were still below him, he was in a good position to catch them, figuring they would climb the small ridge he was on. The sheep preferred bedding on the small knolls from where they could see approaching danger.

Samuel caught movement above the rocks and spotted the sheep angling away from him. They had climbed more quickly than he had figured and were now almost beyond range.

Rising, he moved off the ridge into the draw and began traversing his way upward. His breath came hard. This country was incredibly steep. Several times his legs went out from under him. He caught himself and then gazed downward at the sheer slopes below, shivering at the thought of tumbling.

He edged around a knoll and unexpectedly encountered the sheep a few yards away. He had lucked out; the wind moved upriver during the day, and they did not see or smell him.

Bracing himself, he carefully chambered a round, muffling the *click* with his body. He aimed at a large ewe, behind her front shoulder, and squeezed the trigger. The explosion sent a shockwave through the canyon silence. The ewe went down, tumbled, and then began sliding.

Samuel watched in dread. The animal would tumble to the bottom, breaking every bone in its body, mangling the meat. The remaining band of bighorns scattered, moving swiftly, almost flowing, up and out of sight among the rocks.

The ewe caught on a shrub, spun around, and slid to a stop.

"Thank you, Lord," Samuel breathed.

Carefully, Samuel made his way to the animal, dragged it to a safer spot, and tied it securely to some brush so he could dress it.

He paused a moment to study his position and was surprised at how high he had climbed. Deep snow and timber carpeted the peaks across the river. This side of the river was sunlit and barren where the snow had melted. Upriver, the Salmon wound its way silently toward him, a silver ribbon winking where it ran fast over the rocks.

He gazed downriver, following the sweep of the bends of the mighty river—the River of No Return, people called it. The river glinted, flowing steadily eastward through the sun-drenched canyon. At the junction with the Little Salmon it swept north, eventually flowing past Slate Creek. Miles beyond, it swung west and briefly southwest to where it emptied into the Snake. From there, the Snake flowed northward past the city of Lewiston to where it picked up the waters of the Clearwater. Swinging west, the Snake eventually emptied into the Columbia, which flowed west to the Pacific Ocean. Samuel thought of the salmon that returned each year to this river—many hundreds of miles from the ocean.

He gazed back toward the mountaintops, one piled on the other, an endless sea of broken peaks enfolding the majestic river below. Except where the river cut small gaps, the mountains lay unbroken, heavily carpeted in timber and snow, rocky crags clawing at the sky. *Lord, I can't think of a more beautiful yet treacherous land,* he mused.

Samuel finished dressing the ewe and saved the heart and liver. When he wiped his knife on a grass tuft beneath some exposed rocks, something about the rocks caught his eye. They were stained red and orange like the rich gold-bearing ledge where he had encountered the Sheepeater Indians. He thought of the Sheepeaters—the ghost Indians, as some referred to them. He had never told his father about the ledge. He gazed north. The Sheepeaters lived somewhere in an unexplored canyon beyond the mountains. A feeling tugged at him—a feeling that he should return.

The narrow quartz stringer ran for several feet up the steep hillside. He followed it, checking pieces of rock, finding some that were stained blue and green. He wedged some of the pieces from the earth and broke one. His breath caught at the sight of metallic yellow. *Gold!* Heart pounding, he examined the chunk. Several fragments were locked in the quartz, but then he recognized the brassy color and angular habit. *Sulphurets. Blast it to blazes.* Disappointment flooded him. He remembered Mr. Hinley telling him that many times pyrite could bind with gold and silver, so he collected several pieces for a possible assay.

Samuel looked around, becoming almost dizzy from the height. Even if this rock held valuable minerals, no one could ever mine it. But he was curious about the bright blue-and-green stains. Mixed in around the bright brassy-colored chunks in the quartz, they were quite striking. He took a piece. *Pa might like this.*

Later, as they ate freshly roasted portions of mountain sheep, Samuel spoke. "I like this country, Pa. It's harsh, but it's got promise. It's got an abundance of wildlife. It's got beauty."

"You're telling me that it doesn't remind you of Iowa."

"Not in the least." Samuel laughed. "Chen says the Chinese call America the land of the golden mountain. They're sojourners. They came to find gold to send home to their families and hopefully to someday go back home. I guess you and me are like sojourners. We've come here seeking our fortune. This summer, we'll go back."

"I guess you can look at it that way."

"Kinda not right, is it," Samuel stated. "Most of the miners won't stay. But folks like the Strombacks and the Shearers, they want to stay. They want to make their livings here."

His father pointed with his knife. "You gotta remember something, Samuel," he said. "The wealth in this country isn't going to last. The gold will run out someday. When it does, people will drift away. Right now you see people moving into this country, taking up homesteads along the river, trying to build towns, maybe someday even some churches and schools. They want a future for themselves and for their families. But there ain't any level spots for real farming. Not like Iowa. So they need the gold." He speared a piece of meat.

"I predict people who've come here won't stay," his father continued. "Even the Indians don't live here. Sure, they come through hunting and fishing and such, but they don't live here. They're pretty much all sojourners, as you've put it, using the land for a short time and then moving on. We'll all leave this canyon, I predict, at some point. I guess you can say from wilderness it came, to wilderness it will return."

Samuel did not like his father's prediction. "I understand what you're saying, Pa, but I hope not. Maybe the quartz mines will continue to get better. Mr. Hinley estimates they've taken out over five thousand ounces from them just in the last three years. And I figure someday someone will figure out how to get to the deep gravels under the meadows. Everyone says there's twice as much gold under the meadow than all the gold that's already been mined. I think about it every time I look at the hillside near the Sweet Mary. There's a lot of gold there, Pa. We just need a way to get at it."

Charles grinned. "You figure me out a way, son, and I'll pull up stakes and live here myself." He shook his head and put his plate aside. "I must say, some of Mr. Hinley's optimism is wearing off on you. You may be right. The quartz mines might continue to get better. The O'Riley might even surprise us. If so, the hardrock mines would certainly provide a future. But you know as well as I do, developing the mines will take capital. I went to Slate Creek partly to seek out local investors. Investors aren't going to come into Warren's from the outside. The main problem is access. The mines have been open for ten years, and all you still have are trails. There isn't a wagon around for miles. You can't haul in heavy mining equipment on the backs of mules. Because of that, the mills are hardly efficient, and none of them can process silver."

"Mr. Bradshaw's will."

"And until it does, mines like the O'Riley won't mean much."

"You make it sound pretty grim, Pa."

"Just calling it like it is. We'll be long gone in any case."

Samuel quieted. He was not sure he wanted to be a sojourner.

Mr. Hunt came by the following morning and found them down by the excavation. "Either you have nothing better to do or you think there's gold down there." He was holding out a letter.

Charles glanced up. "Mostly, nothing better to do. I think we've sewed everything there is to sew at least once and fixed our gear at least twice. Might as well chase some of this flour gold."

Samuel took the letter, noting it was from his mother. He wondered about it because she had not had time to receive his last one.

"Do you have a moment for a cup of coffee?" Charles asked. "Pretty cold today."

"Better not. I'll plan on it on the way back. It'll be dark before I make the Shearers', and I'm feeling like a storm is coming in."

They watched as Hunt rode off upstream, his extra mount trailing, snowshoes lashed on top.

At the cabin, Samuel quickly ripped open his mother's letter and began reading aloud:

My Dear Charles and Son, Samuel,

I am very sorry to inform you that my mother has passed away. She passed very quietly last evening, the—

Samuel dropped the letter, unable to read any further. A stinging jumped to his eyes as he recalled his last memory of his grandma, standing with his mother, holding his little sister, waving good-bye as his father and he rode out of the farmyard.

His father picked up the letter and read silently.

A numbing sadness enveloped Samuel. He could not shake his thoughts. "We should have been there, Pa." He could not imagine his grandma being gone.

"I'm sorry, son." Samuel felt his father's hand on his shoulder. "Maybe we should just head home."

Samuel sat silently for a minute. "Does Ma say we should?"

"No. She did not say much, just that everyone misses us." Charles shook his head. "Samuel, your ma has always believed in me—in us. The way I see it, now more than ever, we owe it to her to hit big at Warren's."

"We owe it to Grandma as well, don't we?"

Samuel considered going to the Strombacks'. It was near time, but he wanted to get to bedrock to see if there was any gold. He didn't know what he would do if there wasn't.

This day the sun shone warmly, and he decided to try washing some more gravel. He dug until he finally hit rock. He scraped off an area and filled a couple of buckets with gravel. Together he and his father routed the trickle of water into the flume and on into the sluice.

Samuel watched the gravel slowly wash down through the sluice. As the water cleared, winking in the sun in the black sand was a small, flattened nugget. It appeared brighter and warmer than the sun. He picked it out and held it up. "What do you think, Pa?"

"Well, that's mighty encouraging." Charles took it and rubbed it between his fingers. "All we gotta do is find another thousand or so, and we'll have an ounce."

Samuel studied the pit. The amount of overburden they still needed to remove was nearly overwhelming. "At least we know it's down here," he said. "All you gotta do is clean it off."

"All *I* gotta do?"

"Been meaning to head downriver to the Strombacks', Pa. I promised them I'd be there by now."

"Well, I guess you're right." Charles pushed his hat back. "Now that's good planning. You'll be getting back about the time I have all this cleared off and the water starts running good."

"Just promise to wait. I wanna see the gold."

That night, Samuel wrote his mother, trying to cheer her and his uncle Jake. He told her of hunting in the canyon. He wrote about how beautiful the land was, how full of wildlife, that the cabin they were in had plenty of sunshine, that if a garden were planted it would yield plenty of truck. A nearby stream provided good water. After rereading it, he found himself marveling at his descriptions. *But it's true.* In Iowa you could grow crops. Here you could grow fruit trees, raise cattle, hunt game, fish salmon, cut timber, mine gold, *and* grow crops. This was good country.

SLATE CREEK

Chapter 8

SMALL ROSE BEFORE DAYBREAK and shared some breakfast with his father before leaving. He took the pistol, extra clothes, and his bedroll. He felt strange having the pistol. It was for protection against men, not for hunting. He also took a small amount of gold to send home and for purchasing a few supplies at Slate Creek.

Samuel's mind raced. He had dreamed often of Bonnie. He could see her sparkling green eyes, beautiful smile, and, he had to admit, her figure. But now that he was about to see her again, he grew fearful that his dreams had grown beyond reality. Would she even say hello?

He reached the Strombacks' ranch late evening. Stars were strung across the sky like frozen specks of light. He had pushed through, not stopping except to briefly water Spooky.

Roundup came running up, whining and wagging his tail.

He scratched the dog's head. *At least someone remembers me.*

Heart hammering heavily, he knocked. If Bonnie came to the door, he wouldn't know what to say. It was Mrs. Stromback.

"Good evening, ma'am. I'm here to take Mr. Stromback up on his offer to hire out for a few days—if he'll still take me, that is."

She beamed. "We certainly will, Samuel. Now you just get yourself in here." She called over her shoulder. "Jon, Jon, you'll never guess. That young man from Christmas, Samuel, is here."

"Hey, here you be, lad," Jon Stromback said, entering the room. "Come in. Come in."

"Thank you, sir."

The three children came from their back room, squealing. Josef bounced around, telling Samuel he should see him roping now. The girls stared with their big eyes.

Bonnie appeared absent. Samuel was disappointed, but he forced himself to not ask after her whereabouts.

Mrs. Stromback must have guessed. "Bonnie's away in Lewiston a few more days taking music and piano lessons. She'll be happy to see you when she returns."

Samuel felt crushed. He had taken for granted that she would be here. "I'll sure be happy to see her as well." He wondered if he sounded too exuberant.

"Her mother always wanted her to play the piano and sing," Mrs. Stromback continued.

"We're doin' our best to oblige her," Jon Stromback said, "but I think Bonnie's got more of a liking for ranching."

Samuel figured so as well. "She does have a nice voice."

"She does," Mrs. Stromback agreed. "And someday she may take over from Mrs. Henson and play the piano for Sunday service."

Samuel remembered the woman. She did not play poorly, but the piano had been out of tune.

"The night's long, Samuel. Let's get you bedded down," Stromback said. "I'll get you oriented tomorrow. Mrs. Stromback expects you at breakfast at six sharp."

They headed into the night. "It's good to see you, Samuel. I hope this ranching meets with your favor."

"I'm sure it will, sir." He grabbed up Spooky's reins.

They walked a short distance down a wagon track and across a well-built bridge toward the bunkhouse.

"You can turn your mount out here. Plenty of feed near the fence next to water. He'll find it."

Samuel unsaddled Spooky and brushed him a bit before releasing him. Stromback showed him where to stow his saddle in the tack shed.

Kerosene lamps caused light to dance within the bunkhouse. Two men were playing cards.

"This is the new hand I've told you about. Name's Samuel Chambers."

"We met at Christmas, but not officially," the older man said. "Name's Arthur Shaw. I go by Art." He rose and shook hands. "Welcome back, Samuel. Going to be good to have someone around not so ugly as this here cuss."

The younger man, lanky and with rough face, rose. "Name's Rex Callahan." There was no warmth in either his handshake or his greeting.

"I want you boys to teach him the ropes," Stromback said. "Samuel's a farmer turned miner. Now he wants to be a miner turned rancher."

Samuel wondered about Stromback's comment.

"Art, you might start by riding the perimeter with him. Check to see how the drift fence has held up over winter. Let him get familiar with the land."

"I'll be obliged," Art answered. "Want him to cut out a mount or use his?"

"I'd suggest he use the gray." Stromback eyed Samuel. "Give your horse a few days to strengthen up. That wild grass upriver don't pack as much punch as the hay and oats we got."

After Stromback left, Rex muttered, "And *he's* gonna take care of our stock?"

Samuel did not respond.

The morning saw Art and Samuel following the drift fence to the northwest. The gray was a four-year-old gelding, a bit jumpy like Spooky sometimes was, and Samuel had to keep a tight rein at first.

They passed dozens of mules and several horses. "Packers' stock, mostly," Art explained. "They winter over here. We watch that they don't disappear."

"What, do cougars favor them?"

"Some, but mostly Indians favor them. Not so much the mules, though they might take one and eat it. Mostly we gotta watch the horses. The Nez Perce are quite fond of 'em. They're friendly to us at the present, but Indians can be fickle. They get a notion to do somethin', they just up and do it. And stealin' horses is born in their blood."

"They come here often?" Samuel wondered if he would see any. They moved slowly uphill across the withered grass.

"Often enough." Art paused and swept his arm. "This was their land until '63. Most of them still consider it so."

"So there'll be trouble?"

"Maybe. When gold was found hereabouts, some early folks like Mr. Stromback offered to buy the land from the Indians. So far the Nez Perce have honored that purchase, and Stromback and others treat them well. Not so much some of the newer settlers."

Samuel shook his head. "Then the mining camps were on Indian land?"

"That's mostly why the government renegotiated the treaty. Once gold was found, you couldn't keep the miners out. So they redrew the boundaries. Not all the Nez Perce agreed to that and still consider this their land."

Art eased his mount to the edge of a rocky draw they had come upon and scanned its length.

"This draw is about as far north as the cattle will wander, and usual there's at least a couple that get into trouble down there. I don't see any, though."

Art pointed back uphill toward some grazing horses. "Ever see horses like them?"

"Appaloosas, right?" Samuel noticed the spotted rumps and remembered Bonnie saying that Stromback had some.

"Yep, Mr. Stromback traded for them. They're beautiful animals." He glanced around. "Beautiful country too. I come out here mining up at Florence. Found out I could make a steadier livin' ranchin'." He turned his horse downhill. "Hoping to get my own ranch someday. But I'll be okay if I don't. Mr. Stromback's a good man. He treats us well. When I get a little extra pay, I go into town. That's good enough for me."

Samuel raised his eyes.

"Not Slate Creek if that's what you're a thinkin'. Not even Washington. Too civilized." He nudged his horse over some rocks. "Nope, I go to Florence or Lewiston. That's where the women are."

They returned to the lower fields, and Art angled for the creek.

"Might as well check for ice. We've had to chop ice nearly every day, twice a day, all winter. I sure won't miss doing that."

"I had my fair share of chopping ice upriver near our cabin."

"This has been the coldest winter anyone can remember. We lost some stock a couple weeks back when we had an ice storm. Some animals slid off a bluff into the river."

Samuel cringed at the thought.

Rex came riding in from the east, and they talked. Most of the packers' mules and horses were to the east, up higher toward the timber.

"I saw some cougar sign," Rex explained. "Might have to get the Osmund hands and try to bring the stock down a bit."

"As usual," Art replied. "Don't know why them mules can't figure the grass turns green down here first."

They brought in a wagon next to a crib and loaded hay. Samuel welcomed the work. He felt good as he stabbed the hay and swung it onto the wagon. With Art slowly driving the team, he and Rex pitched it off, some along each side, the cattle stringing along behind and pausing to feed.

"Might be the last we'll be pitchin' hay, boy, now that it's startin' to green a bit," Rex explained.

Later, when they returned to the ranch house, Samuel found Josef outside, practicing roping on the mounted steer horns.

He looked up, grinning. "Want to try, Mr. Chambers?"

"Sure, Josef." Samuel took the rope and began shaking out the loop. "You can call me Samuel."

"Okay, Samuel." He watched, eyes big. Samuel carefully swung the loop but missed. He didn't miss the look on Rex's face.

"Ha," Josef said. "Let me show you." He ran to get the rope, Roundup chasing after, getting in his way. "Down, Roundup," Josef scolded and then coiled and threw the rope, dropping the loop neatly over the wooden steer. "That's how it's done."

Samuel tried again—his second try was successful.

After a couple of days, Stromback decided to move the steers and heifers off the lower fields to make room for the cows that would calve. The men began pushing the cattle downriver toward the creek and some upper range.

Rex rode by, trying to rope a heifer.

Art laughed and addressed Samuel. "Don't have to rope 'em. All you gotta do is herd 'em." He spurred his horse and cut off the heifer, forcing it to swerve toward the creek. "She's all yours, Rex," he hollered.

"Come on, Samuel, fan out. We need to funnel 'em toward the creek crossing and that gap." Art pointed and then started moving toward the bunched yearlings, clucking at them, slapping with his coiled rope. "If they try to break past you, try to cut 'em off without leaving too big a gap around the outside."

Samuel followed, beating his arm, calling to the cattle, "Git! Git along!" Three steers watched him approach, splay legged. His gray hesitated. Samuel tried to nudge him forward, but the horse balked. The gray knew to give the steers time to decide. The animals turned and scampered toward the group moving toward the creek. *Smart horse,* Samuel realized. After that, he knew to let the animal do the work.

Keeping them boxed in from his side, Art hooted and called, forcing them across the creek toward a narrow opening. Samuel saw that they would turn toward the river and moved in that direction to cut them off. Art had given them enough room, and they turned past him, heading upstream. Closing in, the two swept them toward the gap. As the yearlings moved past, they dismounted and pulled poles across the opening. The animals turned up across the shoulder of a barren hillside, now separated from the cows by the creek that cut through the steep ravine.

Rex came up, herding another couple of steers, swinging his rope.

They quickly pulled the poles, but the steers veered away.

"Let's get out of his way," Art said, remounting and heading down creek.

Rex rode past, driving the steers back past them and on up the hillside.

"Kinda a strange man, don't you think, Samuel?"

"He works hard." But Samuel thought he was trying to show off.

"I don't want to butt in where it's not my business," continued Art, "but you'd be wise to watch out for him. He's got this crazy notion that he and Bonnie have somethin' goin', but I know for a fact Bonnie won't have nothin' to do with him." Art swung down and reached for the poles again.

"I appreciate the news," Samuel managed. He helped Art slide the poles back into place.

"Don't know why he's still headin' uphill." Art laughed. "Come on, Samuel, we got some cows to feed."

Chapter 9

With some grass beginning to green, the cows insisted on wandering, and the men were occupied with trying to keep them on the lower fields for when they would begin calving. This day, Art and Samuel drove a couple back up out of a gully.

"Don't know why they always insist on going down there," Art muttered.

Samuel was learning that the only thing predictable about cattle was their stupidity. If they could find trouble, they would. Whenever he noticed any were missing, he figured they would be in the most treacherous spot around, and that was where he usually found them.

Samuel was surprised at how far the animals wandered from the ranch. "At least they don't go to the top of this mountain," he remarked to Art.

"Oh, I've found them close—all the way to the timber, but thank God, they don't keep going. They'd be in Florence." Art laughed. "That drift fence we keep working on above us is pretty good. When they hit it, they usually follow it back down."

They paused to look back on the barren hillsides below them. Cattle were bunched near a draw. Art gazed west across the river. "Might be a storm brewing—they're clumping together, probably sensing it."

Samuel glanced up. The sky was clear, but he felt dampness in the air.

The storm Art had anticipated moved in from the northwest the following morning. Scudding clouds moved in with a steady drizzle, but the temperature dropped, and it quickly turned to sleet and then heavy, wet snow. The wind picked up, howling downriver, driving the snow.

Dinner was quiet.

"We sure could lose some more stock in this one," Stromback muttered. "When it breaks, I want us out checking on the animals. They've been stressed from the last bout. Won't take much to put some more of them under."

"Nothing we could have done about that, Mr. Stromback," Art said quietly.

"I'm not blaming anyone. Worst winter since I been here," Stromback said. "Maybe I shouldn't have had you push those yearlings off the flats yet. I thought spring was here. We better try to push them back. Spread a lot of hay. Maybe they'll remember where the feed is."

They woke to howling winds and driving snow. The northwest sides of the trees and buildings were crusted with thick ice. Deep drifts extended on the leeward sides.

The men clustered about the breakfast table, watching the light come to the sky, considering their options. The snow had weakened, but the wind continued. Over a foot of snow lay on the level, and in places it had drifted to three and four feet. They rode out into the weather, intending to drive the stock back toward the flats. Samuel rode with Stromback. Art and Rex rode the opposite direction to check on packers' stock.

Samuel studied the sky, not sure the storm had passed.

"Some have moved under the cottonwoods." Stromback pointed.

Samuel could make out the brown lumps huddled together, snow plastered to their backs, steam rising from their bodies.

"That's good, isn't it?"

"Not always. Cottonwoods are brittle. That snow will bring down a lot of limbs. I've lost critters under cottonwood limbs before."

Drawing closer, Samuel could see broken limbs scattered about with animals among them. He decided there were not many places where the animals could go to get out of the storm. This country was barren of trees except along the gullies and miles distant toward the canyon rim.

"It's better than the open," Stromback conceded. "Here, let's pull these poles and try to get those yearlings headed back this direction. I'm guessing we'll get more snow by tonight."

They headed up the shoulder to where they had driven the yearlings a few days earlier.

"We'll check this draw and the next one. The upper one is where I had most of my trouble earlier." Stromback pointed to a snow-covered bluff in the distance. "Animals trying to get grass where the wind had cleared off the snow slid into the river. Never seen anything like it in my life. That's when I brought them down to the flats for feed." He pulled his coat more tightly around him as a gust hit.

"Usually don't need to worry about feeding them around here.

Lam'tama, the Nez Perce call this country—'the canyon of no snow.' Except for this winter," he said bitterly.

They crossed a small tributary that fed into Slate Creek and rounded the point, heading downriver. They had spotted no cattle.

"I'm hoping they've holed up in the next draw but not so badly that they're trapped."

They reached the next draw and paused. The canyon walls were rapidly disappearing behind a curtain of descending snow. Samuel glanced toward Stromback, hoping the man was noticing, but he gazed uphill, seemingly unaware.

Moments later, the curtain of blinding white hit. Samuel pulled his scarf more tightly about his nose and mouth, shivering. If they found any cattle holed up, they could do very little to get them moving. It was not as if they could tell them there was better shelter next door.

They snow paused, and they moved onward. Samuel felt wet and chilled. His fingers were numb. He began wondering how much more he could take. Finally, he paused and looked up to call out to Stromback. The man was peering downriver across the draw. Samuel caught sight of two men at work over a carcass lying in the snow. Another curtain of white advanced toward them.

"Indians," Samuel whispered.

"Nez Perce," Stromback said. "Sure looks like they got one of my beef."

"What we gonna do?"

"Let them have it. I've learned if they're taking one, things must be pretty bad."

"What if they see us and come after us?"

"They've already seen us. At any rate, we pretty much have an unspoken agreement."

"An agreement?"

The curtain of snow descended, masking the Indians. Moments later, the wind drove it hard against Samuel and Stromback. Samuel gasped for breath against the numbing cold.

"Come on, Samuel, nothing we can do out here. We better head in."

Samuel urged the gray to turn and follow Stromback, who was now a dark blur fading in front of him. At least the wind was at Samuel's back, but now it drove the snow underneath his clothing and down his neck, chilling him further. He shivered violently, his teeth chattering.

He lost sight of Stromback for a few moments and grew anxious.

The gray trod onward, and Samuel had to trust that the animal knew where it was going. At last, they reached the shelter of the ranch yard. Snow and ice caked Samuel's hat and covered his back. He dismounted and stomped to get it off. They stripped their gear and tossed hay down to the horses. Samuel was shivering uncontrollably by the time they got inside. Art and Rex were already there. Mrs. Stromback had fixed some coffee.

"Not much we can do in this, boys," Stromback said. "Say a prayer we still have some stock standin' by morning."

Samuel was beginning to sense how serious the storm had become.

"Then we'd best be getting things together for the morning," Art said.

Art and Rex rose and headed out toward the bunkhouse.

"You comin', boy?" Rex asked.

Samuel was shivering, barely able to talk. "A-all right."

Mrs. Stromback noticed. "Let him get out of his duds and warm up some."

Samuel hesitated.

"Here ye be, lad. You stay and do as the missus says," Jon Stromback agreed.

Relief flooded Samuel.

Soon he was sitting next to the fire wrapped in a large robe while his clothes dried, feeling a little foolish. He was not so sure it was a good thing. The Strombacks were treating him like some child, but he knew if his mother were here, she would have insisted on the same thing.

Stromback sat in his chair, smoking a pipe. "You surprised me today, Samuel. I pushed it pretty hard. Maybe more than what was smart."

"Yes, sir. I figured you were concerned because of the last storm."

"Sure, but a beef ain't worth a man's life."

"Kind of like gold mining. Some things aren't worth the risk. But it's hard to know when to stop. The next shovelful might turn you rich."

Stromback laughed. "Rich won't happen with cattle. I just seek a good living for myself and my family. We've worked hard to build this place."

"You lost a steer to the Indians."

"It may have already been dead from the storm. Like I said, we have an unspoken agreement. The Nez Perce don't bother me, and if they need a beef occasionally, I don't mind."

He let out a puff of smoke. "Do you know anything about the Nez Perce, Samuel?"

"Art said you bought your land from them, but the new treaty might be trouble. What happened?"

"Back in '55 the government signed a treaty that established a reservation. It included the Wallowas to the west across the Snake, land south of us and up the Little Salmon for a ways, land to the east along the Salmon River for a ways, and land north across the Clearwater—a huge chunk of land.

"When gold was struck in Pierce and later at Florence, miners ignored the treaty and came looking for gold. Likewise, farmers began pushing into the Wallowas for good farm and ranch land. The government was pressured to remove the Indians, so they reduced the size of the reservation to about one-tenth its original size."

"And not all the Nez Perce agreed. Art told me."

"At least five bands of Nez Perce refused to sign the new treaty, especially Young Joseph and Chief White Bird. White Bird's band is who we bought our land from. Those Nez Perce who did sign the new treaty really didn't care because they'd still be living on their own lands and wouldn't be moving." Stromback laughed. "Sure is like me saying you can have my neighbor's ranch."

"Then I don't blame Joseph or White Bird," Samuel said. "Can't we just leave them alone?"

"Too late for that. The land around Joseph is being settled and farmed. We have a couple communities on White Bird's ancestral land, including Slate Creek. It's always the same: people get nervous every time they see an Indian out hunting, and of course every time a horse or cow goes missing, the Indians get the blame, so here we call in the government to wet-nurse us."

Stromback glanced at Samuel. "Trouble is, even if all the Nez Perce agreed to the new reservation, that's not what they want. For certain, the government doesn't care a lick about their ancestral lands. I know I wouldn't want to give up where I lived and buried my kin. Why would *they*? And they look at life different than we do. They're hunters—not farmers or ranchers. They don't want to sit in one place and rot."

"Think there'll be a war?"

"If we push them. Sure is what concerns me. Ever since Lewis and Clark came through along the Clearwater, the Nez Perce have been friendly to the whites. To my recollect, they've never lifted a rifle against us."

"That's good."

"Good for *us*. They're crack marksmen."

Samuel shivered. His father had said something similar.

"If there be trouble, you'll have a part in it." Stromback eyed Samuel.

Samuel stared back.

"Yah, and so will I." He laughed. "If you miners find enough gold in this country, then there will be more towns and ranching and supply communities throughout this region. Eventually, the government will be forced to push the Indians out."

Samuel was not sure what to think.

"Just you remember this was *all* Nez Perce country. Still is to most of them. Here they come hunting and fishing, and sometimes take a beef, and we're happy to let them. To them, it'll always be their land. I'd advise you to remember that."

"Yes, sir." Samuel knew he would remember.

Mrs. Stromback came in and told him his clothes were dry. The three children spilled in as well. Mrs. Stromback had been keeping them at bay, but now Josef wanted to hear stories about Indians.

Later, Art and Rex joined them for dinner. Afterward, when the three returned to the bunkhouse, the wind had finally died down, and the snow had quit. Lying down, Samuel felt like lead, barely able to move.

"Reckon we'll find some dead ones?" he asked.

"I'm sure we will."

Chapter 10

THE SNOW SLOWLY MELTED, leaving drifts lingering in the shaded areas and draws. Rex and Samuel headed out toward the southeast corner to try to account for some missing stock. Stromback feared they had succumbed to the blizzard but also feared a mountain lion was taking its toll. Samuel carried a rifle loaned to him by Stromback in case they spotted the lion.

They worked the perimeter to a spot where it appeared some cattle had wandered beyond. After trailing their tracks for a few hours, Rex suggested they were seeing things. Certainly the tracks were not fresh. About that time, Samuel spotted a carcass. "Lion kill."

Rex scouted about the kill for a moment. "I hate them cats, but you'll never get a shot at one. They sense you comin' and just disappear."

Samuel glanced at the surrounding timber, scanning for the mountain lion, nerves on edge.

"Same as them eagles. They swoop down and take a calf right in front of ya," Rex muttered. "Better to just lace this carcass with strychnine and kill them and anything else that comes to feed." He laughed. "Did that once and got one of Stromback's dogs, so he don't do poison no more, but I say do it."

Samuel thought about Roundup, although the dog never left the ranch. He decided he would rather try to shoot the cougars, but as Rex had pointed out, people rarely caught sight of them. Once a lion started feeding on cattle, it became a regular habit.

That night, Bonnie was home for dinner. Samuel was overjoyed but tried not to show it too much. She was more beautiful than he remembered—a glowing angel with an incredible smile. He found it difficult to concentrate while she politely talked about her stay in Lewiston. After dinner, Art nodded toward Samuel and convinced Rex to head back to the bunkhouse. Bonnie rose and began taking dishes to the kitchen. Samuel followed, offering to help, but Mrs. Stromback stopped him. "Thank you, but I can handle this. You two can sit for a bit and catch up on news."

Samuel felt an incredible rush. "Th-thank you kindly," he stammered. Bonnie glanced at him, a bright smile on her face.

They talked, being slightly cautious, knowing Mrs. Stromback was in the other room. Samuel tried to listen more than he talked. He loved Bonnie's voice and how her cheeks dimpled when she smiled. He loved how the flickering kerosene lamplight danced in her eyes and across her golden hair, bringing out flashes of red.

He was almost oblivious when Mrs. Stromback brought in tea and joined them for a moment. Samuel continued to talk before he recognized that that was her signal for him to leave.

"Thank you kindly again for dinner, Mrs. Stromback, and thank you for tea." He rose. "Thanks for sitting with me, Bonnie."

"Oh my," Mrs. Stromback suddenly said. "Josef and I intended to read. Good night, you two."

"Good night," Bonnie replied.

Samuel was surprised when Bonnie grabbed a lamp and followed him out the door. She whispered. "Don't you worry, Samuel. That was my aunt's way of telling me I could walk with you for a moment."

"B-but ..." Samuel began. His heart raced.

"It is proper," she whispered. She took his hand and they walked toward the bunkhouse. "Trust me."

Roundup padded after them. At the bridge, Bonnie held back, the dog nuzzling her for attention. She glanced toward the starlit sky, looking in no particular direction, rubbing Roundup's ears. "I am much happier here than trying to learn music."

"You sing really well. It would be a shame not to hear you sing." Samuel petted the dog as well, allowing his hand to overlap Bonnie's. She did not pull away.

"I believe I am capable of singing *without* formal lessons," she said with slight disdain.

"That's what your mother wanted."

Bonnie arched her eyes. "Aunt Rebecca told you?"

Samuel nodded.

She turned back, looking away. "I miss my mother. She always wanted me to sing and play the piano. She was magical at the piano. I shall never be like her. Oh, I like playing, but it is not my calling."

"That's okay. You'll honor her with your singing, just the way you are," Samuel said sincerely. "She understands that now."

"Do you really think so?" Bonnie turned, smiling. She peered toward the north where the stars seemed brightest. "Is it not beautiful here?"

Samuel took the hint. "Yes. You truly live on a wonderful ranch." He felt a bit awkward, knowing she wanted him to say something else.

Impulsively he pulled her to himself, looked into her eyes, and whispered. "Bonnie, you know what's beautiful? You are." He meant it with every fiber of his body. "I-I've known so from the first I saw you at Christmas services."

She brushed her fingers across his lips. "And Samuel, you are so handsome."

Samuel felt weak. How could this be happening? "Bonnie?"

Her eyes sparkled from the dancing lamplight.

"I-I like you a lot. I want you to know that, and I'd like to know you better. You're the most wonderful person that's happened to me."

She was quiet.

Samuel raced on. "It might not work, you know."

She frowned.

"I mean … I gotta be leaving come this summer. I have an obligation to my family."

A hurt flashed through her eyes. "Sh, Samuel. You never know what may be possible."

It dawned on Samuel that she had thought of this. He heard the ranch door open. Roundup took off, heading toward the door.

"Oops," he whispered. "Good night, I guess."

"Good night, Samuel." She blew a small kiss and flashed a smile.

Samuel felt his heart beating wildly as he watched Bonnie return to the house. He remained watching until the light from the doorway winked out.

The following day, Samuel rode out with Rex again, intending to account for the still-missing cows. He rode Spooky and was glad for it. The gray was a good cow pony, but Spooky seemed to understand Samuel and anticipate what he wanted. Samuel had decided the horse had a good head for avoiding trouble, except for that one rattlesnake last year.

They had hardly reached the perimeter of the lower fields when Rex turned to him and spat, "I seen you two last night when Bonnie got back. Don't lie to me and tell me I didn't."

"What's there to lie about?"

"I seen you and Bonnie. You stay away from her. She and I are spoken."

"How can it be you're spoken? The Strombacks haven't said." Samuel felt his gut wrench.

"That's exactly what I mean. Mr. Stromback knows about us; we're just waitin' our time. You lay another finger on her, and you and I will settle." His voice was ice.

Samuel felt his anger rising but said nothing. He couldn't care less what Rex thought.

They returned to following several sets of cattle tracks winding uphill until they reached a small saddle. The tracks headed down the other side, following a rapidly flowing stream. Ice floes and snowdrifts still filled it in places. They followed it to where another stream entered from the east and where the tracks turned upward.

Rex paused. "Them old cows might head uphill to a spring about a mile from here, but sometimes they wander down this here gully back to the river." Rex glanced uphill. "I'll follow them that's headed uphill. You take them that's headed down."

Samuel could see the tracks heading uphill but nothing fresh heading down, except some deer tracks. "Those are deer tracks, heading down."

"Hell, boy, take a look. There's cow tracks under them deer tracks. Take my word. They'll show clear in a bit."

Samuel wanted to believe Rex, but he saw little sign. Maybe Rex was right and farther down they would show.

"It's steep, but I've chased them down through there lots a times. You come right out on the trail next to the river. Unless you don't think you can manage," Rex taunted. He turned his horse toward the gully, as if to do the job himself.

"N-no, I'll do it." Samuel did not want Rex telling Stromback that he could not handle the job. He turned Spooky downhill.

"When you get down, make sure you get them cows turned downriver, boy, or you'll end up chasing them all the way to John Day's."

"Reckon I can do that." He eased Spooky downward in the direction of the tracks. He felt foolish and now certain it was a game trail. No cow, even as dumb as they were, would go this direction.

Almost immediately, Samuel was in trouble. The trail quickly dropped into a gully with rushing water cutting through its bottom. In places, rotten snow and thick brush filled it, making travel dangerous and near impossible. He spurred Spooky up and around. The horse slid, nearly spilling him. Spooky turned downhill, trying to regain his footing, fighting to stay upright. Samuel held on. Spooky surged sideways and stopped in the creek, shaking, eyes rolling.

No way anyone's ever ridden down this, especially Rex, Samuel thought.

"Easy boy." Samuel dismounted. He slipped, trying to get his footing. He studied to see which way the tracks went. The deer had to have found a way down, but he knew deer could go where his horse could not.

Buckbrush choked the sides of the ravine. Thorns ripped at him as he tried to urge Spooky upward.

"Come on, boy."

Samuel climbed upward, pulling on the reins. The animal surged up the side of the ravine, caught a foothold, and followed Samuel up and out and across the slope above a sheer drop. The creek emerged from the cleft behind them in a twenty-foot waterfall. No animal was going down where they had just been.

Samuel shook his head. Evening was gathering. "We're in trouble, Spooky." Samuel felt a stab of panic overcoming him. He tried to reason through it. He looked back uphill and studied the tracks where Spooky had slid. It would be impossible to go uphill.

If a cow did come this way, it had to find a way down, or its carcass is in the ravine.

Samuel edged back toward the gully. He saw scattered bones with pieces of red-brown hair. Samuel shivered. Its carcass *was* in the ravine. He knew he could climb out alone, but he would have to leave Spooky behind.

"Somehow we gotta get down, boy," Samuel choked. He studied the wall below. A couple of chutes led through gaps in the rock, ending in sandy talus. The deer tracks went down one.

He mounted up. "It's damn steep, Spooky, but you can do it." The horse shied, but Samuel got him to take a step downhill. The animal took his chance and headed straight down. Standing in the stirrups, Samuel gave Spooky his lead. "Easy, Spook."

The black horse surged, sending gravel downhill, sliding down through the chute. He turned out, standing on the sidehill, shaking.

"Good boy, Spook." Samuel patted him, calming him. He could see the river bottom. "We got her now."

He cut wide traverses on the steep slope until they reached the trail and clattered out onto it. "You did it, boy. I don't care what that bastard

Rex said. Ain't no one ever come down that ravine. Least not until you and I just did."

Night had fallen. Stromback would be wondering where he was. Samuel did not mind. Spooky could find his way from here.

The trail followed high above the river, a thin ribbon clinging to the cliffs. He remembered this section, where part of it was chiseled from the rock. He was thankful Spooky could follow the trail better than what he could see. The river thundered below, spitting white spray from the blackness.

Coming up to the bend, he saw lights flickering ahead and heard horses. The lanterns waved back and forth. "It's Samuel!"

The men rode up.

"You're damn lucky to be alive, son," Stromback said, studying him. "What were you thinking?" His tone was unkind.

"I was following a cow, sir. Found her, but decided I had to leave her." He shot Rex a look.

"You found her?" Rex seemed cautious.

"Yep, she were deader 'n a doornail. Nothing but a bunch of bones and hide," Samuel said. "I told Rex the tracks were old but he disagreed, said last time he went down through that gulch, he chased one out just fine. He offered me to follow this one down."

Both Stromback and Art exchanged quick glances.

"Here, what were you thinking, Rex?" Stromback eyed him. "I've told you before that that gulch is inviting trouble. Any animals go down that way, I've told you to let 'em go. I've said it before—no beef is worth losing your hide over."

"Samuel musta misunderstood me, Mr. Stromback," Rex said, seemingly fighting for words. "He musta *thought* I told him to foller it down. I was askin' him to check if it come back up. 'Most often, they come back up.' That's what I said." His tone was icy, as if daring Samuel to contradict him. "No, sir, I didn't plan on him going down there. When I got back after chasin' them two cows up the ridge, I saw he'd gone down there. That's why I come to get you." He shot another look at Samuel. "That's what I said. You just heard wrong, didn't you, boy?"

Samuel hesitated and then slowly replied, "I reckon. The wind was kicking up something fierce."

The day had been dead calm.

"I got headed down and saw that cow was headed into trouble," Samuel continued. "I would have gotten out earlier, but I was doing my best to get that cow untangled. Too bad I didn't realize right away she was dead. But by golly, I did my best."

Art smiled. Stromback clenched his teeth. Rex glared.

They turned and headed down the trail. "Here you be, lad, I'll tell you one thing," Stromback muttered. "For sure you got yourself one hell of a mount to bring you out of that hole."

Chapter 11

ONCE MORE THEY PUSHED the yearlings back toward the upper range. They had spent a couple of days working on the drift fence, finding where the snow had broken it down, cutting new poles, and standing up the legs. It ran near the timber's edge across the north of the range and then angled down toward Slate Creek. They kept watch for the mountain lion, but there had been no fresh kills.

"The mule deer are moving back uphill. The lions won't be needing to take any cattle unless they've gotten lazy and gotten used to beef," Art explained.

Samuel thought of Bonnie every day. He made it a habit to be early to breakfast and tried to remain behind later at dinner.

This morning, Mrs. Stromback was coming from behind the house with a few hens' eggs, Roundup on her heels. The dog veered off to come and say hello to Samuel.

"You're up earlier and earlier, Samuel."

"I'm just happy winter's finally over," he said. "How can I help?"

Mrs. Stromback never asked for an extra hand in the kitchen, but Samuel hoped she would allow it so he could visit with Bonnie. She again declined.

Samuel made the effort again that evening to help wash up after dinner. Finally, Mrs. Stromback agreed. Rex made an ugly frown, but Samuel ignored him.

Samuel heated water for the dishes and helped Bonnie wash and dry them. Later, he and Bonnie again stood on the bridge, Roundup between them. Again, they gazed at the evening stars, glittering through the tree branches. They talked and dreamed, and Samuel knew with his entire being that he wanted to be with Bonnie.

This time Samuel did not need Roundup's help. He took Bonnie's hands. "Gosh, Bonnie, you are the most wonderful person. If I could … I mean, if it was proper, I would like to kiss you."

Bonnie arched her eyes. She leaned toward Samuel and planted a quick kiss on his lips. Samuel stepped back awkwardly, surprised.

Bonnie laughed lightly. "Isn't this beautiful?" She waved at the stars. A sliver of moon had crept above the mountains.

Samuel glanced at the moon, feeling confused. It was as if she was trying to brush off the most beautiful thing that had yet happened to him.

"Maybe before you go, Uncle Jon will let me take you to our favorite riding spot. It is so beautiful." She smiled.

"I'd like that," he murmured. He wanted to pull Bonnie to himself and hold her tightly.

"Good night." She touched his hand.

"Good night, Bonnie." Samuel turned and headed toward the bunkhouse. He thought he saw Rex at the window. A chill ran through him.

At breakfast, Stromback laid out the day's plans.

"Terrance Vance should be coming in today with a couple of his hands. For sure, he'll want help bringing his mules in. He'll be running them over to Mr. Castle, getting them shod and ready for the season."

Samuel's heart caught. "Does that mean the snow's gone and we can get into Warren's?"

"Nope, now's the time the packers head out to Lewiston and start bringing in goods for when the trails open. Probably Vance will take a short string to the snowline up toward Florence and maybe Warren's so some men can snowshoe some goods in." He pushed back his chair. "Word is coming out that supplies are pretty low."

Stromback nodded toward Rex and Samuel. "You two can head up to the spring and sweep up that direction for any of his stock. Mr. Vance isn't going to be all that happy. I'm guessing he lost four or five head."

Shortly, Samuel and Rex were headed toward the upper spring. When they reached the saddle where Samuel had turned downhill, he paused.

"You know, Rex, that *is* pretty steep country down that way," Samuel managed. "I'm a fool for having believed you rode it."

"Watch it," Rex spat. "You came about as close as a body can to calling me a liar in front of Mr. Stromback a while back."

Samuel sat Spooky. "Well, then, what are you? You sure as blazes never rode down that ravine. You told me clear as day that you chased cows down and out the bottom all the time."

"Watch that mouth, boy. You keep gabbing, it'll be the last thing you do."

Samuel studied the man. He knew he was no match for him. "What you got against me that eats at you, anyway, Rex?"

"Eats at *me*?" Rex laughed loudly. "You don't have to go pretending on me. I've seen you and Bonnie. You know damn well what yer here for."

"No, I don't know, Rex. Maybe you should tell me." Samuel began to wonder if Rex knew something he didn't.

"It's plain and simple, boy. Old man Stromback don't really like me around his niece. He invited you out to interest her away. But don't for one stinkin' moment think it's gonna work."

"I came here to work." Samuel felt his anger rising, but recalled Stromback's hopes that Bonnie might see in him other possibilities than Rex.

Rex's nostrils flared; his eyes bored into Samuel. "I want to work this ranch with Stromback's blessings, but it don't look like he's gonna ever favor me. I work my butt off, but all I get is crumbs. Then he brings in a little runt to court his niece. And you ask what eats at me," he spat. "What Stromback don't know is Bonnie and I got a thing goin'. Soon as she can, permission or no, Bonnie and I are goin' away." He must have reconsidered his comment because he quickly added, "And if you go blab this to the old man"—he patted his rifle—"it'll be the last thing you ever blab. Don't think for a moment I won't."

Samuel saw hatred in the man's eyes. He fought to stay calm and felt his own anger clouding his thoughts. "What you're saying is your business, Rex. I didn't come here to court Bonnie." *Not entirely,* he thought.

"Maybe so." Rex's shoulders eased. "Maybe you're still too wet behind the ears to know what for." He laughed.

Samuel's ears burned.

"Hell, Bonnie and I done things together I bet you ain't never thought of doin'."

Samuel knew otherwise. "I don't believe you."

"You callin' me a liar?"

Samuel turned and headed uphill. He wanted nothing more to do with Rex. He had mules to find.

"I ain't done talkin', boy," he snapped, but Samuel continued moving away. "You turn your back on me, you're invitin' a slug, coward. Turn around you bastard, or I'm the last man you'll ever turn your back on."

Just as Samuel told himself that Rex was bluffing, he heard the whine of the bullet and explosion from his rifle. He flinched.

Rex's laughter reached his ears. He kept laughing. "You're a joke, boy."

Samuel turned Spooky and rode back to within a few feet of Rex, staring at him coldly. "The next time you take a shot at me, Rex, you better kill me. If you don't, I swear to God, I'll hunt you down and put a bullet in your sorry-ass carcass." Samuel tried not to show he was shaking. "And another thing, Rex … I ain't a boy."

Rex must have thought about the idiocy of his actions. His face grew pale. "Look, kid, I'm just foolin' with you."

Samuel saw him grasping for a story. He realized if Stromback knew about this, Rex would be finished. Samuel had covered for him last time, thinking maybe there was a slight misunderstanding, although he knew otherwise.

"Forget it, Rex," Samuel said quietly. "For sure I like Bonnie. Maybe even love her. I can't have her. I'm heading back to Iowa soon as we finish mining. What you saw the other night was me saying good-bye."

Rex's mouth slackened as he must have considered Samuel's comment. "We're okay, then, about me foolin' you by shooting?"

Samuel turned back uphill. He knew they were not.

Although the calves were due, Samuel could no longer stay. The water was running. He had to help at the placer. His last day, Samuel and Art headed out to look for a couple of cows that had strayed.

"They're probably feeling their time to calve and won't show their selves until they've done so. If that happens, the calf is as good as dead. Get eaten by a coyote or cougar," Art explained. "Any cow that calves out in the bush might as well have never carried."

Jon Stromback rode up. "Seeing that you're headed out shortly, Samuel, mind if I tag along?"

Samuel was surprised. "Certainly not, sir."

"You can take Rex for a ride, south, if you want, Art."

"Obliged, Mr. Stromback." Art turned away. Samuel wondered what that meant.

Samuel led out, heading up Slate Creek.

"Sure you know where you're going?" Stromback asked after a moment.

Embarrassed, Samuel glanced back. "I reckon. I'm figuring the cows are holed up in one of the hollows along that side creek that empties into

Slate Creek. Thought I'd check there first." It was the most treacherous place he could think of.

"You might be correct, Samuel," he said. "But first I'd like you to see something." He spurred his horse and headed uphill away from Slate Creek.

It took Samuel a moment before he got Spooky turned and headed uphill, following.

They moved rapidly upward through broken brush and across grassy slopes, winding their way along a ridge that ascended gently toward some outcrops. They reached timber and continued upward, carefully crossing a steep sidehill until they reached a knoll overlooking the canyon.

Stromback dismounted. Samuel did likewise, wondering what the man had in mind. He wondered if this was the spot to which Bonnie liked to ride.

"I sometimes come up here when I got some thinking to do, Samuel." He waved at the Salmon River carving a wide silvery arc below. The ranch house was visible amid trees near the creek. Cattle and horses spotted the river bottom. The town's buildings spread out over the flat next to the river.

"This is my ranch, Samuel." He stood gazing down across the countryside. "Sure proud of it. It's been over ten years in the making. I see a bright future for it. I see a bright future for all this land."

"I agree, sir."

He looked square at Samuel. "Here you be, lad. Tell me what you think of ranching."

"I like it, sir. I like it a lot."

"As much as mining?"

Samuel hesitated. "Depends on what part of mining. Now, not much can beat finding gold, but the work leading up to it can be mighty wearisome."

"An honest answer." Stromback laughed. "But you could handle ranching?"

"I reckon."

"Good." He mounted and turned downhill.

They found the two cows up the draw where Samuel had guessed. One had just given birth.

"Appears you still got a bit more ranching to do." Stromback sat his horse. "What're your thoughts?"

"About like calves back home, I reckon. Too little to keep from getting eaten. We gotta take it in. Momma should follow if she gets the scent and knows I'm carrying her baby." Samuel dismounted.

Stromback was already handing him his coat to wrap the calf in. He held it until Samuel remounted and could hold the calf.

Both cows followed along as they headed downstream back to the lower field. There, they returned the newborn calf to suckle its mother.

It was difficult for Samuel during breakfast the next day. Work had been good. He had felt good. He knew Bonnie was special to him. At last, he said good-bye to Mrs. Stromback, Josef, and the girls and then to Bonnie. Roundup had come out as well and, it seemed to Samuel, had sensed his leaving. He reached down and petted the dog.

Bonnie gave the excuse that she needed Samuel's help with something from the house. They were alone for a moment in the kitchen.

"I wish you were not leaving, Samuel. I don't want to say good-bye."

Samuel could see the pain in her eyes.

They embraced and kissed. Samuel felt the warmth flood him. He felt the woman he knew he loved pressed against him and his own desires. He forced himself to push gently away, and stood, marveling at Bonnie, her cheeks flushed, eyes sparkling. He wanted to say he loved her, but he couldn't, not when he would be leaving.

"I'll see you before we head out," Samuel managed. He wrestled with his feelings. He no longer knew what God had in mind for him. He prayed this would not be the last time he would see Bonnie, but he feared it was.

When they came from the house, Mrs. Stromback studied them. Samuel figured she had to know. He was going to make some excuse but decided against it. Of course she knew.

Jon Stromback rode with him a distance beyond the ranch and paused. This time, Roundup followed, padding along as if he hoped Samuel would stay.

"Hey, Samuel, a few things I didn't get said to you. Mind if I do?"

Samuel sat Spooky.

"About my niece. Here, she's like a daughter to Mrs. Stromback and me. I reckon you know that."

Samuel's heart skidded. Dread washed through him. He desperately wished he had not kissed her without proper permission. He started to apologize. "I-I'm—"

"I know you've got a hankering for Bonnie, and I know she's got one for you. Sure hoped it'd be that way."

Samuel could not believe what he heard. He tried to keep from grinning.

"And judging by what I've seen, Mrs. Stromback and I don't mind. Sure we don't want to rush you, but putting it bluntly, Mrs. Stromback and I wouldn't mind hiring you on, maybe someday see you and Bonnie taking up a ranch and settling down here. Sure would be proud to help you."

Without thinking, Samuel blurted out, "What about Rex?"

Stromback laughed. "Don't worry about him. I keep him on because it's hard to get a hand that's willing to put up with ranching in this country. Most of them want to be near a bit more civilization or go chase gold."

They rode in silence a moment. Samuel was thinking about being with Bonnie, but he was battling his thoughts, not letting them become real.

"Sure ain't any of my business what you and your pa do. He's told me he intends to head back to Iowa and take up a farm, but it seems to me there's land here aplenty to farm, or ranch, if you prefer. I tried to show you that. In fact, I just sent a friend up the Little Salmon to file on a spot. You came in following down the Little Salmon, didn't you?"

"Yes, sir."

"When you do head out, drop by and say hi. His name's Thomas Pollock. You and your pa ought to look around there as well."

"We did look at some good ground when we came in," Samuel remembered. "We even talked about it but figured the Indians might be a problem."

"Treat 'em right, and I don't think so."

"Thank you, sir."

Samuel felt conflicted. He had an open invitation to court the most beautiful woman in the world. He had a job if he wanted. This could be a good life—his future. Then he thought of his own family.

"Here you be, lad. I know what you're thinking," Stromback spoke. "I don't have any answers for you. Sure might be it wouldn't work anyway. You gotta do what's right for you and your pa." He stopped. "Just wanted you to know you'd be welcome back. We all think highly on you."

They were in the narrows above the ranch. The Salmon, high with the beginning of spring melt, surged powerfully through the narrow gap. It was as if they stood at the gates to the wilderness.

Samuel reached to shake hands. "I'm mighty obliged, sir. Please give my best to Bonnie and to Mrs. Stromback and the children. Thank you for everything." Roundup whined. He leaned down and patted the dog. "You too, Roundup." He spurred his black horse down the trail; a terrible ache had risen in his chest.

Chapter 12

THE MONEY STROMBACK paid Samuel for ranching seemed a fair amount, but he had spent most of it for supplies in Slate Creek before heading out—most on some mercury, but also for some staples, and he had sent a few dollars home to Iowa.

About halfway, he camped the night on the trail, reminiscing that about a year ago his father and he had first come to this country. As then, the river was becoming high with snowmelt.

Early morning, he again headed out, keeping watch for trouble, although he had met no travelers. None of the trails over the summits were yet open, despite the hillsides at this elevation being bright green with a carpet of new grass. He had remained longer with the Strombacks than originally planned. Now he was anxious to see his father—to see how the placer was doing.

He rounded the last corner from where he could first see the cabin, smoke rising from the stovepipe. He spotted Molly and Buster and felt a warming.

His father looked up from where he was working at the sluice and hollered, waving.

They embraced. "Good to see you, Pa."

"Good to see you, son." He looked him up and down, grinning. "From appearances, I'd say ranching life has done you some good." He eyed Samuel's pack. "Hopefully, you brought us some coffee."

"I did, and some vegetables."

"I'll be mighty glad for those after this winter." Charles turned toward the cabin. "Let's have some of that coffee, and you can tell me about ranching."

They stoked up the fire, and Samuel put on a pot of water.

"How's the girl?" was the first question his father asked.

Samuel felt a rush at his personal thoughts and began talking. An hour later, he was still talking. A few things he left out, such as chasing a ghost cow over a cliff and getting shot at.

His father shared how he had spent most of the time clearing off overburden, digging nearly every day, and finally getting down to bedrock but not getting much gold yet. The snowstorm had him holed up for a bit. He had been up to the Shearers' once to visit and helped them do some planting.

The good weather abruptly ended with Samuel's return. During the next several days, heavy rains, some mixed with sleet, raced down the canyon, hammering their camp. The tributary streams filled and raced violently downslope, overflowing. White ribbons cascaded from the cliffs across the canyon, emptying into the rising river.

Everywhere, the hillsides were splashed in green; leaves had come to the shrubs and begun unfurling on the cottonwoods. Samuel spotted the band of bighorns across the river and watched the newborn lambs scampering to keep up with their mothers.

Between storms, they worked the sluice as much as possible. Each cleanup showed increasing streaks of gold, and the size slowly increased from fine flour gold to flakes about the size of grass seeds. Occasionally a slightly larger, flattened piece turned up.

"You got back at a good time," Charles said. "Almost half an ounce a day."

"Makes up for all the days when everything was frozen and we were just getting flour gold."

"You're right. All things considered, it hasn't been much, but I'm feeling lucky now. I've been waiting all winter for this run." He took ahold of the sluice. "Help me reposition this."

They realigned the sluice and flume, and Samuel adjusted the head gate until a good flow of water washed a couple of test rocks through. They hoisted the head box back into place and reattached it.

They returned to the pit, where they had finally exposed the heavily fractured, bowl-like bedrock. They took turns with the pick, prying out the chunks of bedrock and exposing the small seams of gravel, which they carefully scooped out.

By midday, they uncovered a thin layer of cobbles between two chunks of bedrock. Samuel pried loose a rock. "Holy jumping Jehoshaphat. Pa!" he shouted. "You can see the gold." He trembled with excitement, blinking his eyes, hardly daring to believe them. So much gold had been trapped that it was visible in the floor.

Charles scrambled down to where he could see.

"Look at this." Samuel reached down and picked out a flattened nugget the diameter of a pea. "Holy Hanna!" he exclaimed. "Here's another."

Gold lay in a streak in the crevice much like it would behind a cleat in the sluice. Samuel started dancing around in the pit, and let out a whoop. His father joined him, and arm in arm, they spun each other around, whooping as they did.

"You fellers must a hit it big." A shadow and voice came into the pit, then another shadow.

Samuel spun around, frantically looking for the rifle. It was yards away, near the sluice.

His father slowly straightened. "Howdy, strangers," he said quietly.

Both men appeared scraggly, clothes unkempt and torn, heavy beards and matted hair. One was skinny, appeared sickly, and had ratty black hair. The other, a bit healthier, had light blond hair and wore a tattered vest. He was the one who had spoken.

Giggling, he nervously headed down into the pit. "We ain't seen an operation like yours, mind if we take a peek?" He stepped lightly across the rocks, waving his arms to keep balance. The black-haired man, slightly balding, followed.

"Name's Andy Stephens," said the light-haired man. "This here's my partner, Clint Boston." Stephens grinned from ear to ear, missing a couple of teeth, his dingy beard sporting tobacco stains and his eyes blinking.

Charles took a step back.

An icy clamminess enveloped Samuel as he recalled stories of people being murdered and buried in the pits they had dug, never to be seen or heard from again. He was slightly relieved to see that neither man wore a pistol, only skinning knives.

"Guess you already did come down," Charles said cautiously and nodded to Samuel who stepped away to get the rifle.

"Heard you guys a hollerin', by gum. Just had to check it out," Stephens explained.

"We just ran into something you almost never see," Charles explained. "Here's a few specks of gold you can actually see lying on bedrock."

The two men peered down.

"Ain't never seen any gold," Stephens said. "Least not in the wild."

"I've seen it, but never enough," Boston said, scratching his balding head.

Charles laughed. "Sounds like me."

Samuel retrieved the rifle. He noted their two mounts, sorry-looking horses, broken and skinny. Their gear appeared similarly shabby. One rifle poked out of a scabbard. Nevertheless, Samuel did not trust the men.

He could hear their excited voices and laughter. He worried a bit about his father. It would not take much to pull a knife on him and overpower him, being there were two of them.

Samuel stood near the pit, making it obvious he held the rifle.

His father looked up. "Remember our visit with Pete and Hallelujah? It's the same sort of thing, Samuel."

Samuel nodded, remembering on their trip in when they had stopped to see how a rocker worked.

The two men jabbered constantly, asking questions, pointing and gesturing, Stephens letting out with a giggle or two. Charles showed them the sluice box, and ran a bucket of gravel through, demonstrating.

At length, his father called up to him, "How about fixin' us some coffee?"

Reluctantly, Samuel turned to do so, but not before he saw the three men coming his direction.

They sat on stumps outside the cabin for a while, talking. Samuel brought more coffee and offered them some cornbread, which they wolfed down. He wished he had more to offer. He had a strange feeling that the gold fever these two had caught was all that was keeping them going.

Later, while they watched them head out, straggling down the trail, still giggling and talking, Samuel laughed. "They sounded just like you and me last spring, didn't they?"

"Sure did."

"Making the same mistakes as well, I'm guessing."

"They might be making the worst possible mistake, son. The trail isn't open. Those horses they're riding will never make it. Last trip by, Mr. Hunt said they still had twenty feet of snow on both summits. Don't know when we'll be able to get in, either."

Samuel felt stunned. "How can that be? We were in there first of June last year. And here I thought by wintering we'd get a jump on it." He felt dismayed. "We can't wait too long, Pa. The snow's probably already off the Sweet Mary. Sitting here, someone might jump us."

"I was thinking the same thing, Samuel," Charles replied. "I asked Mr. Hunt to ask one of the guys I worked with at McLane's to keep his eyes on it. Hunt said not to worry, that there's still three feet of snow on the level in the meadow. Even so, it's hard not to worry."

Samuel felt better. He shifted on the stump and gazed in the direction the riders had disappeared. "We should have offered them some grub to take with, Pa. They were starved."

"I did. I offered them some venison, but they turned me down," Charles said. "They might feel different by the time they reach the Shearers'."

Samuel pushed his hands across his knees. "They don't look like they'll last another day."

His father raised his eyes. "That's what gold fever does to a man, son. That's what's still driving them on. You know that."

"I just don't think they're going to make it."

"Don't fret too much. Nature has a way of telling you what you don't want to hear. I'm guessing when they hit the snow, they'll sit it out at the bottom of the hill until they can get in."

"Hope they can last."

"Better keep the rifle handy from now on, Samuel. We were lucky. The next men drifting through just might intend to help themselves to what we got."

They returned to the pit. Each rock they turned, they found more bits of gold. By evening they had picked out nearly two ounces.

Charles gazed at the darkening sky. "We worked too long, son. We'll have to do a cleanup in the morning."

Wearily, Samuel followed his father toward the cabin. "I could keep going, finding gold like this. Just light a bonfire."

"Hopefully, we'll get another three or four ounces. There's a fair amount of bedrock still exposed."

Chapter 13

SAMUEL WOKE, thinking he heard a horse. "Pa," he said softly, sitting up. "I think someone's out there."

"I hear 'em, son," Charles whispered back. He was standing, fumbling with his trousers.

They heard the soft thud from horse hooves receding. Charles grabbed the rifle and quickly stepped into the night.

Shortly, he stuck his head back in. "Come on, Samuel," he hissed. "I think we've been hit."

Samuel had finished dressing and started to light a lamp.

"No light."

He grabbed the pistol, and they ran toward the sluice. With the moonlight, they could see the damage. The head box had been pried off. It was in a shambles next to the sluice. Several cleats had been ripped up. Water ran sparkling across a bare wood bottom; the black sand and any gold in it had been cleaned out.

An icy feeling clawed at Samuel's stomach. He could see where the brush had been moved. Running toward the bank, his fears were realized. Some of the fines were also missing.

Charles swore. "Bet it was those snoops, Stephens and Boston."

Samuel felt sick. "Not counting the gold we left in the sluice, Pa, we likely lost two or three ounces in the fines. The last stuff was rich."

"Probably more," his father spat. "And they busted up the box pretty good." Moonlight glinted off the splintered wood. "We left it too easy. All they had to do was scoop everything into a canvas bag." He knotted his fists.

Samuel followed the tracks. "They went downriver."

"I don't think so, son. They wanted us to think that. I heard rocks clatter upstream."

They strode quickly to the trail and saw where the tracks reentered.

"They can't get far, Pa. At night, they won't be able to use the ferry."

"And the river's too high to swim it. They'll have to hole up until daylight, until the Shearers' can take them across."

His father turned toward the cabin. "Fetch Buster, Samuel, I'm going after them and find their camp."

"I'll go with you, Pa."

"No," Charles said quickly, and then added more softly, "Your ma would never forgive me."

"And if I don't go, I'll never forgive myself."

Charles glanced away and then back, studying Samuel. "All right, son. I'm hoping to see who they are, maybe get some help from the Shearers."

Shortly, they were on the trail. The fresh tracks showed moisture where the horses' hooves had broken the soil. They rode quietly, pushing as hard as they dared, scanning ahead, watching for any glint of moonlight from metal and searching for a campfire.

"Got to be careful they don't hear or see us, though I 'spect they'll move well off the trail," Charles whispered.

The hackles on Samuel's neck rose, and he cringed at any sound or glint of reflecting moonlight, half expecting to take a bullet.

Charles paused at the Florence trail, studying the tracks. "To blazes, they've headed up this way."

A hollowness washed over Samuel. "For sure, we won't catch them now."

Charles sat Buster a moment, peering up the trail. His jaw tightened. "There's another trail along the ridge closer to the Shearers'. Might be I can get above them and catch them coming up."

"I'm going with you," Samuel protested. He felt chilled, thinking of his father going alone.

"No, I need you here. If it's those two from the other day, I'll have a good chance of stopping them. Their mounts aren't going to get them very far. They probably think we're still asleep and won't be in much of a hurry."

"This is crazy, Pa." Samuel shook his head. "It's just gold. We can get more. It ain't worth killing for."

"I don't intend to kill anyone, son." Charles cleared his throat. "But to us, it's not just gold. This is our life. Besides, if we let them get away with it, they'll just hit someone else."

"Don't go, Pa," Samuel said, desperately. "It's two against one."

"I only saw one rifle." Charles's voice was strained. "Stay here. If they turn and run, they'll not be watching for you. Get a good look at them."

"Yes, sir." Samuel gulped.

Charles pointed up the trail. "Find some rocks up there where you can hide. Whatever you do, don't let them see you."

"Be careful, Pa," Samuel whispered.

His father turned Buster and headed upstream at a brisk trot toward the spur trail.

Heart racing, Samuel headed up the Florence trail, looking for a safe place. Finally, he found where rock outcrops flanked one side. He pulled Spooky into the timber and tied him. Making his way farther up into the rocks, Samuel reached a spot that seemed to offer some protection. Men coming down the trail would never see him until they had passed by, and he could get a good look. At present, the moonlight was good, and depending on when his father could get above the men, it might even be daylight.

Samuel squatted down, back against a rock, another offering a barricade in front of him. It seemed a defensible position. He tried not to dwell on what could go wrong. He had imagined things like this but never expected them to come to pass. This was real. He might get shot at. His throat cracked dry. He shivered in the cold, sweating, wishing he had some water. He strained to hear hoof beats, something that would tell him they were coming, and then he hoped he would hear only Buster's hooves. His hands twisted on the pistol, and he realized he had it pointed at himself. *Idiot. You wanna die?* He aimed it back down the trail.

The night was dead still except for moonlight glinting off a bend in the river and the murmur of water. He waited, cramped, and shifted his position, careful not to let the moonlight glint off the pistol, his heart hammering.

He had to get up to pee. He stood and walked about, wondering about the length of time. He mentally tried to calculate how long he had waited and how long it would take his father to ride up the spur ridge. He worried that his father might miss the men. If so, they would never see who they were.

He returned to his spot, squatted down, and scanned the eastern sky. It was still pitch-black.

The muffled rifle shot, surprisingly near, rocked him awake. His heart skidded. Two other shots exploded the night, echoing off the hillsides. *More than one rifle.* It wasn't Stephens and Boston. A chill washed over him. His heart quickened, and he strained to see. Another shot sounded like his father's rifle. Then in rapid succession, more shots, different rifles or maybe a rifle and pistol; they seemed closer. They were coming.

The noise echoed from the canyon walls, followed by silence. Samuel felt a clawing dread. His hands twisted on the pistol, sweaty. He desperately wanted to go to his father.

Softly thudding hooves descended the trail, drawing steadily closer, but not rushed. Almost surreal, two riders emerged from the shadows into the moonlight directly above him, working their way downslope.

Blood pounded in Samuel's ears. The men were talking and not concerned with running. His father wasn't coming. *Maybe dead.* A sob broke in his throat. *What does it matter now?* A rage filled him. "At least one of you bastards is gonna pay," he breathed. He cocked the hammer.

Cold sweat beaded on his forehead. The pistol wavered.

The riders were beneath him, carrying bulging saddlebags. They could not be Stephens and Boston. Both horses were dark with no clear markings.

He staggered to his feet. "Stop, you sons of bitches. You stole our gold."

"It's the Chambers boy!" The voice was vaguely familiar. The men began laughing.

"I'm serious as the angel of death. I have a pistol leveled on you," Samuel shouted, trying to keep his voice from quavering, trying also to steady his hand. "Leave the gold, and you can go."

"Put it down, boy, before ya blow your fool foot off, or somethin' worse," came the voice, still laughing.

The man's shadowy form settled in Samuel's sights, and he pulled the trigger. The blast surprised him. The man's horse bucked.

"What the hell!" The man clawed the air to regain his balance. "Get that little bastard."

The other man, in a long coat, leveled his rifle and fired, the flash and explosion deafening. A bullet whined high overhead. Samuel took quick aim and fired back. The man spun around wildly, cursing. The flash from a pistol muzzle and explosion caused Samuel to blindly duck and crawl back toward the rocks below. Another round slammed into the rock above him, shattering pieces, stinging his cheek. It was senseless to try to get off another shot. He would save the rounds for when they came at him. Desperately, he wished for his father. *Please be coming, Pa. Don't be dead!*

"I'm going after that little bastard."

Hoof beats headed Samuel's direction, clattering against the rock. The man was coming up. A pounding filled Samuel's senses; he felt icy cold. He strained to see and tried to get into position for a shot. He stood, trembling, leveling the pistol at the shadowy form.

"Let him go," his partner shouted. "The Chambers boy ain't worth it. Let's light out afore his pa gets here."

"Doubt that's gonna happen." The voice laughed as the shadowy form retreated. "Not with a slug in him."

The man's words rocked Samuel. He felt stunned, unable to move or even to think.

"Better go find your pa, boy. He might not be long for this world," the voice continued.

The thudding hooves retreated down the trail, now far below him, heading in the direction of the main river trail.

Samuel felt hot and sick, and started shaking uncontrollably. They had had him pinned down in the rocks. The man could have easily killed him.

In a numb daze, he discovered himself scrambling down, running for Spooky. He mounted and spurred the animal up the trail. The moon would be down before long. He pushed upward into the shadows. How Spooky could see, he didn't know.

A riderless horse came toward him. He knew it was Buster. *No, God. No!* He caught the animal and continued up the trail, thinking terrible thoughts, desperately pushing Spooky, the animal now winded. He slowed for a rocky area, forcing himself to allow Spooky to pick his way through, all the time his heart hammering.

He came into the open on a traverse; a figure stood in the middle of the trail, rifle in hand, limping. It was his father.

"Pa!" Samuel leaped from Spooky and ran to him. "You okay?"

"Banged up a bit," he replied grimly. "What in blazes happened? I heard shooting."

Samuel explained. He found himself shaking as he recounted how the man had come toward him.

"Don't know which of us was stupider, you or me," Charles replied at length. "Either of us could have been killed."

"What happened, Pa?"

"I got past them just fine, but the moment I hollered and fired a warning shot, they started shooting. Buster spooked, and I ended up on my butt. Blazes, I can't remember being unseated so fast in my life." He tried to laugh. "They saw I was on the ground, so they lit out, heading your direction."

His father limped over to his horse. "Give me a hand, will you?"

Samuel steadied his father as he mounted.

"Any idea who it was?" Samuel still struggled to place the voice.

"Not the guys from the other day. Even in the moonlight, I could tell they had better mounts."

"I think they know us, Pa. One of them said 'It's the Chambers boy' when I called them down."

"Then it could have been anybody past our place. Everyone knows us. If you had stayed put, you might have recognized them."

"I'm sorry, Pa. I wasn't thinking. I wanted our gold back. I-I wanted them dead." He found his words hard to believe.

"We were both wrong." Charles pulled up on Buster and was quiet for a moment. "Son, you told me once how this country doesn't care how old you are or what you think—it'll kill you. It's the same thing if ever you go after a man again, and I pray to God you never have to, but keep in mind this country. It has no emotions, no love, no remorse, no hate. If you let your feelings get in the way, you'll end up dead." Charles stared toward the east where faint light now silhouetted the mountains. "I had to learn that during the Southern Uprising. If I hadn't, I doubt I'd be here."

Samuel was finding it difficult to breathe. Never had he felt this way toward two human beings. He wanted to kill them—had tried to kill them—and it scared him, but his father's words scared him more. He did not think he could ever set aside his feelings.

Chapter 14

UPON ENTERING THEIR CABIN, they stopped in stunned silence. Their belongings were scattered and shredded. The beds were turned over; the stove was moved; and part of the floor was ripped up.

Samuel ran to the bag of cornmeal. From the bits of meal, he knew without looking what he would find. Their gold pouch they kept stored in the bottom was missing. He was wracked with disbelief. *Gone!* Their gold was gone.

Samuel sat down hard, unable to breathe, feeling the world spinning about him.

Charles slammed his fist onto the table. He threw the bag and raked the dishes aside, sending them clattering across the floor. He sat, hands clenched into fists.

Samuel caught sight of the anger on his father's face and quieted. It was a look Samuel had never seen. His own distress became fear.

"How could I have been so damn stupid?" Charles breathed. "That's what they wanted. They weren't interested in getting away to Florence. They wanted us away from the cabin." He buried his head in his hands.

Samuel sat stone silent. He guessed it was more likely blind luck. They took advantage when they found both his father and him gone. Luck or not, it didn't matter—their gold was gone. Their dreams were gone. Thoughts of Bonnie, of the O'Riley, and of Chen flashed through his mind. He thought of his mother and sister. Well, going home was settled. What remained for them here?

His father sprang up, grabbed up the meal sack, and began stuffing in food items. "I'm going after them. If I have to, I'll follow them to Hades."

Samuel said nothing but quietly began packing. He knew he was going as well. It didn't matter what his father might say anymore.

In a moment, they were on the trail, heading downstream.

His father didn't speak. Jaw set, eyes flashing, he pushed Buster at a trot. He pulled his rifle and laid it across the pommel. In the growing light, the fresh hoofprints were easy to see.

"Keep your eyes peeled, son. They won't give us a second chance." Charles's tone was ice. It was the first acknowledgment that he knew Samuel had come along.

Samuel forced himself to pay attention, to observe their surroundings, although he doubted the men would try to dry-gulch them. They were running. Samuel wished he had tried for a horse instead of the men. They could have tracked a bleeding horse. But it wasn't worth it. The men probably would have killed him—maybe not if his father had been coming hard on their trail, but he hadn't been. And now they were following the men, presumably to try to get their gold back, but Samuel believed his father had other intentions.

They pushed hard until their horses began to flag. At a small tributary, his father paused long enough to water them.

"I'm afraid we aren't closing the gap, son. They might already be up a side canyon, camped."

Samuel patted Spooky, concerned. His father and he would have to conserve some energy if they intended to pursue for much longer.

"You know, son, it's possible it's two of the men that jumped the pack string last fall."

"Why would they be so stupid? People are still looking for them."

"Might not be looking all that hard. It was the Chinese pack string, remember?"

Samuel understood.

"Like Mr. Hunt told us, the pickings around here are pretty easy. If it's true what you said and they know us, they knew we were alone. They might've been watching me while you were away. When they saw we hit it big, they let us run the sluice a few days, knowing we were stashing the fines and filling up our pouch. Maybe they even saw Stephens and Boston and figured they'd take the blame."

"I can't believe it," Samuel breathed. He felt his anger growing again. He scanned the countryside, now bathed in early sunlight, searching the side canyons, looking for a place the men could be holed up and waiting to dry-gulch them. "It ain't right, what they did, Pa." He choked on his words. Samuel felt empty. He kept trying to reason why anyone would take their gold. How could anyone decide it was okay to bust up someone's property and take what they had worked an entire winter for?

"No, son," his father answered. "It ain't right." He urged Buster back onto the trail.

"But why? We never hurt anyone."

His father was silent a moment. "There's evil in this world, Samuel. Plenty of it. That's all the reason there is."

When they reached Groff's ferry, Jesse explained he had ferried across a couple of men first thing that morning. His description of the men matched what they could see in the moonlight, and they had paid in dust.

"Probably them. That dust was ours."

"Sorry. What happened?"

Charles explained and then requested, "If you don't mind, please pass the word along to others to be on the lookout. Send word to Slate Creek and to Jon Stromback if you can."

"I will." Jesse shook his head. "I respect you for going after them. Least I can do is offer a ride across."

The water had risen considerably. Samuel felt uneasy at the bucking and creaking ferry as they moved across.

"We better not stay on this side too long, Pa. Might end up too high pretty soon."

"I've thought of that. I'm just hoping I can catch sight of them."

They turned up the trail following the Little Salmon and rode a short distance to a side draw. Charles rode over the ground, eyes searching.

Samuel peered up the draw, wondering if the men were up above, watching. He shivered.

"Can't tell if they came this direction. Can't afford to push them if they did. For sure, they'd dry-gulch us now. No one around to be witness."

Samuel quickly scanned the canyon walls again.

"They can turn up any of these canyons and cross over to the Snake River. No one would ever catch them. There's gotta be a hundred ravines they can follow down the other side."

In silence, they turned their horses and headed back toward the ferry.

Near evening, they reached the cabin and fixed some venison and corn mush. Samuel decided he would never look at a meal sack in the same manner as before.

"What we gonna do now, Pa?"

"Not much I reckon we can do. Just go back to work. Hope there's some gold left." His father held his plate; his eyes were far away.

"There may be a couple ounces in the fines that they didn't steal. At least they didn't steal the quicksilver, and there was a little amalgam worth a few dollars." Samuel had earlier found the canister of mercury where he had left it outside the cabin. "Maybe we can clear off some more bedrock."

His father put down his plate, pushed his fingers through his hair, and stared at Samuel.

"You got to understand, son. I spent the entire time you were at Slate Creek clearing off that last spot we been mining. Before we got robbed, we had near fifteen ounces of gold. How much does that come to?"

"Well over two hundred dollars," Samuel replied. "Probably near three hundred with what fines they stole."

"That's about right," Charles said. "You and I spent over half a year working ourselves to near death for three hundred dollars, and for what? Now we got to mend the sluice, and start over. Maybe we'll get another couple ounces. To blazes, Samuel, we'd of both been better off ranching and making a decent wage."

"I'm sorry, Pa. It was my fault." Samuel found himself shaking. "If I'd've stayed at the cabin, they wouldn't have got our gold."

"I'm not blaming you."

Samuel's eyes misted. "But it *is* my fault."

"Look, I've told you before you have to make the best decisions you can, faced with what you know. I considered it before I let you come with me and before we split up. It was the right decision. We can't be second-guessing ourselves. It won't bring the gold back."

Samuel was silent. Despite his father's words, he could sense something different in his voice. The dream was gone.

"Pa, you always been telling me things will work out." He searched desperately for something good he could say. He began thinking about the quartz ledge east of the South Fork, where the grave was—the place where he had met the Sheepeater Indians. Maybe it was time to tell his father. Instead, he continued. "Maybe the Sweet Mary will have a lot of gold, and the O'Riley will prove up good. Then we can go home."

"Got to try." Charles sat and pulled off his boots. "Not much choice is there, son? Not much choice." He stretched out on his bed and closed his eyes. The cabin had grown dark except for the flicker from the fire.

Samuel felt devastated. Last night and this day had been horrible. Not only had they lost their gold, either of them could have been killed.

Even now the thieves could return intent on killing them. Maybe not here. Maybe at Warren's. Maybe other thieves.

"Pa, I got something I need to tell you," Samuel managed. "I found another ledge."

Charles opened his eyes.

"Remember when I went east of the South Fork?"

"Yes. When you saw the Indians and I gave you what for, for going so far alone?"

"I told you I found a grave and a place where someone had been prospecting." Samuel paused, wondering if he should go on. "Well, I didn't tell you the whole of it."

His father studied him.

"The quartz the man was working was rich."

"How rich?"

"I had it assayed. I asked Mr. Hinley not to say anything. It came back over six ounces to the ton."

His father sat up. "To blazes, son, why didn't—"

"I didn't say because I knew we didn't have any time to do anything with it, Pa, and it would be dang near impossible to get the gold out of that country."

"Tarnation! We could have sold it and let someone else worry about bringing it out."

"I know, Pa," Samuel admitted. "But I also wanted to finish the O'Riley because of the work I put in."

"To blazes with the O'Riley, Samuel. It's half as valuable."

His father's troubled eyes made Samuel uncomfortable. "Mostly I didn't say anything because of the Indians. I-I didn't feel right about it."

Having finally spoken of it, Samuel rushed on, not daring to stop. "I had this feeling that the Sheepeaters didn't want me there. I know we could have gone there with a bunch of men and run them off, but that wasn't it. Somehow, I knew that where the man was pointing— where he wanted me to go—was their home. There's nothing there, Pa. For a hundred miles or more, there's *nothing there* but mountains and canyons—land that no whites would ever set foot in—unless *we* did. I began thinking maybe we shouldn't. It just seemed … it belonged to the Sheepeaters."

Samuel was not sure he made sense, even to himself. If there was gold there, why not go and get it? That's why they came here.

"They weren't like the Nez Perce, Pa," Samuel continued. "If they were, they'd have horses and could just up and go to a new place. They didn't own much. Only when they got up close, I could see they had good clothes. They had horn bows, so I knew they were good hunters. They were part of the land like the deer and the mountain sheep. It just didn't seem right. There would be no place for them to go." He looked up, struggling, trying to put into words what he had felt.

"And you think if we leave them alone, no one will ever know about them?"

"That's it, Pa." Samuel nodded. "No one. They'll be left alone."

"That's just not so, son." Charles sighed and gazed out across the river and then back at Samuel. "Whites *will* go into that country. It's· our nature to explore, to always want to go over the next mountain. To blazes, *you* went there. Maybe they'll find something, maybe not. Maybe they'll just homestead and raise a family. Maybe there won't ever be much gold, but they'll go there all right. And those Indians, whoever they are, will get pushed out."

His father was correct. It was like what Stromback had said about the Nez Perce. At some point they would get pushed out. And Samuel knew if he and his father never went after the gold, someone else would.

Charles continued, "What if we go there when we get back to Warren's, son? Let's decide together on this thing."

Samuel clenched his fists. His father would see it was a good ledge and want to work it.

His father lay back and closed his eyes again. Samuel could not. He rose and wandered out toward the sluice box and gazed northeast in the direction of the Sheepeaters and the ledge.

Chapter 15

Troubled dreams filled Samuel's night, but by morning, a tentative calm had returned. His father had risen earlier and had some coffee ready by the time he dressed.

"Well, son, you gave me a lot to think about yesterday." Charles turned the salt pork, its odor making Samuel realize how hungry he was.

"If I was thinking straight, I'd take you and head home. Hell, if I had been thinking straight last fall, we'd already be home. But we made an agreement, you and I, and I'm still in it if you are."

"Yes, sir, I'm happy to be sticking with it." Samuel felt washed with relief. He was not about to give up.

They inspected the sluice and found most of the damage had been to the head box. Samuel found a board to cover the broken side but nails were scarce. Charles recovered a few from the broken wood, and they began reassembling the box. Shortly, they had the sluice operational and were washing the remaining gravel. It continued to be rich.

"We're still getting some decent gold, Pa." The small specks of gold that collected in the black sand behind the cleats warmed him.

"Maybe we'll surprise ourselves and keep finding some for a while." Charles dumped another bucket of gravel into the stream of water. "One thing for sure. We're cleaning up every night in case some other yahoos decide to help themselves."

That night, they moved the fines into the cabin and stored them on a tarpaulin. Samuel decided if any thieves came by to inspect the sluice, it would be empty, and if they wanted anything else, they would have to come through the cabin for it with them in it. He slept with the pistol at hand.

For the next couple of days, the streak continued, and the gold remained coarse. Occasionally, a few flattened nuggets showed. They picked out what gold they could and added the black sand to their growing pile.

They had nearly finished the streak, taking out almost four ounces of gold, twice what they had hoped for, when the river broke through and flooded their pit. Shortly afterward, it drowned most of the bar and continued rising.

"We're done here, son," Charles said. "Except for amalgamating the fines."

They began the slow process, both of them washing pan after pan of black sand with the mercury, slowly collecting small lumps of amalgam.

The canyon warmed. Samuel reflected on the cattle back at Slate Creek. Calving would be finished. The cows would be roaming the hills with their new calves, following the greening grass up the slopes. It was full summer here, and he could not imagine snow in the high country.

Mr. Hunt came through. Samuel had flagged the trail for him to pick up a letter, but it was more for an excuse to talk to Mr. Hunt and to check on the status of the trail.

"Nope, no pack trains yet. There's still a couple miles of deep snow on both summits. Can't get past the freight landing either." He took a sip of coffee. "There's about a dozen pilgrims camped halfway up French Creek waiting for the snow to clear. Several men went in on snowshoes, but they left most of their gear at snowline."

"How much longer?"

"I'd say if the weather holds and we don't get a cold snap, maybe a couple weeks."

"A couple weeks! It's the first of June," exclaimed Samuel. "We were already there this time last year."

"Can't rush the seasons, Samuel," Hunt said. "Remember, some years have been worse."

"Then last season was early?" Samuel wanted to know.

"No, I think about average." Hunt swirled his cup. "By the way, I never did get a chance to say how sorry I was to hear you got claim jumped. Everyone on the river's heard and spread the word, but no one's seen anything that I know of. Any thoughts on who might have done it?"

"Nope." Samuel had some thoughts but declined to share them.

"A lot of problems with high graders and claim jumpers lately. You may have heard Carrol and Brooks got into it over their placer. You know them?"

Samuel shook his head, but he was wondering more about their placer. If Carrol and Brooks were placer mining, that meant the meadow was free of snow.

"Carrol took some shots at Brooks. The sheriff went after him but never did find him. You might want to keep your eyes open for him as well," Hunt explained.

"We will. Anyone who is wanted by the law doesn't have much to lose," Charles agreed.

Hesitantly, Samuel asked, "You said they were working their placer claim. Does that mean the snow's off the meadow?"

"Pretty much." Hunt set down his cup. "Thanks for the coffee. I best be off. The Shearers are going to want to load me up on some more."

They watched as Warren Hunt headed down the trail, his extra mount following with the snowshoes still prominently lashed on top of the pack.

"We have to go, Pa," Samuel said. "The snow's off. We can start placer mining."

"I heard, but you're forgetting our horses. They don't have snowshoes."

Over the next couple of days, they impatiently finished panning down the fines and amalgamating the gold. They stored the amalgam in a canister, deciding they could retort it in Warren's.

"At least we won't be hauling three hundred pounds of fines to Warren's," Charles said.

"I wish it was three hundred pounds of gold." Samuel knew they were recovering very little gold from the fines.

They sat at the cabin in the warm sun, staring at the green grass and shrubs covering the canyon walls. They had gone to the Shearers' and reshod their stock. Nothing remained for them to do except mend some gear and wait for the snow to melt.

"I can't believe the snow's as bad as Mr. Hunt says."

Charles laid aside the shirt he was sewing. "Maybe we should try it. Maybe we could walk the horses in if we try early morning while the snow's frozen."

"We could go until it gets too soft. Maybe we'd have to camp a couple nights is all."

"And it could be, if it doesn't freeze up hard enough, we'd be stuck more than a couple nights."

"Last year we got in and there was some snow." But Samuel knew that by then the pack trains had already broken a trail. Nevertheless, he was willing. He had not seen a rattlesnake yet, but he knew it was only a matter of days. He wanted to be gone before they showed up.

They closed up the cabin and stored the sluice. They doubted they would ever be back. Someone else could use the sluice. Samuel felt a bit bittersweet. It had been a good cabin. With a bit more land it could make a good home. And he knew there was a good deal of gold remaining in the bar, enough a man could mine during the winter for several years.

RETURN TO WARREN'S CAMP

Chapter 16

EARLY MORNING, they were packed and on the trail. The warmth of the canyon was like midsummer. Elderberry and mountain ash were blooming. Wildflowers carpeted the hillsides. Some grasses already had flower spikes.

Mining on the river bars was done whether or not the miners wanted it to be. Snow in the high country was rapidly melting, and the Salmon was at flood stage. The bars were submerged, and now the high water threatened to close the ferries and trail crossings. Where they had been mining was under six feet of racing water. No wonder gold was being deposited there. Each spring, more was brought down. The river acted like a giant sluice, trapping gold below the boulders and sandbars wherever it slowed.

When they reached Shearers' ferry, the water raced past, submerging much of the bank. An upturned tree washed downstream in front of them. The ferry bobbed violently, and Samuel's chest tightened at the sight.

Somehow he forced himself onto the boat and helped hitch the animals. Like before, he held Spooky's muzzle and soothed him. Both of the decked boats that the ferry spanned were submerged, and water poured across the decking.

"The current wants to submerge us," George said. "Don't know if this old boat can take many more of these high-water crossings."

"Just make this one," Charles said. "We got to get into Warren's."

"Hope you brought your snowshoes."

The waves bucked and rocked the ferry, but George jockeyed it across the river toward the opposite bank.

"You won't see the landing, Samuel. It's under water, but it's there."

Water surrounded the pole where Samuel had to tie the ferry. He leaped and splashed into the water, thankful and somewhat surprised that his feet found wood. Quickly he ran the line around the snubbing pole.

They visited briefly with the Shearers.

"I doubt you'll make it in, Charles," Frederick Shearer said.

"Got to try. Can't do any good down here anymore with the bar under water."

Samuel thought about the river creeping up the bank toward their winter cabin.

"Now you mind your papa," Mrs. Shearer reminded Samuel, "and don't stay up at Washington all summer. You get that gold and go home to your momma."

Samuel hoped they would "get that gold."

Shortly, they turned up French Creek, and Samuel peered up toward the direction the trail climbed, toward the dark, timbered ridges. At least no pack trains would be coming out like last season.

Near the first saddle, the trail turned to mud. Shaded areas harbored snowbanks. They were still two thousand feet lower in elevation than the freight landing. The snow had just melted. Grass was yet brown and matted, and the aspens and shrubs had just begun to bud. Musty, damp earth odors wafted on the warm air as they followed Fall Creek downward.

Where they began the climb toward the freight landing, tents and gear appeared, scattered under the timber in the draw. Several parties of miners had camped alongside the trail. Their stock searched for grass nearby. Samuel tried to spot Stephens and Boston, the two men who had visited them, but he didn't see them.

One of the miners came to the trail. "I wouldn't try it yet, boys." He nodded up the trail. "About a half mile up, you run into snow. You're welcome to camp here. We're figuring the first pack string ought to be through in another week, and we can follow it in."

Charles tapped his hat. "Thanks kindly. We may just push on a bit more."

"Nothing level up ahead. The trail gets steep, and there's nothing for your stock unless you're carrying feed."

"Much obliged." Charles pushed on, Samuel and Molly following. After they had passed, Charles turned back to Samuel. "Didn't have the heart to tell them we've been here before."

The trail pitched steeply upward and grew muddier. Rivulets of water from melting snow ran down it. They reached the narrow section where the trail clung to the mountain face with only empty space below all the way to the gorge. Samuel reflected on their encounter with the pack train. Nothing but open, sheer, grassy slopes fell away below the trail. He thought he could still make out the mule carcass in the ravine.

They ran into unbroken snow just beyond the upper switchback where the trail entered the timber. They struggled on for a while longer, the horses and mule floundering, slipping on the snow and rotten ice.

"I can't believe it," Charles muttered. "This morning we were sitting in a tropical paradise, birds singing, flowers blooming—now we're in snow up to our eyeballs." The sun beat down from a pure blue sky, uncomfortably warm. "Guess this isn't so smart. We'll stop next spot we find. With luck, the snow will be frozen in the morning, and we can top the summit."

On the next switchback, they found a level alcove back under the trees. A stream full of melt water cut across the trail.

They cleared out an area and cut and piled limbs to keep their bedrolls up and off the snow. Samuel heated some water while his father cooked up some venison with onions and beans.

"Beautiful country," Samuel said, waving toward the horizon.

Their campsite was like a tiny shelf tacked to the side of an immense wall. Stretching to the west were unbroken, snow-covered peaks rising from the purple depths of the Salmon River canyon. Behind them rose forested ridges. The sky shone blue and the shadows grew long as the sun settled toward the horizon.

"I'm betting we can get through in the morning," Charles said. "We'll start as soon as the snow freezes tonight."

Already, there was an evening chill.

They were up well before light. Ice crystals sparkled from the brush and snow.

Charles kicked the crusted snow. "This should do."

They walked, leading the animals until daylight brightened the sky. By then they had reached the freight landing. Samuel felt strange. No one was around—no tents, no camp, no hay—not like last spring when they had come by. Instead, unbroken snow lay among the trees. He remembered the violent thunderstorm from last year and how Andy Brown hated the lightning.

They rode for a distance, the horses staying on the packed trail, following the snowshoe tracks of Mr. Hunt and others who had gone into Warren's throughout the winter. The trail descended into the trees, and as the day warmed, the snow quickly softened. As they left the snow, they broke out onto long sections of muddy trail crossed by flooding streams.

"There's the steam from Mr. Burgdorf's hot springs." Samuel pointed, feeling joy. They were nearly to Warren's. Chen and he had ridden this trail numerous times. A few miles ahead was the turnoff to the Ruby placer, where his father had worked. This country had been his backyard.

Fred Burgdorf shook their hands enthusiastically. "First folks in on horseback," he greeted. He had the sleeves of his wool shirt rolled up as before. "I hope you haf brought that vhiskey. I been out since March." He snapped his suspenders, eyeing them.

"I did, but it is just a bit, and courtesy of the Shearers." Charles unwrapped a flask he had been carrying. Samuel was surprised, not knowing anything about it—in fact, having forgotten.

"Well, a swallow shall do it," Fred managed. "And a deal is a deal. I hope you haf time for a swim and some chow."

"Been dreamin' about it," Samuel nearly shouted.

"A quick swim and a bite is all. Then we'll have to be off," Charles said. "I want to go as far as possible before we get back into bad snow."

"What I want to know is how you got this far."

"We came across early morning while the snow was still frozen."

Burgdorf nodded. "So you camped in the snow."

"It wasn't bad," Samuel answered. "We cut a lot of limbs to keep dry."

"Yah, that works." Burgdorf found them some towels, and they waded into the hot springs.

"Can't beat this," Samuel said as he kicked out into the warm water.

"For sure," Charles said. "I'd come here more often myself if he was a bit closer."

"I'm kinda disappointed to see Mr. Jenkins still isn't around," Samuel said.

"Why?"

"I was gonna let him know I met Bonnie. See what he had to say about that."

"That's right. The only gal in the territory, he told you. That would have been interesting," Charles said, grinning.

Shortly, they sat down to a hot meal of wild game, a few beans, and some sourdough bread. There were no fresh vegetables.

"Excuse the skimpy fare. Winter is still all up here."

"No apology, Fred," Charles responded. "But do you have a piece of pie or two?"

"By golly, I do. I haf some apple pie. The Shearers had a good crop of apples. I haf kept some in the root cellar all winter. Figured the first pack train would be through this week, so I made up some pie."

He brought out three pieces and joined them, pouring them some stout coffee as well. They visited briefly. Burgdorf wanted to know what the news from the outside was. Hunt had informed him about them being jumped.

"I want you to know I vill keep my eyes open," he said, picking up the dishes. "Next time, Charlie, don't hesitate to put a bullet in 'em. All of us will back you—we will."

"Thanks, Fred." Charles stood. "Mighty obliged for the chance to get a good bath and decent meal."

"Mighty glad to see you two coming through. Now don't you be strangers, and come on back," Burgdorf hollered after them as they turned down the trail.

The moment they turned up Long Gulch, they encountered more snow. Shaded areas were blanketed deep under three or four feet. For a short distance, they skirted the snow by fording the swollen creek and slogging through the muddy marshes, but soon unbroken snow stretched before them and forced them to stop.

Before daylight, after the snow had crusted, they again headed out. They crossed both summits and dropped down along Steamboat Creek, striking the muddy trail before the snow again softened. Willows along the creek were bright red with green-and-yellow tips, showing the beginnings of growth. Some grass was greening around the edges of scattered snowbanks in the timber.

A couple of Chinese placers were operating along Steamboat Creek, and a few whites were operating farther up in the trees. Samuel felt giddy as he realized the men who had wintered in Warren's were already back at work taking out gold. He suddenly became impatient.

They turned up the trail toward Washington. Except for snowbanks along the street, it sat, seemingly unchanged, surrounded by the familiar, timber-cloaked hills. The sight of the buildings sent a rush through Samuel. He recognized the courthouse on the hill with the US and territorial flags. Down from it were Ripson's Saloon, the Washington Hotel, and Hofen's Mercantile. Across the street were Hinley's assay shop and Alexander's Mercantile. Smoke rose from the tin pipe on Ma Reynolds's boardinghouse at the far end of the street, and beyond, he could make out the Chinese businesses and huts. Somehow, he felt he was home, and he was anxious to visit everyone and see how they had fared during the winter.

People swarmed into the street, greeting them. Mr. Ripson asked, "Is the pack string behind you?"

"Not that we're aware of."

"By cracky, we have a crisis. My whiskey's ninety proof water. Been that way since April."

Samuel noticed Miss Lilly and Miss Hattie among the people who had come out to say hello. He waved. His heart raced, but now he had feelings for Bonnie. He knew he would need to tell Miss Lilly the truth and dreaded the thought. Although she smiled and waved, Samuel could not talk to her now, not in front of all the townspeople.

Dozens of Chinese milled about. *More than last season,* Samuel thought. He could see Mann's shop and wanted to hunt up and see if Chen was there, but he knew his father would not welcome going to visit the Chinese.

They dropped by to see Mr. Hinley, to get caught up on the mining news, and to drop off the amalgam for retorting. Samuel showed him the samples from the hillside above their cabin on the Salmon.

"It does not matter where young Samuel is, Charles. He shall manage to find something." Raymond Hinley smiled, and then, adjusting his glasses and squinting, he began inspecting the pieces.

"This is kind of strange-looking rock, Mr. Hinley," Samuel said, pointing to one in particular. "I can see some sulphurets in it and something metallic, but there's a lot of blue and green as well. I thought it was pretty."

Hinley looked up; his eye twitched. "Copper."

"Copper?" Samuel glanced up and strangely realized that he was looking eye to eye with Mr. Hinley. Although somewhat short in stature like Burgdorf, neither Hinley nor Burgdorf had shrunk. Samuel felt a little funny.

"Aye, blue-and-green staining is a sure sign of copper. The only trouble with copper is that it does not take but a wee bit to thoroughly stain everything green." He took out a lens and carefully studied the pieces. "Definitely mineralized." He set the lens down. "I wager you noticed the pyrite?"

"I thought I did."

"Good lad. There is also some chalcopyrite." Hinley pointed out what appeared to be pyrite to Samuel except that it was a brighter yellow. "This is called chalcopyrite. It carries the copper. When exposed to weathering, the copper oxidizes to green."

"Not much value then?" Samuel asked.

"It could very well carry some gold and silver. Most copper deposits do." Hinley retrieved a canister and his ledger. "I imagine you will want an assay." Hinley began writing a receipt. "On copper ores they are very difficult to run."

"Maybe I can help."

"Aye, lad, I was hoping you would offer. And if you wish, you can come in and retort your amalgam." Hinley chuckled. "Like I offered last year, Samuel, should you wish me to grubstake you, I shall. You have a tolerably good knack for finding respectable ore."

Charles laughed. "He does, but he may not be wandering about as much this season. I need his help mining so we can get headed home."

"I expect that is so." Hinley stood back, eyeing Samuel and Charles. "Indeed, it is a pleasure to see you two."

"You as well, Mr. Hinley."

Chapter 17

LATE IN THE AFTERNOON, they reached their cabin a few miles north of Washington along a small tributary of Meadow Creek. Something seemed wrong. At first, Samuel believed the snow had played havoc with the place. The door swung open. Rubbish was strewn about. He wondered if a bear or varmints had overrun the place. But Samuel remembered leaving behind a good pile of firewood, and there appeared to be none. Several rails from the fence were missing—possibly chopped up and burned.

Their cabin had been raided. A clawing, twisting feeling erupted within Samuel. The Salmon River robbery flooded back. *How can this be happening again?* Desperately he sought another answer.

Stumbling inside, a familiar sight met them. The bed frames were torn apart. Shreds of bedding and some tattered clothing, none of it theirs, was strewn about. What utensils had remained behind were on the floor. A plate with moldy scraps of food remained on the table. The stove had been turned over. Luckily the cabin had not burned.

Samuel did not wait to inspect any more of the cabin. He ran toward the placer.

Charles came fast on his heels. "Hold on, son. They might still be here."

Samuel did not think so, not after seeing the moldy food scraps. He prayed whoever had been here had only used the cabin for shelter.

When he caught sight of the Sweet Mary, his worst fears were realized. He saw no sign of the sluice. The pit where his father and he had uncovered and left the boulders was a cavern. Dread and anger flooded Samuel. They had been jumped, and badly.

Samuel began shaking in disbelief. It was almost beyond his comprehension how anyone could have dug up the area as it now appeared. Somehow they had managed to get under the boulders. Both had been dislodged and were now resting downslope of the pit. The pit itself had been dug down several feet.

His father had come up but said nothing.

"I can't believe it, Pa," Samuel whispered. He was reliving his discovery from last fall—how he had anticipated this moment to return, to get some powder, to blast the boulders and to get to the gold that had to be underneath. They had waited all winter for this. Now it was gone.

Water gushed through what once was the catch basin and through the cut where the sluice had been, gullied where the boulders had been, and flowed on out toward Meadow Creek.

"At least we have water," Charles muttered.

Samuel knew how bitterly ironic his father's words were. Most placers in Warren's camp could only be operated a couple of months before the water drained from the hillsides. He had ditched water from around the hill from the spring near the cabin and dug the catch basin to store water for running the sluice. Even so, by midsummer water was insufficient even to fill the catch basin. It had been because of the unusually heavy rain last fall that Samuel had by chance returned to the placer and discovered the rich gravel.

"I'm gonna kill the bastards," Samuel breathed.

Charles remained quiet.

"I'm gonna find out who they are, and I'm gonna hunt them down, and I'm gonna kill them."

"Be easy, son," Charles said. "I know I don't have any words that will make it any better for you, but it's going to be night soon. We need to fix our cabin."

"You can have the blasted cabin, Pa," Samuel shouted. "You can have it all. What in blazes does it matter anymore?" He felt a burning in his eyes.

His father turned toward the cabin.

Samuel found himself wandering up the hillside above the sluice, thinking. He found a smooth boulder and sat, watching the stars emerge. They had found good gold while on the Salmon, at least enough to live on. He had made a few dollars ranching. All of that had been stolen.

All winter he had dreamed of getting back here, of blasting the boulders, and of running the rich gravel that had to be underneath them. Now they found the Sweet Mary robbed, possibly of over forty ounces as he had calculated—well over six hundred dollars—enough to get the land his father wanted.

Who could have known about the Sweet Mary besides his father? No one. Finney and Culler had been suspected of breaking into sluice boxes along the Secesh. Possibly, it could have been them, but after roping Kan Dick, they were run out of town, and no one had seen them. Could Dudgin and Smith have robbed them? He doubted they would work this hard. *Probably just some more ne'er-do-wells,* he thought. Gold camps had a way of attracting scum. He shook his head and watched the sky a bit.

Maybe whoever it was was still snooping around. Samuel began to feel uneasy. His father had warned him to keep his eyes peeled. The hackles on his neck rose.

A branch cracked in the timber below, and he froze. His senses now on edge, Samuel strained to see into the darkness. He found himself reliving the night on the river when he sat in the rocks with the pistol ready. He wished he were at the cabin.

He edged down out of the timber, pausing occasionally to listen, straining to see. He heard another twig crack. *Could be an animal, a deer.* If it were human, they'd be making more noise. He told himself this but could not convince himself. He rushed blindly toward the cabin, where light streamed through the cracks.

Samuel entered, somewhat breathless. His father looked up, a bit startled, and then eyed him. "Glad you're back."

Samuel said nothing but sat, eyes cast downward. He had noticed that his father had cleaned up the mess and had stored their belongings. His bedroll was on the rope frame bed.

His father nudged him with a cup of coffee.

He took it, still not wanting to meet his father's gaze. "Thanks." He had a sip and allowed the heat to fill him.

"I know what you would say, Pa, and I know you're right. You would say there has to be some good in all this. I'd like to believe you, Pa, but right now I'm just not up to it."

"And I don't blame you. All I can say is we're still in one piece."

They sat in silence for a moment.

Charles continued, "It could be they figured someone was onto them. That's why it appears they left sudden-like. Maybe some good gravel is left."

Samuel could not reply. Whoever it was could be watching the cabin at present. The fear that had subsided was again welling up, but then the anger seeped back in.

"I can promise you this," Charles said. "I'll do my best to figure out who hit us. It may even have been the same two on the river. Like you said, they seem to know us. We'll start by visiting Sheriff Sinclair in the morning. Somehow I'll see justice is done."

"Maybe that's all we can do, Pa." Samuel did not share his own thoughts. He was beginning to feel more strongly that it was Finney and Culler, here and on the river. If so, they would not take too kindly to him any longer, not after he had thrown lead at them.

Samuel felt very tired. He undressed and crawled into his bed. He was too tired to think anymore. Tomorrow they would begin trying to set things right.

Chapter 18

THE CABIN WAS COLD in the morning when Samuel woke. Clouds had drifted into the valley and shrouded the trees on the surrounding hills, threatening rain. Samuel pulled himself from his warm blankets and stoked the fire. Usually his father beat him to it. Maybe like him, the robbery had worn on him. Soon he had a fire and water on to boil for coffee. He patted the cold corn mush into cakes and fried them with the salt pork. His father joined him for breakfast.

Except for the robbery, riding into Washington had brought back good memories, as though he had never left. Maybe he would get a chance to visit Chen. He imagined Chen's surprise. Samuel had last told him he was going back to Iowa.

At the combined jail and courthouse, they found a short, wiry man claiming he was filling in for Sheriff Sinclair. "William Stock," the man said and shook their hands. "Been deputized to watch over these men."

Several men were hanging around outside. Inside, the jail held another four or five. Samuel recognized a couple of them. No one seemed particularly under duress, and if Samuel was not mistaken, the door was unlocked.

"What in blazes is going on?" Charles asked. "Where's the sheriff?"

"He's out to Mount Idaho, trying to get some help on this little problem we've got. Won't be back until next week."

Charles eyed the mass of men.

"Howdy, Charles," someone said. "Welcome back."

"Howdy, Lee." Charles nodded at the man and then turned back to Stock. "I need some help out at my placer."

"Unless it's a matter of life or death," Stock answered, "I'm obliged to keep an eye on these prisoners."

"Why?" Samuel blurted. "From the looks of it, most of them could come and go if they had a mind to."

"Hey, it's the kid," another man greeted. "Hey, Samuel, you run into any more bandits?"

Samuel glanced in the man's direction. "As a matter of—"

"Say, you fellows look like the Rescue Mine crew," Charles interrupted. "At least I recognize Pete there and Snyder. What're you guys doing here?" He stepped toward them.

"They *are* the Rescue crew, and they're all in jail," Stock replied. "Come out here where we can talk."

They stepped out onto the street.

"What's up at your placer?" Stock asked.

"It's been hit."

"Had a lot of that going around here, lately. Undoubtedly, it's the Chinamen. Won't do any good to pursue it. Too many of them, and they just play dumb."

Samuel felt a twinge of anger. Anytime anything ended up missing or there was any trouble of any sort, it was always the Chinese receiving the blame.

"These weren't Chinamen," Charles countered. "There was plenty of evidence that said plain and clear they were white, and since that's the case, when can someone come out and investigate?"

"Not till Sheriff Sinclair gets back."

"Not a good answer," Charles snapped. "What if I was to say these men might be back and might not be too friendly to us?"

"Well, I reckon you have the right to protect yourself." Stock shrugged.

"Thanks," Charles responded. "Come on, son, I think we may get better help from Mr. Hinley. At any rate, we're about to get rained on." He took a quick glance at the increasing clouds.

William Stock scratched his head, muttered something, and turned back toward the jail, striking up a conversation with one of the prisoners.

Charles and Samuel reached Raymond Hinley's assay shop as the rain began.

"Gonna be like last season. Could do without the rain."

"Except it will help us run the sluice," countered Samuel.

Hinley looked up as they came in. "I hope you are not expecting your gold or assay results yet, Samuel. You dropped them off just yesterday." He grinned and adjusted his glasses.

"Nope," Samuel replied. "We got trouble."

Hinley frowned.

"The Sweet Mary was hit," Charles explained.

Hinley's eyebrows shot up. "To blazes, you say. Severely?"

Samuel nodded. "Someone's spent a couple weeks there and cleaned us out good."

Hinley stood, unmoving. He glanced from Charles to Samuel, slowly shaking his head. "That is simply intolerable. Just intolerable. I am certainly sorry for such news. I do not presume you have any idea who the scoundrels are?"

Charles shook his head. "We were up talking to that deputy, or whatever he is, up at the courthouse. He didn't seem to be offering much help."

"Aye, that is intolerable as well."

"Looks like the entire Rescue crew is in jail, Mr. Hinley," Samuel said. "What happened?"

Hinley laughed. "I shall take that as an invitation to catch you up." He wiped his hands on his apron. "Just as well. I am in need of a respite." He waved at the crucibles lined up on the worktable. "Would you care for some coffee?"

"Much obliged," Samuel said, pulling up a stool and sitting. The rain picked up.

Hinley filled their cups. "As you will recall, the Rescue has had its share of troubles."

"What now? When we left, they were running a crew of thirty men, around the clock."

"And they're now all in jail." Hinley laughed. "Mr. Isenbeck—the mine superintendent—got shut down. The Pioneer Mill, which Mr. Isenbeck was using, had liens against it. Well, as events progressed, the sheriff shut the Pioneer down and posted an injunction against the Rescue. Both properties are now in receivership."

Samuel felt regret. Everyone touted the Rescue as the richest mine in the district and, in some respects, the pride of Warren's camp. At least it had the best potential. Last season they had hit a rich section of the vein that ran one thousand dollars a ton—the richest rock ever. Unfortunately, it was an isolated pod, and the yield quickly returned to the mine's average of three ounces per ton.

"When the sheriff escorted Mr. Isenbeck from the mine property, I had privileged knowledge that the owners had still not forwarded Mr. Isenbeck any funds for paying his labor. Therefore, the miners took matters into their own hands and continued working. They were high-grading some of the best-paying shoots they could find, attempting to acquire sufficient gold on which to live. They operated for the better part of the winter, taking out whatever they could." Hinley paused and glanced out the window, adjusting his glasses. "Such intolerable weather."

A heavy rattling raked across the building.

"With the Pioneer Mill down, the hands took the liberty to operate it and process their high-grade ore. That progressed until Sheriff Sinclair was directed to arrest and jail them, which he has now carried out a few days past."

"Doesn't seem right," Charles muttered. "They had to eat."

"You shall not hear many argue with you, Charles," continued Hinley. "Each had a five-hundred-dollar bond levied against him. A few were fortunate to bond out, or Sheriff Sinclair would really have a problem. There is problem enough. No one trusts the county, and therefore no one desires to give the sheriff any credit for provisions for the prisoners." Hinley leaned across the counter. "Sinclair has already spent a goodly portion of his own money in trying to feed them. In my opinion, he is a downright decent man just trying to do his job. I say here is a time the county should step in and help out."

Hinley lowered his voice and eyed Samuel. "You shall know, lad, that for the first time in my career, I knowingly reduced some high-grade."

Samuel smiled. "Like my pa said, they had to eat."

"Aye, and living off the land in the midst of winter in this country is nigh on impossible."

Samuel guessed the reason Sheriff Sinclair was in Mount Idaho was to get some financial help.

"It shall be highly entertaining when the judge arrives this summer to hear this case. Attorneys Poe and Gamble, who are representing the miners, and Superintendent Isenbeck have been preparing night and day for their defense. I wager they shall win."

"I hope so," said Samuel.

The rain continued steadily, turning the streets to standing water and mud. No one was in a hurry to head back into it. Hinley poured more coffee.

Chapter 19

To avoid destroying evidence, father and son hesitated to begin placer operations; however, they had searched and found nothing. The real evidence, the gold, was already gone. The best they could hope for was for someone like Mr. Hinley identifying somebody with a good take of placer gold.

They located some of the missing pieces to the sluice, but Charles had to procure additional lumber from William Bloomer's sawmill. Samuel rode into Washington to see Scott Alexander for nails and new canvas.

Scott warmly welcomed him. "Well howdy, Sam. It's good to see you're back and that you survived the winter." His blue-gray eyes sparkled as they shook hands.

"More or less we survived, Scott," Samuel greeted. "Partly why I'm here today. We're in need of supplies."

"If it ain't edible, maybe I can help." He smiled.

"Mostly some nails and canvas."

"I should have that."

"We got jumped and our sluice got tore up."

"Hell of a thing," Scott exclaimed. "Heard you got hit on the Salmon. Didn't know about up here." He took out his pipe and gestured toward the stool where Samuel customarily sat.

They talked for a while. Samuel told him about the robbery on the river as well as the Sweet Mary. Samuel wondered if there was more gray in Scott's black hair. He still wore the same striped shirt with the dingy white apron. For a shopkeeper, Samuel figured he could afford a better-looking shirt. But the smile said he was still the same Scott that Samuel had come to know. Scott had always insisted that he address him by his first name, and it made Samuel feel welcome.

"Well, no one's been in with any remarkable amount of dust," Scott said.

"Mr. Hinley said the same. Apparently, no one noticed anything unusual."

Another customer came in and Scott excused himself to greet and help the man. Samuel knew where to find the nails and canvas from helping Scott before. He gathered what he thought he would need and measured it out.

"That wasn't much of a sale," Scott muttered after the man had left. "Wanted some butter and eggs and flour. All I had was a little flour. Then he said if I didn't have eggs, how about some vegetables. I told him the Chinamen have vegetables. Probably have eggs as well. I tell you, Samuel, those Chinamen are going to run me out of business."

"Now, that's not true, Scott. They don't have nails and canvas, or candles, or ..." Samuel waved his hands about the store looking for items he knew Sing Mann didn't have. He noticed it was not much, so he decided to be quiet.

"Well, I hope you and your pa brought enough grub to last till the pack trains can get in."

"Now that you mention it, we could use some cornmeal and beans if you got any."

"Beans are okay, but the cornmeal might be more bugs than meal. You might consider waiting if you can."

Samuel shook his head. "We're out."

Scott scooped out some cornmeal for weighing. "You must have come by some spending money." He dumped the meal onto some paper to wrap it.

"Nope," Samuel replied. "I'm going to ask you to start a ledger page for us, if you can."

Scott stopped midway to wrapping and raised his eyes. "Next you're going to want a grubstake."

"Not yet," Samuel replied. He thought Scott seemed overly delighted by the manner in which he opened the ledger. He stroked his moustache and began writing down items. Before, Samuel and his father had always paid with gold. He laughed to himself. That was after the first visit, when he had only coins and made Scott give him change. He had also tried to use coins at the Chinese store and found out they only accepted dust. That was how he had met Chen. Chen would not take the coins, and he returned later to pay Chen with the first gold he had mined.

Samuel walked out of Alexander's Mercantile over twenty-six dollars in debt. He headed toward the far end of the street, where Sing Mann and Chen had their store. He glanced around, hoping not to spot Miss Lilly or Miss Hattie. He was not ready to meet them, although his heart flip-flopped at the thought.

The two Chinese who always sat outside Mann's store smoking their long-stemmed pipes smiled broadly and quickly rose to greet him. They bowed and chatted exuberantly. Samuel wondered at how happy they seemed, apparently because of him. Before, they often got up and left whenever he visited Mann or Chen.

Sing Mann must have heard. In a flurry, he was outside, bowing and smiling.

"Vehlie good to see you, Mistah Samyew." Sing Mann's long, black queue swung as he bobbed his head. He was dressed in his red tunic with gold buttons and braid and wore a small rounded red cap.

"It's mighty good to see you, Sing Mann." Samuel noticed Mann's much-improved English.

"You see, Samyew, I am right. I say snake and dragon are tied strong."

Samuel remembered the story. Last fall when he was saying good-bye, thinking he would never return, Sing Mann predicted Samuel and Chen would see each other again.

"You were correct, Mann. I'm glad to be back to see you as well. Is Chen here?"

Mann shook his head. "He is at garden with Sang Yune. He be back tomahlow." He excitedly waved his arms as if he wanted to hug Samuel.

Samuel had looked forward to seeing Chen, but it was just as well that he was not in. He had work to get underway back at the placer.

"You tell him I'm back and for him to come out to the cabin if he can."

"Yes. I will tell him," Mann replied. He shook his head and bowed. "He be so happy you are home. Yes."

Samuel caught the word *home.* "Yes, you tell him I am happy to be home as well."

Back at the cabin, Samuel helped his father finish repairing the sluice, and they began working on the catch basin. The claim jumpers had dug into it, and the water had cut down through its bottom. They hauled rocks and rebuilt the berm, patching it with mud. Digging until near dark, they were finally satisfied they had a basin again sufficient for storing water.

"That ought to keep us running awhile after things start drying out."

Samuel followed his father toward the cabin. "Hope we didn't do all this work for nothing."

"Could be we did, but I'm guessing you'll find something the claim jumpers missed."

Samuel began cooking up the cornmeal to make hasty pudding. Tasting it, he nearly spit it out. It tasted like sawdust. He added more molasses. Maybe his father wouldn't notice.

When it had finally thickened, Samuel served it up.

"Thanks," Charles said and took a bite. "No thanks." He wiped his sleeve across his mouth. "Terrible. Just terrible. That stuff must have sat all winter."

"Sorry, Pa," Samuel said. "I think it did. Mr. Alexander is nearly dry on food stocks."

He took out the last of the salt pork and cut off some pieces to fry. Salt pork made anything palatable. He added the drippings to the pudding.

His father took another bite and eyed him. "Better. At least it's edible."

Samuel tentatively tasted some. It still tasted like sawdust.

The following day, clouds scudded into the meadow early. They began work, expecting rain would begin shortly.

Like before, they loaded buckets with gravel and carried them to the head of the sluice. Samuel dumped in the dirt, allowing the strongly flowing water to wash it into the box, where it bumped against the cleats and flowed on out the far end. After each bucket, Samuel peered into the head of the sluice for the sight of gold. A few encouraging flakes gathered behind the cleats, but it was nothing like last fall.

By midday, a steady drizzle began. They worked through the rain, shoveling the muddy gravel into the box, washing it through. By late day, they were soaked.

"Enough of this," Charles said. "Let's do a cleanup and go dry out."

Samuel blocked the flow of water, and they washed the black sand into a couple of pans. Samuel washed his down. "I'm afraid it doesn't look good, Pa."

"I've been noticing."

Tiny specks of gold winked from the black sand but nothing was larger than a grass seed.

"It's hard to believe there was so much gold before." Samuel poked at the two largest pieces.

Charles set his pan aside. "That's the way it is with these gravel deposits." He studied the surrounding hillside. "There could easily be another pay streak, but then again, we likely won't find it. The trick will be getting enough gold to prove up the O'Riley." He straightened up and pushed back his hat. "We won't know that for several days."

Samuel dumped the black sand back onto the pile for later amalgamating.

"At least we don't have anything for any claim jumpers to steal," Samuel said, bitterly.

A couple of days later, after similar dismal results, they decided to check how much snow remained on the O'Riley.

Samuel led the way. The Chinese were in full operation on Baroon's claim on Slaughter Creek, and he noticed there was plenty of water.

Charles nodded across the narrow valley toward the Pioneer Mill. It was silent. "I'll need to head up to the Summit Lode and check on Mr. Bradshaw's mill. I haven't heard if he got it in or not."

Last fall, when they were looking for a mill to process their ore, William Bradshaw had been the only mill that offered to fit them in. Both the Charity and the Hic Jacet mills had full contracts, and now the Pioneer was again shut down.

They worked their way through the dense timber along the ridges that rose to the north above Meadow Creek and the summit above the South Fork of the Salmon River. Long before they reached the O'Riley, Samuel guessed it would be inaccessible. Scattered snowbanks quickly became consolidated into an unbroken snowfield. Clouds had sifted in from the northwest and threatened rain or possibly snow.

"Don't like the looks of that," Charles said, nodding.

Samuel guessed they had a couple of hours at best before the weather closed in.

Finally, he recognized the area where he had discovered the O'Riley. One of his claim posts stood out of the snow. A deep snowdrift covered where Samuel had exposed the vein.

"Almost like it was supposed to keep it buried for us," Samuel observed.

"Means we have at least a week or probably more to continue work at the Sweet Mary before coming up here. Probably about the time the first pack train makes it in."

Muted thunder rumbled to the north and the rain began.

"Like last season," Charles observed. "Remember all the trips looking for O'Riley's ledge and getting soaked?"

"How could I forget?" Samuel pulled his coat up around his ears.

Halfway back to Washington, the rain turned to snow—wet, thick, sloppy flakes. By the time they reached their cabin, several inches had accumulated.

Chapter 20

SUNDAY, as was customary, they headed into Washington for business.

"You don't need to accompany me while I visit Mr. Bradshaw, son," Charles said. "You can catch up on some of your own business. See if Mr. Hinley has the assay done and our retort gold."

Samuel had hoped his father would turn him loose. Before seeing Mr. Hinley, he intended to visit Chen. He caught up to him in the back of Sing Mann's store, where he was putting crockery on a shelf.

He had never seen anyone smile as much as Chen smiled when he walked in. He bobbed a quick bow, his long, black queue swinging as he stepped toward Samuel. They embraced. Samuel had never been so happy to see someone.

"Sam, you surprise me vehlie much," Chen said. "Uncle tell me you are here. You said you would never be back, but I told myself sometime you would be back. Sing Mann tell us you will be back." Chen was dressed as usual in his dark blue cotton tunic. His bony ankles were showing, sticking out from his short baggy blue trousers. He wore the traditional cotton shoes. Many of the Chinese miners wore Western clothes, but except for a Western-style hat, Chen wore traditional Chinese dress. It was more fitting for his work as a merchant and farmer.

"Yep, Chen. Mann was right. The dragon and the snake are tied strong together. I am glad to see you."

"I am glad to see you, Sam. You tell me about your winter. How is your father and mother? How is your mine?"

Samuel joined Chen at the table in the rear of the store where they often spent time reading. Sing Mann stood aside, listening and smoking his long-stemmed pipe.

Samuel told Chen about Bonnie and ranching.

Chen laughed. "So you will marry her and live here?"

Samuel blushed. "That is my business, Chen."

"At least you have a woman. No women for Chinese men." Chen glanced away.

Samuel knew what Chen thought. Without the presence of women, the Chinese men whiled away their time by smoking opium, drinking rice whiskey, and gambling. Not infrequently, fights broke out. A few Chinese had been hacked to death by their countrymen over gambling debts or other disagreements.

"My father and I do not plan to stay, Chen. We came back to finish digging the gravel I found last fall and to prove up the O'Riley so we can sell it."

A shadow crossed Chen's face. "Like last season."

"Yes, only someone jumped the placer and got our gold."

Chen startled and then frowned. "You should have told me, Sam. I would have watched."

"You went to the Sang Yune's gardens, remember?"

"Yes. Now I am coming from the garden for two months. We have a good trail through the snow."

"How is Sang Yune?"

"Good. We grow vegebows all winter. Bring them here as soon as we can to sell. Maybe go in a few days to sell. You want to go?"

"It might come to that, Chen. It doesn't look like there's much gold left on the Sweet Mary, and we need money for the O'Riley."

Chen paused and then smiled brightly. "Hey, let me show you what I can do." He jumped up and brought out the book Ma Reynolds had given them, now tattered and dog-eared.

Chen flipped open a couple of pages. "I know many words now." He began pointing to words and reading them.

Samuel was stunned by the many words that Chen remembered and more so by those he had figured out on his own. "You have our paper and pencil?" Samuel asked.

"You bet." Chen produced several sheets of paper that were filled with words—carefully crafted words, not scribbled.

Samuel laughed. "I need some with room to write."

Sing Mann had been listening and soon brought them a couple more sheets. "Vehlie good paper."

"Thank you." Samuel knew that paper was scarce, except the rice paper they wrapped merchandise with. "Here, try this, Chen." He wrote a few words into a sentence.

Chen read, "My name is Sing Chen. I sell vegetables." Only he still pronounced it "vegebows."

Samuel laughed. "You're amazing, Chen."

Chen stared back, stonily. "I want to learn to write and read English."

"I know you do, Chen, and you are doing well." Samuel wrote, "You are doing well."

Chen read it.

"Exactly."

Chen smiled. "See, I tell you that I study. Now you are back and can help me more."

Samuel felt good about Chen's comment. He hoped he was of help to Chen. They worked for a long while until Samuel realized he still needed to visit Raymond Hinley.

Hinley had several crucibles in front of him. "I was beginning to believe you had forgotten your assay and your gold."

"No, sir." Samuel took his customary stool. "Just been mining."

"How is it proceeding?" Hinley was measuring flux for some samples, something Samuel had learned to do. He added the soda ash to the crucibles and wiped off his hands.

"We've hardly been at it, and it doesn't look good. The claim jumpers cleaned us out."

"Simply intolerable." Hinley began measuring out the borax.

"Want me to take over?" Samuel asked.

"If the winter has not caused you to forget everything I taught you."

Samuel laughed. "Maybe some."

"First, let us take care of business." Hinley went to his safe and pulled out a cloth bag. "Here's your paperwork and the gold from your amalgam." Hinley laid two small shiny ingots on the counter along with a few silver coins. "Forty-two dollars and forty cents."

Samuel picked up the two one-ounce ingots and hefted them. "Praise the Lord. These sure feel nice." He could not help but think of the stolen gold, maybe another fourteen or fifteen ounces after refining. His stomach knotted.

"I shall never grow tired of seeing fresh-cast gold," Hinley said. He pulled out a canister and unfolded a sheet of paper. "Now here is your assay. It did not show strong gold, Samuel, but it is a respectable amount."

Samuel read the assay: "Gold: 1.2 ounces. Silver: 8.4 ounces. Copper 6.4 ounces."

He set the paper down. "So, if I hauled out a lot of ore, I might have something. You once said you needed about an ounce a ton to make it worthwhile."

Hinley shook his head. "Unfortunately, this is not likely with this sample. The metals are bound in sulphurets, and there is no nearby mill that can reduce this type of ore. I do believe there is some free gold, but most likely that will be a fraction of an ounce per ton."

Samuel shrugged. "I guess I'll keep prospecting."

Hinley harrumphed. "The winter has not been so long that I have forgotten about that good prospect you should already be mining."

"The rich sample I brought in?"

"That is the one."

"I did tell my pa about it, Mr. Hinley. We agreed we didn't have enough time or money to get it out of that country."

"Poppycock. I wager I could find someone who would be delighted in hauling out that type of ore."

"You have been mighty kind to me, Mr. Hinley. If I decide to give it up, you will be the first to know."

"I shall hold you to that, lad."

"So how are the mines doing, if I can ask? You're always in the know."

"And you also know I am bound to keep secrets."

"But I work for you, and I'm sworn to secrecy," Samuel protested.

"Then you shall work for me, and you shall be quiet." Hinley handed Samuel an apron. "I am in the process of running this set of assays; however, those two samples await the muller." He nodded toward some ore next to the muller.

"I figured." Samuel stepped over and tossed some of the pieces onto the metal plate. He began rolling them under the muller, watching the tiny fragments pop as they gradually turned to powder. "So how *is* the season looking?"

"Several of the quartz mines ran all winter and are anxious to get their ore milled. Most of those mines are still operating, except, of course, the Rescue."

Hinley set the crucibles next to the furnace and opened the door, allowing a blast of heat to escape. "Here, bring me that bucket of charcoal and help me pack these crucibles."

Samuel assisted. He wanted to ask where the assays were from. Maybe when he saw whether or not they were any good he would ask, although Hinley would likely not say.

Samuel worked for as long as he dared and as long as Hinely was sharing the mining news. When at last he left, he spotted his father coming up the street. "How'd it go with Mr. Bradshaw?"

"Maybe we should talk about it at the cabin."

Samuel knew things were not good.

At dinner, they talked.

"Took a bit of doing getting into the Summit Lode. More snow up there than at the O'Riley. But they were operating. Mining, that is. There is no mill."

Samuel stopped midway in taking a bite of venison and stared at his father.

"They ran into trouble last fall getting it shipped out of Lewiston. Some of it's still sitting at Mount Idaho waiting for the trails to open, and some other pieces got shipped south to Oregon Territory by mistake. The best guess Mr. Bradshaw thinks he'll be operating by is mid-July or so."

"That's better than a month, Pa." Samuel felt dismayed.

"He asked if I still wanted to be on his list. I told him I had no choice."

"What about the Charity and Hic Jacet? Any chance on them?"

"I went by the Charity. Mr. Sanders said they're full up with contracts. He guessed the Hic Jacet is also booked up. I talked to some of the other miners. Some of them were talking about bringing in a mill out of Florence. Might get it in by this fall. If we'd a been sticking around, I'd have offered to go in with them."

"Guess we'll be here awhile, then," Samuel said. He wondered if his father would change his mind and head back to Iowa now. Probably, they should. Nothing was working.

Chapter 21

WHILE WAITING for the snow to leave the O'Riley, they began trying new places on the Sweet Mary, checking for richer gravel. One spot they tried under the lodgepole pines, stripping the thin soil underneath, hacking through the roots, and shoveling the upper layers of dirt to the side. When they had dug down a couple of feet, they reached a thin seam of gravel packed on top of a layer of clay. The gravel held moderate gold, but for the work, it proved nearly worthless.

"We gotta be able to find some cobbles like you had last fall," Charles said.

They moved to another area where a bit of gravel showed and began a new hole.

"Certainly doesn't look like the pay streak from last fall," Samuel observed.

"Maybe we'll get lucky."

Maybe the next pick or shovelful, Samuel hoped.

Both continued swinging their picks, shoveling gravel, carrying it up to the sluice, washing it through, and checking it. Very little gold showed.

The following morning, they woke to several inches of snow. It melted by noon under a good sun, but clouds again thickened and by evening, the drizzle had begun anew.

"Weather like this makes you want to mine hardrock underground."

"True, but now the mines are filling with water," Samuel said. "I've heard some of the miners that come by Alexander's say that during snowmelt, working underground is like working under a waterfall."

"What's the difference, this time of year?" Charles gazed up at the rain. "Certainly underground has to be warmer."

"Maybe not. It's surface water coming into the mine. A lot of the time it freezes."

Charles paused, leaning against his pick. "I guess if a man is going to make a living, none of it's easy. Seems I remember something like that from the Bible."

"And for sure, we won't eat if we don't work." Samuel thought of his family back in Iowa. They had not received any letters since they last sent one of their own. "Wonder how the crops are going."

"I'm guessing your uncle Jake and your cousin Daniel got them in okay." Charles pulled his collar up. "I figured we'd be headed back by now."

Despite the rain soaking through, they continued work. A small line of gold grew behind the uppermost cleat.

The following day, the weather held, and they worked all day without any interruptions.

"We stick to this hole, maybe we'll start to get lucky," Charles observed.

They had been working downward into an area that held more cobbles and gravel than usual.

"It's certainly looking better." A few more specks began showing.

That night, they cleaned out the box and piled the black sand.

"I can't believe we got a full day in without rain," Samuel said. He had stoked the fire and they had hung their clothes to dry. "Maybe tomorrow our clothes will stay dry."

But the next day, a steady drizzle sifted down, drenching the woods and meadow. They worked for a while, each pulling his coat about himself, trying to keep the rain from running down his back.

"Figured it was too good to be true," Charles muttered.

"At least the snow is melting. A few more days and we should be able to get into the O'Riley."

"And the camp has good water," Charles said. "I've even heard some fellows are ground sluicing."

They continued work and spoke little. The cold rain soaked through their clothing. It trickled from their hats and down their necks and backs. The gully where they ran the sluice turned to mud, sucking at their feet as they trudged uphill with the heavy buckets, snatching their legs from under them when they returned downhill to the pit. Their trousers were soaked and clung to their bodies. Their boots filled with mud and water. If it had been warmer, they might have stripped like the Chinese did in the heat of summer during the summer thunderstorms, but today, the rain, sometimes mixed with snow, was bone-chilling. By noon, they shook with numbing cold.

"Enough of this," Charles finally said. Without waiting for Samuel, he set aside his pick and shovel, and, holding his hat firmly, headed back to the cabin.

He built up the fire. "Just like last season, son. You would think summer would come a bit earlier. When I get home to Iowa, this is the part I will definitely not miss."

"Nor I," Samuel managed. He rubbed his numb hands over the stove. They stung with needles as his circulation returned.

Charles put a pot of water on to boil.

In the morning, the sun shone and the meadow warmed.

Samuel recognized Sheriff Sinclair on his bay, riding up the trail.

"Hello, Mr. Chambers ... Samuel," he greeted, dark eyes squinting, and dismounted. He glanced at Samuel. "Seems I'm riding out here to check on you more often than I should be, Samuel."

"I reckon." Samuel remembered the last time after his encounter with Dudgin and Smith. Sinclair was younger than his father was by a few years and of medium build with dark hair. "We seem to have more than our fair share of trouble."

"That you do." Sinclair smiled. "My deputy told me what was up, Charles. I came out as soon as I could get away."

"I appreciate that, Sheriff," Charles said, pushing his hat back. "I may have covered up any evidence, though. I didn't have much choice but to get started mining."

Charles walked about, pointing out the damage as he explained the robbery. "A lot of garbage left behind. Seemed to be pretty lazy. Instead of cutting wood, they burned half of my pole fence."

Sinclair followed, taking note. "Can't say any of my other cases show this pattern. What I have seen, Chinamen have been suspected. In those cases, I think it's a misunderstanding about boundaries and such. Maybe not always." He paused and glanced around. "In your case, they were camped here and knew what they were doing."

"Anybody you would guess?" Charles asked.

"Maybe those two I suspected of hitting placers down on the Secesh," Sinclair replied.

"Finney and Culler," breathed Samuel.

"Yes." Sinclair eyed him. "Hell, Charles, I thought Finney and Culler, and whoever else was with them, would have taken the lease on life we allowed them last fall and left the country. No one has seen them otherwise that I know of."

Charles shook his head. "They weren't who we were chasing last fall, Sheriff. Samuel figured out it was Dudgin and Smith with a new partner that we chased. Samuel recognized my description of their horses."

Sinclair tightened his jaw. "For sure you better hope it's not them. They won't hesitate in killing somebody else." Sinclair glanced at Samuel. "Nor is it much better if it *is* Finney and Culler. Someone's going to be slinging lead at them one of these times, and when that happens, I'm guessing they won't hesitate to start slinging it back."

Samuel wondered if they had not already done so.

"You two better keep your eyes peeled."

"We're getting accustomed to keeping our eyes peeled," Charles replied.

"Hell, Charles, soon you're gonna have all the scum in the county after you." Sinclair laughed and swung back onto his bay. "Do me a favor. Take them all with you when you head back to Iowa."

"Unless we hit some decent gold, they won't have any reason to follow."

Samuel wanted to laugh but couldn't.

That evening, while his father fixed dinner, Samuel did his best to separate what gold he could from the black sand. He panned it down as far as possible, scrapped out the largest particles, and then dried it over the fire in a pan. Next he used a magnet to remove most of black sand—magnetite, an iron mineral, Hinley had explained. The remaining lighter sand he gently blew away, leaving mostly clean gold. When paying for merchandise, the lingering impurities did not matter as much, but for large amounts, the dust needed further refining, which is what Hinley did.

Charles examined the gold Samuel had separated. "How much do you figure?"

"About like we been doing, about five dollars." Samuel scraped the gold into the small canister in which they kept their dust. "There might be another four bits or so in the black sand."

Charles pushed back on his stool. "That keeps us in grub but not much else."

Samuel nodded. "Only the Chinese work a placer this poor. Hinley said as soon as yield drops below half an ounce a day per man, owners are looking to sell."

"Only we can't sell. This is all we got," Charles said. "And we still need about a hundred dollars for tools and powder for the O'Riley." He set his jaw. "My concern is as before. Can we get our investment out of the O'Riley and still have some money to take home? If not, we should start packing."

Samuel gulped. "We can, Pa. I'm sure of it." He didn't want to go. He wanted to make it work, but he also realized how difficult staying would be.

"Okay, but at this rate, it may take all summer to get any gold, and I don't want to be here all summer. Maybe I'll ride out and visit John McLane. You can keep running the Sweet Mary and keep an eye on the cabin. Who knows? Maybe you'll hit another rich spot."

"I know Mr. Alexander will let me do some packing as soon as his wares get in. That might help a little."

FIRST PACK TRAIN
COMES TO TOWN

Chapter 22

THE MORNING HIS FATHER headed downstream to see Robert McLane, Samuel set off for Washington, intending a quick visit with Raymond Hinley about possible work until the pack train got in, after which he hoped to do some sales trips for Scott.

The moment he dismounted from Spooky in front of Hinley's, Miss Lilly stepped from Ripson's Saloon and headed directly in his direction, her red hair flashing from underneath her large, feathery pink hat. *As if she was watching for me,* Samuel thought. He felt his heart do a flip-flop. *Blazes, why does she have to look so beautiful?*

He recalled the first day he had met Miss Lilly. Her beauty and presence in a remote placer camp had mystified him. Since then he had come to know both she and Miss Hattie were dancehall ladies. It didn't help that he was attracted to Miss Lilly and she to him. He glanced around to see if the older woman was standing by ready to ambush him as well.

Samuel politely touched his hat. "Hello, Miss Lilly."

"Well, howdy, stranger." Her hazel eyes sparkled as she smiled broadly. "I tried to say hello when you come to town the other day, but you were busy at Mr. Hinley's shop."

"I'm sorry, ma'am," Samuel stammered. "I had a lot to do." Samuel felt nervous. He wanted to tell her about Bonnie now, before it became too late—to get it over with—but he could not muster the courage. His throat was dry. She wore the same low-cut, frilly, pink-and-white dress as when he had first met her. Her standing just inches away, all cinched up and pushing up her breasts, didn't help matters.

"Don't call me 'ma'am,' Samuel. We're still friends, ain't we?" She nodded for him. "Well, then, you just call me Lilly."

"Yes'm, Lilly." Samuel remembered. Although she was but four or five years older than he was, the respect he had learned for women was too difficult to overcome—despite that she entertained men with her singing and stories and other possibilities. But that thought only made Samuel more uncomfortable. He wanted to think of her as a regular woman—a real lady.

"I sure missed you over the winter. Not a lot of people wintered over," she continued.

"I missed you too, Lilly," Samuel admitted. She visited him when he fell from Spooky because of the rattlesnake and was nearly killed last year.

"How was it on the river? I heard you and your pa got jumped. Did you lose a lot of gold?"

Samuel nodded. "Yep, except for that and the fact our placer up here also got jumped, we managed the winter okay." Samuel wanted to melt into Lilly's arms. The feelings in the pit of his stomach made him ache.

"Your placer here as well? That's where your cabin is, ain't it?" She frowned and then raced on. "You get a good notion of who they were? You see 'em? If'n you do, you gotta put lead in 'em, Samuel. That'll settle it."

"We have an idea who they might be, and yes, we aim to put lead in them if they return." Samuel smiled, thinking how easy it was for Lilly to tell him to shoot someone. "How was your and Miss Hattie's winter?"

"We survived. Miss Hattie better'n me. You know how she is." Lilly sighed. "My winter wasn't good." She stepped closer to Samuel, and he took a quick step back. He could feel her warmth.

"I been a mite sick."

Samuel could now see a grayness to her skin, partly masked by her heavy makeup.

"If you'd've come back sooner, I would've been better." She smiled and reached to brush Samuel's hair. He desperately wished she would not do that … not in the middle of the street. He glanced to see if anyone was watching.

"I-I'm sorry you were sick—" Samuel could not tell her about Bonnie, not at this moment. "You look good now," he lied. "I hope you're better."

"If you'd've come visit me like you promised, I'd feel *much* better." She cocked her head. "Just come by Ripson's."

Samuel felt a rush. He remembered his promise. What he had said had been somewhat accidental, but since that day, he had been troubled by it. He often imagined what it would be like to visit Lilly. Now he felt emboldened and warmed by the idea.

Samuel noticed Chen walking his direction from his uncle's store.

"I have to excuse myself, Lilly. I'm here on business. I'll see you, okay?"

"I'll be here, Samuel." She smiled broadly.

Samuel walked quickly toward Chen.

"Hehwoh, Sam," Chen greeted. He bowed slightly.

"Howdy, Chen." Samuel bowed in return. "Shake." He extended his hand, which Chen took.

"Good. It's important to shake if you are going to do business with us Americans."

"And it is important you bow if you do business with Chinese." Chen laughed.

Shortly, they were seated in the back of Sing Mann's store. A couple of Chinese were present, finalizing a purchase, talking excitedly with Sing Mann. Samuel always worried that when they became as agitated as they now appeared, out would come the cleavers and hatchets. Of course, this never happened, but due to the many stories, it was hard not to expect it.

Samuel took out some paper. "Write me a sentence, Chen." He offered the pencil.

Carefully and deliberately, with well-crafted letters, Chen wrote, "My friend Sam looks for gold." He used no punctuation, but it was of no concern to Samuel.

Samuel shook his head in wonder. It had taken him years to learn to read and write. Chen was doing so in a few months.

Chen wrote another sentence: "Someday I will teach Sam how to write Chinese."

Samuel smiled. "I don't have the patience you have, Chen, and I don't plan to go to China."

Chen grinned. "So you do business with Chinese here. You do more business."

Samuel paused. Sometimes when talking with Chen, he wondered about China. He felt comfortable here in Mann's store. He enjoyed coming in to see and smell and sometimes taste the merchandise from China, the mysterious and wondrous food—crocks of pickled eggs, beans, onions, pig feet, pickled everything. The teas of different tangy smells mingled with the aroma of ginger and with the pungent, sweetish odor of burning joss sticks from an altar near the rear of the store.

Most Chinese items were strictly functional, but Samuel appreciated the clean design of the different crockery types—those of light and dark brown with red Chinese lettering, and those with all white glazes and bright blue characters. And he appreciated their simple clothing designs, the wide-open blue tunics, the baggy and loose pants, and the slip-on cotton shoes. And then there were some items that appeared to be more for decoration than function—tall, narrow vases containing brilliant peacock feathers; brightly colored silks that hung and floated on the air; several bright brass figures representing animals of the Chinese zodiac; and fluttering squares of red-colored rice paper pocked with holes. But the pocked rice paper, he remembered, was to ward off the devil. He decided the decorative items must remind the Chinese of their homeland. Samuel smiled to himself. In many ways, the Chinese had brought their homeland to America.

Inexplicably, Samuel felt a longing for Iowa, for his own mother and sister. He reflected that he would never again see his grandma, but when he thought of home, he could see her there as well, cooking at the stove or playing with his little sister.

"Uh, Chen, do you hear news of your family in China?"

A shadow crossed Chen's face. "Not for vehlie long time. Not since after you go."

Chen was born to a San Francisco slave woman and escaped with Sing Mann to Idaho Territory after the saloon boss had murdered his father. Mann had taken in and raised Chen as his own, giving the boy the name Sing to help protect him. Even so, all Chen dreamed of was getting enough gold to go to China to seek his own relatives.

"What of your mother?"

Chen appeared troubled. "Sh. Do not ask." He frantically glanced around, even though only Mann was present. "I do not know where saloon boss have his men." He wrote a few words: "Someday I will go to China to see my family."

Samuel wrote, "Maybe I will come with you."

Chen smiled. "Then see, Sam, you should learn Chinese."

Early afternoon, Samuel headed back toward the assay shop, where he had left Spooky. He was met with dozens of cheering men, both Chinese and white, running into the street. They gathered around a man who sat his horse in the center of the road, waving his hat and shouting.

"Pack string's a comin' in. Binnard and Grostein's string's comin' in with thirty-two mules," he cried, "and they're fully packed."

"Told you'd it'd be them," someone else shouted. "They always beat Hofen's string."

"That means whiskey, gents. Whiskey!"

His words were nearly drowned in answering cheers.

The bell mare led the way down the street's center. A rider alongside urged people to step back. Mule after mule trotted in, aparejos swinging and bulging with goods.

A second rider came up along the opposite side of the mules.

The mules, heaving and clamoring, sensing they had arrived, slowed and stopped, heads mostly down, standing uneasily in the street, occasionally twitching their tails and shivering from muscle fatigue.

A rider instructed, "Stand back unless you want to help unload."

There was a sudden rush of men, most making a beeline toward the whiskey kegs, arms reaching to unlash the mules' burdens.

"And not just the whiskey," the rider protested.

Piles began growing along the street, and one of the packers began directing bundles to the appropriate merchants.

Samuel noticed one large stack being deposited in front of Scott Alexander's Mercantile, where Scott was busy examining the material.

"Want me to give you a hand hauling this inside?" Samuel asked.

"Just as soon as it's checked off, Sam. You'd be more'n welcome to help." Scott was reviewing items with one of the packers.

A couple of men started rummaging through the items. "Now hold on, Mr. Thomas, and you too, Mr. Baker. Let me get this inside. There'll be plenty of time to get what you want—tomorrow."

The men looked in Scott's direction and grumbled.

"You're not going to starve in a couple more hours. I'll have it ready in the morning," Scott insisted. "Maybe you've forgot about Mr. Ripson? Just as soon as he gets that whiskey unloaded, he'll offer a round. He does that every season after the first train comes in."

The men's expressions lit. "Well, we just might go by then." Turning, they nearly tripped over each other, heading toward Ripson's Saloon.

"Didn't have the heart to tell them Ripson won't be opening for business for an hour or so." Scott grinned, his eyes sparkling. He pointed at the pile. "*Now* you can start hauling those bundles inside."

Scott waved at the packer. "Come on in, Carey." He nodded to Samuel. "Just keep bringing that stuff in, Sam, while I settle."

Scott hung a Closed sign on the door, went behind the gold scales, and dug out a large pouch of dust. "Want me to weigh it for you?" Scott asked.

"Nope, I trust you, Mr. Alexander." Carey hefted the pouch and headed out the door. "We'll catch up later for your order. Like you told those other fellows, I'm heading over to Ripson's."

"That's all anyone's been talking about all winter, Sam. 'When's the whiskey comin' in?' We get this unloaded, I just might join them." He pushed at his moustache and then began undoing some ropes on some boxes. "You might as well come along and say hello. Everyone in camp will be there."

Samuel's heart caught. Lilly and Miss Hattie worked there. Lilly was always telling him to visit. He was also fifteen—not an age to be drinking. But he knew about whiskey. He had seen what it did to men on frequent occasions. His father never seemed to take part. Something in Samuel's memory, a time after his father returned from the war, he was eight or nine, he remembered his grandfather bringing his father home. His mother had been upset. It had something to do with whiskey—and his father and Uncle Jake.

He said nothing but helped Scott undo bundles and stock shelves and bins. Within the hour, they had the necessary work finished.

"Come on, Sam. I can work on the rest later. I'll credit you four bits for your help." Scott took out the ledger and entered a line.

Together they headed toward Ripson's Saloon. The place was packed and noisy, and bottles clinked as they were being passed around. It seemed that the entire town was present, even some of the miners who should have been on shift. He caught sight of both Lilly and Miss Hattie as well as a couple of other ladies. They were serving drinks and bustling about.

Lilly saw him and came up. "This don't count," she whispered. "This is a town doin's."

Someone hollered for her, and she turned away, carrying a whiskey bottle and a couple of shot glasses. She winked back at Samuel.

Scott stepped up to the bar. "We too late, James?"

James Ripson was behind the bar filling bottles from a keg. As fast as one was filled, another was handed to him.

"By cracky, *we* ain't, Scott." He poured a glass and handed it to him.

"What you staring at, Samuel?" Ted Rankin, the county recorder's partner, had shouldered up to Samuel. "Come on, no one's gonna bite you. We're celebratin'."

Scott held his glass; somehow Samuel found one in his hand; he swirled it and watched the amber liquid smoke the sides.

James Ripson clinked a glass for attention. "All right, gentlemen, who'd ever of thought it would be the middle of June afore we got ourselves rescued?"

Men roared, "Hear, hear."

Ripson held his glass high. "Here's to us. Here's to survivin' another blamed long winter, by cracky." He drained his glass.

In unison, a couple dozen men noisily tipped their glasses. "Hear, hear."

Samuel swirled his, watching the amber reflections.

"Come on, kid. No one here cares how old ya are. If you can reach the top of the bar in these parts, you're old enough." Rankin nudged him. Other men watched.

Samuel took a swallow and tried not to grimace as the liquid burned its way down. The men cheered, laughing.

Rankin slapped him on the back. "Whatcha think, kid?"

Samuel swallowed some more, a bit too much. He nearly choked. "I guess I can take it ..." He coughed, sputtering. " ... or not."

The men laughed and cheered and tipped their glasses. "To the kid! Hear, hear."

"It's official," Scott said. "He ain't a greenhorn no more." He thumped Samuel's back and took his empty glass. "But we best not overdo it."

Scott led him back outside. The warmth Samuel felt was more than just the whiskey.

"Too bad your pa wasn't around to join in."

"Thanks, Scott." But Samuel didn't think his father would approve. He gazed at the western horizon. The sun was settling into the trees, sending long shadows across the land. Likely his father was back at the cabin, wondering where he was.

"Well, Sam, like the first robin that marks the start of spring, the first pack string of the season marks the start of summer. Must be summer."

"I reckon."

"By the way, you and your pa should come to town tomorrow. There's a miners' meeting taking place. The new mining law is out. Mr. Rayburn will give a rundown on it."

"I'll tell my pa." But Samuel wondered about its use, because they would be leaving in the near future.

Samuel met his father back at the cabin.

"You stayed in town quite a while today."

"Yep, it was an interesting day." Samuel set down the supplies and began making up some supper. "The first pack string came in. Mr. Ripson offered everyone a round of whiskey to celebrate."

Charles studied Samuel a moment. He sat and began removing his boots. "Not a good idea to make that sort of thing a habit. Maybe when you got a few more years on you, but not even then if you can help it."

Samuel threw some venison into the hot skillet. "I don't plan on it, Pa." He searched for some explanation. "Mr. Ripson was being kind to everyone; I felt I couldn't refuse."

"Nor would have I," Charles replied. "But just remember—we fatten up steers, but it ain't for the reasons of being kind to them."

Samuel laughed.

"Don't read too much into it," his father continued. "Mr. Ripson gives the men a free drink, they'll be sure to buy the next one and the next. Same with those dancehall girls like that Miss Lilly you like. You might think they just want to be kind and visit and tell stories or entertain you with a song, but they're just working you up to get you to buy another drink."

Samuel thought of Lilly and Miss Hattie. He felt a little confused.

"I ain't condemning liquor, son. You just gotta know your limit and what it can do to you." Charles spread his hands. "Next time, come get me so I can join you."

Shortly Samuel had some dinner of beans and fried venison. He offered a plateful to his father.

"How's Mr. McLane?"

"Actually, he's quite well. I managed to pitch in today and earn three dollars."

"Hey, I got paid four bits for helping Mr. Alexander unpack."

Charles laughed. "Well then, we've had a banner day, son." He stabbed a piece of venison. "No, Mr. McLane is doing well. The placer is up and running. He said anytime I wanted to give up on this placer of ours, he'd give me my old job back."

Samuel expected as much. If anyone worked harder than his father did, he had never met the man.

"He asked about you. Hoped you hadn't had any more run-ins with desperados. I told him about our luck on the river and up here. He said apparently you weren't learning."

Samuel grinned.

"He also said if you got tired of mining gold, he'd sure like a new cook."

"I hope you didn't volunteer me." Last season, when Samuel had his arm in a sling, he had helped Gabe Whitman with some of the cooking. Later, when Gabe left, he had taken over.

Charles laughed. "Nope, I knew better."

"Thanks."

"I did say you might like to run a sluice with me."

Samuel paused. "I'd rather run ours."

"I figured, and you can keep your eyes on things here. Besides, you have a knack for finding rich spots."

"Only the one, and we didn't get to mine it." Samuel felt the bitterness wash over him.

"All we can do is try to catch up. Come Monday, I'll work for Mr. McLane until the snow's off the O'Riley. Should only be a few days."

"I can do some packing for Mr. Alexander."

Charles nodded. "Then how about tomorrow we go to town, clean up, and have a decent meal?"

Samuel frowned.

"I'm not saying anything bad about our cooking, son, but even you'd have to admit we're no match for Ma Reynolds."

"No, sir, I won't argue with that." Samuel felt a rush of joy.

Chapter 23

SAMUEL DREAMED about visiting with Lilly, seeing her in her frilly pink dress with the low-cut bodice, and then seeing her come out of her bodice. Lilly was talking and serving him whiskey, insisting he keep drinking, unaware of her dress. Other men were gathering around, staring, and laughing. Samuel wanted to cover Lilly, but she kept talking as if nothing was wrong, and then she was no longer beautiful. She turned angry with him and began yelling. It was because of Bonnie she was angry with him. Bonnie was arguing with Lilly. Bonnie began crying and would not talk to him until he took her in his arms and held her—held her very close—and felt her warmth.

He woke to the images of Bonnie in his embrace. Emotions of helplessness and anger and desire overwhelmed his thoughts. He sat up, noticing that his father had already left the cabin. Samuel shook his head. If a shot of whiskey did this to him, he would never have another.

He pulled on his trousers, glad his father was not around to see him. He could not shake the images. This could not just be the whiskey, he told himself. He busied himself with lighting the fire and putting on the coffee pot.

His father came in with a bucket of water. "Bring some wood in when you're done."

Samuel slipped outside into the damp mountain air, not missing the clouds that were scudding in from the west. *Probably more rain before the night,* he figured.

Samuel thought of the upcoming day and began to feel better, more settled. He wondered about the dreams and his feelings. He returned to the cabin, dropping the wood into the box next to the stove.

"You were tossing around a lot last night, son, so I let you sleep," Charles said. He poured some coffee and handed it to him. "Must have been something you drank." He smiled.

Samuel felt embarrassed. "Thanks for reminding me." He mused,

Must have been someone I met. The coffee helped. But instead of Lilly, he had an overwhelming desire to see Bonnie.

By late morning, the clouds had increased, mostly blocking the sun. A beam shone on the Sauxe Saloon, where Reverend Weatherspoon would hold Sunday services. Samuel wondered if it was a sign.

As before, the paintings were turned and the bar was covered, but Samuel felt pretty uneasy about the entire business. He knew he was due some preaching. Christmas service had been his last occasion, and he had done a few things, mostly fancied a few things, that the good Lord might find untoward. In addition, Reverend Weatherspoon was doing a good job of reminding people about the evils of spirits. Samuel figured it might have something to do with the pack string coming in and the more-than-average celebrating. He noticed that the women were standing pretty tall and stoic. More than one man seemed a bit under the weather and subdued.

As before, they still had no piano, and the Bibles didn't quite make it around the room.

By the conclusion, Samuel was feeling a mite better, perhaps a bit more redeemable.

People visited in the street, catching up after the long winter. Several of the families had just returned from their winter homes, some on the main Salmon, a few on the South Fork. Others came back from as far away as Oregon Territory or northwest from Lewiston. All returned to resume mining and related commerce. Some, the Penningtons included, did not return.

The gathering reminded Samuel of the Independence Day celebration last year. The young children, those not in their mothers' arms, ran about, chasing each other and playing games while their parents talked. For some reason, the children all converged on him, jabbering and laughing.

"Sam! Sam, can you play with us?"

The Manuels' daughter Julia, maybe four, and the Osborns' oldest children, William, five, and Caroline, three, remembered him. Sam noticed how the children had all grown. They reminded him of his own sister, now six, back in Iowa, and his cousin Daniel, now ten.

Charles found him. "We better get on over to Ma Reynolds's before the line gets too long for getting a bath. Either that or we can skip dinner."

"I'm coming." Samuel broke away from the children. In truth, being with them reminded him he was still caught somewhere in between them and the men.

A spattering of rain began falling.

"Just what we needed," Charles muttered. "More rain."

Samuel pulled his collar up and his hat down, shrugging his shoulders to keep out the water.

Ma Reynolds bubbled with joy when she spotted Samuel. "You've growed like a weed, Samuel. Can't see you growin' anymore or you'll be taller than Mr. Chambers." She pushed at her large, voluminous print dress, which Samuel took to be new but already well worn.

They asked how she and her family were doing. Her hair was pulled back as Samuel remembered and was the same salt-and-pepper gray. She was rather stout and bosomy. Maybe the only change was a few more lines etching her face.

"'Bout the same, 'bout the same. Winter was really hard on us. I'm thinking if Mr. Reynolds can take care of things for a bit I just might go down to the river for some sun. This rainy, snowy, cloudy weather is making my bones ache."

Samuel thought she looked good. She was very much the same warm person he had come to know and love.

She eyed them closely. "Now are you two here for a bath or just some grub? You missed breakfast. Won't serve dinner until later."

"We're figuring on both," Charles explained.

Samuel glanced at his father to make certain he was not hearing things.

"Well, you know where to go. Mr. Reynolds will be fetching in the water." She wiped her hands on her apron.

George tumbled into the room.

"Sam! Sam!" The boy clapped with glee and ran to his mother. "Sam is here, Momma."

"Yes, now you let him and his pa alone. You help me make this dinner."

But George did not let them alone. He promptly followed Samuel and Charles to the room off the kitchen where they had the bath facilities set up, jabbering all the way.

When Samuel settled into the tub, he could not help but recall his accident. He examined the scars from where the limbs had punctured his side and abdomen. They were white splotches, stretched like melted white cheese. He also examined his arm and the scars from where it had been skinned.

"I know what you're thinking, son," Charles said. "It's a miracle you survived."

"The good Lord and Sang Yune's medicine."

"Yes, I admit, the Chinamen saved your life," Charles replied. "You ready for some hot water?"

"You bet."

Samuel felt the rush of the luxuriant liquid heat wash over his head and shoulders. If there was one pleasure in life, it was taking a hot bath. He resolved he would never pass up the chance when going past Burgdorf's. Somehow, they would have to visit Ma Reynolds's more frequently.

Later, they settled in for dinner. Samuel hardly had an opportunity to answer the many questions the Reynolds and other diners directed his way, let alone eat. Fortunately, Ma Reynolds kept pushing more toward him: mashed potatoes with rich gravy, wheat biscuits with butter, sliced apples, some greens, and beefsteaks. Samuel ate until he was stuffed and then started on a second round.

Charles eyed Samuel with a look that said not to overdo things.

Ma Reynolds must have caught the look. "Now, Mr. Chambers, you just let young Samuel have all the fixin's he can hold. You two are no better than last time, still as skinny as spring chickens. You musta not et anything at all when you were down on that river. You can both use some fattenin' up. You all just better come by here more often."

Samuel paused from a bite of beef. "It wasn't all that bad, Ma Reynolds. We had a few good meals. Got to Slate Creek for some Christmas dinner—"

"Long time past, that Christmas is," she said.

"And we got out to the Strombacks'. In fact, I got to work for them for a while. Mrs. Stromback can rustle up a pretty good batch of grub." Samuel caught himself. "Of course, she doesn't best you."

"Why, thank you, Samuel."

Peter Reynolds glanced up. "Is that the Strombacks that bought the land off the Nez Perce? A waste of money, I tell you. It's all part of America."

"I reckon." Samuel didn't offer any further argument.

"They have a daughter, don't they?" Ma Reynolds eyed Samuel.

"Bonnie, but she's their niece. She's a really nice girl."

Samuel now caught all eyes on him.

Mr. Reynolds leaned back. "Now doesn't that beat all? If you play your cards right, Samuel, you could marry that gal and own a cattle ranch. Sure would be a better living than placer mining."

Samuel felt himself blush. "Maybe."

Despite the rain, a good number of men, including the Rescue Mine hands who were supposed to be in jail, gathered for the miners' meeting at Ripson's Saloon. Michael Rayburn had seen a copy of the new mining law and knew some of the changes.

As usual, Rayburn was the chairman. Pat Townsend acted as secretary. The Blakesly brothers, two huge hardrock miners for the Charity, were sergeants at arms.

"We have a couple items of order for the night, so settle down and find a seat. And yes, Mr. Turner, the bar is closed," Rayburn harrumphed. A few boos echoed throughout the room.

Samuel sat on a stool with his father, elbow to elbow with other miners. Most of the men stood along the walls. The rain had settled in and made a constant drumming on the roof.

"Bloody rain," Turner muttered. A leak had sprung above him, and he moved. It gave Samuel a little more room.

"First order of business is to review the new mining law," Rayburn continued. "It's made some mighty fine improvements, I think. Makes it easier for a man to file a claim and prove it up. The main point is it allows any citizen the right to enter onto government lands, make discovery, file a mining claim, and eventually own it."

Cheering broke out.

"Then the gov'ment cain't come and take my claim anymore."

"Right, Smitty."

"Then the Chinaman issue is settled," Clarence Johnson, a large, boisterous man shouted. "Chinamen can't be citizens. In that case, they can't enter onto lands and can't own mining claims."

Clapping ensued.

A man stood, waving his hand, and Rayburn tapped his gavel. "The chair recognizes Attorney Poe."

Raymond Poe addressed the men. "In my understanding, the new law is explicit that no foreigner can enter onto lands, make discovery, and file a mining claim. But I do not read that as meaning they cannot buy and own a mining claim. This very miners' assembly gathered here three winters ago and voted near unanimously to allow the Chinese in."

"Bah, most of the men who voted to let 'em in ain't even here anymore.

And back then, no one knew what thieves they were." Johnson peered around the room. "Hell, you know about McLaren's boots that were stole. Had to be Chinamen."

Muttering increased and Ben Morton, a small, wiry man, stood up. "Excuse me. If the law says you have to be a citizen to have a claim, I think it's pretty clear the Chinamen can't own claims. Explain what's different from owning a claim and owning land."

Others joined in voicing their agreement and Rayburn rapped his gavel. "Order, order. Each of you will get a chance to talk."

"What I'm saying," Poe continued, "is this law does not change our decision to let the Chinese into Warren's camp or to allow them to buy or lease claims from legitimate owners. However, it does mean no one can file a claim and later patent it if he's not a citizen or if he has not declared his intention of citizenship, whether Chinese or of any other nationality. In short, it really changes nothing as it relates to the Chinese. The Chinese can't file for patents to own the land. But please allow me to do some more research for discussion at a later meeting."

Ben Morton turned toward the others. "All you know me—how my claim got stole by the Chinamen. I think it's pretty clear what the new law says. I don't need any more interpreting. I want them off my claim."

Rayburn harrumphed. "Mr. Morton, you need to address that with the sheriff after the meeting. I'm not saying I disagree. But it sounds like we need to give Attorney Poe more time to look at the law. Now let's move on." He glared at Morton.

"There's another important change due to the law. You will now have to recertify your claims and recertify your labor on the claims. In summary, go pay Mr. Watkins another dollar. After that, you will need to do a hundred dollars of improvement on your claim each year in order to keep it—that is, until you receive a patent."

"That's a hell of a lot of money," someone groused amid other loud grumbling.

"You figure on five dollars a day. That's twenty days of work. Who here isn't going to spend twenty days working their ground?" Rayburn demanded.

The arguing decreased.

"I see the main thing is to refile your claim and certify that the work has been done. It's pretty straightforward. If you don't, then the claim can be relocated by someone else."

"What about claims where they ain't come back to camp yet?"

"If they don't recertify in sixty days of the posting of this law, then the land is open to relocation."

Samuel saw a number of eyebrows raised. He realized some potential ground might come open. He could also see some arguments arising if someone didn't return to check on his claim for a couple of months. Someone might shoot first before asking questions.

A man held up his hand. "Vhat must you do to declare intent to become a citizen?"

"Hey, Fritz, you wanna be a citizen?" A couple of men laughed.

"No. I just vant to own der claim and make a living. I vant to get enough golt and go back to Prussia and get my wife and kid."

Another man spoke up, "Yah fer sure, how do you declare intent?" The room quieted.

"Anyone wanting to declare intent to become a citizen can see me after the meeting," Poe said. "I'll draw up the papers for the judge for when he comes through next month. And God bless you. We can use more good citizens."

"Yeah, no more yellow heathens." Ben Morton's comment cut at Samuel.

Melvin Crukshank, who had seemed to be simmering during most of the discussion, raised his voice. "Request to speak, Mr. Chairman."

Mr. Rayburn recognized him. "You have the floor, Mr. Crukshank."

"Now, you all know I come here afore the Celestials come. I weren't in favor of them comin' in, and I still ain't." The veins on Crukshank's neck bulged as the man began to work himself up. "Now, what I'm a sayin' is it ain't right to allow them here. The biggest form of thievery is the gold they's a takin'. Them Celestials live on a few cents a day, grub out all the gold, and ship it back to China. *It ain't their gold.* It belongs to us Americans. It's our gold, and by our rights as Americans, we can take it back."

Smitty muttered, "Mel, you said that last time."

"My turn to speak, Smitty, and I aim to set things right," Crukshank snapped.

Other men began arguing. Rayburn banged his gavel. "Order, order."

Pat Townsend stood and turned the paper and pencil over to Raymond Poe. "You can record."

Poe grumbled but took over.

"I was one who voted to allow the Chinese," Townsend said. "Maybe we do have some thievery problems, but we can solve that by watching out for each other a bit more."

An undercurrent of booing began to grow. Samuel squirmed on his seat. He was beginning to see why Sheriff Sinclair had once cautioned him not to take sides—that he could be caught in a cross fire.

"I wanted to remind you since we voted to bring them in, I guess we could vote to throw them out," Townsend continued. "But before we do that, remember why we wanted them here. We couldn't afford to operate our claims with our own labor. It was plain and simple. And most of us just wanted to move on to find new ground.

"Keep in mind, Sheriff Sinclair collects a five-dollar tax on each Chinaman every month for their privilege to mine. What is that … two thousand dollars a month for this camp alone? We let them work. That's about all. Looking at it that way, they don't cost us much."

Samuel guessed that if Sheriff Sinclair were present, he would correct the amount to more around five hundred dollars, based on the stories he had told him about his inability to catch the Chinese and make them pay up.

"Keep in mind some of you are collecting lease money on your old claims, and many of you sold your claims you thought were wore out for some pretty good sums of money."

Another man stood up. "Ya shoulda been a bleedin' heart preacher, Mr. Townsend. Fact is, I'd a much rather have less thievery. Them Chinamen are nothin' but heathens, corruptin' folks. You said yourself, Pat, we voted 'em in—I say it's time to vote 'em out again."

The cheers and boos increased. Rayburn hammered his gavel, and his face began turning red. The Blakesly brothers moved about the crowded room, encouraging men to settle down.

Samuel felt a crawling feeling enveloping him. He glanced at his father, but his father didn't seem overly concerned. Samuel thought of Chen and Sing Mann and Sang Yune—all of them his friends. They were not evil. He had seen a man murdered, and it was not by Chinese.

Rayburn got the men's attention.

"I can see we still have some disagreement on the law and, more importantly, on our Celestial brethren. How about a motion to continue discussion in a couple more weeks when we can get a better reading on the law?"

People sounded their agreement.

"The night's getting long, and I think some of that whiskey that arrived yesterday is still available. Is that so, Mr. Ripson?"

Ripson stood up. "Somebody give us a motion to adjourn, and I reckon we can open the bar, by cracky."

The meeting adjourned amid cheers and clinking glasses.

"They can celebrate, but I'm not sure what for, son. We got work tomorrow," Charles said. He pulled his hat down about his ears and stepped out into the night. The rain had stopped except for a chill mist and occasional spatter. The street was deep in mud.

"Not sure I like the tone of things, son," Charles said. "I'm not too crazy about the Chinamen either, but it's not healthy to blame them for all the evil and misfortune in this camp. Some men are dead set to hang whoever stole McLaren's boots."

"Hang him!" Samuel exclaimed. "They're just boots. You can buy a new pair for three dollars, not even a good day's wage."

"My point. You and I both know if they get rid of the Chinamen, there'll still be plenty of trouble. We should know."

They reached the livery, caught up their horses, and headed north toward their cabin.

"I'm also not sure how much to trouble ourselves with all this if we aren't going to be sticking around."

They rode in silence for a time.

Chapter 24

As THEY HAD AGREED, Charles began work at McLane's placer, and Samuel arranged with Scott Alexander to deliver supplies to some of the outlying mines, mostly tools and hardware.

"Not a lot for this trip, Sam. Take some orders," Scott said and handed him the list.

"Sure will."

Samuel mounted Spooky and headed out, leading Molly. He met Chen at the trail intersection. Scott may have guessed Samuel would accompany Chen, but Samuel did not make it apparent. He sensed that Scott was becoming less tolerant of the Chinese. They were excellent merchants and brought in fine produce, along with chickens, eggs, and fish. An increasing number of white miners were buying from the Chinese, and the Chinese did not hesitate to deliver the merchandise. What miner could refuse fresh vegetables when he was miles outside the nearest town? Samuel had picked up the idea from Chen last season, and Scott had allowed Samuel to take out supplies—mostly mining tools, but also buttermilk, cheese, and bread, all items the Chinese were less likely to peddle.

They turned up Steamboat Creek, and though they passed a couple of placers up in the trees, Samuel and Chen intended to visit other areas. Samuel tried to make deliveries based on requests coming in to Scott from the miners. Chen customarily rotated among areas.

Unlike last season when Chen insisted on leading his packed mule, he now rode. He had two wicker baskets that straddled the mule and towered behind his saddle. Sometimes, Chen put his feet up on the saddle yoke and leaned back into them. The mule plodded onward, following the trail.

Molly followed Spooky without protest. Most mules had their own notions about where to go and how fast to get there, but Molly had seemed to have given in to her fate of following the horse.

"So, do you have any holidays coming up?" Samuel asked. He reflected on the Festival of the Moon.

"Sure. We have fourth of youlie," Chen laughed.

"I mean Chinese holidays."

"Maybe. Maybe we have feast for dead."

Samuel was intrigued. "What's that like?"

"You come see. I will tell you when."

They rode in the direction of Burgdorf's hot springs. Movement on the hillside startled Samuel, and his heart caught. Immediately, he ducked into the brush, hissing at Chen. "Off the trail, Chen."

Chen did so and studied Samuel, concern in his eyes. "What's wrong, Sam?"

Samuel studied the timber, seeking the flash of sunlight off metal or something that would tell him it was a man and hoping it would not be. "My pa and I have some men who may be wanting to dry-gulch us." He pulled his rifle.

"They are the bandits?"

"Could be. We slung some lead at each other last winter on the river."

"Not good, Sam."

"Nope." He studied the brush for a while longer, finally deciding it had been nothing. He knew if he was dry-gulched, he would likely never know it was coming.

"Guess we're good, Chen." Samuel urged Spooky back onto the trail.

Beyond Burgdorf's place, they soon reached a new trail, turning off Lake Creek. Several new two- and three-man placers, known as Willow Creek, were situated to the east along some of the smaller tributaries leading into Lake Creek.

There was hardly a trail. No one had cut more than a horse width through the dense timber, and Samuel and Chen painstakingly threaded their way around and over downed trees. Both mules protested. Samuel led, pulling Molly. The sun beat down, and with the recent rains, the humidity was high. Sweat trickled from Samuel's brow, stinging his eyes.

"Maybe we do not come here again," Chen muttered.

"Maybe we raise our prices," Samuel suggested.

Chen laughed. "Yes, good idea."

Wherever they found the small camps, the men came out of the timber and up from their sluice boxes along the creek, cheering. Samuel thought it was often more for an excuse to take a breather than for any other reason. Besides picking up a few badly needed supplies, the miners were eager for any news and goings-on back at Warren's camp and the other placer diggings.

It was the way in the camps: Each miner was anxious to hear if anyone had hit it big but secretly happy to hear when no one had. It assured them their chances were a mite better where they were. The fewer the miners who made big hits, the more likely it was it could soon be their turn. But if news came in that someone had made a good strike, then they were torn between leaving their own strike and trying to cash in on richer ground elsewhere. Often those who tried were disappointed, and often they left better diggings behind. Mining was a battle of nerves and second-guessing. It was a fear only a miner understood.

Samuel sold canvas, nails, two pans, an ax, and a pick—all items that Scott knew the miners would need at the new diggings. Chen sold most of the vegetables. Deftly, the two took the men's gold and weighed it on a hand scale. Chen figured that the gold was richer than most and gave fifteen dollars an ounce for it. Samuel agreed. He had now seen enough himself to be a fair judge of its purity.

Somebody muttered, "That's the way to get rich. Sell vegetables for their weight in gold."

Another miner countered. "Well, if you want 'em, nobody but the Chinamen can seem to grow 'em."

"Be thankful these two are willing to bring us anything at all." The man, skinny, ragged, turned to Samuel. "Thanks, lad." He giggled.

Samuel recognized Andy Stephens. His blond hair was darker, rattier—his beard, more scraggly. He wore the same tattered vest.

"I know you," Samuel called after him.

"By gum, I thought it was you, lad," Stephens grinned, showing his missing teeth. "Me and my partner paid you a visit down on the river when you and your pa struck it good a while back."

"How you doing? I see you made it in. Where's Mr. Boston?"

Stephens glanced away. "Just me, now. Clint didn't make it."

Samuel felt as if the wind was knocked from him.

"It's okay. He knew he wasn't gonna make it. Got caught in snow, we did, by gum. Got wet, he did. Just sort a went to sleep. Afore that, he had tolt me if he didn't make it, just to bury him on a hill overlookin' the river. That's what I did. I know that was fine by him," Stephens said brightly. "And you, you're lookin' good. Your pa?"

Samuel kept fighting the realization that Boston was dead. He knew death happened. It happened a lot, but he could not shake it.

"Uh, he's fine."

By late afternoon, they had finished visiting the scattered camps and had headed back. Thunderheads were moving over the ridge.

As before, they found an area to camp near the main trail. Samuel considered continuing on to Burgdorf's. He longed for a swim in the hot springs, but he knew Chen would feel uncomfortable. He also didn't have the money to spare, although Mr. Burgdorf might not charge him.

Samuel felt strange to be peddling merchandise with Chen. All last season he had prepared to leave, never expecting to be doing so again. Now he was back. The feelings warmed him. He no longer felt uncomfortable with Chen's strange customs as he had when they first met. He accepted Chen's company and his strange ideas. Samuel appreciated Chen's passion for life in his own manner.

Chen boiled water for rice and tea. Samuel had cold cornmeal mush and venison.

They talked while watching the sun set, catching the tops of the thunderheads and turning them orange. Occasionally lightning lit the clouds, and muted thunder reverberated from the mountains.

"Might get caught in rain tonight."

Chen studied the clouds. "No. Tomorrow, late maybe."

"The placers are doing better this year because of more water."

"Yes, all men do well. Chinese do well. We have good gold."

"But it will dry out soon."

"Maybe by then we all get rich and go home." Chen laughed.

"Will you?" Samuel wanted to know if Chen still intended to go to China. He had trouble understanding why Chen felt he had to go, other than that his relatives were there, but none of whom he personally knew. At least Sing Mann told him he had relatives. Chen had said they had written. Samuel wondered, but he knew no reason Sing Mann would mislead Chen unless he wanted to provide him with some hope for his future.

"Not for long time. Not Sing Mann either. We give money to tong."

Often there were disagreements among the tongs—fraternities of Chinese somewhat like competing gangsters—but Chen's tong included the merchants, and as near as Samuel could determine, the other tongs tolerated the merchants because they brought in the supplies.

"Well, after more claims open up and more people come, you can sell more stuff."

Chen frowned slightly and shook his head. "Not as many new claims. Most are Chinese. White miners do quartz."

Samuel could not deny Chen's observations. Scott and others often reminisced about the boom days when gold was everywhere. Everyone now realized Washington would prosper only if the quartz mines began producing.

Chen pulled out his flute and played for a time. Samuel enjoyed listening to the hollow, melancholy notes. It brought to mind China, a faraway land he could only imagine, but one he somehow had come to know by knowing these people and their customs.

The mountain air chilled. Samuel pulled out his bedroll and found a fir under which to sleep. Chen found an area a few yards distant.

In the morning they were soon back on the trail and intersected the main trail that ran beside the Secesh.

Samuel immediately noticed a pungent odor and spotted the tracks and droppings. Spooky pricked his ears forward.

Chen laughed. "We in trouble now. Kan Soo bling in pigs."

Samuel could see the churned up earth where apparently dozens of animals had passed. He could make out the small cloven prints, as though a bunch of small deer were in front of them. They followed until topping a rise, where they spotted a long string of pigs stretched out, clambering, grunting, and squealing. The pungent stench enveloped them. Several Chinese were jogging alongside, all with long switches, directing and prodding.

"How in blazes do you herd pigs?" Until now Samuel would not have thought it possible.

Chen laughed. "One man have corn. Pigs start to follow. When on trail, they keep going."

Samuel noticed a man with a gunnysack.

They soon found themselves trailing behind the pigs. Chen called out to the closest man. They waved and chatted. Chen and Samuel kept pace, wondering if they would ever get past the swarm of animals.

"Maybe soon they let us go past." Chen hollered to the Chinese man again. The man turned and waved and smiled but kept walking, switching at the rumps of the pigs. The pungent odor grew more intense.

They followed a good half an hour before the Chinese with the gunnysack enticed the pigs off the trail and down toward the creek. The animals immediately spread out, rooting around, grunting, splashing into the water, guzzling. The Chinese paused along the trail, waving and bowing as Samuel and Chen passed. Chen greeted them and chatted for a moment.

"Good to get by," Chen said. "Even better to see pigs. Good to eat."

Samuel was more pleased to be able to breathe.

At Alexander's Mercantile, Samuel returned the few remaining items. Scott offered him some coffee and took out his pipe.

"I see you went with the Chinaman boy again."

"Yep, but don't worry, Scott. He sells things you don't."

"Maybe I'd sell what he's selling if he wasn't."

Samuel knew better. The Chinese had the vegetables—what the miners wanted and needed, especially after the long winter. "At least I'm out there making some sales that he isn't."

"True."

Then Samuel remembered. "How about some pork? Some Chinese are herding in a bunch of pigs."

Scott straightened. "Jay DuBois might object, but most likely it won't matter. Pigs are Chinaman food for sure. They aren't about to let any go to us." He smoothed his moustache. "Oh, don't mind me, Sam. Things seem to be turning down around here. I really don't know how much longer this old camp will keep providing a living."

Samuel felt disheartened. Scott seemed less optimistic than last season. "I'll find a new strike, Scott. You'll see. We'll have a new rush."

"I hope you do, Sam." He tapped his pipe.

Samuel met his father back at the cabin in time for dinner.

"Figured you might be back, so I thought I'd come on in from McLane's and see how it went," Charles said. "You seem to have a knack for attracting trouble."

"I did good, Pa, but you remember Andy Stephens and Clint Boston, those guys who tried to get in over the snow early?"

Charles straightened, nodding.

"I met Mr. Stephens at a new placer. Mr. Boston didn't make it. He died in the snow."

"That's a shame." Charles shook his head. "I remember you and I worried about those two fellows. Boston was the skinny one, wasn't he?"

Samuel nodded. "How'd it go for you, Pa?"

"So far, it's good. I'll get paid at the end of the week, about the same as last season."

"You finding any nuggets?"

"We're still trying to get down to the pay streak, but good color is showing in all the boxes."

"That's what I like most about the Sweet Mary—seeing the gold in the sluice."

Charles heaped some stew onto a plate and handed it to Samuel.

"You want to head up to the O'Riley and check how things look? I'd have you start hauling some of the ore out, but it makes no sense until we have a mill to haul it to."

"Any word on it?" Samuel took the plate. The stew was good and hot and had better than usual flavor.

"Last I heard, it's still at Mount Idaho," Charles said. "Maybe you should take a trip over to the Hic Jacet and see about them running our ore. We might have to get in line."

Samuel shook his head. "That's another six or so miles past the Summit Lode. We better hope Mr. Bradshaw gets his mill."

Chapter 25

SAMUEL TOOK HIS FATHER'S suggestion and headed up toward the O'Riley. He felt nervous about heading back alone into the country where he had run into Dudgin and Smith and witnessed them murder their partner. He figured they still wanted him dead as well, and he could only hope they had left the country. He kept his rifle across the pommel and scanned carefully for tracks. Thankfully, he saw nothing fresh.

When he reached the O'Riley, the snow was completely gone. The ore they had hidden to one side was untouched. The claim itself appeared forlorn, lifeless, and barren like any of the many other abandoned quartz ledges scattered throughout the country.

He checked along the cut where he had dug out the ore and examined it for mineralization. The snow and rain had washed off much of the dirt, and the quartz was startling white, showing traces of gray metal. In one spot, Samuel felt certain he could see some tiny specks of gold. His breath caught. *It's still here. All we got to do is mine it and get it to a mill.*

He spent nearly two hours at the cut, chipping out more assays from the richest-looking spots. Carefully, he recorded their locations, pacing the distance off from his center post. He knew that the more sampling he did, the more accurate the results would be and closer they would be to the vein's actual potential.

Samuel turned toward the South Fork, intending to hunt deer. When he neared the summit, he noted a party of men in the gulch below, working a ground sluice. He hollered for their attention so as not to surprise them. Normally, a gulch like this did not hold enough water for mining. This season, the heavy snow and runoff had made it possible. Three men were shoveling dirt into a thirty-foot long ditch that ran with muddy water and emptied into a small sluice box installed at its end.

They recognized Samuel and talked for a moment.

"What you up to, kid?"

"Just doing a little hunting. I'll probably head on over to the South Fork," Samuel explained. "You fellows doing any good?"

"Nah, just about to call it for the season. When we first started we got good gold. We're so high up, you'd think someone would find a ledge nearby."

Samuel glanced around, half wondering where the source was.

"You haven't seen anyone about that's got other ideas than mining, have you?" Samuel asked.

"Just folks like you out hunting."

Leaving, Samuel made a wide arc toward the summit so he could check for rock. He spent more time than usual, studying the outcrops. The gold in the gulch below had to have come from somewhere nearby.

He also scanned the woods. Maybe he was too edgy, but he kept watch for any startled birds or any unnatural movement. He watched Spooky. The animal could hear much better than he could, and Spooky would alert him, especially if a horse was around.

Samuel crossed the summit and angled off the trail toward Sang Yune's gardens. It was dangerous country, steep and rocky. As he descended, the country transitioned from heavy, dense conifer forests to broken trees and brush. Eventually, it opened into barren grass and sagebrush hillsides that fell steeply toward the river. The lower elevations were dotted with towering yellow pines on the north-facing slopes that stretched to the river's edge. Most of the south-facing slopes were open, covered with thorny brush that mingled with prickly-pear cactus. It was also favored country for rattlesnakes, as Samuel all too well knew. He shivered. He was not far from the ridge where he had run into the rattlesnake that nearly cost him his life. Had it not been for Sang Yune, toward whose stone hut he now angled, he would have died.

Samuel came out above the terraces. The garden was lush green with growth. Samuel laughed to himself. Both Chen and Sang Yune must have worked all winter broadening the terraces and cutting a new, lower one. Water sparkled in the ditch that carried it from the creek across them.

He spotted the two Chinese hoeing along one of the rows and hollered. They looked up, set aside their hoes, and headed his direction.

Sang Yune could not contain his wide grin. He repeatedly bowed and chatted exuberantly.

"He say he is vehlie happy to see you and that you look well."

"I am happy to see him and thankful again for what he did for me."

159

Chen explained. Sang Yune spoke again.

"Come, Sam, he say we should go to his house and visit."

They made their way upward toward the stone hut. Samuel found it hard to believe Sang Yune lived here all winter. The room was tiny with no window and only a door covered by a simple flap of cloth. And where did Chen stay when he was here as well? There was little room. But Samuel noticed two pallets of blankets inside along with a tiny table and oil lamp. He wondered how Sang Yune survived the winter with just an oil lamp.

"You *did* work all winter," Samuel exclaimed. "The garden is even more incredible."

"Yes. Now we grow even more."

"Anything new?" Samuel asked.

"Potatoes. Turnips." Chen brightened. "Some squash."

Samuel shook his head, amazed. Sang Yune listened closely, bowing, nodding as Chen interpreted.

"Does Sang Yune ever come to Washington?" Samuel had never seen him there.

"Yes. Sometimes he comes. But he stay here most of time to chase away animals from garden."

Sang Yune took the pot from the fire and added some tea leaves. He found three small cups.

It occurred to Samuel that the man did not live in the stone hut at all. He lived outdoors, where he also cooked his meals. He came to the hut for shelter at night or in the worst of weather.

Later, Chen lugged up some water from the nearby creek and set it on to boil.

"That's going to make a lot of rice," Samuel observed.

Chen laughed. "Not for rice. For bath. Almost every day take bath. Not like you stinky, white foreign devils."

Samuel stared at Chen.

"I joke, Sam," Chen managed, starting to grin. "But it is custom to take bath almost every day. You can if you want."

"That's okay. I'll just have to stink." Samuel shook his head. "Besides, I just had a bath at Ma Reynolds's." *Last Sunday,* he thought. Samuel felt uneasy. Every night? He was lucky to get one once a week.

When the water was hot, Samuel took his leave. Chen did not ask where he would stay the night, but Samuel had figured on continuing down to the canyon floor for his camp. He planned on hunting at daybreak when the deer would be near water.

He spent the night with a small fire for company and the sounds of Spooky cropping the nearby grass. He also kept his rifle ready and at arm's reach. Muted thunder reached him from a far-off thunderstorm, but for once, it did not rain.

In the morning, Samuel shot a doe and headed back toward Warren's. It began raining by the time he reached the cabin.

"Blasted rain." He pulled his collar up and his hat down more tightly. He remembered last year. Most of June it had rained.

He checked the sluice. Water gushed from the catch basin.

"Lord, you've sure given us water this year. Just wish you would have given us more gold."

He studied the gravelly hillside. How could there be gold in one spot but not elsewhere?

Samuel walked toward the end of the hill to where a small drainage came in. Another meadow stretched beyond. Samuel was certain a bed of gravel lay beneath it as well, along with gold. But like the main meadow, the soil and gravel were too deep, and there was no grade. Any prospect would have to be at least eight to ten feet deep before it hit any consolidated gravel or bedrock. Sure, flour gold could be found throughout the gravel, but it didn't amount to much, not until just above bedrock.

Making his way back, Samuel noticed a few cobbles sticking above the mat of needles beneath the lodgepole pines. An area about ten feet square formed a slight mound.

His heart began to race. Where he was standing, gold-bearing gravel could exist only a few feet down, but he would need water. He gazed back uphill toward the cut they had made. It would be tough to do, but he could build a flume and bring the water another hundred feet to the west and then downslope past this new area. For the first time, he might even be able to shovel gravel directly into the flume and have it carried into the sluice. It would cut his work in half, making this spot pay even better—if there was any amount of gold.

Samuel started laughing. There was bound to be more rich spots on this hillside, possibly many more. This could be one. He shrugged. Until the mill was operational and they were hauling ore from the O'Riley, he might as well continue mining right here.

Rain settled in while he began his first hole. Like last season, he planned to dig a series of prospect pits and sample the area. It could be there was no gold. But if he was right, there would be good gold.

Reaching a depth of three feet, he began running into larger cobbles—a good sign. He fairly shook with excitement. This matched exactly what they had dug before when they had hit the rich pay streak.

He eyed the distance to the sluice and figured it too far for lugging forty-pound pails. Shortly, he had Molly. She protested, but Samuel counterbalanced two pails across her, and led her to the sluice. He made several trips until he figured he had a good sample of gravel.

The rain continued to increase.

"Won't need to carry it to the sluice pretty soon. Could just build a ground sluice here and shovel in the dirt," he muttered. Water ran from his hat brim and soaked through to his skin. He was tempted to quit. *I won't melt*, he told himself. *I gotta see if I'm right.*

He dumped a bucket of dirt into the sluice, sprinkling it into the stream of water, watching it wash through. Immediately, a few flecks of gold caught behind the upper cleat. Samuel's heart began hammering. "Thank you, God," he breathed. *It's the same!*

Oblivious now to the pelting rain, he continued digging and washing buckets of gravel. The gold remained consistent. He picked out a few pieces the size of grass seeds. The Sweet Mary had a new life.

Shaking with cold, his hands numb, his teeth chattering, Samuel finally gave up. He washed some of the black sand from the upper cleats and took a panful back to the cabin.

In its welcome warmth, he stripped off his soaked clothing and built up the fire. He returned to panning the black sand in a tub of water. Samuel stared in disbelief, a solid line of rich gold showed at the edge of the black sand. He had spent only a couple of hours after reaching the gravel layer and had at least a third of an ounce.

Samuel had the pan on the stove, drying out the sand, when his father came through the door. They both stood still a moment, Samuel in his underwear.

His father laughed. "Don't blame you." He began pulling off his coat and shirt.

"Pa, you ain't gonna believe it." Samuel grabbed the pan and shoved it in front of his father. "I did it."

Charles peered in. "That's good gold, but where's it from?"

"The Sweet Mary."

"What, the past two days while I was gone? I thought you were going to check the O'Riley and get another assay."

"This is from a couple hours today, Pa! A new spot."

"Glory be," Charles exclaimed. "Tell me about it."

Samuel explained while his father continued to pull off his own wet clothing. Soon they were both sitting amid hanging, dripping, steaming clothes, talking about Samuel's new pay streak.

Samuel explained his plans for a flume.

"I don't know about lumber for a flume. That might cost a lot," Charles said. "I really don't know our best options anymore."

"A month, Pa," Samuel said. "I figure we can work the Sweet Mary until Mr. Bradshaw's mill is in. Once the mill is running, it won't take us but a couple weeks at most to get enough ore to get the assays and convince someone to buy the O'Riley. In the meantime, I can be finding gold."

"I'm guessing you're right. If there is anything we should've learned by now, it's to stay on the gold when you've got it. It appears you have some."

Chapter 26

IN THE MORNING, Samuel immediately headed to Washington to see Raymond Hinley and Scott Alexander.

"I got a couple more samples off the O'Riley," Samuel said, placing the canvas bags on Hinley's counter.

"Aye, this may help if you get any inquiry," Hinley replied. "You have done admirably well in obtaining assays."

"I could see some gold in a couple of the pieces," Samuel said excitedly. He dumped out the best samples and searched through the ore before handing a piece to Hinley. "Ya gotta look close, but I swear, I could see gold."

Hinley positioned his glass and began scanning the specimen, his eye twitching. "Without a doubt, Samuel, without a doubt. Take yourself a look." He handed the glass and specimen to Samuel.

Under the lens, Samuel thought the gold stood out like yellow stars in a field of snow. "Looks really good, wouldn't you say?"

"I wager these will be good samples," Hinley replied. "Will you be doing the work, or shall I proceed with them?"

"I 'spect you better go ahead," Samuel admitted. "You see, I need to do some work on the Sweet Mary. I might have another rich spot."

"Should I be surprised?" Hinley shook his head. "I shall hope you do, Samuel." He offered Samuel some coffee.

Samuel was impatient to get going, but for as many times as he had bothered Hinley and interrupted him, now was not the time to run off. "Thanks." He took his customary stool.

"You should know the Celestials are doing well."

Chen had alluded to that when they were out peddling, but something bothered Samuel. If Hinley knew, then word would get out. Rumors of gold in the air were to highwaymen like blood in the air was to a pack of wolves.

"I do not refine much of their dust. They take it out directly to

Lewiston, but I have examined some of it, and I have heard they are finding some beautiful gold."

"Do you know from where?"

"Aye, It appears most of it is from the claims up Slaughter Creek." Hinley shook his head. "Those claims were supposed to have been played out a long while ago. Indeed, they had been abandoned."

"Until Lance Baroon refiled on them and leased them back to the Chinese."

"Aye, for a few dollars a year to keep him in whiskey." Hinley frowned. "I did not share this with your father. I did receive an offer on the O'Riley ... for all of fifty dollars."

Samuel felt as if he had been punched. "It's a good thing you didn't say anything. Was the man joking?"

"Actually, I told him he should go seek his own ledge."

Samuel laughed.

"Based on your assays, Samuel, I am certain you shall have ore that goes well over fifty dollars a ton, and you are likely to hit some high-grade pods similar to those on the Rescue. Some of the Rescue crew were following some rich leads last winter before they were locked out. They were getting as much as fifty dollars a day on the high-grade they found."

"I knew it. The O'Riley has to have some ore like that." Samuel was anxious to get out to the mine and would, just as soon as they had money for drilling and blasting.

Another man whom Samuel didn't recognize came into the assay office.

Samuel rose to leave. "Thanks, Mr. Hinley, I got to get some stuff from Mr. Alexander." Samuel was out of the door and headed across the street.

He clumped across the puncheon floor a little more louder than usual as he entered Alexander's Mercantile.

"I need a small grubstake if I can, Scott."

"Well, well," Scott mused. "I've offered before, but now you'll have to convince me."

Samuel explained. Soon he had packed his saddlebags with nails and some new canvas and was leading Molly, headed out toward William Bloomer's sawmill for some lumber.

Maybe his father would not approve, but this was between him and Scott. Samuel knew he would have at least another sales trip, and with the gold off the Sweet Mary, which he was bound to find, he would have the grubstake paid back quickly.

Procuring the wood, Samuel began at once fashioning the boards into a U-shaped box. He tapered one end so it would slip into the head of the next section. He cut lodgepole pines and prepared to elevate the flume for most of the distance, but the rain returned.

Curtains of rain marched across the meadow, and the clouds descended, masking the treetops. Large areas of the meadow had turned to standing water. The steady drum quickly soaked through his clothing again. He worked until chilled and unable to continue before he turned for the cabin.

He half expected his father to return as he had the previous night. Again, Samuel spent much of the night drying his clothing.

That night, the rain increased in intensity, driving into the cabin through the walls and roof. Flashes of lightning lit the night with crackling, booming thunder reverberating through the meadow. Nearby strikes almost deafened Samuel. He thought about his father. They slept in canvas tents at McLane's. The wind and driving rain could easily rip them and, by now, probably had. He worried about the cabin—worried that it might not hold up. Places inside were like small waterfalls.

Unable to sleep, his bedding soaked, Samuel got up and dressed and huddled near the stove in one of the few somewhat-dry areas of the cabin. He shivered. If he was going to be wet, he might as well be somewhat warm. Samuel added some small twigs to the dying fire and blew on the remaining coals, coaxing a small blaze. He added more twigs until the fire was able to dry and consume the fuel.

Outside, the lightning continued to flash, followed by instantaneous exploding thunder. He hoped that the rain would not wash out his catch basin or destroy his sluice box and flume.

He boiled some coffee and then sat, shivering and wet, through most of the night. Toward morning, the rain finally tapered off. The water rushing in the spring creek and the rivulets of water cascading down the hillside toward the meadow drummed a constant rhythm.

As the sky began to grow light, Samuel built up the fire and strung up their bedding and clothes to dry. Almost unbelievably, the sun rose into a cloudless sky. Lingering fog rolled from the meadows.

Doesn't matter—it'll be raining by evening, he told himself.

He returned to the flume. Water coming from the catch basin

thundered through the cut, washing quantities of muddy gravel with it. It could have been worse; he could repair the breech. He only wished he could have positioned the sluice in the cut during the night. It would have trapped some gold for sure.

The boards were soaked and difficult to hold and nail at the same time. He cut the lodgepoles into short lengths and configured them into tripods to prop up the flume. Finally, he had a hundred feet of flume crossing the shoulder of the hill and over to the edge where he had discovered the new gravel. He tapped into the catch basin and watched as the muddy water flooded the flume and flowed swiftly along. The water moved with such force that it slammed into the end and shot high into the air where the flume turned downslope toward the sluice. Samuel had no choice but to build a wall and a baffle to dampen the water to keep it in the box, but he had run out of nails. *Guess it's back to Scott's for more.*

The trail was flooded. When he reached Meadow Creek below the cabin, he found a raging river. He urged Spooky into the torrent. The animal hesitated and then surged out into the water, lunging through until he caught the opposite side, where it ran less deep.

Most of the trail was under water, much of it a small creek. Spooky splashed along it and sometimes hesitated when he was not sure of the depth. Fortunately, where Steamboat Creek entered Meadow Creek, it spread over a relatively shallow area, and Spooky slogged through.

Samuel could see men milling about the streets of Washington, and then he could see damage from flooding. At least three buildings near the creek had been swept into the torrent. Hinley's assay shop escaped, but the water was up to within a few feet of it. A section of interlocked logs of the boardinghouse next to the shop now hung over the raging creek.

The east end of town was completely flooded. The creek had burst onto the street near Ma Reynolds's boardinghouse and cut a new channel down its center for a number of yards before swinging back into its bed below the town. It was a pounding muddy torrent, carrying timber and boards and broken bits of buildings.

Samuel rushed toward the boardinghouse. Belongings had already been carried out onto the street and stacked to one side. Ma Reynolds, appearing worried and forlorn, stood nearby with her small son, George.

"Are you okay?" Samuel asked.

"We are all out safe, Samuel." She held George, patting his head. "The first floor got flooded."

Peter Reynolds came over. "Hope things are a bit drier out your direction."

"I survived." Samuel gazed about. People were trying to remove belongings from the buildings that had been swept into the creek. Another building was leaning crazily and badly damaged.

At least three dozen men, including some Chinese, were upstream where the creek had left its banks. They were shoveling dirt and hauling rocks to fill the cut and form a berm, trying to divert the water back into the channel.

"Should start to drop fairly soon, Samuel," Reynolds continued. "Not a lot of country above us."

"Lord sakes, we got waked in the middle of the night. Lightnin' and thunder all about, and then a terrible crash from the buildings goin' in," Ma Reynolds said. "I came out of the bedroom and water was just a gushin' in, fillin' the house. I thought I had lost poor George for sure." Her face was strained. "Terrible feelin', Samuel, terrible feelin'. When I got ahold of George, I didn't care so much for the stuff. You get that way in close times." She pulled George more tightly to herself. George's eyes were wide.

Samuel realized that the ground sluices and other placers upstream had most certainly been washed out. Any trapped gold had been liberated and was now washing past the town.

Samuel pitched in with the other men, forming a human chain, passing rocks one at a time from the old tailings above the town and tossing them into the cut. Toward midafternoon, they had blocked the creek and forced it back into its old channel. Water began draining from the street and buildings. Samuel decided he had done as much as possible and would let the townspeople finish the work of filling the cut.

Scott Alexander and he talked for a moment.

"I feel bad about just getting nails and heading back to work."

"You did your share, Sam. I saw you out there," Scott said kindly. "I know you have little time, and this isn't putting any grub on your table either."

"I know more than a few people just lost everything. At least my pa and I still have our cabin and a chance to get gold."

"I'd say a lot of folks just lost a chance to get gold that washed down that creek, in other ways as well." Scott smiled and tapped his pipe. "I'm guessing some may pull up stakes now and leave. I've been hearing rumors from a few who've been thinking about it anyway."

"Like who?" Samuel worried it might be some of his friends.

"The Manuels and the Osborns. This town hasn't been exactly favorable to raising families."

Samuel's heart sank. He liked the comfort of the families. They meant civilization and reminded him of his own family. "I sure wouldn't want to see them leave."

Scott started to speak and then was quiet. Samuel wondered if he had intended to remind him of his own intentions to leave.

Samuel headed back toward the cabin, his thoughts bothering him. The creek had already dropped considerably. The flash flooding had stopped. Best of all, the sun remained shining. _Maybe this was Old Man Rain's last effort,_ he thought.

Samuel was surprised to find his father at the cabin busy stretching the bedding and clothing in the sun across some shrubbery.

"Might dry faster in the sun, especially since the fire was out," he explained.

Samuel was slightly embarrassed. He explained how he had been helping in town.

"Then you are forgiven."

Samuel finished helping his father and together, they returned to the flume. By evening, it was complete. For the first time, Samuel would be able to shovel dirt directly into the flume and have the water carry the slurry into the sluice.

"Hope all this time and expense pays off for you."

"It will, Pa. And if not, I 'spect I've already got buyers for the lumber. Some buildings in Washington were ruined."

Samuel fixed dinner and shared what he had seen in town. The businesses uphill had completely escaped any damage. None of the Chinese, as far as he knew, were harmed, because their huts were all built on a hill.

His father shared that some of the sluice boxes at McLane's had washed out and some tents were ruined, but otherwise, they should be operating by Monday.

Chapter 27

SUNDAY, THEY VISITED Alexander's for supplies—cornmeal, beans, a few potatoes, and some salt pork. Charles added another gold pan to their stack along with some kerosene and more candles.

Charles dumped out their gold. "After this, what will we owe?"

Scott glanced at Samuel.

"Include his bill as well, Scott. We're in it together."

Samuel realized that his father had guessed about his grubstake from Scott.

Scott shrugged and put the dust on the scales. He did some figuring in his ledger. "I can carry you on some of this, if you wish. Keep some dust for whatever else you might need."

"We'll manage."

Scott smoothed his moustache and tapped with his pencil. Finally he said, "Adding in what I think you will need for powder and the rest of your supplies for the O'Riley, you will still need about a hundred dollars."

Charles whistled. Samuel said nothing but fidgeted. He wondered if they should not leave town today. They would never get that much gold in a few more days.

Back on the street, Samuel turned to his father. "I just know we'll do okay, Pa. But if we don't try, for sure we won't get anything."

"We could have saved what we just spent."

Samuel couldn't answer, and an ache crept into his chest.

Charles softened. "We'll just have to keep at it a bit longer, son. But by the Lord, I swear we shall be home by Christmas. We sure won't spend another winter around here."

Nothing they did seemed to get them ahead, and Samuel wondered when a person should quit—how long should one keep trying? He rode in silence back to the cabin and dropped off their supplies.

"I'm going to start running gravel," Samuel said.

"It's Sunday, son," Charles reminded him.

"I gotta be doing something."

"They have another miners' meeting tonight. Being we're likely to be here for a time, you and I should attend," Charles said. "Besides, we got other chores. We'll have some of those potatoes for dinner and head on back."

As before, they met in Ripson's Saloon, and Michael Rayburn officiated the proceedings.

"The main issue from last meeting was the Chinaman issue. We were debating if a Chinaman can own a claim or not. If you read the new law, it's not totally clear. I quote, 'All valuable mineral deposits in lands belonging to the United States, both surveyed and unsurveyed, are hereby declared to be free and open to exploration and purchase, and the lands in which they are found to occupation and purchase, by citizens of the United States and those who have declared their intention to become such, under regulations prescribed by law …' and so on and so forth."

Ben Morton spoke loudly, "It's pretty clear to me. Like I said before, Chinamen can't be citizens, so the lands aren't open to exploration or purchase by them. They cannot own a mining claim, plain and simple."

A muttering of agreement erupted.

"We have the right to remove them yellow heathens from every scrap of land hereabouts, and now." Morton emphatically flayed the air.

Clarence Johnson and Melvin Crukshank shouted their assent.

Rayburn searched the room. "Look, I have asked Attorney Poe to further address this issue. Please give him the floor."

"Thank you, Mr. Chairman." Raymond Poe stuck his fingers into his lapels, acting as if he were about to give a great speech. "I did examine the law in some detail since last discussion; furthermore, I took the liberty to discuss it with others at Mount Idaho and Slate Creek. They come to the same interpretation and agreement as do I. Simply stated, the Chinese cannot enter lands and file claims, but they can purchase them, or, better stated, they can purchase the mineral rights. They cannot own the land. But just as a citizen initially does not own the land, the citizen still has the right to mine and extract valuable minerals. The difference remains the patent. Any citizen, after proving up a claim, can apply for patent and purchase the land, which gives him and his heirs title. Chinese cannot be citizens and thus cannot get patent."

Even after Poe's explanation, fierce muttering and angry replies continued.

Samuel was surprised when his father raised his hand.

Rayburn recognized him, "Mr. Chambers, you may have the floor."

"Watch this," a man next to Samuel whispered to his partner. "His boy's good friends with them Chinamen." He glanced Samuel's way, but Samuel pretended not to hear.

Charles rose. "Samuel and I have been here since last season, and I reckon you should know that we're planning on heading out soon, so what I have to say needs balancing with that. That being said, we wish for a good future for you and this camp.

"I can't say what I really think about the Chinamen. I've not had any problems with them—they seem to keep to themselves. My son's had considerable amount of doin's with them. He and that Chinese boy do some packing and peddling together. He tells me most of the Chinamen don't really want to be here. They're trapped, you might say. Isn't that right, son?"

"Yes, sir, Chen tells me that, and other things as well." Samuel felt everyone's stare.

"Like what?" someone asked.

Samuel glanced nervously around, reluctant to continue.

"Why don't we let Samuel tell us?" Townsend asked.

"He ain't twenty-one," Johnson muttered. "He can't vote on mining proceedings."

"Nothin' says he can't talk. I'd like to hear what the kid thinks."

Samuel was uncertain. He didn't think he could say it the way Chen had shared.

"I reckon he can talk," Rayburn said. "Any objections?"

Samuel found himself standing. The room had gone silent. "I reckon I really don't have much to say. I'm just saying what Chen and some of the other Chinese tell me. The Chinese didn't come here to stay. They came here to escape what was going on back in China. They lost a war with Britain and were being made to pay huge taxes, which has pretty much ruined Canton—that's where most of the Chinese have come from. Most of them lost their farms and many are starving back in China. They came here to get money to send home to their families to feed their families and buy back their land. They call this the land of the foreign devil. They don't want to stay here. They want to go home."

"We're the devils, hey? *They're* the devils, thieves, *and* heathens. For sure, I say, send 'em back," Johnson hollered.

Muttering erupted.

"Let the kid talk."

Samuel stumbled on. "That's just it, Mr. Johnson. Not many of them can go home. They also had a war in China. Now some of the Chinese are hiding out from the emperor. They'd be dead back in China. And a lot of them that came here have to work for the bosses who paid their way here. They can't make enough money to ever go home—sort of like slaves."

The muttering began dying down.

Charles said, "I don't know about all what my son says, but I will say this. Many of us just fought a war to end slavery in America. If that's what it's like for them, maybe it wouldn't be so wrong for us to allow the Chinamen an opportunity. Besides, as all you know, it wasn't Chinamen who robbed me and my son last winter or here back at the meadows."

The miners had become silent. Some clapped a bit. Several got up and left.

Samuel sat down. "Thank you, Pa," he whispered.

"'Fraid a few people don't take cotton to your point of view," Charles whispered. "You may have just made us a few more enemies."

Samuel was silent, wishing he had not talked.

The formal meeting ended. The independent miners remained to discuss bringing in a stamp mill to process their ore.

Matt Watkins caught them on their way out. "Mr. Chambers, those were mighty fine words you and Samuel had," he said, "and I respect your opinion."

Charles paused under the overhang of Scott Alexander's store.

"Now, I know you haven't been able to prove up and sell your quartz mine, and I know you got jumped on your placer."

"In other words we're busted. What have you in mind?"

"Sorry," Watkins continued. "It seems pretty clear to me, even more so now, the Chinese don't have claim to O'Riley's old placer. I know Lance Baroon, who leased it to them, isn't a citizen. I'd wager he won't even be in the country until this fall. Past the time for refiling." Watkins paused. "Well, that claim is rightfully yours. All you got to do is refile."

"Thank you, Matt," Charles said and then gazed down the meadow. "Wetter this year than last when we got here, don't you reckon, Samuel?"

"I understand your feelings, Mr. Chambers, but if I know the status of that placer, someone else is also likely to figure it out. As your friend, I advise you to stake it. If you don't want ownership, you could sell the mining rights back to the Chinese. It's got to be worth at least five hundred dollars."

Samuel's heart caught. For a fleeting moment, he imagined what five hundred dollars would look like. Then he considered the Chinese. They might not have the money.

Charles turned to Watkins. "I appreciate your thoughts. Unfortunately, the way I see it, those Chinamen wouldn't understand. They've already paid for the lease, new law or not."

"You don't leave me much choice then, Charles. If you don't stake it, someone else will. They'll throw the Chinamen off." He paused. "Sleep on it, Charles. Let me know in a few days?"

Charles remained silent. They caught up their horses and rode back to the cabin.

Samuel stoked the stove and pulled the coffeepot to the front. "What do you think, Pa? About what Mr. Watkins says?"

"There's things Mr. Watkins didn't figure on. We won't be here long enough to do any good, just you and me. The reason those claims are doing well right now is *because* of the Chinamen. There's a lot of them, and *they can* live on two bits a day. I think we'll still have a better bet with the O'Riley."

"If the mill ever gets here," Samuel muttered.

"It will," Charles replied. "Got to be careful about the Chinamen, though. I know you're friends with the Chinese boy, and I don't cotton to seeing the Chinamen being pushed around. Just be cautious."

"I guess I shouldn't have said anything tonight. Maybe you're right and I made us more enemies."

"No, you did good speaking your opinion, and you backed it up with some grit, not like Crukshank and Morton."

"Do you think they'll vote to throw out the Chinese?"

"After what you said, I doubt it. Unfortunately, those like Ben Morton will be even more stubborn." Charles rose and dished up some beans for himself and Samuel.

Samuel didn't know what to think. People were angry, and in truth, some of the Chinese did cause problems.

"We'll have to figure a way with those Chinese placers. Maybe I'll partner up with Mr. Hinley. He'd watch out for our interests."

"At least we got through one day without rain," Samuel said.

Charles gazed off toward the mountains. "Even though the Sweet Mary might be looking good, I'm going to head back to McLane's where the pay's reliable. If you hit it really big, come and get me."

Samuel woke to cold. The moonlight showed that a ground fog had filled the meadow. Its dampness had seeped into the cabin. He rose to stoke the fire. His father turned in his bedding. Samuel realized he had not been asleep.

Lord, maybe we do need to restake and sell the rights back to the Chinese. Even for a few dollars. Samuel had trouble falling back asleep himself. He thought of his mother and sister, alone now that his grandma had died. He thought of Uncle Jake and his family—how difficult managing the farm alone had to be, especially with only one good leg, and how much they depended on Samuel and his father to send some money. The last had been when he was at the Strombacks' ranch, and that was very little. He thought of his words at the meeting. In a sense, he and his father were slaves as well. They were slaves until they had the wherewithal to go home, and that might never happen.

Chapter 28

SAMUEL FELT A LITTLE ODD when his father headed down the meadow toward McLane's placer, leaving him to dig the promising new spot by himself. Maybe he knew how much it meant to him. He had invested several days and good money in building the flume and relocating the sluice. He felt a little trepidation now that he headed there to operate for a full day. Maybe he had been premature; maybe he had misjudged the gold. Repeatedly, there had been color in the pan, only to prove later that it was a misfire.

He felt good this day. The weather had warmed, and the rain had turned the meadows into a riot of color-spangled green. The conifers sported bright green tufts of new growth. The sky was deep azure.

He opened the gate to the flume and directed the water into the sluice, checking that he had a good flow strong enough to roll a small cobble through.

With high spirits, he swung and sank his pick into the earth, dislodging some gravel. *So it begins,* he told himself. One swing became two, then became three—became dozens. But this time, he didn't need to load buckets. He shoveled the dirt and gravel directly into the flume next to him. This gave the water more time to break up the clods of dirt and clay and tumble it for a longer distance, allowing more time for the gold to be released. Most importantly, it gave time for it to settle to the bottom of the box where it would be washed into the sluice and trapped in the cleats.

He ran to the sluice to check its flow. A good, steady turbulence curled over the top several cleats. He had learned to judge the flow and the turbulence. Too much and the gold could not settle. Too little and the cleats packed and allowed the gold to slide over and out. Now the flow was good. Already a fair amount of black sand had collected, as well as numerous tiny particles of gold.

It's still here, Samuel breathed. It had not been a dream.

He returned to his small pit and resumed wrenching free the gravel and shoveling it into the sluice. He paused only to remove cobbles and to make certain that the sluice was not packing up on him.

At noon, he wandered back to the cabin for a bite to eat and a chance to ease his arms and back.

As he returned to work, the sun shone warmly, making it difficult to believe there had been so much rain. But the good flow of water in the box was proof of the recent rain. He shucked his shirt.

He had learned to pace himself. His hands had long ago become calloused. This had becomes his life: hard work, hope, and reward. Most of it was of hope—always the next swing of the pick, the next shovelful of dirt, the next swirl of water in the pan—always the hope it would reveal gold.

Late afternoon, Samuel began to tire, but the light remained good and the water and weather held. He pushed on until dusk, near nine o'clock, when he at last blocked the water and cleaned the black sand from the upper cleats into his pan. He also washed the canvas into a bucket. If the sluice was set correctly and the water flow was correct, the upper cleats usually trapped 80 percent of the gold. The canvas trapped only a small amount, most often the flour gold, but it all added up.

While the light faded, he squatted next to the catch basin, washing the fines. The sight was incredible. Samuel could see better than three quarters of an ounce, maybe ten dollars, not counting the gold he could not see—more than what his father would earn in two days.

He jumped up and did a jig, threw his hat as high as possible, and yelled. This was what it was all about.

In the morning, he could hardly force himself to make some breakfast before he headed back to the sluice. The long flume was clearly one of his best accomplishments. As long as the water held, he could process a lot of gravel.

The gold continued to accumulate in the sluice, but it did not appear as much as the previous day, and this concerned Samuel. He wondered if he had the water flow wrong or the angle of the sluice wrong. He adjusted both and ran for another hour. The gold remained about the same.

He surveyed his pit. The walls appeared consistent, which meant there were no obvious rich streaks or deposits. There was no apparent difference between the gravel from a day ago and this day. He puzzled as to what had happened.

He dug deeper. The gold did not appear to increase as it should have. Samuel began to wonder if the gold occurred in a thin zone, not necessarily on the bedrock, but in a deposit that had been swept down during some unusual event, maybe by some severe flooding.

By late afternoon, he called it quits. He had recovered about half an ounce. It was good, but not nearly as good as the previous day.

The next day he continued digging downward. The sides of the pit sloughed in as he did so. For every couple of inches that he worked downward, several feet fell in.

There was gold in the gravel, but not as much. He began to feel discouraged. He was beginning to realize that streaks of gold ran throughout the gravel. The only way to work the Sweet Mary profitably would be to wash the entire hillside. His sluice was simply too small, and even if he had adequate water, he could never shovel enough gravel by himself.

His pick hit a rock, larger than what he had been finding. That was good. Heavier gold could be trapped around or underneath it. He worked around the rock, and then hit another. His heart quickened. Large rocks usually meant more gold.

He pried loose the small boulder and began pushing it out of the hole.

A trickle of dirt and gravel spilled into the hole, and at the same time, a voice said, "You need a hand with that?"

Samuel froze. He spun away and scrambled back from the boulder, letting it slip back into its place. His rifle was several feet away.

The man laughed. "Don't worry, I'm not going to jump you."

Samuel remained cautious. He studied the man, who appeared about his father's age, decently dressed in a vest and coat with light-colored eyes, light brown hair, and a stubble beard. He seemed pleasant enough. Samuel's heart began to settle.

"Howdy, what can I do for you?" Samuel asked.

"Actually, Samuel, I was thinking I could do for you." He jumped into the hole. "Come on, let's get this out of here." He put his hands to the boulder and began rolling it up the side of the pit.

Samuel was too surprised to move.

The man straightened. "Sorry, name's Terry Cochran." The man offered a hand.

Hesitantly, Samuel shook.

"You *are* Samuel." He leaned down and grasped the boulder again.

Samuel still didn't move.

"I know because you're the only kid in these parts."

Samuel figured his explanation made sense, and together they rolled the rock from the hole.

"Thanks," Samuel said.

Samuel had noted that Cochran's horse was a good-looking bay. He had a decent outfit, not worn out and ragged like most, especially like those coming into the country prospecting.

"You wouldn't be looking to buy mining properties?" Samuel speculated.

Cochran laughed. "Nope, I'm just riding through."

Samuel doubted that. The Sweet Mary was not exactly on the main route.

"So, if I can ask, Mr. Cochran, what's the nature of your business?"

"Saw you needed a hand is all."

"There's plenty more rocks where that one came from. You could be lending a hand for a long while."

"All right, let's see about that."

Cochran took up a pick and began working. Samuel stood by, surprised. Finally, he picked up his shovel and began pitching gravel into the flume.

Shortly, they changed positions. Samuel started to explain how to feed the sluice, but it was obvious from the first shovelful of dirt that Cochran knew how. Samuel did not ask. Instead, he swung the pick and dislodged more gravel.

They worked steadily, moving double the amount of gravel, astounding Samuel. Good gold began showing in the sluice, but Cochran did not seem overly interested in checking on the gold.

"I gotta take a break," Samuel finally said. "Can I offer you some chow?"

"I'd be obliged."

Samuel heated the coffee. Cochran ate as if he had been hungry for some time.

Samuel guessed that the man was just in need of some grub; however, things seemed out of place. His dress said he had money, and if so, he could have gone into Washington to resupply and have a plate of chow. Maybe he didn't want anyone to see him. Despite Samuel's unease, something told him that he could trust the man.

"Here's something for dinner later on." Samuel wrapped up some cold corn mush with some venison and handed it to Cochran.

"Much obliged, Samuel."

They returned to work and worked steadily for several hours. A crack of thunder rumbled through the valley. Cochran eyed the building thunderstorm. "If you don't mind, I reckon I best be off. I have a long trail ahead."

Samuel walked with him to catch up his bay and gave him a hand while he saddled up.

"Mighty fine horse you have, Mr. Cochran."

"He has served me well," Cochran said and pulled down tightly on the cinch. He flipped the stirrup back into place, swung into the saddle, and reached his hand down. "Thank you for not asking, Samuel. I know it's been on your mind since the moment you set eyes on me. Just let me say people have a way of disappearing in this country. Some don't realize they've disappeared. I may be through again sometime. Do me a favor, however. I'd appreciate it if no one knows."

"How about my father?" Samuel asked.

"Tell him." Cochran turned the bay, but instead of heading west out along the trail or north down the meadows, he headed east back into the timber toward wilderness.

Samuel watched until Cochran had disappeared. He found himself wondering if the man had even existed.

He walked down to the sluice to check how the gold was accumulating. The sight surprised him. A respectable nugget had wedged itself above the top cleat. Shaking, he examined it. It was more rounded than those he normally found. There were two others but smaller, also wedged in the riffle.

He ran back to the pit and shoveled more gravel. He went and checked the riffles. The gold was as he customarily found it—nothing bigger than a grass seed.

Samuel stared back at the timber where Cochran had disappeared, his thoughts troubling him.

Lightning streaked across the sky to the north, followed shortly by reverberating thunder.

He stopped running the sluice and began a cleanup in case of heavy rain. He finished just as it came—hard, cold rain with some hail. Samuel carried the pan with the best gold he had ever mined back toward the cabin.

He noted his father turn up the trail. He ran to the cabin, lugging the pan and meeting him.

"So how'd the flume work out?" his father asked after they had settled down to dinner.

"Incredible," Samuel managed. "I think I have over three ounces of gold."

"In three days?" Charles's eyebrows shot up. He pushed his hands through his hair. "Must of hit a pay streak."

"I had some help," Samuel said. He went on to explain Mr. Cochran's visit. "Do you know him, Pa?"

Charles stared at him hard. "You're lucky, son. If it had been somebody else, you could have ended up dead."

"So you know him?"

His father hesitated. "I cannot say I do."

Samuel felt even more confused. "The way he talked, I think he was looking for someone. He said people have a way of disappearing around here."

Charles tightened his jaw. "I don't know, son. Many reasons to be here other than just gold."

Samuel knew men didn't just show up and disappear. He would think on Cochran's visit for a while. He had some comfort knowing that usually he could piece things together and figure things out. "He said he might be coming back through."

"I 'spect by then he'll let us know. Probably he has some unfinished business he doesn't want word to get out on." Charles began pulling off his boots. "I'm tired, and this thunderstorm seems to be hanging around. Might get some sleep while I can. I 'spect you'll be running the sluice tomorrow."

"I'm hoping to finish getting the gold we need for the O'Riley."

Chapter 29

Samuel worked the sluice for another day, but by midmorning, his eagerness had diminished. Despite the large nugget he had found when Cochran left, the gold decreased. He knew some of the reason he had done well was Cochran's extra set of hands, but it was clear he had worked through the pay streak.

The catch basin was now draining and not quickly replenishing. Samuel blocked the flow into the flume, and while the basin filled, he dug and hauled buckets of gravel to a spot from where he could shovel it into the flume. He removed the cobbles, washed them, and stockpiled the remaining gravel. In the afternoon, he released the water and began running more gravel. He avoided checking the sluice, making certain he could run as much gravel as possible with the limited water.

Samuel shook his head and stood back. How could it be that they had had so much water a few days ago, a steady supply, and he had been able to run the sluice without let-up? Now it was nearly gone. He suspected that much of his water leaked from the flume and drained into the gravel under the catch basin. Unless there was constant rain and the ground was saturated, the catch basin was near useless.

The following morning, Samuel headed into Washington to meet up with Chen. He loaded up Molly at Alexander's, and soon they were both headed back toward Steamboat Summit, both fully packed. Chen had vegetables sticking out of everywhere, more than usual.

Lake Creek was full of salmon.

"Maybe on the way back, we get one," Chen said.

The huge fish raced under the shadowy banks toward cover. Last season, men had brought them into McLane's camp, and Samuel helped fix them for chow until he and the men had tired of them. "Salmon aren't filling," they had told him.

They turned down the Secesh for a distance and stopped at some of the placer camps. None of the camps was of much size, partly because there were very few good gravel benches. Some of the miners were salmon fishing. When they recognized Samuel and Chen, they warmly greeted them and came up from the river to trade.

The day had been sultry, and now that evening was on them, the mosquitoes were thick and swarmed about Samuel's face. He swatted at them ineffectively and sought higher ground, looking for a drier campsite. Shortly, he found an opening in the timber among the beargrass clumps.

"We'll need to haul some water, Chen, but up here we shouldn't have as many mosquitoes."

"Yes, they are vehlie bad." He waved his arms wildly.

Chen began a small fire while Samuel rounded up water containers. He kept a wary eye out for other men, thinking briefly of Cochran. It seemed he was always encountering someone. Thankfully, Cochran had seemed a decent man.

Chen had his customary rice and chopped vegetables. Samuel ate dried beef with beans.

Samuel started to tell Chen about Cochran but then remembered the man's request that he keep quiet.

"You haven't seen any strangers about, have you?" Samuel asked.

Chen appeared surprised before slowly shaking his head. "Other Chinese have."

"What do you mean?"

"Ahn Kwan and Lok Ming see the men who rob Chinese pack train and rope Kan Dick."

Samuel froze; his mind raced. The Chinese still thought Finney and Culler had robbed the pack train, not Dudgin and Smith. "How many men?"

"Ohnee see two men," Chen replied.

Samuel breathed easier. Dudgin and Smith had a partner. "Probably it is Finney and Culler. They've been known to break into sluice boxes. I think they were the ones that broke into ours on the river."

Chen's eyes widened. "You tell the sheriff?"

"Yep, but until now, no one's seen them. When I get back, I'll let the sheriff know." *So Finney and Culler are snooping around again.* "Where did Kwan and Ming see them?"

"Maybe near here."

"This is near where they broke into some sluice boxes. We best keep our eyes open." Samuel glanced around, feeling a shiver. They might not hesitate to jump Chen and him for the gold they now carried, even a small amount.

"Uh, Chen, you should know it wasn't Finney and Culler who jumped the Chinese pack train—it was Quinton Dudgin and Ramey Smith and some other man."

Chen paused and studied him, questioningly.

"Dudgin and Smith were the men who killed Bender and also tried to kill me. My pa described their horses, and I remembered them."

"Yes, you told me." Chen shook his head. "Many bad men are here."

"I doubt Dudgin and Smith are here. They probably went to Canada. If they're caught here, they'll be hanged."

"Should catch and hang Finney and Culler."

"As far as anyone knows, they haven't killed anyone."

"They almost kill Kan Dick," Chen said bitterly.

Samuel was quiet. If they had killed Kan Dick, he doubted anyone would have done anything.

"Not matter, Sam. Many think the Chinese should leave. Say the gold is Ahmehlican gold."

"Like Ben Morton," Samuel said.

Chen nodded. "We want to go back to China. We have to find gold so we can."

"I know, Chen. You've told me this." Samuel felt troubled. "I don't want you to leave, Chen, even when you do get enough gold. You and your uncle are hard workers."

Chen shrugged. "Maybe we never get enough gold. But you are vehlie good at finding gold. Maybe you will go soon." He rose and retrieved his flute and, squatting, began playing.

Samuel understood why Chen identified with the other Chinese. He also realized that if any Chinese person could succeed in America, Chen could. He had learned to read and write English, not only so he could conduct business but also so he could help his countrymen.

The Chinese were odd, that was true. They had their problems— their opium and rice whiskey, gambling dens and slave girls, but they seemed happy and worked hard. They seemed much happier than many of the white miners, Samuel decided.

In the morning, Samuel and Chen continued on to Ruby Meadows and Miller's camp. Samuel visited with Mr. Thomas at the Ruby placer, where his father had worked, and caught up on news. The gulch now appeared mostly played out.

Thomas seemed to notice his look. "We got our eyes on another gulch up creek," he explained. "If you had an interest, you might be able to horn in on some good ground south of here. There's some new placers opening in the meadows in that direction." He pointed. "Problem will be getting water to them."

Samuel laughed. "That's the problem everywhere."

"Yep, the early days, it was easy pickings along the streams, but now we gotta work to get water to where it's needed."

They visited a few placers on the lower meadows and then turned back toward Warren's following the Secesh trail. At Lake Creek, they turned up toward Burgdorf's place and paused at a deep hole, where they trapped a couple of salmon. They loaded the huge fish into the baskets in which Chen had carried his vegetables.

"We could catch more and sell back at Warren's," Chen said.

"Perhaps," Samuel agreed, "but not for much. There's far too many." The stream was thick with swarming fish. Besides, he knew the miners preferred beef.

Back at the cabin, during a dinner of fresh salmon and potatoes, Samuel compared pay with his father.

"Dang near enough to outfit for the O'Riley, son. I've got over fifty dollars." He handed Samuel his pouch. "I can keep on at McLane's for a few more days to make certain."

Samuel mentioned how the Chinese had reported seeing Finney and Culler.

"All kinds of visitors coming to town," Charles said. "Must be the Chinamen are preparing to take out some gold." He laughed.

Samuel paused with his bite of salmon, realizing the truth. "Placer season's ending, Pa. Could be that's the case."

July 1, the sun baked the meadows. Samuel hoped to get in at least half a day of mining before the catch basin drained. All morning he stockpiled gravel but mostly dug downward into the pit, hoping he would find some cobbles and some richer gold. He ran some of the gravel for a while and watched nervously as the water level quickly dropped. He sprinkled some of the remaining gravel and dirt into the stream of water. A few pieces of gold winked out of the black sand.

This is better. Some of the pieces were larger than grass seeds.

He threw in more dirt and washed it through. More gold.

Finally, he thought. Now that he was out of water, he was back into a pay streak.

185

He studied the pit. He was down a good eight feet, and just like last season, the water was gone—drained from the hills.

He shut down the flume. After cleanup, his pan held a third of an ounce, a great find for only a partial day. He stood and stretched.

Maybe I am done. He studied the gravelly hillside. The spring creek wasn't enough. If he could get sufficient water ditched around to this side of the meadow from another source, he could operate longer. It might be possible, but it would take a lot of manpower and several weeks, maybe months, to do so. But then the entire hillside would be opened up for mining.

Surprised, he saw his father turn up the trail. Normally, he worked well into the evening as long as daylight remained.

"How's your fortune today, son?"

"Toward the end, I was getting some good gold, but now I'm out of water."

"Ain't that the way. McLane's is also feeling the pinch. We're only operating one of the boxes."

"Does that mean you're done? That why you're home early?"

"No, there's still plenty of work." Charles laughed. "I realized I got a couple things to take care of in town. Bring your gold."

Samuel was beside himself wondering what his father was up to. On their way to Washington, his father talked about plans to begin work on the O'Riley, but Samuel knew enough to recognize when his father was avoiding what was really going on.

"Let's drop in and see if Mr. Hinley has those assays done that you dropped off."

"He won't. I just took them in a few days ago."

Entering the assay shop, Charles called out, "Ray, you got those O'Riley assays done?"

Hinley came out from the back, wiping his hands, adjusting his glasses. "Aye, Charles, I should say I do."

Samuel was taken aback. It was as if Hinley had been waiting for them.

"These are fine assays, Samuel," Hinley commented, sliding them over. "Your values are still running close to three ounces per ton. You should be up there beginning a drift."

"We will be, but I'm still finishing up on the Sweet Mary, and we're still waiting on a mill."

"Aye, I have heard nothing new about the mill. It may be you shall never get one. If you wish, I may allow you to use the hammer." Hinley nodded at the muller, smiling.

"Not funny, Mr. Hinley." Samuel could hand work some ore but not the volume they would need.

"Come on, it's not too late. We may still be able to catch Mr. Alexander," Charles abruptly said. "Since we're here, I have a few things to pick up."

Samuel traipsed after his father as they entered Alexander's Mercantile.

"I'm glad you dropped by. This is for you." Scott handed a letter to Samuel.

The letter was from his mother, of course. Samuel stuffed it inside his shirt, where it could be considered on the ride back to the cabin—where he could wonder what news it held and cherish it.

His father picked out a few items, including some dried beef, dried fruit, some salt pork, cheese, crackers, and other items that Samuel took to be trail food. Samuel guessed his father was preparing for the move to the O'Riley. It made sense. If the assays had been low, his father would have told him they were heading home to Iowa.

Charles tossed over his pouch. Scott measured out some gold and handed it back. Charles glanced into it. "You're leaving me some?" he joked.

"No sense in leaving you broke," Scott said. "By the way, how's your flume working out?" He eyed Samuel.

"You just saw some of the gold," Samuel said proudly. "I was averaging better than half an ounce a day for a while."

"That's better'n most placers these days." Scott finished the packages and reached for his pipe.

"But now the water's drying up."

Scott shook his head. "You'd never have guessed based on the flooding we had." He began packing tobacco into his pipe. "You guys going to Slate Creek for Independence Day? Nearly the whole town is, the way I hear it." He struck a match and began drawing on his pipe, letting out a puff of smoke.

"Why would that be?" Charles asked.

"Slate Creek is really going all out. I hear they're bringing in a whole passel of fireworks—Sam'd like that."

Samuel immediately thought of Bonnie and tried not to think anymore.

"It's close to eighty miles, Scott. Not likely we'll go," Charles answered. "Need to pay you and finish up here as soon as possible." He handed one of the packages to Samuel and grabbed up the other. They nodded to Scott and stepped from the store.

"I know you'd like to go, Samuel," his father said, loading the packages into the saddlebags. "It's just not possible."

Samuel knew that. Besides, he had gold to dig.

When the two reached the cabin, Samuel anxiously opened the letter. It was not as cheerful as the last. Samuel guessed it was because his mother had expected them to be home by now. He had previously mentioned meeting Bonnie and visiting the ranch, but it was before he had gone to work there.

> *My Dear Charles and Son, Samuel,*
>
> *It shall be over a year when you receive this letter since I have seen you. Not since the Southern Uprising have I been so lonely. I must say the truth, but I am confident when you receive this letter you will be informing me about the sale of the mine and your imminent return to your family. I truly miss your companionship and desire for you, both of you, to be here. Charles …*

Samuel recognized his mother's longing for his father. He was beginning to understand the need that a man and woman had for each other, and he found himself thinking of Lilly and then Bonnie. *Why did Scott have to bring up Independence Day at Slate Creek?* It could never work for Bonnie and him. He wished he were home in Iowa.

He skimmed the remainder of the letter before going back and rereading it, cherishing his mother's words.

His mother talked about his grandma's death. She mentioned how Elizabeth was growing and helping with the cooking and the garden. She mentioned his cousin Daniel again and how he was helping Uncle Jake till and plant the fields. Daniel was shooting squirrels and rabbits for game. But Samuel found himself wanting not to be tilling fields and planting crops. He thought of himself finding gold or perhaps of running cattle across the hills.

He handed the letter to his father, who studied it for a long while.

"She sounds good, does she not, son? It sounds as if the farm is doing well. That's good. It makes it easier to be away." He talked cheerily.

"She misses us, Pa," Samuel blurted out the truth.

"Yes, she does, son." Charles's tone softened. "It's okay. Things will be all right. We'll be at this at most another month."

In Samuel's reply to his mother, he talked glowingly of the strike on the Sweet Mary and how they would soon be bringing ore out of the O'Riley. He also told of his ranching with the Strombacks and meeting Bonnie. He labored over using just the right words when talking about Bonnie, not wanting his mother to think into it too much. He ended by writing glowingly about their prospects.

> *When you see us riding in, dear Mother, we will be packing a goodly amount of gold. We will all go to the town and you will be able to buy all sorts of things. For sure a new dress for you and one for Elizabeth. For sure now, we will be laying out a new farm. Pa and you and Elizabeth will have a wonderful new home.*

Only after he signed the letter and reread it did he realize he had left himself out.

He watched as his father read what he had written and caught a slight frown. His father added some lines, folded the paper, folded an envelope around it, and sealed it.

"You can post this from Slate Creek."

"What?" Samuel could not believe what he thought he had heard.

"To blazes, son, you're going to Slate Creek," Charles said. "I was thinking on it, and your ma's letter convinced me."

Samuel broke into a huge smile and then bit his lip. "It's okay, Pa. I can stay and run some more gravel. We need the money."

"No, Samuel. You're going," Charles said. "I had sent word to Mr. Hinley for the assays. We have to take things into our own hands a bit. I want you to go back and see that man you saw last December and try to sell the mine, and I'd like you to advertise the O'Riley around town."

"Is it worth it?" Samuel wanted to believe his father, but going that far only to advertise their mine didn't seem prudent.

"We haven't had any offers on the O'Riley sitting around here, except that fifty bucks you didn't want to tell me about. We sure as blazes need a better offer than that," Charles said. "And if you're really wanting to, you can drop by and see that girl."

Samuel felt his heart quicken and a knot formed in his stomach.

"That will be tough, Pa. When I finished up ranching, I told Bonnie I was leaving. I don't know if I can tell her again."

His father was silent a moment as if searching for something else to say. Awkwardly he continued, "Well, go see some of the festivities at least, but I don't recommend you go racing Spooky. We can't take a chance on losing him before we head back." Charles pulled off his shirt and poured some water for washing.

Samuel did not move.

"Better get your things together. You'll need to get on the trail early. It's going to be two days there and two back." Charles doused himself with water. "You need some time for business as well."

Later, as Samuel slowly undressed, things he thought he had buried began boiling up within him. He stared through the twilight; a couple of stars had appeared. *God, where are you taking me now?* he wondered.

SLATE CREEK,
INDEPENDENCE DAY 1872

Chapter 30

Samuel was on the trail before sunup. He felt strange traveling the distance alone with no one to talk to or with whom to share a camp. He took his father's advice and kept watch for strangers, especially for those they had run into before who could be trouble. He saw only a few men off the trail working at some of the placers. He paused briefly to say hello to Fred Burgdorf but passed up the obligatory swim at his hot springs. He would reach Slate Creek by tomorrow afternoon only if he pushed straight through.

Late in the evening he stopped for the night, a few miles short of Shearers' ferry. He paused at the only level spot he could find near where he could find water. He checked for rattlesnakes and unrolled his bedding under a huge pine, thankful that there were no evening thundershowers. Instead, as he had descended into the canyon, the heat had steadily built. He figured it was still a sweltering eighty degrees.

Samuel was again up before sunrise. Spooky had grazed all night along the stream and seemed ready to go. To Samuel, Spooky always seemed eager to travel. When he reached the Shearers', other travelers were just preparing to head down the trail. He visited for a short while, catching them up on their mining progress.

At the winter cabin, Samuel paused. The cabin was much the way they had left it. He walked down to the river. The sluice, undisturbed, seemed to be awaiting his return. He knew there was a goodly amount of gold in the bar—not enough by which to get rich, but enough to pay a decent wage, much like the hillside at the Sweet Mary.

He studied the bench. It was too steep for plowed fields like those that his father was used to, but a man could put in a good-sized truck garden by terracing the land like the Chinese did. Fruit trees could grow on the hillside, especially if a ditch was run higher up and the trees were watered. Between the two drainages, there was some grass for grazing, and a meadow near the second creek might produce enough hay to winter a few head of cattle. If necessary, his father could buy hay or trail animals out to Slate Creek for the winter, similar to what the packers did.

Samuel pushed at his hat. The day was already uncomfortably hot, far warmer than Warren's camp in the mountains.

He passed Groff's ferry across the river from him, and farther downstream, he again took notice of the Chinese stone hut. Several Chinese were busy at a couple of rockers along the river. He saw no white miners. They had returned to the mountain placers or quartz mines. Others were likely headed to Slate Creek for Independence Day as was he.

Late afternoon, he reached the town. Red, white, and blue bunting surrounded doorways and windows, and banners stretched across the street. Every building sported a flag. A crepe-covered grandstand had been erected in front of Slate Creek House.

People were milling in the street, and already Samuel sensed excitement. Scott had been right. Everyone from miles around was here. He wanted to go to the ranch and say hello to Bonnie, but he refrained. He would not impose on the Strombacks. Besides, Bonnie could be here in town attending some of the festivities. He glanced around, half expecting to see her.

He immediately sought out Ralph Clark, the man who had expressed an interest last Christmas. Clark looked over the assay reports but handed them back. "I shall pass. I'd much rather grubstake you and have you look for a better one."

Samuel's hopes were dashed. "There aren't many quartz claims that go better than three ounces a ton, Mr. Clark. This one's rich."

"Yup, but times are changing."

Samuel puzzled at Clark's meaning. This was the man he had come so far to see.

"Anyone else you know who might be interested? I've come eighty miles to see you." Samuel could not hold back his disappointment.

"Sorry, son." Clark drummed his fingers. "There's been a lot of speculation coming out of Warren's camp but not a lot of results."

Samuel fidgeted, not knowing what else he could say or do. He had come too far for a simple no.

"There is a guy in town who's expressing interest in mining properties but mostly up at Florence," Clark said. "But then, everyone's interested in Florence. That was one rich strike until it played out. People still dream of the early days in Florence. They don't think of Warren's. His name's Jesse Williams. He should be over at the hotel."

Samuel thanked Clark and headed to Slate Creek House. A fancily dressed man in a white collared shirt, string tie, and black vest sat at a table with a newspaper, smoking a cigar. He appeared to be in his midthirties with dusty blond hair and a ruddy complexion.

"Name's Samuel Chambers," Samuel said, stepping to his table. "Heard you were looking at mining properties. I got one."

The man looked up, his expression showing that he questioned Samuel's youth. "Jesse Williams." They shook. "How is it that a kid is offerin' to sell me a mine? And how'd you know I was interested?"

"Mr. Clark referenced you."

"Here, sit down." Williams indicated the chair.

"Thanks." Samuel sat. "Legally, the claim's my father's," he explained. "I just happened to find it."

"Well, that takes some spunk." The man laughed and asked Samuel to tell him about it. Samuel recognized the interest. He was more hopeful when Williams carefully studied the assays.

"How accurate are these?"

Samuel explained his care in acquiring the samples.

"Not many folks know about cutting a good sample for an assay," he said. "It sounds like you knew what you were doing. Too bad you don't have a mill-run for me to consider."

"Mr. Hinley does assays in Washington. He instructed me," Samuel said. "We had hoped to have some mill-runs done. We're waiting on Mr. Bradshaw's mill. It's still hung up in Mount Idaho, I believe."

"Actually, I think it's now on the trail."

Samuel grinned. "Then you'll for sure want to be looking at our mine."

"Perhaps." He folded up the assays and returned them. "I have a full schedule; however, I am taking out a couple days for celebration. Mostly because my guide is already overcelebrating." Williams laughed and drew on his cigar, letting the pungent smoke encircle them.

Samuel stopped himself from fanning the smoke. He preferred his father's pipe.

"He'll be taking me up to Florence. I'm most interested in some properties up there."

"You ought to drop by Warren's first," Samuel suggested.

"And why's that? Properties in Florence not as good?"

"Actually, sir, they probably aren't. It was the placers up there that were rich. And they're mostly played out. The quartz ledges are proving real shallow. In fact, I hear they're dismantling one of the stamp mills and taking it to Warren's."

Jesse Williams raised his eyes. "And you know this how?"

"The independent miners are looking to bring it into Warren's to run rich ore such as ours." Samuel emphasized *rich*.

Williams tapped his cigar. "I appreciate the news, son. I committed to seeing a couple of gentlemen up at Florence. I didn't plan on going to Warren's. That's at the end of the world, if you get my meaning. That adds a steep cost to everything, but who knows? Maybe I'll pay a visit."

"Visit Warren's first," Samuel said again. "It's a good trail along the Salmon all the way to the trail up to Warren's. On the way out, you can cross the Salmon and go directly into Florence. Either way, it's about the same distance."

"You're a convincing young man," Williams replied. "I'll see. I'll see."

Samuel felt a glimmer of hope. He had done his best. He talked to other merchants and posted information about the O'Riley. He could not help but see other "for sale" notices.

He led Spooky out into the field north of town and picketed him where he could get good grass and water. He set out his gear nearby. Others had pitched camps in the same area, and those present greeted him. After checking for rattlesnakes, Samuel unrolled his bedroll. The day had been scorching hot, well over a hundred degrees. Someone had said the firecrackers wouldn't need help being lit.

Samuel wanted to be near town within walking distance of the river. Ralph Clark had told him General Wood had a detail for firing the cannon and launching rockets at midnight. The sun had set and the air was finally cooling. He lay down, meaning to rest just a few minutes. The booming of the cannon awakened him. Samuel hurried toward the river, seeing the flash from the muzzle, belching fire out over the river. He cringed at the reverberating explosion.

Throngs of people gathered along the flat with their colored lanterns winking where they had gathered in groups, sitting out on blankets, some with small children. Samuel glanced around for the Strombacks, anxious, but a little nervous, to see Bonnie. What would he say to her?

"Hey, Samuel. Here you be at Slate Creek," Jon Stromback called from behind him.

Samuel turned, seeing the children coming running and Bonnie and Mrs. Stromback farther behind. His heart quickened. Josef reached him and gave him a hug. He ruffled the boy's hair.

"Good evening, sir." They shook hands. He waved to Bonnie and Mrs. Stromback.

"Oh, Bonnie," Mrs. Stromback exclaimed, pointing. "It's Samuel." She waved.

Samuel grinned and greeted them.

"Hello," Bonnie said cheerily but then quieted and frowned. The good feeling Samuel had suddenly died.

"Samuel, what a nice surprise," Mrs. Stromback bubbled, reaching him. "Is your father with you?"

"No, ma'am."

"It is so wonderful to see you. We thought you and your pa had packed up and gone back to Iowa."

"We're still fixing to, but we're still trying to sell the mine."

"When'd you get here?" Stromback asked.

"Late afternoon," Samuel answered. "I had some business to attend to; otherwise, I was figuring on coming out to see you."

"You should stay the night with us," Mrs. Stromback offered. "After the rockets, you just come on out."

"Thank you. I don't wish to impose." Samuel began to feel funny.

"Oh, posh. You're practically one of the family," she said. "And then you come with us tomorrow for all the doin's. Josef asks about you almost every day."

"Yes, ma'am."

Josef tugged at Samuel's hand. "We'll do some ropin' tomorrow. You should see me and Ol' Blue ropin'."

"You betcha," Samuel said, but he wanted to talk to Bonnie. He wondered if she had been asking about him. *Why should she? I told her I was leaving.*

Samuel excused himself and made his way toward her. "I'm sorry I couldn't send word, Bonnie. It just came up a couple of days ago that I could come. But I was aimin' to see you before we left Warren's no matter."

Samuel saw the disappointment in Bonnie's face. She had yet to say anything more than hello.

The Strombacks moved the children to a spot where they had thrown the blanket where they could watch. The cannon boomed again. They shrieked with joy and covered their ears. White smoke drifted across the river.

One of the men manning the cannon barked orders as it was loaded and fired. The explosion shattered the night, sparks skittering across the ground. A flame erupted from the barrel, a long tongue reaching into the darkness, its orange-and-yellow light reflecting off the river. The momentary flash lit up the faces of the nearby people and then faded. They clapped and cheered as the white smoke enveloped them.

"I've never seen anything like this, Bonnie." He peered at her for some response.

"You said you were leaving," Bonnie whispered. "I didn't expect to ever see you again."

"I said I'd be by to say farewell."

"You also said you would be leaving by June. It's July." She bit her lip.

"What's wrong, Bonnie?" Samuel whispered.

"Oh, Samuel, I agreed to see Rex."

"Rex!" Samuel hissed his name. "That no-good fencepost!" He felt like he had been kicked in the belly.

"He was here, Samuel," she hissed back. "You were gone." Her eyes flashed, but Samuel could also see some pain.

"Should I go?"

"No!" Bonnie exclaimed. "The Strombacks invited you out to the ranch. You worked for them. They would be offended if you left now."

"What about Rex?" He lowered his voice.

"He's off with friends somewhere," she said and then offered somewhat bleakly, "probably at a saloon."

Samuel shrugged it off. "I mean, you're courting him. Do you really have feelings for him?"

"Maybe." Bonnie covered her face. "I-I don't know, Samuel. You weren't here."

Samuel saw Mrs. Stromback turn around.

"Bonnie says it's going to be really hot tomorrow."

A curious look came over Mrs. Stromback. "That it is," she replied, frowning and then turning back around.

The cannon boomed again.

"I'm sorry, Bonnie," Samuel whispered. He began to touch her shoulder but then rapidly withdrew his hand. He was thinking dark thoughts about Rex bragging about doing things. *To blazes. She's right. I'm leaving. But Rex?* Samuel felt sick. He wished he had not agreed to stay at the Strombacks'.

Bonnie nodded her head, her attention now on the rocket crew. Samuel could see more in her eyes than what she said, even in the dark.

"Is it official courtin'?" he asked.

"Might as well be … the Strombacks know. They are insisting our behavior be proper."

Samuel felt sick all over again. *Anybody but Rex.*

A loud *whoosh* startled him. With sparks flying and dancing, a rocket raced upward until it disappeared into the night, its trail of luminescent red-and-orange flame reflecting in the still waters of the Salmon. White smoke enveloped the cheering people. Samuel wanted to enjoy the sight, but he could not. He felt like catching Spooky and heading for home.

They watched for a while until the children began to nod off. Kerstin and Sophia had curled up with Bonnie. Even spunky Josef had slowed down, but he stubbornly kept his eyes fixed on each rocket, showers of sparks reflecting in them.

Samuel no longer watched the rockets. He watched Bonnie's eyes. Despite what she had said, Samuel knew she cared for him. It would be a very long day tomorrow. He resolved to pretend things were as they had been, at least while Rex was not in sight.

"Here you be, we should get the children home," Stromback finally said. They had fallen asleep. "Sure they'll be launching these rockets and celebrating until daylight."

Samuel rose, nudging Josef to get up. He helped by carrying Sophia while Stromback carried Kerstin. They loaded the children into the wagon, and Samuel threw in his gear. He brought up Spooky, tied him to the back, and climbed up with Bonnie. He wanted badly to hold her but did not dare. The Strombacks rode up front.

Chapter 31

THE NEXT THING SAMUEL KNEW, Josef was bouncing on him to get him moving. "Come on, slowpoke. We got some ropin' to do."

Samuel lurched up. "We got some breakfast to do first." He could smell the bacon. He remembered Bonnie and Rex, and the ache returned. Maybe this was just as well. Now there would be no reason to return to Idaho Territory.

Josef insisted on sitting next to Samuel. He wondered what had gotten into the boy to make him want his attention so. In a way, Samuel was glad for it.

"Excellent breakfast, Mrs. Stromback."

"Better thank Bonnie—she's doing most of the cooking."

"Great breakfast, Bonnie," he said sincerely.

She smiled and curtsied. "Why, thank you."

Is she putting it on? Samuel wondered.

About ten, after roping with Josef and sparring with Roundup until he was sore, Samuel helped Mrs. Stromback and Bonnie load up the food for the afternoon picnic. They rode back into town in the wagon. Already the Independence Day procession was gathered in front of the hotel. It was a wild assortment. Led proudly by the Florence Brass Band, it wandered through the brightly decorated streets, banging, clanging, and dancing as it wound around the livery and blacksmith at the far end of town and returned to the hotel. Rex and Art rode Jon Stromback's appaloosas, both decorated with red, white, and blue crepe. Samuel cringed when they rode past, catching the threat in Rex's eyes. Bonnie waved and hollered more vigorously when Rex turned their direction.

At the grandstand, the Reverend Nathan Earl opened with a prayer, thanking the Lord for the abundance from the land and for the country's freedom. A couple of songs were acted out and sung. Samuel recognized Washington's quartet club. The Honorable Alex McDonald read the

Declaration of Independence. Samuel listened. He had studied it in school, of course, but it sounded great.

"Why didn't King George III just give us representation?" he whispered to Bonnie. "He could have saved the colonies, and a lot of good people wouldn't have died." Bonnie shushed him. He found himself thinking about his father fighting against the South. *A lot of good men died there as well,* he told himself. *A lot more will go on dying, keeping our country free.* People clapped when McDonald finished, nodding to each other.

Professor Noggle stood up, and people were clapping before he even began speaking. Samuel wondered why until he launched into a fiery speech about the country and its independence, its strength, and the opportunities it held for all its citizens. Samuel was immediately caught up in his words and found himself thinking about his own journey west, to mine, to ranch, to homestead—to do what he wished. He also thought of the Chinese. They had come here from a war-torn and impoverished country to get a chance to help their families as well. Noggle's speech warmed him. Truly, he did live in a great country—one that would soon be a hundred years old.

The picnic meal was unbelievable. The women had all prepared their best dishes and laid them out on several tables. Everything that could be grown and that was in season was somewhere on a table—new potatoes, new beets, radishes, lettuce, peas, beans. The meat dishes consisted of mutton, venison, elk, and beef. Bonnie had helped Mrs. Stromback prepare a dish of sliced beef in a rich gravy sauce flavored with salt and pepper. Someone had prepared some salmon and trout. There were also biscuits and breads of all types and pies made from berries, apples, and rhubarb. And to wash it down, there was fresh buttermilk and lemonade, kept icy cold with blocks of ice kept over from the winter.

Shortly, some men poured whiskey and began making toasts. Samuel was offered a glass, but he thought it prudent to decline, especially in front of Mrs. Stromback and Bonnie. However, the presence of women did not slow anyone else. They toasted the town, they toasted the county, and they toasted Idaho Territory. Then they toasted each other: they toasted General Wood, especially because his cannon crew got through the night without an accident; they toasted the Honorable Judge McDonald; and they toasted Professor Noggle. Soon, everyone had toasted everyone, and everyone began toasting everyone all over again.

The whiskey, mixed with the heat of the day, quickly took its toll. Fewer toasters remained standing as more and more drifted off toward the shade of the cottonwoods.

The ladies gathered up the dishes and packed up the remaining food. Samuel insisted on helping. Something was telling him not to give up on Bonnie, and this was a small way to stay near her. He wondered what had happened to Rex. He had not seen him since the earlier procession. Maybe Rex was off smoldering because of his presence.

The men still standing politely allowed the women to do their work. Eventually, they joined their companions under the trees, where they smoked and told lies, the latter arrivals having the good fortune of being able to outdo their predecessors. Samuel overheard some recounting their days during the Southern Uprising. Others turned the topic to the Indian depredations and then to the problems with the Chinese. Soon joined by the ladies, most dozed off in the shade of the cottonwoods.

Samuel first tried his best to help Mrs. Stromback but also found himself nodding off. Fortunately, Jon Stromback and Bonnie had gathered the children under the trees out of the sun. The parents were more than pleased when a few of the adults took the children to participate in gunnysack races and finish off the watermelons someone had brought in.

It wasn't until evening when a breeze kicked up that people again began to stir—the children first, beginning to run and play, Josef wanting Samuel to practice roping.

The cannon signaled the start of fireworks down near the river. Samuel scrambled up to see. The launching team angled them to rise over the river, and in an orange trail of sparks, they raced up over the reflecting waters and burst into brilliant colors of red, yellow, white, and green to the gasps and cheers of the gathered crowd. The exploding fragments trailed white tendrils earthward, and clouds of pungent smoke drifted across the bench.

"I hear they brought these things all the way from Chicago," Stromback commented.

"Far better than exploding black powder," Samuel admitted. "Certainly nothing like this back in Iowa."

"Sure must admit, Slate Creek folks know how to celebrate."

Samuel thought that all of Idaho Territory now knew about the Slate Creek celebration.

"We're going to run the children home, Samuel," Stromback

addressed him. "I'm guessing you and Bonnie will be at the dance. I'll be back later."

Samuel was confused. "I-I thought Bonnie ... Rex."

"Oh, hell, that Rex, he still don't know what he's doin'," Stromback said. "I thought he was comin' around some, but then he up and disappears for the whole day. Probably out drinking. I saw he got started pretty early today."

Samuel thought the comment strange. He had kept a close watch for Rex. He was trying his best not to get between him and Bonnie.

"Maybe we should all just take it in. I've had a day of it as well."

"Hell, Samuel," Stromback swore again. Samuel realized Stromback had also had a few drinks. "That niece of mine has sure had her heart set on that dance for weeks. She's at that age if'n you didn't notice, but I reckon you did. Be just about the first time for her. I'm not that old, but I figured that's why she was wanting to look past all the rough spots Rex has to offer so she could attend."

Samuel's heart skipped. He felt a fool. That explained her putting up with Rex.

"She was sorer'n a stuck pig because she hadn't seen you, and she was 'spectin' to. 'Course she didn't tell me all that direct-like."

Samuel took Bonnie to the dance. "We can just sit if you like. I'll let the other men ask you to dance," he said.

She shot him a hurt look but, despite Samuel's hope, did not ask him for a dance.

The Woods had done as before for church services. They hauled away the tables and set up chairs around the perimeter. The orchestra, so to speak—a few violins and a banjo—took over one of the corners. Samuel recognized Charlie Bemis and a couple of other men who played at Washington for the stag dances. They were remarkably good musicians.

Older men immediately took the opportunity to dance with Bonnie, each staring in obvious disbelief at Samuel before doing so. He heard one mutter to his friend, "Someone ought to take that young'un out and explain the facts of life to him." Samuel's ears burned.

That's it, he thought. "Bonnie, I'd like this dance." He looked at her sternly and took her hands. They moved out onto the floor. The feeling he had for Bonnie was wonderful and miserable. Twice he stepped on her, vaguely reminding himself he should have paid more attention when his grandma had tried to teach him to waltz. He pulled her close as the dance ended. The people clapping around him were encouraging Bonnie and him—Samuel knew it. He led her back to her seat.

"It's Rex," Bonnie hissed.

Samuel's heart skidded. He knew Rex had seen them on the floor.

Rex pushed his way directly through the crowd until he stood inches away, face red, huffing.

Cursing, he lifted Bonnie to her feet. "Don't even think it, boy," he hissed. "I watched you all day. This is my girl. Everyone here knows it."

He was speaking rather loudly, words slurred. Men had stopped and were probably wondering if they would have to stop a fight.

"I know," Samuel said quietly. "Bonnie told me. Congratulations."

Eyes bulging, neck straining, Rex suddenly relaxed. He sputtered, apparently not knowing how to reply to Samuel's comment.

"What the hell you touching her for, then?"

"Your employer has returned home. He asked me to accompany Bonnie to this dance. Mr. Stromback had not heard from you and asks for you to accept his apologies."

Rex's face grew redder. "Don't take me for a fool, boy," he hissed.

"No, sir, I'm not." Samuel felt himself warming up. His fear had eased. "I'm simply doing as Mr. Stromback asked. Of course, you know I'm returning to Iowa shortly. I was just offering my good-byes to the family, to Bonnie, and to you as well, now that you're here. I'll be seeing everyone off tomorrow. Please enjoy the evening."

He turned to Bonnie. "Thank you, ma'am, for the dance." He bowed slightly.

Rex sputtered. The music started up. He pulled Bonnie onto the floor and, crushing her to himself, danced awkwardly.

Samuel did his best to act composed. His feelings inside were a flood of ice and fire.

Some of the men nodded knowing looks toward him.

Samuel was still sitting when Stromback returned. He did not ask anything but sat a moment with Samuel while Rex and Bonnie finished their last dance.

"Here you be, I see *he* showed up."

"And how," muttered Samuel.

"You sure you want to go back to Iowa?"

Samuel shrugged. He could say nothing.

In the morning, Bonnie met Samuel as he packed to head out. Rex was sleeping off his whiskey.

"Maybe you could find work in Iowa," Samuel suggested. He wondered about his comment. His own family could barely feed themselves. He suddenly felt bitter about coming west, looking for gold. Their lives would be no better after he and his father returned.

She peered steadily back, her greenish eyes unwavering. "Maybe you could find work and stay here, Samuel."

Samuel felt miserable. He was drawn to her. Unlike Lilly, Bonnie was a person he could feel good about and live with forever.

He found himself shaking. "I-I can't. I got to go back with my pa."

"I know," she said simply. "And I *am* so thankful I got to see you again, Samuel."

"Does that mean you'll go back to Rex?" He couldn't believe his own words.

She shrugged. "I told you before—he's here."

Samuel felt sick again and looked away. It made him somehow feel dirty.

"Don't say that. You're young. We're both young. Lots can happen. You once said something like that," Samuel managed. "Look, at least let me see you when we're leaving out. Probably a month yet. We got to mine some ore from the O'Riley and get it proved up enough to sell it. Then we'll be on our way. M-maybe things will be different by then."

"Are you asking me to wait, Samuel?" Bonnie asked, a slight smile tugging at her lips, her dimples showing.

"I-I don't know," Samuel stammered. His thoughts raced.

She nodded and then reached her arms about him and kissed him.

Chapter 32

TWO DAYS LATER, Samuel climbed out of the Salmon River canyon toward the freight landing. A thousand thoughts had plagued him the entire distance. Mostly he thought about Bonnie.

Just off the saddle beyond the freight landing, he reached the long section of trail that traversed the dense timber and caught sight of movement and a flash of horses ahead. Samuel reached for his pistol. Edging closer, he recognized the black and the dun and their two riders. A chill shook him. *Reuben Finney and Orwin Culler.* He felt his stomach tighten. The Chinese were right; they were back. He quickly turned off the trail, hoping the two men had not seen him.

Samuel carefully moved up through the timber to where he could see them more clearly. There was no mistaking the two men. It was Finney, derby askew, vest and shirt showing even more dirt and wear. Culler wore the same long, black frock and was shaking his head. Samuel remembered his dark, sunken eyes and matted black hair and beard.

Samuel wanted to move past them, but he dared not. Finney had pulled a pistol on him before when he had interceded to help Kan Dick. And Samuel had made Culler appear a fool in front of the sheriff, which Culler was unlikely to soon forget. Meeting these two here ... maybe they would just rough him up, but they also might put a bullet in him. Samuel could not risk either.

He had no choice but to stay back and to let the men move on. Maybe they would turn off the trail for one of the new placers. They were certainly up to no good.

He waited a long while after they had moved off down the trail before he cautiously began following. After another hour, he topped a rise where he could see a good length of trail. Hesitantly, he moved into the open. He caught sound of someone and whirled around, expecting Finney and Culler to be behind him. Instead, it was a party of three men, leading a heavily packed mule. He waited for them to catch up, keeping his hand near his pistol. He recognized the men as being from Warren's and having been at Slate Creek for the Independence Day celebration.

"What's going on, kid?" one of the men asked. Samuel recognized Max Barnhart, a hardrock miner.

"Heading back to Warren's is all. 'Spect like you, Mr. Barnhart."

They moved up to where they could talk. The horses and mule paused impatiently.

"You look a little jumpy, kid," Barnhart said, glancing at Samuel's hand near his pistol.

Samuel wondered if he should tell him about Finney and Culler. "Could be I don't want to meet a couple men up along the trail," he confided.

Barnhart nodded. "Not good to be travelin' alone in this country." The other two men nodded as well.

Samuel knew it was never wise to travel alone. Men were not the only kind of trouble, although they were probably the worst kind.

He was not surprised when they met Finney and Culler on the opposite side of the clearing. He wondered if they were fool enough to take on four men.

"Howdy," Finney called out. Barnhart and the others returned his greeting.

"Need help?" Barnhart asked.

"Nah, just taking a spell," Finney said, smiling. He eyed Samuel. "Well, well, if it ain't the Chambers boy."

Samuel's heart caught. He recognized Finney's voice. "Howdy, Mr. Finney ... Mr. Culler." He nodded toward each man.

Culler glared, his dark eyes glittering. He rested his hand on his rope, and Samuel knew.

"You still in the territory, kid?" Culler asked.

"I reckon. We were supposed to head out last winter, but our sluice got robbed." He stared unflinchingly at Culler.

"That's a hell of a thing, now isn't it, men?" Culler glanced a bit nervously at the others.

"We heard about it," Barnhart muttered. He flashed Samuel a strange look. "Ever find out who might've done it, Samuel?"

Samuel shook his head. "Likely it was the same two men that pilfered the sluices last summer on the Secesh. Sheriff Sinclair never did find them."

Both Culler and Finney stared stonily at Samuel. Samuel knew he was pushing it, but he had to be certain, and now he was. He clucked to Spooky to move on. The men pushed past.

Barnhart rode near him. "You and your pa sure did have a run of bad luck. Your placer was jumped as well, wasn't it?"

"It was."

"And you never figured out who?"

"Nope." Samuel felt it wise not to involve Barnhart.

Finney and Culler really are back, Samuel reflected. He doubted they would dry-gulch him just for his suspicions, but he knew he had to be careful.

Samuel rode with the other miners until he reached the trail down the Big Meadow toward his cabin.

"Much obliged for the company," he told them and turned downstream.

When he reached the cabin, he continued past, intending to visit the Sweet Mary and see if there was water.

"Pa, you're here working."

"Hello, son," Charles replied, smiling and swinging another bucket of gravel into the sluice. "Good to see you made it back. How was the trip?"

"Tell me why you're here and not out at McLane's."

"Just checking to see what you left me." Charles chuckled. "Still some good gold, son, but not much water."

Samuel felt a little disappointed. He had wanted to run the pay streak.

"Help me button up, and we'll visit over dinner," his father said. "Sure is good to see you again."

His father explained he had finished up at McLane's and had tried running the Sweet Mary for a while.

"We get our hopes up on this placer, run into some decent gold for a bit, and then it peters out, or like now, the water disappears," Charles said.

"Or it gets jumped," Samuel said. "Speaking of which, I ran into Finney and Culler on the way back."

Charles stopped short.

"Luckily, Max Barnhart came along about then, and I rode with him and a couple other fellows coming back to Warren's."

Samuel saw concern in his father's eyes.

"Pa, it was Finney and Culler that hit us on the river last winter. Finney calls me 'the Chambers boy.' I recognized his voice and Culler's voice this time. It was them, all right."

Charles lowered his plate. "I know. I figured it was them, but I wasn't completely sure. I told the sheriff they were my suspicion."

"He ought to round them up; we'd be better off."

"For sure," his father agreed. "Do they know that you know?"

"Yes. Mr. Barnhart asked if we had any suspicions of who hit us, so I said it was the same fellows that jumped the sluice boxes on the Secesh. I was with Finney and Culler when the sheriff said he suspected them of the sluice break-ins on the Secesh. So I figure they know."

"Maybe not the smartest thing to say."

"I had to know, Pa. At least I know who to watch for."

"I'm going to the sheriff, son. With what you said, we might be able to get an arrest. At least Sinclair needs to know they're back in the country."

Samuel nodded. He would need to keep the pistol handy. Maybe he should practice a bit more.

"So while you were in Slate Creek, was there any interest in the mine?"

Samuel informed him of Clark's decision to not make an offer but also of Williams's possible intentions to visit.

"Figures Clark would get cold feet, but Williams's interest might be good. And now that we have someone coming up to visit the O'Riley, I think our marching orders are clear. We need to quit fooling around down here and get the O'Riley looking as good as we can so we can sell her, even if we don't have a mill. What do you think?"

"I reckon, Pa."

They sat for a moment.

"Now, son, I'm not one to pry, but I haven't heard you say one thing about the Strombacks. You did go out to visit them, didn't you?"

"I visited them. They are doing well. They said to tell you hello."

"And ... "

Samuel gazed out toward the timbered mountains. "It didn't work, Pa. She's courtin' Rex."

"Rex?" Charles almost choked and then shook his head. "Guess I know the answer to that one. He's there and you're here, right?"

Samuel nodded.

"I'm sorry, son. I thought you might have been thinking of taking her to Iowa. She seemed to be a mighty fine gal."

"She still is, Pa."

His father was silent a moment. "Times like this I wish I kept a bottle of whiskey around."

"I can manage," Samuel said.

"Not for you, son. For me."

HARDROCK MINING

Chapter 33

SAMUEL NOW LOOKED FORWARD to returning to the O'Riley. The Sweet Mary was not the dream come true that they had envisioned, but it had helped bring in a few dollars for the O'Riley. They headed to town.

"Besides taking care of the amalgam, do we need anything else, Pa?"

"Let's see what our yield is first," Charles said. "We'll be back tomorrow getting tools and supplies we'll need for the O'Riley. I don't think I'll get back from the Hic Jacet until late, so you can plan on meeting me back at the cabin. You can start packing if I'm not there."

"They said that Mr. Bradshaw's mill was on the trail, you know."

"I do, but I also know how people change their minds. The Hic Jacet has been running the Rescue ore, and now that the Rescue is shut down, they might be able to accommodate us, rather than us waiting for Bradshaw's mill. And you don't know the problems Mr. Bradshaw's likely to have trying to put up that new mill."

Samuel nodded. He did know. It seemed as much as any mill in Warren's camp operated, it was also down.

As Samuel guessed, Hinley had other work to do rather than retort some amalgam, but he allowed Samuel to proceed on his own.

"If you should have any questions, just come in and fetch me," Hinley instructed.

"Thanks," Samuel answered. "I should be okay." He walked around behind the assay office to where the retort kiln was located. He placed the amalgam into the retort chamber, packed the furnace with charcoal, and ignited it. He checked the tubing and the collecting flask.

He reentered the assay shop. "Got the fire going."

"Wonderful. Now if you would like to assist me while you are waiting, I would be obliged."

Samuel found an ore sample awaiting him next to the mulling plate and began rolling the muller over the quartz chunks, pulverizing them.

"You should know that the Celestials have discovered a cinnabar deposit," Hinley said, as he marked crucibles and set them in a holder.

"They did? Anywhere near here?" Samuel knew part of the reason mercury was expensive was that it came from only a few mines, most in California. The production was controlled and freight was expensive.

"Aye, leave it to the Celestials. They found good ore somewhere near Ruby Meadows."

Samuel shook his head. "They'll make a fortune. They'll have a market here and at every other camp in the territory."

"And they know it." Hinley straightened. "Lend me a hand as I pour these, will you?"

Samuel monitored the furnace while Hinley removed a crucible and poured the smoky orange liquid into a buttonmold.

"I hear they built some ovens and are retorting the ore on the spot. They just packed out their first seventy-pound flask." After pouring the last crucible, Hinley dusted his hands and positioned another four.

"The Celestials are managing to keep the exact source quiet, and since they cannot file a mining claim, it is a safe wager that they do not have one. Nevertheless, knowing the Chinese, they will not hesitate to protect their newfound treasure."

Samuel wondered if Chen knew about the mine. *Somewhere near Ruby Meadows.* He had no idea what cinnabar looked like. As much time as he had spent in the area, he could have walked right over it, not realizing the fortune underfoot. Seventy pounds of mercury could sell for over two hundred dollars. Processing it would be as simple as what he was doing in the kiln out back.

"Makes me realize I better go check my amalgam."

"Aye, you should."

Samuel found the kiln was sufficiently cool. Even so, he was cautious about being near any lingering mercury vapors. Using long tongs, he removed the crucible and carried it back to the shop.

Hinley took a quick look. "It appears you have a fair amount of gold. We shall proceed in treating it."

"Part it with nitric?"

"No, nitric shall not be sufficient." Hinley reached for a flask and unstoppered it. "This is aqua regia, a mixture of nitric and hydrochloric acid." He transferred the retort sponge to a flask and carefully poured in the aqua regia. "This may take a couple of hours, but it completely dissolves the metal into a solution that I later treat to recover the gold and silver."

"Is it something you can teach me?"

Hinley laughed. "I say again, lad, if you want to remain here in Washington, I should be happy to have your assistance."

"I've thought of that."

"I know, we have discussed it," Hinley agreed. "That shall be your decision, of course."

Samuel returned to mulling the ore. Something inside him told him it would be a good living. Although he loved the chase and the hunt for gold, this was good work, but he also wondered about the camp's future. The placers were nearly done. The quartz mines were struggling.

"Things may be looking up for our camp," Hinley said.

"I could use some good news," Samuel replied. He wondered if Hinley had read his mind.

"John Crooks is in town. He is the receiver for the Pioneer Mill. That should be settled soon, and that mill shall be operating again soon. The judge shall be here at the end of the month, and I expect soon after, the Rescue will be back operating along with its old crew. The Charity, Sampson, Hic Jacet, and other quartz mines are going strong. And, as you know, Mr. Bradshaw is getting his mill in for the Summit and Keystone lodes." Hinley eyed Samuel. "I believe those are good signs the quartz mines will be producing for a long while. Warren's camp still has a bright future."

Samuel grinned. "You forgot the O'Riley. That should be coming on line."

"I hope that shall happen, Samuel," Hinley said. "There are some other good signs as well. Many of the longtime miners are relocating on the rivers. You shall recall Salon Hall and his family, James Rains and his brothers, and Sylvester Smith—they all have twenty to thirty acres on their ranches on the South Fork under cultivation. We shall soon have all the good produce we need, other than depending on the Celestials' vegetables. And you are personally aware that Miller's camp is doing quite well, mainly because it has better water. You should consider prospecting for a new placer yourself in that direction."

Samuel felt a surge. That was the second person suggesting he prospect that area. He wished that he could strike a good placer—one with water.

A commotion outside in the street caught his attention. A Chinese pack train was coming in.

"Drop by later, Samuel. I shall go ahead and finish refining your gold. I can see you have other things on your mind at the present."

"Thanks, Mr. Hinley." He raced out the door.

Chinese began boiling out of their small huts, several running down the street toward the pack train, raising a ruckus. Samuel watched as the heavily laden mules passed by with several Chinese riding alongside.

He counted thirty mules. In addition to the heavy packs, he noticed several mules had riders, which struck him as strange. The Chinese who arrived in camp always walked, a dozen or more arriving each day.

Chinese excitedly pushed past, chattering. Along with several of the other townspeople, Samuel jockeyed to where he could watch. A pack string coming in always brought a strange excitement—even a Chinese one.

Chen found Samuel. "Hong King pack string finally here," he said, breathlessly. "It brings lots of things from China."

The mules halted, swaying and stamping, spread the length of the street. Several Chinese quickly spilled among them, grabbing and unloading packs. That was when Samuel noticed two of the riders were Chinese women. A number of men gathered about each woman, chattering to them.

"Jumpin' Jehoshaphat, Chen. Hong King has brought in a couple women." Fascinated, Samuel watched as one of the men helped down the younger of the two. She appeared maybe eighteen or nineteen.

"Well, well," one of the townsmen standing nearby exclaimed, "here's Polly."

"'Bout time you Chinamen brought in some women," another said loudly, while others clapped and cheered.

The Chinese chattered more excitedly. Both women appeared quite small—dainty.

"Look at Polly, Chen, she ain't much older than you." Samuel elbowed Chen. "Maybe you could marry her someday."

Chen glared at him. "Not marry anyone. Owned by Hong King. These are slave girls like my mother." A shadow crossed Chen's face.

Samuel quieted, remembering. He wondered if Chen would ever try to find his mother, if she were even still alive.

Samuel noticed how tiny Polly's feet were—like a doll's feet—and that she bobbled as she walked. "How come she walks funny?"

"As little girl in China, she had her feet bound," Chen explained. "She is a very special woman. Hong King is a very lucky man."

"I think she's pretty," Samuel admitted. "They both are, but Polly's prettier. You sure you can't court her?"

"Sh," Chen hissed, deeply frowning. "She someone else property."

Samuel did not push the point. He recognized how serious Chen had become.

"So when will you go on another sales trip?" Samuel asked.

"In one day or two," Chen replied. "You should come."

"I'll see if Scott has anything for me to deliver." Samuel excused himself and headed toward Alexander's Mercantile.

He noticed Miss Hattie with another woman and wondered where Lilly was. Lilly and Miss Hattie were always together. Two men stood outside the saloon with them where they had been watching the Chinese pack string.

"Hello, Samuel," Miss Hattie called.

The men, whom Samuel recognized as hardrock hands, stepped aside, curiosity on their faces.

"It's the kid," one of them said, grinning. "Sorry, kid, these two ladies are occupied."

"Sorry, sir." Samuel greeted Miss Hattie, "Hello, ma'am." He touched his hat and also greeted the other woman. She was younger than Miss Hattie and wore a dark blue dress that clung tightly to her body. A frilly top accentuated her breasts.

"Uh, where's Miss Lilly?"

"Oh, Samuel," Miss Hattie began. She nodded and whispered toward the two men before stepping over to Samuel. "She's not been too well, Samuel."

Samuel felt distressed. "What's wrong? She gonna be okay?"

Miss Hattie hesitated a bit, appearing to be thinking on her answer. "She's getting better. She asked about you."

Samuel felt even more concerned. "Where is she? Upstairs?" He nodded toward the saloon.

Miss Hattie shook her head. "Heavens no. Not those rooms. Those rooms are … She's at the ladies' cabin up the hill. But you can't go there."

"Then how do I see her?"

Miss Hattie did not reply. The men and the other woman beyond were watching.

"She came to see me when I was laid up," Samuel stumbled on. "I should like to do the same."

One of the men interjected, "Hey, kid, you got your answer."

"I'm sorry, Samuel," Miss Hattie said. "I'll tell her you asked about her." She and the other woman turned toward the saloon, accompanied by one of the men.

Samuel stood, confused, not knowing what he should say or do.

"Look," the remaining man said. "I know you got the desires," he said. "If you need something, go to Florence and visit the Moonlight. That's where the women are."

Samuel felt himself flush.

The man continued talking. It reminded him of the time Jenkins kidded him about girls.

"Warren's is too civilized. The women here are all like the hurdy-gurdy girls. Oh, they might take you for a swing if they like you. Miss Hattie will, but you'll do better going to Florence, I tell you."

Samuel stared at the man, dumbfounded.

"They're dancehall girls," the man explained. "You buy a dance with them. Maybe they'll sing for you or sit at your table. They get you to talk with them and get you to buy more whiskey." He must have noticed Samuel's expression, and he laughed. "Sorry you didn't know that, kid."

Samuel found himself stumbling away from the man—the man's laughter chasing after him.

He found himself walking toward the ladies' cabin. He no longer cared what others would think. Lilly had cared about him. He knocked.

Another woman answered, a puzzled look on her face. "You're at the wrong place, child."

Samuel flushed at her comment.

"Is Miss Lilly here? I would like to see her."

"That's not possible, child. No men allowed here," she said firmly. "You got to leave."

"I heard she was ill. I want to visit. She visited me when I was laid up."

The woman's face softened. "You're the boy that was nearly killed last year."

"Yes'm."

She shook her head. "Sorry, can't let you in, but Lilly's doing much better. She'll be back at the saloon soon. Go and visit her then."

Samuel heard Lilly from the back. "Who is it, Katie?"

"It's some child asking about you."

Lilly pushed her way to the door. "Samuel," she almost shouted. "What are you doing here?"

"I promised to visit you," he blurted out. It was the truth. He had made that promise last year, not knowing why or understanding how, but it had eaten at him nearly every day since. "You came to see me when I was laid up. I heard you were laid up—so I'm here."

Lilly laughed gently. "It's okay, Katie. This is Samuel. We're friends. He won't be a bother."

"You know the rules." Katie frowned and scrutinized Samuel. "Well, a child … maybe he don't count."

Samuel's ears burned.

Lilly did not argue but gestured for Samuel to come in. "I can make us some tea, if you would like. You are such a gentleman, comin' to visit me like this." She smiled.

Samuel melted, thankful for her comment. He didn't think Lilly would soon return to work. Her skin appeared gray. But her smile, her hazel eyes, and her flowing reddish hair diminished all that. She was still beautiful.

They talked. Samuel told her how the mining was doing. He told her about the winter on the river and about going to Slate Creek for Independence Day. He held off telling her about Bonnie.

Like before, Lilly listened.

Samuel realized he was sharing all his dreams, but he knew nothing of Lilly's.

"Do you have dreams, Lilly?" he blurted.

Lilly hesitated. "Well, I guess I used to."

"Not now?" Samuel pressed. "What would you do if you could do anything?"

"I'd like to travel, to see the world," Lilly replied finally. She appeared troubled.

"I'd kind of like to go to China," Samuel admitted.

"China? Whatever for, Samuel?" She laughed.

"Chen makes it sound so fascinating, all their strange customs and such."

"I suppose so," Lilly replied. "For me, I would like to go to France. I'd like to see some real ladies. Maybe see a real princess."

"Maybe someday you can."

Lilly shook her head.

"Why not?"

"Well, for one, it costs way too much."

Samuel laughed. "Then marry a rich man."

A shadow crossed her face, and Samuel caught a look that penetrated him deeply. He shook it off.

"I'm sorry," he blurted.

"It's okay, Samuel. Who knows? Maybe someday." She poured some tea and glanced at Katie. "Would you like some?"

Katie shook her head. She stood, huffed around for a moment then took her shawl and headed out. She gestured toward one of the back rooms. "Shouldn't be anyone back until midnight," she muttered. "If you have a mind." She glanced at Samuel.

Lilly did not acknowledge. She just smiled thinly and sipped her tea.

Samuel caught the meaning of Katie's gesture and felt mortified. He told himself that it was all right. His intentions were only to keep his promise to Lilly.

Samuel felt conflicted. He had to tell her his thoughts. "I like you, Lilly. I like you a lot. From the first day I saw you, I liked you. I wanted to get rich and move away with you."

Lilly sat quietly; a strange look crossed her face. "Oh, Samuel—"

"But I didn't find much gold and then last winter on the river … I met a girl. Bonnie is her name. I like her a lot too. She's my age."

Lilly swallowed; a pained look flooded her face. "That's wonderful, Samuel." But her tone seemed hollow.

They sat in silence. Samuel had not touched his tea.

"Really, Lilly. I wanted to marry you. Before I met Bonnie. I-I'm sorry." A choke caught in his throat.

Lilly studied him, eyes sad. She laughed gently. "I ain't the marryin' kind, Samuel. Not now, anyways. Once, I wanted to be, but it didn't work out."

The silence became awkward. Samuel slowly stood. "Well, I guess I best be on my way." He stepped toward the door. "I hope you're feelin' better."

"Please, Samuel, don't go just yet." Her eyes pleaded. "J-just keep me some company. I like your company."

Samuel thought she was about to cry. He was confused that she should be so upset.

"No man ever told me he wanted to marry me." She was shaking.

"Don't, Lilly. Things will be okay."

She took a drink from a small flask that Samuel guessed to be laudanum.

"No, Samuel, they won't be. You aren't like the other men."

Samuel sat again, confused.

"Don't you understand, Samuel?" She touched his shoulder, caressed his neck. "To them, I'm just entertainment."

Samuel pulled back. The thought seemed so cold.

"They don't care a hoot about me or Miss Hattie or the others," she explained, returning her hand to his shoulder. "They don't have to. We just dance with them, sing for them, pour them whiskey, and you know what else on occasion. And that's all there is to it. Nothing nice about it. They don't care if I have any feelings or not." She pulled her hands to her lap.

Samuel saw tears in her eyes. "Then … why do you do it?"

"Somebody's gotta do it. It's a job. I gotta eat."

"There are other jobs."

"Not in my case," She replied. She was quiet for a moment. "Even if'n they don't say, I know the men appreciate me. Some are nice to me. Give me nice things." She paused. "Besides, I'm doing something good for them."

"Something good?"

"We all lead hard lives, Samuel. You know that," she said. "That's why I'll never go travelin'."

Samuel felt distraught. She sounded so hopeless. He had a sudden urge to hold her and found himself touching her shoulder, trying to console her.

She put his hand on his; traced his fingers where he touched.

"It's okay you met another woman, Samuel. I'm glad for you. Really I am."

Confused emotions began to overwhelm Samuel. He suddenly wanted Lilly. He wanted to melt into her. To hold and kiss her. He wondered how her touch did to him what it was doing. He could no longer stop himself, and he leaned over and kissed her. When he did, Lilly's hand fell and brushed across him. He saw her glance. She had to know.

"If'n you want, Samuel, we could … you know … Katie said no one would be back."

Samuel was burning with thoughts of what he had dreamed. He knew about his own powerful feelings and wanted this. He found himself shaking.

"I'm sorry, I just can't." It was as if someone else was saying the words for him. "I'm owing to Bonnie." But he was lying. He was leaving Bonnie. He forced himself to stand.

Lilly became quiet. Samuel felt coolness where her fingers had touched. "It's okay, Samuel. It's better this way."

Samuel stumbled from the cabin, finding himself feeling sick—not because of Lilly, but because of himself. *God, why can't it be the way it was?*

Chapter 34

CHARLES AND SAMUEL returned to Alexander's Mercantile for their supplies for the O'Riley.

"Last season you told Samuel what we'd need for hardrock, Scott. Guess it's time."

Scott began rounding up items, a couple of bundles of drill steel and a long-handled eight-pound iron hammer. "Do you want your powder and fuse?"

Charles shook his head. "Save it for when we have some holes drilled. We got some ore to haul for a couple of days and can probably break out some more rock before we need the dynamite."

By afternoon, they had reached the O'Riley. About a quarter of a mile away near a seep where Samuel had camped before, they unloaded their gear and pitched their tent.

They were soon in the main excavation, wedging loose some remaining pieces of ore and stacking it with that from last season.

"Looks like we'll need to wait for Bradshaw's mill to begin operations after all, son. When I checked the Hic Jacet, it was still working ore they had stockpiled from last winter."

"How soon do you think?"

"No one can say. I just keep hearing it's on the trail."

"Must be using one mule, if it's taking this long."

His father grinned. "No, but I'm guessing the mules have to trade off a lot. The stamps are five hundred pounds each. A mule can't go long carrying that kind of weight."

"How in blazes do the packers load them?"

"As I understand, they use a tripod and raise it up, then position the mule underneath. They do the same to give the mule a rest—just let the tripod legs down and raise the load enough for the animal to walk out from under."

"More likely, crawl out from under." Samuel grinned. He threw another chunk of quartz onto the pile. "How much ore do we need?"

"Mr. Bradshaw wants a full run, if possible. That would be close to seven tons if everything works well. I'd say with the time we have, that will be about all we can muster."

"We have a bit over three."

"And if we don't commit to drilling and blasting, that's all we'll have."

They paused for dinner. Samuel glanced around. Finally, they were working the O'Riley. It had taken them a month and a half to raise enough money; still, most of their supplies were on credit. They were sinking everything they had into this mine and then some.

The following morning, they located the area along the vein, which Samuel believed was the richest. They marked a square eight feet by eight feet for the start of a shaft and situated the vein across one side to where it dipped toward the center.

Charles gestured at the marks. "You know, we're going to be drilling and blasting a lot of worthless rock."

"If you want, we can just try to work along the vein."

"That might be the smartest thing. I know when the O'Riley gets picked up, the owners will go down the hill about a hundred feet and cut a drift to intersect the vein anyway. Instead of digging down like we'll be doing, they'll drive along the vein either direction and stope upward, blasting the ore out of the ceiling, making it easier to load into a cart."

"Who says that?"

Charles laughed. "I spent a lot of time talking with Mr. Thomas last season at the Ruby. He spent time as a hardrock stiff, and I figured we were eventually going to come to this ourselves."

Samuel peered down the hill. Even as steep as it was, someone would have to drive a tunnel nearly two hundred feet. The cost would be enormous. He and his father had to prove the ore was rich enough to warrant that amount of work and expense, or no one would ever consider buying the O'Riley.

Charles continued, "Of course, they might drive in a drift and not hit the vein, or find that the vein is barren."

"Or they might hit two veins and find even more gold," Samuel replied. "I'm guessing that's what they're gonna find."

Charles smiled. "I've heard of it happening before."

"I just wish I could be here and see it whenever someone does."

They began laying out a pattern of drill holes. Charles marked three equally spaced marks near the center.

Samuel studied the marks. "Why don't we just mark them in a square?"

"This isn't like drilling and blasting boulders where all you do is drill to their center and blast them apart," Charles explained, "The center holes are relievers. We drill them at an angle so they lift the rock out of the way, giving room for the rock coming in from the edges. This pattern takes fewer holes and is more effective, or so Thomas tells me."

"Sounds easy," Samuel said lightly.

"It is. We drill fifteen holes at least two feet deep, load them with dynamite, shoot them, and muck out the rock, and we'll be about a quarter of the way done."

Charles picked up a shorter, slightly larger diameter drill steel and the four-pound hammer. "This piece is called the starter. Once I get the hole down a couple of inches, we'll change to the regular steel. Then you can hold and turn it, and I'll swing. Double jacking goes faster, and you get a bit of a rest when you're doing the holding."

Samuel had watched a couple of drilling contests, but he had never tried it, nor had he paid attention to the details. All he had used the steel for before was chipping and prying.

"The trick is to drill the hole straight and smooth so the steel doesn't bind. You do that by turning the steel a quarter turn after each stroke."

Charles positioned the steel on one of the outer marks and hit it, sending tiny granite fragments and dust flying. He swung the hammer and turned the steel. The strong, metallic ring echoed from the surrounding rocks.

Charles paused. "Give her a go."

Samuel took the hammer and steel. What had appeared easy was not. The hammer bounced off the steel and the steel vibrated off the rock. He swung and missed the steel, barely missing his hand.

"Better learn the length of that hammer if you don't want a busted hand."

Samuel shook his head, repositioned the steel, and struck it. He hit and turned the steel. Hit again. In a few minutes, the resemblance of a hole began to appear amid the dust and rock chips. It took him twenty minutes to near two inches.

"Good enough, son. Time to get serious." Charles chipped an area on the rock and handed Samuel the long-handled hammer. "Hit this spot, full extension of the hammer precisely each time. Use a full swing. Get your back and legs into the swing, not just your arms, and keep your back straight. If you don't, you get all stove-up. I learned that the hard way at McLane's."

Samuel took several swings, only occasionally hitting the mark. His father watched, saying nothing. Samuel swung again. Although similar to swinging an axe, there was less room for error. The hammer's tapered head was not quite two inches across; the steel was an inch and a half across. He dared not miss. His father's hands would be holding the steel, and he knew men could have their arms busted by partners who missed. Samuel already knew what it was like to spend a summer with a broken arm.

"The most important thing is to keep your eyes on the spot. Your swing will follow your eyes. Don't try to swing to the left or right. An easy swing all the way through. Same spot. Let the weight of the hammer do the work."

His father took a few swings. He was dead-on. "Okay, time to get started."

Samuel placed the steel back into the hole and gripped with both hands. His father hit it. The vibrations jarred his hands. He turned the steel a quarter turn. The hammer hit again. Dust and tiny fragments bounced from the hole. He turned. His father hit. The loud metal on metal ringing echoed through the woods.

They switched positions. Samuel took a few practice swings.

"Don't think about it. Just keep your eyes on the steel. Get a full swing. Let's do it."

Samuel gripped the hammer, his hands sweaty. He swung, felt the jar of steel on steel, and felt relieved to hear the metallic ring. He continued swinging. His father turned the steel. Slowly, slowly, the steel penetrated the rock. Rock dust bounced out of the hole.

Thirty minutes later, they were down six inches. Samuel began making mental calculations. *Fifteen holes at twenty-four inches*—he quickly dismissed the idea.

The hole filled with dust and rock particles, binding the drill.

"Hold it," Charles said.

Samuel paused as his father poured water into the hole.

"Now take a few more licks."

Samuel did. His father grasped the steel, pulled it free, and knocked off the mud.

"That's how you free a piece of drill steel and clean out a hole."

They finished the first hole in two hours. They drilled a second hole, one on the outside that Samuel had started, saving the angled holes until they were both more practiced. Samuel was already tiring. They paused for lunch and a short rest.

Samuel ate in silence, thinking. His shoulders and arms already ached. His back ached. He examined his hands. Although calloused from swinging a pick and shoveling dirt all season, they were red and sore. They had thirteen holes to go, and that was just for the first round of explosives.

They resumed work. His father talked and joked as if he had been born for drilling, but Samuel found it difficult to concentrate and talk.

Samuel missed. The hammer came down on its handle.

"That's why handles get replaced," Charles muttered. "Just remember my hands don't."

A bead of sweat trickled from Samuel's scalp. He resumed swinging. His father turned the steel. Shortly, he missed again; this time to the side of the steel. His father moved in time.

"I'm sorry, Pa," Samuel managed. He twisted the hammer in his sweaty hands.

"Don't be sorry. Hit the steel, Samuel. Nothing else."

"Do you want to change out?"

"No, hit the steel."

Samuel wiped his hands on his trousers and took several practice swings against a spot on the rock, returned to the steel, measured his swing, and hit the steel. He tried not to think about missing, just hitting the steel. Eyes on its end, he swung and hit. He kept swinging and hitting, eventually losing track of the count. Finally, his father stood up, indicating it was time for their rotation, after approximately two hundred strokes.

His father did not miss. Samuel turned the steel and counted. They finished the third hole and prepared to drill the fourth. Between holes they broke to drink some water, to take a short break, and to try to relax their muscles.

When the sun had set, the fourth hole was done. Samuel struggled to build a fire and help prepare some dinner. They ate in silence. Samuel was used to hard work running the placer, but this was much worse.

They finished the beans and cold cornmeal mush they had brought. "I could use some more," Samuel said.

"I could as well," admitted Charles. "Tomorrow, get up early and make up a little more chow."

"Maybe a deer will wander within range."

Samuel washed out the dishes and examined his hands. Despite his callouses, blisters were forming.

"You can see why I didn't care to work in one of the quartz mines," Charles said. "It's the same type of work, only you're underground in the dark."

"At this rate, Pa, it'll take a month," Samuel whispered. "We'll never get done."

"Not very optimistic, are you? We'll get faster."

They did get faster. Each hole was an accomplishment that made Samuel proud, but it was also brutal, demanding work. Sweat dripped from his hair and stung his eyes. His hands were now bleeding. His back ached. His legs ached. He could hardly lift and swing the hammer. He could hardly move. Whenever he rested, it took a painful effort to get up and resume work. How men did this for ten hours a day, six days a week was a pure mystery.

At night, he slept like the dead, except that toward early morning, he woke from the pain in his shoulders and back. He could hardly rise up from the stiffness that had set in, and he ached with hunger. He ate everything in sight and was still hungry.

By Friday early afternoon they had finished two more holes. Two remained to be drilled, but the drill steel had dulled down next to useless.

"Guess we have no choice but to go to town," Charles said. "I didn't realize how quickly the steel would wear. We had plenty of steel out at McLane's whenever we needed it."

Samuel was too exhausted to argue. Town, for whatever reason, would be welcome.

"Let's get loaded, son. We can drop off the steel on the way through town. A night in our beds at the cabin will do us good."

"And a stove to cook on."

They packed the steel and headed back toward Washington, stopping at Andrew Faust's blacksmith shop.

"Should have brought it in days ago," Faust said.

"That would have meant the first day," Charles replied.

Faust scratched his chin. "Either that or you get yourself a blacksmith out at your mine." He grinned.

The producing quartz mines had their own blacksmith and forges on site where they sharpened the drill steel around the clock.

"What are my options?" Charles asked. "I can't afford the time to bring it in every day and wait around for it to be sharpened."

"Bring it in and trade out for steel that's ready to go," Faust said. He indicated several piles of various lengths. "I outfit a couple small mines that way."

"Thanks," Charles replied. "Not sure I can afford to go and buy any more steel."

"I can sell you some of this pretty cheap if you don't mind a few dings and odd lengths."

Charles nodded. "Wish I'd known that before I bought all this."

Faust laughed. "Someone has to buy the new stuff." He kicked at a pile of steel. "Just pick out another sixteen to twenty pieces. If you can trade it out at midweek, that ought to be enough. I'll even buy it back when you head out."

Charles waved at the pile. "Go ahead, son. Get what we need."

Samuel selected equal amounts of the four lengths, including some starter steel, bundled them in canvas, and began strapping them onto Molly.

Faust took out a pencil and made notes in a ledger. "Of course, I buy it back based on condition and length."

"To blazes, son, I wished I'd have known this before we bought it new," Charles said as they rode toward their cabin.

Samuel grinned. "Yes, but like he said, someone had to buy it new."

"That's going to save us a lot of time, but I'll have to trust him to keep track of everything. There will be the cost of the steel plus the cost of sharpening it each time we bring it in. Hope he can figure all that out."

They reached the cabin, turned out the stock, which seemed appreciative to be back where there was more grass, and began supper. Samuel checked on the Sweet Mary. Enough water had collected to where he could make another run. He was tempted, but his body ached, and he was hungry.

They ate in silence.

"I don't know about you, son, but that drilling business has just about worn me out."

Samuel was comforted to hear his father admit that he was tired as well. He had questioned himself. He was near his limit.

Chapter 35

ON THEIR WAY to Alexander's Mercantile, they noticed Sheriff Sinclair up the street talking to a couple of men.

"Think you can manage getting the fuse and powder?" Charles asked. "I need to see the sheriff a moment."

"Sure." Samuel thought it might have to do with Finney and Culler. Samuel greeted Scott and asked about the powder and fuse.

"So you got some holes drilled. Congratulations. Now you're about to become a real hardrock miner." Scott set out a spool of fuse and box of caps. "If you have any extra, bring it back." He swung a wooden case of dynamite onto the counter.

Samuel backed away.

"Don't worry about this stuff, Sam. It's not like black powder that can blow up by being looked at cross-eyed. Mr. Nobel's invention is truly miraculous. When nitroglycerin is mixed with clay, it's stable. It takes another explosion to set it off—that's these fuse caps."

He opened the box and held one up. "These are far more dangerous than that powder. You hit them hard, they'll explode." He handed a cap to Samuel. It resembled a brass bullet casing. "They're a lot like a Chinese firecracker. You crimp it to the fuse, stick it into the stick of powder, and light the fuse. When it explodes, the powder explodes. Otherwise, you could lay a stick of powder on a fire and nothing would happen."

Charles came in and assessed the pile. "Our credit still good?"

Scott frowned. "Well, I can't very well grubstake you with drill steel and hammers if I'm going to leave you with empty holes, now can I?"

"Just checking." Charles smiled and grabbed the case of dynamite. "I'll strap this onto Molly, Samuel. It's probably not a bad idea for you to carry that other stuff separate." Charles headed out toward the mule.

Samuel whispered to Scott. "How much is all this?"

"Considerably more than a couple sales trips," Scott whispered back.

That meant it was expensive.

Even though Scott had explained that the dynamite was stable, Samuel still felt nervous with Molly following so closely. He reminded himself it was more likely to detonate the caps.

Samuel considered what else Scott had told him about dynamite. "The main thing is to keep the powder dry," he had said. "This time of year you don't have to worry about it freezing, but if ever it does, you want to thaw it gently next to a fire. You also got to watch old sticks of powder that've been sweating. If any nitroglycerin leaks out, it'll explode just by being jiggled. Build a fire you can toss it into and run like hell."

Still, Samuel did not completely trust hauling dynamite, and he watched Molly's steps.

At the O'Riley, they found a rock crevice in which to store the dynamite and then drilled the final two holes.

Charles laughed. "Makes a difference having sharp steel." He stood back and surveyed the fifteen holes. "See that they are clean, and then let's load them up. Based on a drill hole of two feet, one stick should do it, son. All we want to do is break the rock, not pulverize it. But first, we need to test burn our fuse."

They retrieved the fuse, and Charles measured and cut a three-foot length.

"Count with me, one thousand, two thousand, until the fuse burns out. That will give us an idea on how fast this fuse burns per foot and how much we need so we have time to get away."

Charles lit the fuse and they counted until it went out. "About three minutes. That should be enough."

Samuel had no idea how far away he had to be in order to be safe. He imagined a huge blast sending up columns of shattered rock that would rain down everywhere.

"I figure we should come back down here, son. This is plenty far. We can walk this in a minute. That gives us a full minute to light fuses and another for safety."

Samuel gingerly wrapped the dynamite into a canvas and carried it toward the excavation, following at a distance his father, who had the fuse and caps.

At the site, Charles cut another three-foot length of fuse and crimped a cap onto the end.

"Now, when you're handling dynamite, you want to use gloves. Nitro can be absorbed through your skin, and it will give you the worst kind of headache you can imagine."

He pulled on a pair of gloves, cut the dynamite in half, and then cut one of the halves lengthwise. "Pack half a stick into the hole, then place in the primer and pack the remaining half stick around it." After tamping in the half stick, he gently sandwiched the fuse with cap between the two remaining quarters and tamped them in. "Now we pack the remainder of the hole with dirt." Charles scooped up double handfuls and trickled them into the hole until full. "By compacting the dirt around the powder, the blast will be forced down and out rather than up and back out of the hole. That does a better job of fracturing the rock. In fact, if you just laid a stick of powder on top of a rock and detonated it, it'd hardly chip it. All the force would be directed up by the rock underneath."

Charles packed the dirt down. "Fourteen to go." He cut another piece of fuse and began attaching a cap. "Go ahead and cut yourself a fuse and start loading a shot."

Samuel cut the fuse and then cut into a stick of dynamite. The consistency was like thick clay. Despite Scott's assurance that it was safe, Samuel handled it with nervous trepidation, not quite believing it wouldn't explode. He set his knife aside and packed the half into the hole, tamping it in firmly.

As his father watched, he took a cap and crimped it to a fuse, squeezing the open metal ends down around the fuse, feeling nervous the entire time.

"As long as that cap doesn't explode, there's no danger," his father reassured him. "Just don't grate it against the rock when you slide it in."

He slid the primer into the hole, gently pushing it into the dynamite, and then sandwiched the remaining dynamite around it.

"I think you've got the hang of it," Charles said. "Just don't get cocky."

They continued working until all fifteen holes were loaded. Charles made a final check.

"Now we trim and split the fuses," Charles said. "We want the center holes to go first, so I'll shorten those fuses about an inch. The next ones out, we shorten half an inch."

Charles cut an inch from one of the center fuses and cut a notch into its end. "Try to shake the powder down into the cut. It will ignite easier."

Samuel copied his father as they quickly trimmed and notched the fuses, leaving the outermost ones their original length.

Charles took another section of fuse and cut fifteen notches into it about an inch apart. He lit two candles and handed one to Samuel.

"Yours is in case my candle is spit out. We don't have time to fumble around lighting another." He held up the notched fuse. "After it's lit, the fuse will burn to each notch. When it hits a notch, flame will spit from it, making it easier to light the fuses. If you try lighting fuses with a candle, either a spitting fuse or the wind will snuff it out. You don't want to be caught with a short fuse while trying to light another candle."

Samuel understood. He felt a tenseness building in his chest.

"Okay, you ready?"

"Ready."

His father lit the notched fuse and held it close to one of the fuses. When the flame started spitting, the fuse ignited. He moved to the next fuse, and when the notched fuse again began spitting, that fuse also quickly ignited. White smoke and sparks began filling the excavation. Samuel thought the fuses were burning much faster than their test fuse. He fought a desire to immediately leave the hole and get away.

His father worked unhurriedly, continuing to light each fuse, counting loudly, until all fifteen were lit.

"Okay, come walk with me. We don't run. We walk away—together."

They climbed out of the shallow excavation and walked toward the camp. Samuel fought the impulse to run. He peered over his shoulder; white smoke poured out of the hole. Heart hammering, he expected the blast at any moment.

They reached the dynamite cache and waited.

"We both count the explosions to ourselves and then compare," Charles said.

As if on cue, the rounds of dynamite exploded in rapid succession. Samuel counted and thought he had fifteen but was not certain. The explosions echoed throughout the valley, and tiny fragments of rock rained down. White smoke rose above the excavation.

"How many?"

"I'm pretty sure I got fifteen."

"I know I did," Charles replied. "You have to be certain. If not, we wait a few minutes in case one hang fires." He smiled. "Now, a hang fire—that's a dangerous stick of powder."

Samuel was eager to get back to the excavation to see if a vein of gold had been exposed. It had been his dream since he had begun looking for a quartz ledge.

Dust and smoke lingered over the hole.

"Let it clear out a minute, Samuel. No sense in breathing in that stuff. About like nitro, it'll give you a headache."

They took their time in returning to the excavation. Even so, the stench of burned powder hung in the air and stung Samuel's lungs and eyes.

Samuel studied the broken rock, somewhat dismayed. A few jagged gray chunks lay askew, and smaller fragments were strewn about, but overall, the rock appeared hardly disturbed.

"It was no good."

"Looks pretty broken up to me. Remember, all we wanted to do was fracture the rock so we can muck it out."

Samuel jumped into the pit, looking around for chunks of ore. Gray dust coated everything, and the ore was indistinguishable from gangue. He knocked pieces together and blew off the dust, looking for the quartz. "Can't tell what's what with all the dust."

"Most of the ore will still be in the vein. And if you miss a piece, it'll show after the next rain." Charles heaved a heavy chunk over the lip.

Samuel began turning over the pieces, checking for quartz, tossing out the pieces that didn't have quartz and stacking those that did.

They broke free the larger pieces with their picks. Those too large to lift, they broke down further with their hammers and tossed them out of the hole.

"Get any pieces too large, we'll have to drill and blast them."

Samuel noted that none of the rock below the drill holes had fractured, nor had any rock behind the four corners fractured. Although his father had explained it would not, Samuel had to see it to believe it.

"How much ore do you figure we blasted loose?" he asked.

"You're the one who's good at numbers, son," Charles replied. "Figure your vein is a foot wide. We've just gone down two feet."

"Sixteen cubic feet," Samuel quickly replied. "That's a bit more than a ton." The realization was sobering. *All this work for just a ton,* he told himself. He could almost not bear the thought.

Charles leaned on his pick. "Being it's Saturday, we should load what ore we can and take a trip to the Bradshaw and see how the mill's coming along. It's about eight miles. We'll have just about enough daylight to get there, drop this off, and head home."

They began packing ore into the packs for Molly until they figured they had about 350 pounds. They packed an additional 150 pounds of ore each onto Buster and Spooky.

Four of the miles were without trail. The worst portion was coming off the steep ridge below the O'Riley, where they had to head east along a heavily timbered slope. They cut long traverses to keep from rolling an animal and painstakingly wound their way around the numerous blow downs.

"Might be we need to do some trail work," Charles observed. "Cut a few of these fallen trees and straighten out our trail."

Striking the Meadow Creek trail, they turned down it for a short distance back in the direction of Washington and then cut up the drainage that led toward the Summit vein. Here the trail was well established, and they encountered no further difficulties in reaching the Bradshaw mill site.

Samuel was relieved to see that the mill had arrived. Pieces were arranged next to a crude foundation and a partially completed frame that had been erected near a strongly flowing stream.

Lloyd Stanton noticed them ride in and greeted them. "Howdy, Charles, I see you're finally bringing us something."

"Didn't think there was a rush." Charles nodded toward the pieces.

"Give us a week or so, we'll be firing it up." He nodded toward Samuel. "This is your son, I take it."

"Yes, sir, I'm Samuel." He remembered seeing Mr. Stanton about town, but had never been introduced. He was a heavy-built man, apparently used to swinging a hammer. He had dark hair, and like all the men in this country, his face was etched by the wind and weather.

A couple of men came over to greet them and take a breather. They introduced themselves as Michael O'Shaughnessy and Liam Connolly.

"We've already been hauling down ore from the Summit and Keystone," Stanton explained. "You'll see the piles uphill adjacent to the mill. I'll show you where you can unload yours."

They followed Stanton to a level area next to the mill. A large platform that had been built into the hill extended out to the mill frame.

"You're still going to be our first run," Stanton said, "unless you've decided to keep mining. In that case, I'll run the Summit ore, and you'd be up in early August."

"Way we're going, it might end up *being* August. It's going to take a bit of time to mine and haul seven tons."

"We could run less, but I'd like to see how this plant is going to operate at its capacity."

"And I'd like to see a convincing result so we can sell out," Charles added.

They unloaded the ore. O'Shaughnessy and Connolly helped. To

Samuel, the pile appeared pitifully small. No one commented, but Samuel had begun doing some figuring. They had over four tons at the O'Riley ready for hauling. They had just dropped off about six hundred fifty pounds. They could drill at best five holes a day. He shook his head. A week and a few days would not be enough time to mine and haul seven tons.

They turned back down the trail at dusk, heading for Washington and their cabin.

Chapter 36

Samuel desperately wanted to cling to his sleep. His father rose before him, and the tantalizing odor of bacon and coffee drew him from his bed.

"We got a fair amount of figuring to do, son," Charles said. "Mostly we need to figure out how to haul seven tons of ore to the mill and also be drilling and blasting."

"Maybe I can borrow another mule and make a trip at night."

"We'll think on it." Charles poured some coffee. "For today, we prepare what grub we can for the week and get ready."

Samuel rubbed his hands and examined them. They were calloused and cut. "I can see why the hardrock stiffs board at Ma Reynolds's. They don't have to worry about things like cooking. They can get a bath once a week. Get their clothes washed. Wish we could do that."

"We could if we were drawing eight dollars a day."

Later, Samuel headed into town with a list for supplies his father had decided they needed. He noticed several Chinese in the street. A number of townsfolk stood by as well, some talking. It seemed to be a procession of sorts. Samuel glanced around for Chen.

Instead, Samuel found Scott. "What's going on?"

"Seems they hung that poor Chinaman that stole the boots."

Samuel's breath left him. "I can't believe it." He felt queasy. "I heard they were looking for him, but hanging him for a three-dollar pair of boots?"

"Four," Scott corrected. "But I guess that's what they value a Chinaman's life at. Caught him on the trail. Poor cuss said he just found the boots in an abandoned cabin. Claimed he didn't know they belonged to anyone."

Samuel sat down, a numbness enveloping him.

"They had him in jail last night, but while that deputy wasn't looking, someone hauled him out, and they hung him." Scott shook his head. "Trouble is, I believe the poor bastard. He probably didn't know."

Thoughts of Chen, Chen's uncle Mann, and Sang Yune overwhelmed Samuel. It could have been any of them. He pushed his hands through his hair.

Scott studied him, a deep frown. "I wouldn't get too involved, Samuel. They're just Chinamen."

Samuel shot Scott a look and staggered to his feet. "They ain't just Chinamen, Scott. Chen and Yune ... they saved my life."

Scott said nothing more.

Angrily, Samuel left. He headed to Mann's to check on Chen, the sick feeling storming his stomach. The store was closed.

The Chinese had gathered, and Samuel realized that the bundle they held was a body. Townspeople stood by, observing. A procession of Chinese, burning numerous joss sticks and carrying the body, slowly headed up the hill behind their huts.

Samuel spotted Chen and caught up to him. Chen looked away.

"I'm sorry, Chen."

Chen bit his lip. "It is okay," he answered at length. "It is okay he is dead. Life is not so bad now."

Is that what their lives mean to them? Samuel wondered.

"Can I come?"

Chen stopped and shrugged. "Okay."

A man handed Chen a wad of bright red rice paper perforated with holes. Samuel remembered the holes had something to do with the devil. Chen tossed bits along the path.

"For the devil?" Samuel asked.

"Yes. If devil finds him, he takes him to hell. But devil will get lost going through all the holes and so cannot get to his body by time he is buried."

Samuel followed with Chen until they had reached the cemetery. The Chinese and some white miners gathered around. Some of the Chinese bowed politely, recognizing Samuel, but none spoke.

A man standing waist-deep in a freshly dug grave reached out to help with the body. Several men removed the shrouds, and sets of hands gently lowered the clothed body into the ground. In death, the man had no color, neither white nor yellow—just gray. Quickly they filled the grave. Chen and others scattered more brightly colored perforated rice paper around the site. "More paper, devil get confused," Chen commented. "Now we go back and eat." Chen turned toward the Chinese section of town.

"I guess he doesn't get to go home," Samuel said quietly.

"Oh, he go home," Chen quickly replied. "In year, maybe two, the bone collector come around and take his bones back to China, back to man's family."

Samuel was mystified. "He won't be bones for years."

"He will. Buried shallow. Worms eat flesh, so his bones will be ready. His spirit is in his bones. Devil is in his flesh, not in his bones. Bone collector cleans his bones so there is no devil," Chen affirmed, nodding.

"I go to eat now. But just for Chinese." Chen made a quick bow toward Samuel.

"I understand. I figured as much." Samuel did not intend to eat with the Chinese. He didn't figure the whites were too popular with them at the present.

Samuel turned to go. "I'm sorry about this, Chen. It's not right."

Chen returned a steady gaze, his dark eyes solemn.

Bradshaw Mill

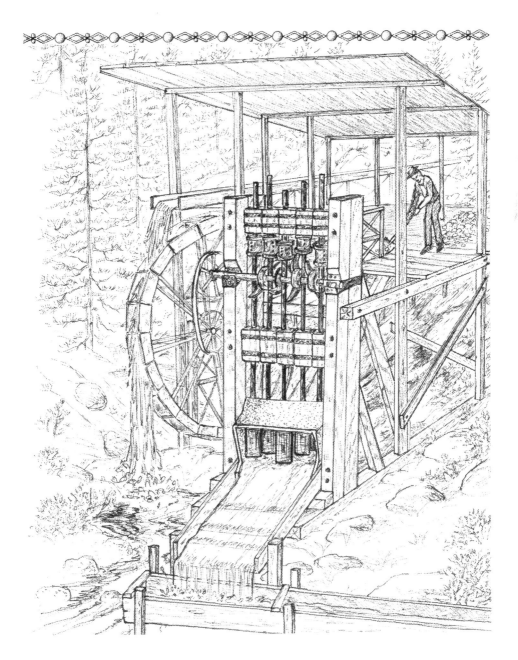

Chapter 37

ON THEIR RETURN to the O'Riley, Charles and Samuel stopped at Faust's blacksmith shop and picked up newly sharpened steel.

"Swap it out in a couple days," Faust reminded them. "You'll need to do that if you're drilling steady."

"I'll send Samuel in."

They reached the O'Riley, and after stowing gear and taking care of stock, they returned to the excavation.

"We still got some rock to muck," Charles observed. "But we need to figure out how to get more of this to the mill or figure on staying here all summer. When Mr. Stanton gets that mill operating, he isn't going to be wanting to wait on us, and I'm not waiting until August."

"I know, Pa. I should have been hauling it already."

"Buster ain't going to like it, but I've been thinking—you can load him with three hundred pounds or so and maybe get close to eight hundred pounds a trip. I'll stay here and muck and drill. We won't be drilling as fast, but you'll be hauling ore a lot faster."

"I'll get the better deal."

Charles laughed. "I don't know about that. See how it works."

They began loading ore. Molly was used to standing still while being loaded. Buster was not. The moment he felt the added weight, he wanted to start moving. It took some doing to get him to stand steady.

Samuel headed out, winding his way off the timbered ridge toward the saddle. In a few places, he tried to move some of the downed logs and straighten the trail. The area reminded him of the ridge where he had come out of the timber and stumbled upon Dudgin and Smith. He shivered, remembering Bender's bleeding body lying in the dirt. He scanned the deep undergrowth, half expecting to see the men. And now Finney and Culler were about. He felt dangerously vulnerable. This was about midway from the mill, and even farther from any help. He pulled his rifle out and checked it. He did not feel at ease until he finally struck and turned down the Meadow Creek trail.

At the mill site, he greeted O'Shaughnessy and Connolly and began unloading. Each bag was near seventy pounds, and he struggled to untie and lower them to the ground. He lugged each to their pile and dumped the ore. He glanced at the ore from the Summit and Keystone. Some had the same gray specks running through the quartz. He assured himself that the O'Riley ore appeared no worse. If anything, it had more gray.

Stanton came over. "Howdy, Samuel. Got time to check it out?" He waved at the mill.

"Sure." Samuel needed to see how the mill was progressing and get an idea of how soon it would be ready.

"Not much to look at yet. They should be trying to install the stamps in a day or two. But you can get an idea how she's gonna work."

The frame stood nearly finished.

"That waterwheel is my best accomplishment. Mr. Bradshaw didn't think we could get that to work up here, but I got a flume built coming out of the creek farther uphill. By the time that water reaches here, it has a lot of force behind it. Turns the wheel, no trouble at all."

Samuel could tell Stanton was proud of his work. The catwalk where they presently stood was about twenty feet above the floor. The wheel *was* impressive. It stood about twelve feet in diameter and had been fitted to the mill for turning the camshaft that would lift the stamps.

"After the ore's cobbed, it'll be shoveled into this hopper where it feeds down into the stamps and is pulverized." Stanton indicated a yawning hole that fed into a chute. "Water mixes with the powdered rock, and the slurry that contains the gold washes out onto a table where it will be amalgamated and then run through a sluice."

Samuel crossed the catwalk to look down into the mill.

"What if we don't have our ore here by the time you're ready?"

"I won't wait. Mr. Bradshaw has ore from the Summit ready to go."

"Then I better get these critters back up the mountain." Samuel stepped off the catwalk toward the stock.

"You've still got a few days. If need be, you could hire Mr. Baker or someone to haul it down for you. Baker's been the one packing ore down from the Summit."

Samuel thanked Stanton. He knew his father would not hire anyone, not if he could figure a way on his own. He glanced at the sun. They might be able to get in two trips a day, about sixteen hundred pounds. The stock probably couldn't handle much more.

Back at the O'Riley, Samuel explained what Stanton had told him.

"We can only do what's possible, son," his father said. "You figure on it, but I'm thinking one of us drilling and one of us hauling will be the most efficient."

"Want me to take my turn drilling?" Samuel asked.

"Maybe tomorrow. For now I'll see how I hold up," Charles said. "I got a bit more weight behind my swings than you."

Samuel didn't argue. He knew his father had more muscle, and anyone could pack animals. He prepared to load more ore.

"I can take the ax and cut a few of the downed trees. I think I can straighten the trail a bit below us here and save some travel time."

His father helped him load another eight hundred pounds and returned to drilling. Samuel headed back toward the mill. He stopped several times and cut timber. After an hour, he had connected several switchbacks that would save a couple hundred yards. *Can't do too much of this,* he realized, *or I won't get anything packed.*

Late evening he had made the round trip. His father had completed four holes. Hardly speaking, they ate and turned in for the night. Samuel remembered thinking that maybe swinging a hammer wouldn't be as bad.

In the morning they returned to double jacking, Charles swinging the hammer, Samuel turning the steel. When they switched, Charles examined the steel.

"Dulls pretty fast. We're going to need to rotate it already," he said. "I guess I can pack a load of ore, and you can drill. We'll switch when I get back, and on your trip out, you can head into Washington with the steel."

"And then come back here?" Samuel was confused.

"No, stay at the cabin. Bring the steel back in the morning."

Samuel helped load the animals and saw his father off. In the resulting silence, he had the urge to relax for a bit, but he could not bring himself to do so. If he only had a single hole drilled by the time his father returned, he would not be able to live with himself.

Soon he was at the excavation working at one of the drill marks. They had agreed to forgo trying to do an eight-by-eight-foot shaft and instead go after more ore. They extended the drill holes along the vein and narrowed the excavation. They figured that if the future owners wanted to use the site as a shaft, they could widen the hole.

Within several swings, the ache came back to his shoulders. He ignored it.

Samuel could take more swings single jacking, but each swing had less power and cut less rock, and the work went more slowly. With each crack of the hammer against steel, hardly any dust or chips flew. The steel sank almost imperceptibly. He turned the steel, hit again, ringing his hands, releasing mostly powder. He flushed the hole. At this rate, he would not even get one hole drilled.

He settled into his work, losing track of time. He did not expect his father could make the trip in much less than four hours. He missed having his company, not so much to talk to, but just the comfort of having someone near.

The sun climbed to its zenith, and the day warmed. Sweat stung his brow. Samuel stripped off his shirt, hoping for a cooling breeze. There was none. At this elevation the sun had an unusual intensity. He was tanned, but he knew he would burn from too much exposure.

He frequently gazed downhill for sign of his father. He had finished the one hole and had begun a second, drilling it to a foot when his father finally returned.

"Your turn, son." His father greeted and immediately began sacking ore.

In half an hour they were loaded, and Samuel was headed down the trail. "I'll see you in the morning, Pa."

"I'll be here. You have my horse." He grabbed his hammer and headed toward the excavation.

By evening Samuel had dropped off his load of ore and had reached Faust's blacksmith shop in Washington. The man was gone, but Samuel left the steel, planning to pick some up in the morning.

At the cabin, Samuel scrounged to find enough food for a meal. He ended up boiling some cornmeal for mush. There were a few dry beans, some sugar, and salt but little else.

In the morning, still hungry, he headed toward the O'Riley. When he was still well below the mine, he could hear his father's steady blows ringing against the steel. He rode up to let his father know he had arrived.

"Everything good?" Charles asked.

"Yep, but we forgot we didn't leave any grub at the cabin." He began unstrapping the steel and easing it to the ground.

Charles studied Samuel. "I guess you're right." He set down his hammer. "Take a moment for some chow, then."

"I'm okay." He really was not, but he wanted to get packing immediately.

"Come on, then, I'll help you load these animals. You can make the first trip."

Shortly, Samuel was on the trail back down the ridge, heading for the mill. Again, he felt strangely alone. He cut a few more trees but decided to wait until later to see how their time was going.

O'Shaughnessy and Connolly greeted him when he arrived. They were working on putting the camshaft into place. The stamps would be installed next. Stanton assured him they were on schedule and would soon need the ore.

Samuel unloaded the ore and headed back toward the O'Riley. Again, he could hear steel against steel as he neared the mine. It was a good sound, but it reminded Samuel of how difficult it would be to meet their goal. His father would not quit trying, he told himself, nor would he.

His father had drilled two holes and begun a third. Samuel helped him load the ore and then took over the drilling. By evening, when his father returned, he had finished the third hole and nearly a fourth. Not quite four holes and sixteen hundred pounds a day, he realized. He continued drilling and finished the hole while his father fixed dinner.

Samuel sat with his father for dinner. He mopped up every scrap of the cornmeal mush and wanted more.

His father eyed him. "Guess you better get us some more grub when you go in tomorrow night."

Samuel thought about the cost of supplies. They had not mined any gold for some time and were now living completely on credit.

The next day was much the same. Samuel drilled and his father hauled ore. They switched when his father returned. Samuel was barely into the trees when he heard his father's hammer, but he felt good. Tomorrow they should be able to blast.

He reached the Bradshaw, unloaded his ore, and headed toward the cabin. The sun had set and evening was upon him. More than ever, he worried about being dry-gulched, and he carried his rifle at the ready.

Even at the cabin, he felt spooked and slept uneasily. He thought about his father miles away at the mine, without even a horse.

In the morning, Samuel had some time before Scott would be at the store, so he wandered down to check on the Sweet Mary. He surveyed the hillside and came away with the same feeling he always had. There was gravel with good gold but little water to run it. He eyed the water in the catch basin. It held water now but not enough to run more than a couple of hours.

Samuel longed to see some gold. They had spent days at the O'Riley and seen none. Carefully, he released the water into the sluice and shoveled some dirt into the flume. After a few minutes, he checked the upper riffles. A few sparkling yellow specks sent shivers through him. There was nothing as good as seeing gold.

Finding the O'Riley had been good. Mining it was discouraging, brutally hard work. He missed placer mining; it was hard work as well, but at least there were moments when he could see the gold.

When he reached Alexander's, Scott had not yet arrived. Men were loading a pack string that stood outside Ripson's Saloon. Samuel thought it was unusual in that it was midsummer—too early for people to be heading out for the season. Then he noticed Lilly standing by. Miss Hattie held an arm about her.

Lilly immediately began waving. "Why, Samuel," she said. "I'm so pleased to see you. I didn't think I'd get to." She was shaking, coming toward him.

She had no color to her face and, strangely, reminded Samuel of the dead Chinese man.

"I haven't been in town for a few days." Samuel touched his hat. "Lots of work lately."

"I don't care what people think, Samuel," she whispered. "You are the kindest gentleman in Washington." Her words were slurred.

Hattie came up. "Don't pay too much of a mind to her, Samuel," she whispered. "She's not well."

A queasy feeling rushed through Samuel.

"I don't care if you found someone else, Samuel," Lilly whispered. "You're still my man."

Samuel glanced frantically around. Only the packers were present, but he hoped she wouldn't say anything more.

"It's okay, Lilly," he said. "Are you okay?"

"She'll be okay, Samuel." Hattie tried to steer Lilly toward a horse. "She's leaving us."

Samuel felt stunned. "Going?" He could not imagine Lilly being gone.

One of the packers gave her a hand. "You hang on good, you hear, Miss Lilly? I'll be right behind you. You holler if you need to stop."

"W-where you going, Lilly?" Samuel asked, his voice quavering.

"Lewiston." Lilly smiled faintly. "Going to go get me some sunshine and have me a vacation." Her voice wavered.

"You take care of yourself, Lilly," Samuel called. The pack string began to move out.

"You come visit me in Lewiston, Samuel."

Samuel was careful not to agree. "I'll keep that in mind if ever I get there. Thank you, Lilly." He waved.

"Thank you, Samuel." She blew him a kiss. "The most handsome man in the territory."

Samuel watched as the pack string passed through town, Lilly swaying in motion with the horse, heading out toward the main trail. He no longer cared what people had heard or what they thought. An emptiness filled the pit of his stomach.

Miss Hattie came over to him. "She'll be all right, Samuel."

Samuel shook his head. He knew she would not be all right.

"Look, Samuel, she told me if she didn't get to say good-bye to tell you that she really did care for you."

Samuel felt hollow. He had been right about her feelings for him, and when he told her about Bonnie, she had hidden them. Underneath, Lilly really was a good person.

Samuel turned to Hattie. "She's not going to get better, is she?"

Hattie tried to look away but could not. "No, Samuel, most likely she's not."

"How long has she known?" Samuel asked.

"Last winter when she got sick."

Samuel realized she had known during his visit.

"I know what you're thinking, Samuel," Hattie said. "She was so happy after you visited her. That's all she talked about. She was glad for you that you met someone."

Samuel felt a knot in his throat. He realized what he could have shared with her. "Even though I—"

"She told me you wanted to marry her," Hattie said. "She said she never had a man tell her that." She lowered her voice. "She said you refused her when you visited, that it would not be honorable to your gal at Slate Creek. She wished she was that gal. She really loved you, Samuel."

Samuel felt the ache inside break and wash through him. He wanted to sit down, wanted to be left alone, wanted to run after Lilly. It was not so much what she could have given him; it was what he could have given her.

Chapter 38

ON HIS TRIP back to the O'Riley, Samuel found himself thinking about Lilly and Bonnie—that things would have been different had they found the real lost ledge, had the Sweet Mary been rich, had anything worked out better for his father and him. Instead, they faced returning to Iowa the same way they had come—broke.

He reached the excavation, not realizing things were silent. His father was packing dynamite into the drill holes. Samuel had almost forgotten and rushed up to help.

"Thought I'd get a jump on this, knowing you'd be getting grub and supplies."

"But this is the best part, Pa."

"Here, I've saved you a couple holes." Charles pointed.

Samuel began loading the holes, and when he finished, his father cut two starter fuses and notched and ignited them. Samuel lit half the fuses with one while his father lit the second half.

They walked toward their camp, getting distance between them and the blast. Something about watching and hearing the dynamite exploding, seeing the shower of rock fragments, and watching the plume of white smoke rising was extremely satisfying to Samuel. It seemed a perfect finish to hours and hours of drilling and offered a rare moment of rest.

Shortly, tightly spaced explosions began rocking the woods. After the smoke cleared, they returned to the excavation, eager to see the exposed ore.

It was about the same yield, maybe three or four cubic feet more, but anything more helped. The vein seemed to be holding its width. If anything, it appeared to be getting wider.

After cobbing and stacking rock for a while, his father paused. "Best get you loaded while we still got daylight. You can get another load to the Bradshaw and see how they're doing on the mill."

In a few hours, Samuel reached the mill and unloaded the ore.

"You gonna make it?" Stanton asked. "We should be running by midweek."

Samuel knew they couldn't. "We're tryin'." Stanton wanted to run seven tons. They had mined less than six and had hauled four. He pushed the animals, heading back to the O'Riley. Tense minutes passed into hours. The desperate need to get the ore mined and hauled pressed upon him.

At the O'Riley, his father had finished mucking and had stacked the ore for sacking.

"Mr. Stanton says he should be ready to run midweek."

"Best we keep drilling, then." Charles picked up the long hammer.

Samuel grabbed the steel. *Why try?* It would be impossible for them to drill and blast another ton, let alone haul three tons by midweek.

When his father called it for the day, Samuel could hardly stand. His entire body ached. He hardly remembered dinner, and after he pulled his blankets around himself, morning came all too soon. He forced himself to stand and took a few minutes to knead his sore muscles. After a quick bite and some coffee, they resumed double jacking.

"We'll need to take the steel in tonight. And I'm guessing when Stanton gets the mill done, he'll want a test run before they can get to us. That should give us another day."

Samuel felt a little hope. He held and turned the steel; his father swung, ringing steel against steel, making Samuel's hands vibrate. With each turn, small chips bounced from the hole. Occasionally, he flushed the hole and removed the mud. After two hundred strokes, they changed positions.

Samuel swung the hammer, striking steel. His father turned it. He swung, feeling his shoulders, feeling his muscles bring the hammer down, swinging and striking the steel. He brought up the hammer and swung it down in a full arc onto the steel. He lifted again.

He no longer worried about missing, and he and his father talked.

The day heated. They stripped off their shirts. Sweat stung their brows. They switched positions, took a few moments for water, and returned to swinging the hammer and turning the steel.

At noon, they broke for more water, something to eat, and a short rest, and then they were again at it. As difficult as it was to swing the hammer, it was almost more difficult to pause. Each time they did so, Samuel found that his muscles tightened, and the ache quickly returned to his neck and shoulders.

Samuel led off with swinging. His father held the steel. They drilled another hole and then another. By late afternoon, they had five holes drilled and another started.

"That's more like it, son, but we better load some ore and head to the Bradshaw if we want to get back to the cabin before dark."

They began sacking the ore.

"Ho, the camp." A voice reached them.

Samuel glanced up to see Sheriff Sinclair riding up from below.

"Welcome." Charles straightened and adjusted his hat.

Sinclair swung down and eyed their work. "Got a mighty good-looking operation here. Always wondered where you guys were." He eyed Samuel. "So this is what you discovered?"

"Yes, sir," Samuel replied. They both knew Sinclair was not just visiting.

"We can rustle up some coffee back at our camp," Charles offered.

"No, thanks. I'm up here to let you know I rounded up Finney and Culler."

At first, Samuel could not believe what he had just heard. An immense weight lifted from him. The two men who had robbed them were in jail.

"I read them the charges you and Samuel have against them after we talked the other day," Sinclair explained. "They just laughed. Said it was a misunderstanding, said that they'd have their bond money in a couple days and be out."

"They shot at me," Samuel managed, now shaking. The sudden relief had turned back to fear.

"Seems to me *you* shot at them." Sinclair eyed him. "At least, that's what they're saying. Saying they were just minding their own business."

Samuel felt a burning tightening in his chest. He glanced frantically toward his father.

Sinclair must have sensed Samuel's desperation. "Well, for now they're in jail, but I'm going to have to let 'em go if they can bond out." He frowned. "I didn't think they'd have any money."

"Probably ours they stole last winter," Charles spat.

"Likely is, but you might be thinking on your statements. The judge should be here around about the end of the month to hear the Rescue case. If Finney and Culler do bond out and stick around to be heard, you two will be testifying."

Charles nodded. "Then I doubt we'll be testifying. They won't stick around."

"Right. Which is why I'm here. They might want to come after you." Sinclair adjusted his hat. "Maybe you might have some other information you've thought of so I can have more of a reason to keep 'em."

"Nothing more than what we've told you." Charles gazed toward the horizon. "How long until you have to turn them loose?"

"Probably when I get back."

"Maybe you could take a trip to the South Fork to check on things."

"I was thinking that, but it won't matter much—three or four days at best."

"Good. We're shooting one last round here, and then we'll be packing ore to Bradshaw's mill. We should be done about then."

The sheriff swung back into his saddle and turned his horse toward the South Fork. "Good luck."

"Thanks," Charles called after him.

Samuel stared at his father. His heart was pounding. "If Finney and Culler are turned loose, there's no telling what they might try—especially after having been thrown in jail on account of us."

"We'll just have to stick closer together, son," Charles said. "Come on, help me load these." He hefted a sack of ore.

At the mill, Stanton met them. "I told Samuel yesterday we should have the mill running midweek. I'll finish the table and do a test run. I'm obliged to tell you if your ore's not ready, I'll have to get going on the Summit ore."

"We'll be ready," Charles assured him.

They unloaded and piled the ore.

"We need more ore than this, or we won't recover enough to even begin paying for what we've spent," Samuel muttered.

"We still got a couple days for mining and hauling," Charles said.

They reached their cabin after dark, took care of the stock, and fixed a simple dinner before turning in for the night, exhausted.

In the morning, Samuel woke to his father preparing some coffee. He stood and dressed, surprised to find himself not as stiff and sore—surprised to realize he had toughened to the hard work. He took a cup of coffee.

"Thanks, Pa. It's kind of good not to be swinging a hammer or packing ore."

"It is at that. I'm glad the good Lord invented Sundays."

They sat a few minutes eyeing each other.

Samuel spoke first. "You once told me the good Lord said that when the ox is in the ditch, you have to get it out. And I reckon those holes aren't going to get drilled by themselves." He drained his cup. "I'm willin' if you are."

Charles laughed. "Glad you said so, son."

They packed and headed toward the O'Riley, picking up new steel on the way out of town.

They put in three more holes before Samuel headed toward the Bradshaw with another eight hundred pounds of ore. When he returned, his father had completed another hole. Six remained. It was evening. They called it quits and had dinner.

"We're nearing five tons at Bradshaw's," Samuel said.

"Then when we get this round finished and hauled we'll have something over six," Charles said. "That may be the best we do."

"Maybe this last round will show a solid vein of gold."

Charles laughed. "You don't give up, do you?"

"Not as long as there's quartz showing."

They began the next morning again double jacking, putting in three holes before deciding to load the remaining ore and sending Samuel on to the mill.

"I can finish another hole, son, maybe two, but the steel's pretty shot. You better swing by Washington and rotate it out. We can finish tomorrow and blast—that'll have to be the last of it."

"You bet, Pa," Samuel said. "If you can, maybe drill another hole on the vein. Get some more ore."

"I'll see how far I get."

Samuel reached the mill and unloaded. It stood essentially finished except for the sluice table. O'Shaughnessy and Connolly were pulverizing ore, breaking the pieces down, and getting them ready for shoveling into the hopper.

"You really think what you're finding at your mine is going to be worth all your trouble, lad?" O'Shaughnessy asked.

Samuel took offense. "The assays came in really good. I'm thinking it's better now that we're deeper."

O'Shaughnessy laughed. "That's what everyone who's ever tried to sell a mine says. The deeper ye go, the richer it gets."

Samuel hesitated. "A dollar says it will go richer than that stuff you're fiddling with."

Both O'Shaughnessy and Connolly laughed. "Save your dollar, lad. We all be gamblers in this business."

But O'Shaughnessy's comment got Samuel to wondering. Maybe the ore wasn't richer the deeper they drilled on the O'Riley.

It was late when Samuel left the Bradshaw and headed toward Washington. He wanted to check on the Sweet Mary and see some gold. He was tired of mucking and hauling rock.

He dropped off the steel and headed through town. On the outskirts he noticed cattle in the meadows and figured they had been brought in for slaughter. At first he thought they were Burgdorf's, but then he recognized some of the animals. They were Jon Stromback's cattle. Excited, he started looking for Art and Rex. He dropped by Jay Dubois, the butcher, and found Art there, completing the sale.

"Art," he hollered. "What you doin' at the end of the world?"

Art glanced up. "Well, I'll be. If it ain't Samuel. I figured you'd be long gone by now."

"We would be, but we still haven't finished work on the O'Riley. How is everyone?" He hoped Art would say something about Bonnie.

"Everyone's good, even Bonnie," Art replied. "But your run-in with Rex had a lot of people talking. Cooled his heels for a bit."

Samuel ran his hands through his hair and grinned. "Anyone not heard?"

"Probably a few folks up here." He turned to Jay Dubois. "Hey, you heard about how this kid dances with another man's gal?"

Dubois looked up. "Samuel? You got the wrong kid. He's the most honorable man in these parts. No foolin'."

Samuel felt himself turning red. "I was honoring Mr. Stromback's wishes," Samuel sputtered, half thinking that Art was serious. He was thankful folks had not heard of his visit with Lilly, or maybe if they had, they were not saying anything.

Art grinned. "Actually, it was the other way around, Mr. Dubois." He leaned over the counter. "You saw the ugly cuss who rode in here with me? *He* was dancing with *this man's* gal."

Samuel was really red now.

"Bless my stars. That gives us folks here in Warren's hope for you." Dubois grinned. "We were getting mighty concerned there wasn't going to be a followin' on generation around these parts. Fact is, people around here were startin' to take bets on whether or not you'd ever land yourself a gal, or if you'd just spend the rest of your life being a sourdough chasin' gold around these hills."

"Come on, guys," Samuel tried to get a word in. "You musta noticed there ain't too many gals around these parts."

Art laughed. "Fact is, Mr. Dubois, he's right about that one. That Bonnie is a real nice-looking young woman. She'd have this entire town stood down because they'd be too smitten to do a lick of work." Art finished signing the papers that Dubois had handed him. "They're all yours, Mr. Dubois. I'll pick up the payment in the morning if I can."

"That'd be fine," Dubois replied. "Have a good night."

Samuel turned to Art as they left the butcher's. "Where you guys staying? Where's Rex?" Samuel had to ask, although he didn't really care to see Rex.

"Don't have a place yet. Gotta find Rex and see what he wants to do. I'm sure he's over at one of the saloons. Don't mind if I join him."

"I'll go with you."

Art eyed him. "You ain't growed up that much since I last saw you."

"I can have coffee." Samuel laughed. "Or we could go to Ma Reynolds's. She serves up some wicked pie and buttermilk."

"You know, Samuel, pie's a better idea."

Shortly, they were seated in Ma Reynolds's dining area, and she was setting down a huge slab of apple pie with fresh buttermilk in front of them.

"Sure is good to see you, young'un. How's your pa doin'?" she bubbled. "How's the mining goin'?" Young George came over, eyes big, and said hi to Samuel.

"Thanks, ma'am. Pa's fine. We're finally about to run some ore." He gestured at the pie. "Best pie in these parts, Art."

Art took a bite. "Yep, might even give Mrs. Stromback a run for her money."

Samuel felt a bit guilty having pie. All he had was four bits to his name.

"So, how come you weren't at the Independence Day celebration?" Samuel asked. "I saw you riding the appaloosas with Rex. Then you were gone."

"You really don't want to know."

"I do." Samuel paused with his next bite of pie.

"I was trying to keep you alive."

"What?"

"Rex saw you standin' there next to Bonnie and went crazy. He literally swore he was fetchin' his gun to kill you. I told him to calm down—that I knew for a fact you were leaving this country and he'd have Bonnie all to himself again."

Samuel stopped eating.

"Fact was, I didn't know with certainty, because you and your pa hadn't been by, and the expressman, Mr. Hunt, didn't know what you two were up to. I took Rex out for a drink. You might say I kept my eye on him most of the day."

"Did Mr. Stromback know?"

"He might have guessed," Art replied. "We were nearby at the saloon. Rex'd wander out to spy on you, and I'd convince him you weren't any competition, to let Bonnie visit with you one last time, and so on. Eventually, though, I ran out of stories."

Samuel knew Rex was crazy. Rex had already taken a shot at him once to scare him.

"I didn't see you at the dance when Rex showed up."

"Nope, he slipped out on me. Guess he figured what I was up to. Luckily, you handled it like you did. He didn't know what to think."

Samuel almost laughed.

"Unfortunately, he figured it out later. He ran on and on to me how you made him look like a fool."

"He could've looked in a mirror and saved me the trouble," Samuel said almost seriously.

"Yep." Art chuckled.

"He still seeing Bonnie?" Samuel could hardly bear to ask.

Art was quiet. "How about some more pie?"

Samuel sat back. "I guess that means yes." His stomach tightened.

"Look, Samuel," Art said quietly, "unless you and your pa have changed your minds, I'm guessing you two are still planning on leaving. Bonnie's going to have to find someone. Rex works hard when he's got his head on straight."

"But *Rex*?" Samuel almost shouted. He saw Ma Reynolds had been listening. She turned away.

They sat in silence for a moment.

"Well, I guess I better get on down to my cabin, Art. You can spend the night there if you want. Don't have much grub, though."

Art laughed. "Thanks, I think I'll stay here."

They got up to leave.

Ma Reynolds came over, taking the plates. "Now, Samuel, don't you be a stranger. You come visit, okay? George likes it when you come by."

"I'll try. Thanks for the pie."

They headed out into the street and walked toward the butcher's for their horses.

Samuel heard Rex holler a greeting at Art. He recognized the man and his stubble of a beard, unkempt, coming down the stairs from one of the rooms from above the saloon, adjusting his trousers. Samuel felt his stomach turn, and a blinding fury filled him. He walked toward the man, fists clenched.

"You filthy scum," Samuel spat. "This how you honor Bonnie? You want me to share with her what you do with other women soon as you leave the ranch?"

Rex walked directly to him. "Mind your own damn business, little boy. I'll bed who I want, when I want." He cursed.

All reason fled Samuel. He saw only hatred and disgust. He ran at the man and blindly swung, his fist barely grazing him as Rex stepped aside.

Light and numbing pain exploded in Samuel's head. He felt Rex's punch before he saw it coming. He tried to strike back, but his arms felt like lead.

He felt two more punches, one to his nose sending another blinding flash through his head as he felt the blood spray across his face, the second to his gut, doubling him over, causing him to gag and cough, to spit blood.

"Leave him alone. He's just a kid."

"Bastard of a whore." Rex spewed filth, cursing Samuel, and landed another punch.

Samuel felt a force hammer into his chest; he couldn't raise his fists. He doubled over, blood streaming down his shirt. He pitched headlong into the gravelly dirt. He felt a blow into his ribs as he began to vomit, trying to get to his hands and knees so he did not choke.

"That's enough." He heard shouting and scuffling. Other voices and shadows above him were fighting.

He felt a boot smash into his side, knocking him over, back into the dirt; he rolled over, seeing vague shadows of men, seeing the dimming sky, hearing far away voices.

"He's a kid" were the last words he remembered before the blackness came.

He woke at Ma Reynolds's, groggy and in throbbing pain. Dr. Sears, dressed in his high-collared shirt and a string tie, was looking him over. Ma Reynolds dabbed at a cut on his nose.

"Welcome back to the land of the living," Dr. Sears said. "How many fingers am I holding up?"

Samuel could see three, but said, "Four."

"Work on it."

"Okay, there's three."

Dr. Sears harrumphed. "He'll survive. Nothing broke I can tell. Just cut up and got the senses knocked out of him." He made a note.

"I didn't mean for you to be back so soon, Samuel," Ma Reynolds said, continuing to dab at his cuts.

Samuel tried to smile, but the pain caused him to flinch.

Samuel saw Art. "Where's that bastard Rex?"

"A couple men were going after him. He lit out for the ranch, I 'spect." Art studied him. "You okay?"

Samuel tried moving. He could flex everything okay; it just hurt. "That's twice," he muttered. "I dang near get killed being dragged by Spooky; now I get laid out by a crazy man."

"You did call him on his morals, and you were swingin' at him with murder in your eyes. The way you took off after him was somethin' else. I never seen you like that, Samuel."

"You defending him?" Samuel asked, incredulously.

"Not in the least," Art replied. "You just set the record straight for anyone around who might have had 'spicions about Rex's character, though."

Dr. Sears returned his attention to Samuel. "You're going to be sore for a few days, lad, but nothing worse than that, far as I can tell."

"I'm getting used to hurting ever so often." Samuel tried to smile again.

"You're probably also going to look like you went through a stamp mill." Dr. Sears pulled out a couple of small bottles. "Here's something for the pain and some salve for the cuts. I'd recommend you stay here the night, just in case." He stood.

"I'd be tickled to have young Samuel," Ma Reynolds quickly replied.

"I'll check back in the morning." Dr. Sears closed up his medical kit and stepped out.

"Where's your pa, young'un?" Ma Reynolds asked.

"He doesn't need to be here," Samuel said, sitting up. He didn't want to think about his father coming in to see him laid up again. "Doc says I'll survive. I'll get back out there tomorrow like planned." He lay back.

"It's good he's half a day away, Art," Samuel said. "You think you saw me mad, wait till he hears about this. Rex might just want to keep on heading west. My pa's liable to do something more than just think about killing him."

He lay in bed, looking out the window at the trees on the hillside as he had done a season ago. The view was all too familiar. He half expected Lilly to come through the door. He suddenly wished she would. He had defended Bonnie; look where that had gotten him. Lilly would not have needed any defending.

Ma Reynolds stuck her head in. She seemed to do that at the most inopportune times. "You be needin' anything, young'un, you just ding the bell. Now you get yourself some sleep."

Samuel did not fall asleep for a very long time. He listened to the noises of the boardinghouse—men snoring, one he thought was Art, George waking up and wanting water, and the rustle of Ma Reynolds.

Chapter 39

SAMUEL WOKE to the late morning sun. It must have been the laudanum, he guessed. Still, he was angry with himself for sleeping so long. Gingerly, he sat up, swinging his feet over the side of the bed. Pain wracked his side. His face was swollen. He could barely see from the one eye, but he had to get out to the O'Riley and help his father.

"Lord sakes, he's finally movin'," Ma Reynolds exclaimed when Samuel stumbled in to the kitchen. "Set yourself down and I'll prepare you some fixin's."

Two miners looked up when he came in. Neither said anything, but they stared hard at him.

Samuel managed to sit. "Mighty obliged."

Art showed up and joined him. "I was waiting before I headed out to see how you were farin'."

"Greater than a honey bee in a field of clover." In truth, Samuel could hardly lift his arm, and his side was on fire.

Ma Reynolds frowned. "I'm a thinkin' I ought to fetch Doc Sears again. You may a had your ribs busted."

"Could be," Art said. "He had you laid out, Samuel. I sure don't know why he had to go and kick you."

One of the miners at the nearby table interjected, "I think it were me, boy, I'd a be huntin' that feller down and be packing me ol' six-shooter when I did."

"Fer sure," the man next to him agreed. "I'd put lead in him fer sure. Kickin' a man when he's down—that calls for it, fer sure."

Samuel nodded, wincing. Right now he couldn't even *lift* a pistol.

Ma Reynolds brought him a heaping plate of eggs, ham, cornbread, and jelly. He found himself famished and despite the pain managed to get some of it down.

He looked up to see Dr. Sears coming in. "Mrs. Reynolds says I ought to give another gander at those ribs of yours."

Samuel protested but not too strongly.

Back in his room, shirt off, Sears prodded him some more. When he touched one spot, Samuel felt numbing pain; he could hardly breathe.

Sears kept muttering and prodding until Samuel wriggled out of range.

"Can't rightly tell for sure," he muttered. "That's the thing about busted ribs. Don't often know unless they're sticking out of your carcass."

"Believe me, Samuel—that you don't want," Art said.

"No, sir, you sure don't." Sears stood. "I'm going to get you a bandage and bind these up, just in case. I'll want you to leave it in place for a couple of days, and if your ribs don't feel better, come back and see me."

"Yes, sir."

"At least I see you've managed to put some meat on those bones. You're about one of the best fit human specimens I've seen in some time."

"That's from drilling and blasting."

Sears harrumphed. "That'll do it for you faster than anything I know." Sears eyed him. "Now if you don't want mushrooms taking root under those bandages when I put them on, I'd recommend you take a good washing." He turned to Ma Reynolds. "Would that be workable?"

"Certainly. I'll get Mr. Reynolds to bring in a tub." Ma Reynolds left.

Samuel began to panic. He remembered the last bath. He was too embarrassed to say anything but just hoped Ma Reynolds would not be too much of a help.

Art said, "Well, I reckon you're going to be all right, Samuel. I best be heading down the trail. You take care if I don't see you again."

"Uh, Art," Samuel said, "maybe you should get word to my pa. He's expecting me back with the drill steel this morning. We were fixin' to do some blasting."

"I suppose I can do that. Better give me directions."

Samuel explained. In his current shape, he didn't care to see his father, but his father needed some explaining, or he would be out looking for him.

Peter Reynolds dragged in the tub and began filling it.

"All set for you, Samuel." He left a towel. "Leave your clothes outside the door. My missus will get those washed for you while you're bathing. Need any help?"

"I'll be fine, thanks." It was not like before when he had no use of his hands.

Soon he had undressed and was sitting in the hot, steaming water.

A bucket of hot water with a dipper was within reach. He began soaping and washing, enjoying the warmth, feeling better already.

He heard a soft knock. "Sure you don't need some help, Samuel?"

Samuel flushed with embarrassment. *Ma Reynolds.* He gulped. "No," he almost shouted.

"Won't be a problem, young'un." Disappointment touched her voice.

Samuel felt bad. She was just trying to be a mother. He knew it. "Maybe a little. Maybe my hair."

She came bustling in, looking proud and happy, and reached for the dipper.

What is it with these women? Samuel wondered.

"Now, I won't notice anything," she said as she scooped up water to wet his hair.

Samuel grimaced. Of course she would. There was hardly enough water to cover his toes.

She began lathering. Samuel forgot his embarrassment. He was in heaven. If this was what it would be like to be married, to be fussed over, he was all for it, but those thoughts sent another kind of pain through him. He was here with busted ribs because of a woman.

George came in and stood at the edge of the tub watching. "I wanna bath."

"Lord sakes, you get more baths than what's good for you, George. Now go on and help your pa."

"I wanna be with Sam."

"It's okay. George can stay." Samuel liked having George around. It was like having a younger brother. He wished he did. He thought of his sister.

"You ready for some rinsing?"

Samuel nodded and felt the warmth of the water running about his head and shoulders. Nothing was ever this good.

"Thank you, ma'am."

She left; George stayed behind. Samuel dried off and sat with the towel, awaiting his clothes and Dr. Sears. He and George talked. The youngster had a lot of questions.

"Bad men come back?" He wanted to know.

How could he explain Rex? He remembered Finney and Culler. "You might say. They're in jail."

"They are?" His eyes went big. "Are they gonna get hanged?"

Samuel considered it. He doubted it. "It depends on who the judge believes." *And it depends on whether or not they stay in jail,* he thought. He gulped. He would soon have to testify against them.

The clothes came first, still warm from the iron. He dressed except for his shirt.

Finally, and much later than expected, Dr. Sears arrived. He prodded his ribs again, still muttering, still uncertain. He unraveled a long bandage and wrapped him solidly, creating a momentary pain, but the constriction from the wrap felt oddly comforting.

"Just in case, I wouldn't go swinging a hammer or lifting too much for a while."

Samuel knew that wouldn't work. "What if I do?"

"You'd be a fool, as most men are, lad, but it probably won't damage things. You just won't heal up as fast as you should."

Samuel began putting on his shirt. He was ready to leave this place; ready to get back to mining. He heard his father greeting Peter Reynolds and felt frustrated. He had hoped his father would not see him this way.

"Can't keep yourself out of trouble, I see," his father said matter-of-factly as he came into the room.

"I'm sorry, Pa." Samuel felt like a little boy again.

"It could have been worse. At least you're alive."

"Rex did his best to make sure I wasn't going to be."

"The way I heard it, you had every intention of making sure he wasn't going to be."

"Probably so."

"And rightfully so," Charles said, "but you said about the worst thing you possibly could have to him."

Samuel looked up. "You defending him?" Samuel felt confused. A man just didn't do what Rex had done—not when he was spoken for.

"I ain't defending Rex in the least, Samuel. He went way too far, but you called him out is what you did. I don't disagree with you doin' that, but you might have picked a better way."

"I couldn't see a better way, Pa."

"Looks like you couldn't see at all." He was silent a moment. "I know we talked about how powerful feelings between a man and woman can be. Hate feelings are worse. They can overcome a man if he isn't careful. You were right, but you could have ended up dead mixing it up with a man like Rex. Being right wouldn't have mattered."

Samuel shivered. He remembered the blinding rage that had overcome him. What Rex had done was pure wrong. But something nagged him, and he felt shame. He and Lilly had come mighty close. He tried to tell himself that it was okay. He had walked away from Lilly because of Bonnie, but that had made no sense. Despite what he told Bonnie about having time—that things could change—he knew it was not true. What would it have mattered between Lilly and him?

"I did get some good news," Charles said. "Finney and Culler are staying put until the judge gets here."

Samuel felt a weight lift. "What happened?"

"Alan Parsons and Brad Jessips got word they were in jail and identified them as the men they saw when their box was broken into on the Secesh."

"Did they catch them breaking in?" Samuel could already see a problem.

"Enough that the sheriff said they'd have to sit in jail until the judge gets it all sorted out. That didn't set too well with them. They wouldn't be in jail except for us, you realize."

That was exactly what Samuel was thinking.

"So we're staying at least for the hearing?"

"I reckon for the hearing."

Samuel nodded.

Charles glanced around. "Since I'm here, wouldn't mind taking a bath and having some chow myself."

"You'd best be careful. Ma Reynolds might insist on helping."

Charles laughed. "I take it she gave you a hand."

Samuel nodded. "I couldn't lift my arm very much."

"Well, it's instinctive for women, you know. She took care of you before. You mean a lot to her."

"I know, and I'm grateful, but I'm not a little boy anymore."

"No, I reckon you're not." His father grinned. "I admit, it sure will be good to get home. Not having the comfort of a woman can tear a man apart. We've been gone over a year now, son."

"I know." Samuel was not sure he wanted to hear what his father was confessing.

"Most of the men in this camp aren't married, and there aren't many prospects for them. They have nothing they can look forward to except some occasional comfort from a dancehall lady. But you do. You're young. You'll find another Bonnie."

"I sure hope so, Pa."

"But you gotta watch yourself, son. Blind anger can get you killed."

Samuel considered his father's words.

Art stuck his head in. "Looks like your pa found you okay."

"Yep. Thanks, Art. Thanks for everything. And when you get back, give my regards to everyone. Don't know if I can make it by to say good-bye. I'll try." Samuel knew he didn't want to ever be around Rex again. It was over now. It was Bonnie's choice.

His father declined to take a bath, but they had a meal together, and then he prepared to head back to the O'Riley.

"No sense in you coming out until tomorrow, son. I can finish drilling and set the charges. I doubt you can swing a hammer anyway."

"I can come with you. I feel okay."

"Well, you don't *look* okay. Get another night of rest. Maybe go by Alexander's and pick up some more grub. We'll probably be hauling ore for a few more days."

Samuel said farewell to his father. He didn't know if he had paid Ma Reynolds or not.

"I think I'll head to our cabin," he told her. He felt all right with the bandage tightly holding his ribs.

"Now, young'un, you should stay the night. I heard your pa talking with you."

"I'll be back later." Samuel wondered how much else she had heard.

He changed course and headed for Alexander's intending to get the grub his father wanted.

He saw Chen leading his mule, heading out on a sales trip. He tried to avoid him, but Chen spotted him and hollered a greeting. When he got close, Chen's dark eyes shot up.

Samuel knew his purple eye and cut nose had to be startling.

"Next time pick on someone your own size," Chen chided.

"Worst of it is, Chen, I didn't even get to land a punch."

"What is it all about?"

"A girl," Samuel sputtered. "And that's all I'll say about it."

"Romeo and Yuliet?" Chen grinned.

"No. Cain and Abel," Samuel snapped. "I said I wouldn't talk about it."

"Cain and Abow in Bible. They were brothers, not lovers."

Samuel threw up his hands. "You know what, Chen?" He stared at him. "You're getting too dang smart for your own good."

"I try." He smiled.

Chen talked to him about another selling trip. "Go in two days."

"Sorry, Chen, we're still trying to bring ore out of the O'Riley to get it milled. We might be finished later this week."

Chen shook his head. "Going to be a good one, Sam." He grinned. "Lots of vegebows. Make lots of money."

Samuel thought a moment. At best, the hearing would be early next month. He guessed they would need more money than what they would get from their ore, and now he had another doctor's bill to pay. "Maybe later."

"Sure, Sam."

Samuel was not certain he wanted to visit Scott.

"Howdy, Scott," Samuel said after he entered the store. Scott was in the back, pipe clenched in his teeth, studying a newspaper. No one else was in the store.

Scott glanced up and continued to stare. "What in blazes—"

"You mean this?" Samuel filled in the blanks. "You got to be the only one in town who didn't see me get laid out in the street last night."

"Sorry, I didn't know. You look like you been mule kicked and snake bit at the same time." He kept staring. "Hope the other guy looks as bad."

"Nope, I didn't even get to land a punch." Samuel shook his head. "Rather not talk about it today, Scott. Maybe when it quits snowing."

Instinctively, Scott glanced out the window—clear blue sky. "Okay, I guess we can talk about women in a moment."

"I'm done with them."

"I thought you said you didn't want to talk about it."

Samuel shoved his hands into his pockets. "I don't."

Silently, Scott smoked his pipe, letting out a long puff.

"I need to pick up some grub to last us a couple more days."

Samuel wandered about the store, picking up a few onions, some potatoes, some dried meat, and some dried fruit. "Do we still have credit?"

Scott still didn't say anything. He just tallied up the items and put the numbers into his ledger.

"How's the mining coming?" he asked.

"We're about done. We're running what we got at Bradshaw's mill in a couple days."

"That's good news."

Samuel was certain Scott was wondering if he would ever get paid.

"It can't be Miss Lilly—she's gone. Must be that gal at Slate Creek," Scott finally said.

"I said I wasn't talking about it."

Scott poured a cup of coffee. "Maybe you'd like something stronger?"

Samuel shook his head, but he soon found himself sitting on the stool, having a cup of coffee and talking about Bonnie with Scott listening.

Much later, not having any other answers, but feeling somewhat better, he returned to Ma Reynolds's. He slept less troubled than he had in weeks, although his ribs bothered him.

Chapter 40

SAMUEL FELT BETTER in the morning but looked worse. His bruises were darker purple, and his eye was still nearly swollen shut. The constriction bandage helped his ribs feel more normal.

After breakfast, he headed out toward the O'Riley, anxious to get back to work. He still might not be able to swing a hammer, but his father should be ready to blast. At least he could haul ore. They should be doing the test run today, and he wanted to see it.

He heard the explosions from down the valley before he reached the O'Riley.

"Sorry, son, I couldn't wait."

"I'm the one sorry, Pa. I like seeing stuff being blown up."

He jumped down into the pit to examine the exposed ore, feeling his side pain him when he did so. The vein was looking good.

It was now a good drop to the bottom. When they were finished mucking, it would be over eight feet deep. The vein showed strongly across the floor. Despite what O'Shaughnessy had said, it *was* getting wider and now measured fifteen inches across. Samuel washed it clean, exposing a stringer of gray metallic specks. If it carried gold, it would be even richer than the assays.

He began helping his father sack ore. An angry pain caused him to catch his breath, but he struggled on, reminding himself that he wouldn't worsen the injury. He tried to haul one of the bags but stopped short in agony. His father noticed and took over the loading.

"I'll keep mucking this until you get back. I might put in another couple charges to break out some more on the vein. Maybe you'll be back by then."

Samuel agreed. He could see that at this point, drilling into the vein and blasting might give them a few more pounds.

Samuel was near the steepest section of their trail when he spotted Rex's horse wandering, limping, on a narrow ridge across from the one he was descending. His stomach turned and he felt his blood begin to boil. He checked the load of his rifle and put it across his pommel.

"Maybe I'll be lucky and find someone dry-gulched the bastard," he muttered.

Gently, he turned Spooky toward the horse, wondering what it was doing here in the opposite direction of the trail to the Salmon. Maybe Rex had stupidly thought he could go down the South Fork to reach the Salmon, taking a roundabout way back to Slate Creek.

He reached the horse. It had been fresh ridden. Long gashes were raked across its rear flank. Samuel figured it must have been tree limbs. It was a good chance Rex had been knocked off somewhere.

"I hope he broke his neck," Samuel breathed.

Samuel began retracing the tracks. He reached the edge of the ridge and, from the marks in the soil, could see where the horse had struggled. It reminded him eerily of his encounter with the rattlesnake when he had been thrown and injured last year.

Though he felt Rex was near, he refrained from shouting. He left the packed animals and the trail and walked downward into the ravine. If Rex's horse had slid down here, it was miraculous it had lived. He spotted flecks of blood on a rock. *Could be the horse.* He expected to find Rex's body.

The man was an almost unrecognizable lump wedged against the trunk of several downed trees. He was awake, watching Samuel.

"You alive?" Samuel half expected him to pull his pistol and shoot him.

Blood stained the boulders where Rex lay, holding his knife.

At first Samuel thought he was going to use it on him when he drew near enough.

"Put it away, Rex, or I'll kill you." Samuel raised his rifle.

"N-no, Samuel. You gotta help me."

"Get me up close to where you can slit my throat?"

"I-I was fixin' to cut my leg free."

Samuel felt himself go weak, but he managed to keep his voice steady. "Good, I'll leave you be, and you can get back to work sawing on it."

Rex glared at him. "You bastard."

Samuel could now see the man's leg pinned under the log, the boulders firmly holding it in place. His hands were bloody from trying to wedge the boulders free.

"You gotta help me," he rasped.

Samuel could see where Rex had done some damage to his leg. It bled freely. Everything inside of him told Samuel to leave the man. If Rex bled to death, he would be deserving. Samuel stepped back.

"I'm fixin' on leaving you to die."

A frantic look flashed through Rex's eyes. He began cursing, spewing out filth about Samuel and Bonnie. Samuel plugged his ears; squeezed his eyes shut; felt his anger rising. He could not handle it. He fingered the rifle, cocked, and raised it.

Hate feelin's are the worse. He remembered his father's recent words.

"No," Rex pleaded. His face was white.

Samuel lowered the rifle, eased the hammer down. He grabbed Rex's knife, pulled it from his hand. The man blubbered. Quickly Samuel sliced through the man's trousers, cutting the cloth away, revealing the injury. It wasn't deep. Samuel slapped the cloth back onto it.

"Got to stop the bleeding," Samuel explained. "I ain't gonna let you die, no matter how much filth like you deserve it." He tied the cloth tightly in place, causing Rex to wince. "You ever cheat on Bonnie again, I'll pray to God he lets the devil take me to blazes for allowing you to live."

"I'll be owin' to you, Samuel," Rex kept sobbing.

"Be owing to Bonnie. She deserves a good man." Then Samuel could not help himself. "Others have said you could be a good man, Rex. I don't believe it myself, but they do. Be good to Bonnie." He found an ache in his throat.

He found a limb and wedged the boulders off the log pinning Rex. The man scrambled up. Samuel took his arm and managed to help him hobble back to the ridgeline where he had left the horses.

Samuel collapsed from the effort; the ache from the beating Rex had given him raked his body. His ribs throbbed in pain. He sat a moment, breathing hard. Rex had collapsed beside him.

"What ... can I ask, are you still doing here, Rex? You headed out a couple nights ago."

"Just wandering," he said quietly. "Thought maybe I could get out to the main Salmon this way."

"You can, but it'd take you a week longer."

"I found out." Shakily, he stood. "I got to get goin'."

"That doesn't make sense, you being out here."

"No, it don't." He limped to his horse and tried to mount. His foot slipped from the stirrup. Samuel stood and helped him.

Rex peered down at him. "You should know. I wasn't lookin' to goin' back after I laid you out. I knew Mr. Stromback wouldn't look too kindly on me. I knew he'd cut me loose."

Samuel had not thought of that. "You go back to the Strombacks', Rex. I'm leaving in a few days. I won't be seeing Bonnie, except maybe to say good-bye. At least own up to telling Mr. Stromback yourself." Samuel choked. "At least tell Bonnie."

Rex sat his horse, looking around. "Ain't you headin' back to Washington now?"

"No, I'm hauling ore to Bradshaw's mill." Samuel gestured at the packed animals. "Besides, I'm not up to ever riding with you again, Rex."

Rex glanced away.

"Think you can find your way back?" Samuel asked.

"Head up over the hill." Rex pointed to the timber-covered mountain above.

"Trail's off to your left." Samuel pointed.

Samuel watched as Rex disappeared into the timber, snapping branches and brush as he made his way back toward the ridgeline and the trail leading back to Washington.

I couldn't do it, Samuel thought. *If I ever had a right to take a man's life, that was it.* But he was thinking of Bonnie. He could not imagine meeting anyone finer than her. He had no right—he could not support her and start a family. It was just not his time. At least Rex would be there.

He gazed east. He thought of the Sheepeaters. Maybe theirs was a harsh life, but it seemed simpler. Gold did not mean anything to them. Even growing crops did not concern them. He thought of just forgetting about everything, just heading east—to see if he could find the Sheepeaters—not to even ask questions of them, but just to forget all he had been through.

This is crazy thinking, he told himself. He stumbled to his feet, mounted Spooky and began leading Buster and Molly back toward the trail to the Bradshaw.

Samuel heard the stamps from nearly half a mile away. *A good sound,* he told himself. They sounded steady. *Thump, thump, thump.* He imagined the five stamps rising and dropping, pulverizing the ore under them, turning it to powder, releasing the gold.

Stanton was cheering and shouting to O'Shaughnessy and Connolly, who stood on the catwalk, shoveling in pulverized ore.

Samuel greeted them. Everyone stared in return. Samuel was fully aware of what they were seeing. He briefly explained.

Connolly muttered, "I hope if ever you meet up with that cuss, you put lead in him. Not one of us would blame you if you did."

Samuel said nothing but began unloading his ore. O'Shaughnessy must have noticed him struggling. He lent a hand.

"Thanks," Samuel said. "Busted up my ribs pretty bad. It's hard for me to swing much weight."

"I find him," O'Shaughnessy said, "by me soul, he won't have anything left to swing."

Stanton came up. "Anyone tell you that you look like hell?"

"Just about everyone."

Stanton chuckled. "Well, the good news is my mill's running perfectly. At least it appears to be. We haven't checked recovery yet." He waved at the strong stream of muddy white water running from the mill into a secondary sluice.

Samuel watched the wheel turning under the weight of water coming from the flume. What a sight it was. What a marvel.

"I might need to adjust the table angle to get better flow."

"You gonna have enough time for that today?" Samuel asked worriedly.

"That's why I agreed to run your ore, Samuel. If we miss it on yours, we still got time to fix it for ours."

Samuel stood, dumbfounded.

Stanton laughed. "Just funning you, Samuel. It'll do just fine getting your gold. I swear, by gum. But I'm testing the outflow throughout the day just in case."

Samuel didn't think the joke was funny. The mill could very easily be off. If so, it would mean losing everything in their ore—everything they had worked night and day for during the last several weeks.

"Here, have a gander."

Samuel followed Stanton to where they could see the five-hundred-pound stamps, loudly pounding down.

"The wheel turns a camshaft with various spaced cams. As the shaft turns, a hook on each cam catches one of the stamps and lifts it," Stanton shouted, demonstrating with his hands. "When it turns over, it disengages and allows the stamp to fall. Anything under the stamp is pulverized."

Samuel watched the cams rapidly lifting the stamps, one after the other, allowing first one and then another to fall and then lifting them again.

"The cams are spaced differently so the stamps fall in a specified sequence. That allows the ore to be pulverized equally, and it prevents uneven wear on the shoes and dies—that's the plate under the shoe."

Stanton reached a large, inclined table that emerged from the bottom, a sheet of milky water flowed evenly over its surface. The noise was less.

"The pulverized ore is pushed out onto this table. Much like in a sluice, the gold and silver are trapped behind the cleats and amalgamated with quicksilver."

"So I won't be seeing any gold."

"No. You might see a line of very fine gold, but nearly all of it is being drawn into the quicksilver."

Samuel thanked Stanton. "We'll be bringing in our last load soon."

"We're ready to go tomorrow."

Samuel headed back toward the O'Riley. When he greeted his father, he didn't mention anything about Rex. He intended never to do so.

"Did they get the mill running okay?" Charles asked. "You must have been watching—you're running late."

"Yep, it seems to be going good. Stanton doesn't know how well it will recover gold yet."

"I'll assume it will, because our ore is going in," Charles said.

"I told him." Samuel inspected the remaining stack of ore. "Looks like we got a good amount."

"The good news is we got quite a bit more than I thought we would from the last round," Charles said. "The bad news is we might not be able to get it all hauled. Come on, I got two holes drilled."

Samuel was elated. He lit the fuses with his father and then got out of range. Watching the final two explosions—and imagining Rex going up in them—was the best feeling he had had in the last several days.

They quickly loaded nearly seven hundred pounds and headed toward the Bradshaw, reaching it well after dark. The mill was shut down. Stanton gave them a place to throw their gear and spread out their bedrolls.

The thumping stamps awakened Samuel.

"Guess that's our signal to get up," Charles muttered. "They're running our ore."

Finally. An odd elation washed Samuel.

"See if you can give them a hand here, son. I'll get the last of our ore before this is all run."

Samuel tried to get up. During the night he had become so stiff, he could hardly move. He groaned, bit his lip, and tried to stretch a little. Turning on his side, he pushed himself up and then stood.

His father watched. "Still hurts?"

Samuel nodded.

"I ever run into that bastard again, I'm going to put lead into him," Charles muttered.

Everyone but me is willing to put lead into Rex, Samuel thought.

They made up a quick breakfast. Charles headed back toward the O'Riley, and Samuel walked up the hill toward the mill. The thumping was almost more than Samuel could stand. He figured part of that was due to his head being pummeled by Rex.

O'Shaughnessy and Connolly were busting ore and shoveling it into the hoppers. *From the O'Riley,* he thought. *Our ore.* His heart quickened. A year ago he had found the ledge. It was finally happening.

"Well, the least you could do is give us a hand," Connolly said. "This is yours."

"I'll be happy to." Samuel scrambled to the pile. "Got another hammer?"

Connolly nodded toward one, and Samuel picked it up and began swinging. He stopped short. The pain wracked his side.

O'Shaughnessy noticed. "Maybe ye can help shovel." He swung another shovelful of broken ore into the hopper, which angled down to feed into the bins behind the stamps. An opening near the bottom of the chute allowed a few fragments at a time to fall under the stamps.

Samuel shoveled some crushed ore into the hopper, grimacing.

Stanton came up to see Samuel. "You don't need to be doing anything, son. You and your pa are paying me a percentage to do this."

"I don't like standing around."

Stanton laughed. "I've noticed that about you, Samuel, and about your father as well."

"How was your recovery yesterday?" Samuel asked.

"For the ore we ran, it seemed to be very good. Mostly I was just making sure everything worked, and it does." He nodded and headed back down to watch the table.

Samuel pitched in again, despite what Stanton had said, and resumed shoveling some of their ore. "So whose ore looked better," he asked Connolly, "yours from yesterday or ours?"

"To me, it all looks the same," he replied. "It's just rocks—big rocks that need to be made into little rocks."

At length, Samuel spotted his father coming up the hill, leading Spooky and Molly, the animals heavily packed with ore.

"I almost overdid it," Charles said. "I didn't want to make another trip."

"Do you think we have six tons?"

"Well over six. That should make Mr. Stanton happy."

Samuel did a quick calculation. If the ore went three ounces a ton, they would have close to four hundred dollars—a decent amount.

Charles was soon at work with O'Shaughnessy and Connolly, cobbing and feeding the pulverized ore into the hopper. Stanton stood below, gauged how the stamps were doing, and directed the flow. He explained that it was important to have an even feed and not to allow any one stamp to hang up.

The men cobbed and shoveled, occasionally taking a break for water but nothing else.

A slurry of whitish mud washed over the copper plates below.

Stanton addressed Samuel. "This is probably the most efficiently it will be run all season. You sure you don't want to hire on and help keep this thing running?"

Samuel shook his head. "You sure it's working?"

Stanton ran his hands across the table. "The quicksilver seems a little frothy, so it's definitely picking up some gold."

Small particles that were trapped in the mercury and behind the cleats created small riffles in the smooth water. Samuel hoped it was all gold.

Toward evening, they had run their ore. Stanton rerouted the water, and the stamps went silent. Samuel returned to the table, where he could watch Stanton do the cleanup.

"You can give me a hand if you like." Stanton took some paddles and scrapped the slurry and amalgam off the copper plate. He placed it into some cloth and squeezed out some of the mercury. "That's the stuff that did not amalgamate."

Samuel was surprised by the amount. "Did we get *anything*?"

Stanton laughed. "Oh, there is definitely some gold." He hefted the cloth.

"You can help me collect the material from around the stamps." He used the paddles and scrapped more slurry down across the table into a pan. Samuel worked around another stamp, doing the same.

"Most of this is just rock dust," Stanton said. "But I don't think you'll mind panning it down with me in case there are some large particles of gold."

"That means I get to help work it down?"

"Yep." Stanton handed Samuel a pan. They took the fines to a couple of large tubs and began working them down with some mercury, much like the black sand Samuel had worked from before.

"I can retort the amalgam tomorrow and run it through the furnace. We can also separate out your silver—the only mill in the district that can do that." Stanton smiled. "You and your pa can drop by in the afternoon. We should have everything by then. You'll know how you did."

Samuel and his father collected their gear and headed toward their cabin, leading Molly.

"It's hard to believe we're done, Pa," Samuel said. He rubbed his arms. "I think I was actually building some muscle. Doc Sears thought so."

"No question." Charles eyed him. He clucked to Buster. "Maybe we can get a good yield and pay our debts and have enough proof to sell this mine."

"Have you heard any news about Mr. Williams?" Samuel had not. He was beginning to believe the man had backed out.

"Nope." Charles pulled his hat down more tightly. "Guess we just got to keep advertising."

Chapter 41

LATER, SAMUEL AND HIS FATHER returned to the O'Riley and tore down their camp. They gathered up the drill steel and hammers and packed up the remaining dynamite. It occurred to Samuel that they were really done. He gazed at the pit where they had labored so hard, still not sure if it was worth it or not. His post with O'Riley Lode written on it still stood near the pit. He wondered if this was the last time he would ever set foot here. He felt numb. He had invested so much of himself—sweat and blood—that it hardly seemed possible. He had found it and mined it. It had become part of him.

They returned to Bradshaw's mill, anxious for the news.

Stanton handed them a sheet of paper. "Not a bad yield, I think," he said.

But Samuel was not talking, nor was his father; instead they were staring at the numbers: "Processed ore, 12,700 pounds. Silver yield, 26.8 ounces. Gold yield, 12.6 ounces."

The yield should have been closer to forty ounces of silver and eighteen ounces of gold. The assays had been nearly seven ounces of silver and three ounces of gold per ton.

"You look like you've seen a ghost, Samuel," Stanton finally said.

Samuel explained the assays.

"You realize that even the best mill is not going to get over 70 percent recovery? The dry stamps won't even get fifty. This is now the best mill in the district."

"I figured as much," Charles said, handing back the paper. "Both Samuel and I were hoping."

"Look, being it's our first run, I can give you two hundred sixty dollars, if that will help."

Charles agreed and Stanton paid them.

"Spread the word for us," Charles said. "We need to sell the O'Riley. I'd settle for five hundred dollars."

Samuel stomach tightened. In a month, they could produce that much. They would be selling the mine for a fraction of its value.

"Actually, son, we didn't come away that bad."

"It wasn't that bad if you don't count my work last season and everything it took to get to this point," Samuel said quietly, bitterly.

"Maybe so, but I like to look at it this way. No one was paying us a wage. We created real money that anyone anywhere in the world can spend."

Samuel considered his father's words. They had created *real money*. And there was more in the ground. He just wished it would be him taking it out.

They could do nothing more but wait. The hearing might be late next week, assuming the judge arrived by then.

They returned what steel they could to Faust and paid him the difference for sharpening it.

"The mine has good potential," Charles told him. "The vein is strong and seems to be getting stronger."

"I'll keep my eyes open, if someone expresses interest," Faust said. "What I'm doing now seems a lot more dependable."

Samuel visited Dr. Sears. After the first couple of days of leaving the bandages tightly binding his ribs, they had come loose. He had grown accustomed to removing them and then replacing them, tightening them again for support.

"Guess my ribs weren't busted."

"Probably were, Samuel." He massaged Samuel's ribs and checked his jaw and eye. "Good to see your eye looks okay. The bruising is nearly gone."

He poked him some more. "Ah, to be young again. You youngsters heal up mighty fast."

"Thanks, Dr. Sears." Samuel jumped off the table, pulled his shirt back on, and refitted his suspenders.

At Scott Alexander's they asked to settle their bill. Scott showed the numbers to his father. His father nodded, and Scott measured out some of the gold, returning some. At first Samuel thought they had made money, but Scott had simply returned some spending money. They still had an unpaid balance.

"I have some things you can deliver if you wish, Sam," Scott suggested.

"Thank you. Pa and I have some settling up to do at the claim, but I'll be glad to do some packing."

They rode in silence back to the cabin. Samuel walked to the Sweet Mary. The catch basin was nearly dry.

He helped fix some dinner.

"The O'Riley's a good mine, son," Charles said. "It's got a lot of gold."

"I know, but like so many have said, it may cost as much to get it out as what's in it."

Charles shook his head. "Not with a good crew, a good mining engineer, and some serious work. It could make someone a good living."

Samuel felt comforted by his father's assessment.

"I regret to say it, son. We still have some debts to pay. We have nothing to go home on."

Samuel had figured as much. Together they had spent over a year nearly killing themselves or getting killed, chasing one dream after another, and still had nothing to show for it.

"It's okay, Pa. Like you always said, we can make it without the money. It sure would have been nice for once to try making it with some."

"I don't regret trying," Charles said. "I don't regret bringing you out here anymore, either. We did our best. You've learned a lot. To blazes, like Mr. Hinley says, you're the only man he knows who made three strikes in a season."

Charles spread his hands and glanced down the meadow before continuing.

"I reckon I got to admit this: I figure you're your own man now. I know Bonnie might be spoke for, although if I find that Rex bastard she'll be in need of another man, but you haven't said anything lately about Miss Lilly."

Samuel could not speak. He knew the implications of what his father said. Slowly, he shook his head. "I said good-bye to Miss Lilly a few days ago, Pa, before I ran into Rex. She's left Washington and gone to Lewiston. But I never forgot what you told me." Samuel smiled. "Can't say I wasn't mighty tempted, but the cart's still where it belongs."

His father laughed. "Not entirely what I was getting at, but it's good to hear you say that." He studied his son. "I believe Miss Lilly is a good person. You aren't the same youngster you were a summer ago, that's all."

"Thank you." Samuel studied his father. "I'm still going home, Pa. We have a future ahead of us in Iowa. Ma needs us."

"Thank you, son," Charles said quietly, handing him a plate of venison and potatoes.

Inexplicably, Samuel remembered the quartz ledge where he had found the grave and met the Sheepeater Indians.

"Pa, we didn't get back to the ledge across the South Fork. You think we should? Maybe we should stake it and sell it?"

"No time for that now. Something I've learned since coming into this country—for every rainbow you chase down, there's two more springing up somewhere else. The harder and faster I've worked to pin them down, the harder and faster the others spring up. I reckon I know when I'm done. Most important now is our family. Best we just stay here and get this hearing over and head out."

Samuel nodded. "I just owed it to you to say it again. I'm ready to head out as well." But deep down, Samuel was not. He would always wonder what was beyond the next ridge—what the next ledge looked like. He ached to know what was beyond the South Fork. He wondered about the Sheepeaters.

He took the arrow down from the wall and fingered its tip. "I'll always wonder why the man gave this to me."

"Perhaps he thought someone would recognize it. The Indians paint their arrows differently so they know whose arrow made the kill."

Samuel nearly dropped the arrow. His father was right. It could have been meant as a message to the boy's father or to someone who knew something about the grave. He swallowed hard. If only he had shown the arrow to others, perhaps someone would have recognized it.

"He kept repeating *'Dugumbaa'naa Buih-nee'* and pointing at my eyes. Maybe the boy's father had blue eyes like mine. He would have recognized the arrow."

Charles shook his head. "Another mystery, Samuel." He laughed. "Another one I'll have to add to my list to ask the Lord when I get there. You can too."

Samuel held the arrow up, further eyeing it and thinking about its mystery.

Charles watched. "Won't be likely we'll ever be back here, son. We might as well take a gander," he said quietly. "How about we head out tomorrow? Won't have the hearing for a while. Maybe Mr. Williams will show when we get back."

"You sure?" His father had just talked about chasing useless rainbows and never-to-be-solved mysteries. Samuel felt strangely elated and somewhat scared. He wondered what he would find going back to the grave. Could he walk away from the gold again?

"When we get back, I might rustle up a few days of work somewhere," Charles said. "Think you can do some packing?"

"Mr. Alexander has already asked me."

"Good, that should give us enough traveling money."

STORY OF THE GRAVE

Chapter 42

EARLY MORNING SAW them on the trail moving past the Chinese huts, heading toward the summit above Warren's. By late afternoon, they reached the South Fork, wide and placid, reflecting green from the trees along the shores, sparkling where the sun caught the ripples. They forded the river, picking their way across the scrubbed gravel bottom. Several large salmon scooted past, moving upstream.

Climbing the far shore, Samuel took the lead, riding upstream and then turning up along the East Fork, where he located the old trail, appearing much as before, only fainter.

They soon reached the Sheepeater camp. It also appeared much as before, although the poles on the shelters were more barren, and the brush and few hides had further deteriorated. The shelters were but shadowy skeletons among the cottonwoods.

"I can see why they call them the ghost Indians," Charles said. "Doesn't appear to me they've been here for quite some time."

"Could be they know there are settlers downriver from here and are avoiding them."

Samuel located the dim trail upstream of the old shelters and found where it traversed up out of the canyon. Almost invisible in places, he gave up trying to follow it and headed toward the head of the gorge, where he remembered the saddle to be. Occasionally he found he was on the trail, and then it again disappeared.

"Unless you know where you're going in this country, Samuel, I'm pretty sure no one is going to find this spot. Certainly not by following this trail."

"Hasn't been much used." Samuel paused to look back. "It has to come out near the saddle, though." He pointed upward.

They climbed to a small bowl just below the saddle. A trickle of water emerged from beneath a boulder field and ran across before disappearing into the gorge beyond.

"This is where I camped last year," Samuel said, pulling up and dismounting. "Above here there's no water until you cross over and drop down into the lake."

They stripped the gear from the animals and hobbled them. The country to the west appeared as beautiful as Samuel remembered. The summit above Warren's camp was blocked from sight—they were too far east—but he recognized the other ridges piled one upon the other, receding into the purple shadows that marked the South Fork canyon.

Samuel built a fire against the evening chill and began frying up some venison with some salt pork for fat. The sun shone yellow orange on the rocks above, reminding him of the time he first saw this country. On that trip, he believed he had been the first white man to ever set foot here—until he found the grave.

They woke to a morning chill. The rising sun lit the western ridges in brilliant light. Charles fixed some breakfast. Samuel quickly rose, dressed, and stooped to help him.

"Coffee?" Charles poured a cup.

Samuel held it to his face, allowing the steam to bathe him in its warmth before taking a sip.

"Mighty fine, Pa. Thanks."

"You get to do tonight's meal."

"A deal."

When they returned to the trail, Samuel had even more difficulty following it. He remembered it had traversed up the grassy slope above the basin, but he could no longer see any trace. He led out and began a long traverse the horses and mule could manage. Shortly, he rediscovered the trail. Without use, the lengthening grass and brush had hidden it.

They reached the saddle, and as before, Samuel paused, taking in the splendor. "What do you think of *this* view, Pa?"

They sat a moment. In every direction, gray crags rose, etched in the morning light, some carpeted in thick timber, others jagged—rocky pinnacles, ragged fingers jutting into the pale blue sky. A breeze kicked across the saddle, rippling the late-July grass, causing Samuel to pull his coat more tightly around himself against the mountain chill.

"This land could grow on a man," his father replied. "Too bad you can't farm it."

Samuel shrugged. His father was right. This country was too high for farming or grazing. For sure, no one would ever build a cabin here.

He studied the ridges fading into the distance and dropping into the shadows of a myriad of canyons. Somewhere beyond lived the Indians called the Sheepeaters.

He headed in the direction of the ledge and soon came out where they could look down on the shallow lake. Several cow elk stood near the outlet, watching them as they came into view. The elk turned quickly, their hooves thudding in the damp soil as they strode up over a grassy knoll into thick timber beyond.

"Good game country," his father remarked.

"I got a ptarmigan down near the lake last time," Samuel said. "No fish, though. I'm pretty sure it freezes to the bottom during winter."

They dropped down into the lake and skirted the shore toward the rock outcrops at its head. Samuel's heart quickened as he recalled the details, everything familiar once more. He recognized the quartz veins and spotted the rust marks left on them by the oxidizing minerals.

He turned Spooky up along the flank and crossed the ridge into the next basin. Now his heart raced. He could not help but recall the Sheepeater father and his son. He glanced toward the trees, half expecting to see them. A chill raced down his back.

He reached the rock outcrop and remembered the broken white quartz, some pieces stained red and yellow.

"That's the pile of ore, Pa." He pointed to the mound, partially overgrown by grass. "You can see where they worked the face."

"I can. They worked at it quite a while. It goes in a ways."

"Wait until you see the gold." Samuel felt his voice getting away from him as he dismounted. Until he saw gold in the rocks again, he had a scary feeling that all of this would turn out to be a dream that over time had become bigger than the truth. It had been almost a year since he had been here. He grabbed a chunk of quartz and studied it closely. *Nothing.* Feeling a slight panic, he examined another piece. Specks of bright yellow shone among spots of blackened silver. "Here, Pa." He tossed the piece to his father.

"This *is* rich," Charles muttered. He glanced at the outcrop and then peered back the direction from which they had come. "I can see it would be difficult developing this. Probably the best a man could do would be to come in here and mine for a while and then pack it out to Warren's by mule train."

Samuel felt torn. He wanted gold but not from here. Here, he felt unwelcome.

"Come on, Pa," he said. "I'll show you the grave."

He led his father up onto the bench and showed him the rusted pick and shovel and the fire ring. He pointed out the grave, exactly as he remembered it, a crude pile of stones and a weathered piece of wood that at one time must have been a cross.

"The man had to have been buried by whites. Indians don't bury their dead," Samuel said.

His father picked up the piece of wood that had been the crossbar and examined it. "Too bad they didn't carve in the person's name." He retrieved a short length of rope from his pack, laid open a few strands, and refit the cross member, once more forming a cross. "Might last another year or two."

Samuel wondered why last year it had not occurred to him to do the same when he had discovered the grave, but he recalled that was also when he had spotted the Sheepeater man and boy. He glanced toward the spot under the tree. An eerie feeling returned. Only the empty alpine hillside, wind whispering through the grass, answered his gaze.

"So where'd you meet the Indians?"

"They were under that tree over there when I first saw them." Samuel pointed. "I was scared at first, but then realized they must have been watching me for a while. The man had a really strong-looking horn bow, but he didn't have an arrow ready. I also noticed he wore a white man's knife. He could have killed me had he wanted. Instead, he just stood up and raised his hand.

"He kept motioning at me and saying, *'Dugumbaa'naa Buih-nee.'* Something like that. I pointed at myself and told him my name. I'm pretty sure he told me his and the boy's names, but I don't remember them now. I remember *'Dugumbaa'naa Buih-nee'* because he said it so often. I figured the boy was six or seven, and I'm pretty sure he was part white."

"A half-breed?"

Samuel nodded. "I gave them some of the ptarmigan I shot, and that's when the man gave me the arrow. He also looked at my eyes really close, maybe because they're blue and Indians' eyes aren't. He kept pointing to the sky and repeating *'Dugumbaa'naa Buih-nee'* and pointing at the boy. That's when I realized the boy was part white. Maybe it's his father who's buried here." Samuel waved toward the grave.

"Anyway, the Indian pointed toward the canyon and beckoned me, wanting me to follow. I guessed that's where they live. Maybe he was telling me to go away. Maybe he gave me the arrow to tell me to go away."

"Pretty mysterious country, this is," Charles said.

"I didn't say anything to anyone—except to you. Of course, Mr. Hinley knows about the gold, but he has no idea where I found it."

"Probably a good idea not to say anything. Even if we can't develop this property, a person could probably work out several tons of good ore and pack it out of here." Charles shook his head. "It's ironic we spend over a year in this country, and the day we decide to leave, we find a good-paying mine."

"I'm sorry."

His father laughed. "I could have checked it out as soon as we got back after you had told me. I just figured the O'Riley was a better bet, being close in and all. Never know how things for sure will turn out."

Samuel was silent.

"Time to head home, son. We've been gone too long. At least in Iowa we can eat what we grow. Funny what life can send your direction. Come on, let's load some of this ore."

They packed the bags and loaded about three hundred pounds onto Molly. They strapped an additional hundred pounds onto both Spooky and Buster and turned back toward the ridge they had come down. Gaining the summit, they paused a moment, looking back toward the hidden ledge.

Samuel took in the view, studying the crags and the heavy timber; he noticed movement near some trees by the head of a gulch.

"Someone's there, Pa." He pointed. Already he knew it was an Indian. His heart quickened. He thought it was the man and boy again.

A man had emerged from the timber, leading a heavily packed pony.

"Let's visit." Charles turned down the ridge toward the Indian.

Samuel had no choice but to follow. "What if he has a gun?"

"Look at his pack. He's a trader, Samuel."

Charles rode down toward him, raising his hand, and greeted him.

The man waited patiently, watching, and raised his hand in reply. He appeared elderly. Dressed in a fringed buckskin shirt with breechcloth and leggings, his nearly white braided hair fell to both sides of his shoulders. A lock of hair in the middle of his forehead was chopped short. His deep-set eyes held steady; wrinkles of age deeply creased his face. He closely studied Samuel, making him feel uneasy.

"Trade?" his father asked.

The man nodded and walked back along Molly, patting the bags, a puzzled look on his face.

Charles dismounted. "Here," he said, pulling out his tobacco pouch and pipe, motioning to the Indian. "Fetch the cups and the coffee, Samuel. We can trade those."

The man's eyes lit up. He began pulling apart his wares and spread them on the ground.

Charles opened his tobacco pouch, prepared, and lit his pipe, and offered it to the Indian. The Indian took it and smoked it, grinning. Samuel noticed he was minus a few teeth.

"My name is Chambers." Charles pointed to himself and then to Samuel. "This is my son, Samuel."

The man seemed to understand. "Broken Blade." He tapped his chest.

Samuel froze. Incredibly, the man understood and spoke some English.

Charles spread his hands. "Do you know of the people who live here?"

Broken Blade nodded and grunted. "Tukudeka live here. For many seasons the Tukudeka and I trade." He continued to study Samuel, making Samuel feel more and more uneasy until at last Broken Blade spoke. "I know of you." He pointed a slender finger toward Samuel.

Samuel felt shivers up his spine. "How?"

"White Eagle tells of white boy with eyes of sky he sees. You have eyes of sky."

Samuel nodded. "Yes, I was at the grave."

"Bad place." Broken Blade shook his head. "Evil men kill man who digs in dirt."

This Indian knew of the grave. Samuel felt stunned. He knew of the Sheepeaters he had met.

Broken Blade inhaled deeply from the pipe. "White Eagle sees you. At first he is afraid. He thinks you are ghost of his brother. But then he sees you are like the man who digs in the dirt and comes to talk to you."

Samuel nodded. "He had a boy with him."

"He is Laughing Boy, son of the man who brings life. I know the man who brings life when he was still Sky Eyes. It is said he saved his brother's life and killed the evil men who killed the man who digs in the dirt. All Tukudeka speak of him. Some of his spirit is painted on the memory rock."

"Man who brings life?" Samuel asked, confused.

"We no longer say his name. Spirits will confuse him as he walks the sky stairs."

"He is dead?"

"He does not return to the people. He must be dead," the old man continued. "We trade when he is Sky Eyes. Man who brings life is brother to White Eagle. You remind White Eagle of his brother when he was Sky Eyes."

Samuel tried to make sense of what the old Indian said. He knew he reminded the man of someone else—someone whom he had known when he was Samuel's age.

The old Indian turned toward Charles. "You are not the man who brings life. When I see you, at first I think you are."

Charles shook his head.

"White Eagle asks always of me to watch for his brother when I return to my own people and when I trade. He will be pleased when I tell him I have seen you." He looked at Charles. "His heart will hurt because you are not his brother." He pointed toward the canyon. "You should come to visit."

Samuel glanced at his father, but already his father shook his head. "Much obliged, Broken Blade, but we are several moons away from our own home."

The old man nodded. "Then you will not come to the place where man digs in the dirt? That is good for the Tukudeka if you do not come. The white men bring good things, but soon the shaggy necks and the curved-horns will go away if the white man comes here." He stood and returned Charles's pipe. "Good tobacco. Now we trade."

Charles traded the coffee cups for a fox fur. Broken Blade tried to give him several, but Charles refused.

When they parted, Charles also gave him his remaining tobacco. Broken Blade smiled. "Very good tobacco."

They packed and rode to the ridgeline before glancing back. Broken Blade had not moved.

"A miracle they can live in this country without crops," Charles observed. "I can see why you weren't anxious to tell anyone. These people wouldn't stand a chance."

"It didn't feel right, Pa."

Charles nodded. "I see no difference if we try to sell the ledge to anyone or not," he said. "If we decide to, we'd need to properly stake it and record it. Once we do that, there will be a flood of prospectors into this country. They might come anyhow, but that ledge is tucked away. I'm still not sure how you spotted it."

"I saw the rocks from the ridge and thought they looked like those near Warren's camp. I got lucky."

"It's your ledge, Samuel. If it was proved up, it could be worth a lot of money. As is you could probably get a couple hundred dollars," he said. "Money or not, I'm inclined to leave it."

"Then what are we hauling this ore out for?"

"Might as well. Someone will give us something for it." Charles laughed. "Home is a long ways away yet."

"I reckon so." Samuel was torn. He knew the gold would pay for good land and a new home. Yet he didn't want to disturb these people, and now he wanted to visit the man called White Eagle—to ask him about his son and his brother.

CHINESE GOLD

Chapter 43

Upon their return, they said nothing about the ledge.

"If we were staying around, it might be a different story," Charles said.

When they dropped by Alexander's Mercantile, Scott asked about the placer.

"I guess that's yours. You put us on it last summer," Charles said.

Scott pushed at his moustache and chuckled. "I'll be fair about it. I don't intend to mine it. You two showed there's some gold there, but not much. If I sell it, I'll send you something."

"We're going to be around for a few days for the hearing and try to get some traveling money. Maybe we'll get lucky and Mr. Williams will show up, or someone else will, and buy it."

"Maybe. People are always showing up," Scott said. "By the way, I hear one of the attorneys in the Rescue case just showed up. He came in over the Payette River trail. He could not say enough about that country. Said the grass for grazing in the long valley south of the big lake is unmatched with anywhere he's been. He can't figure why we aren't trying to put a wagon road through there all the way to Fort Boise."

Something tugged at Samuel. He wondered about the untouched land to the south.

"He's trying to recruit support for it. It would help unite north and south Idaho Territory, ensuring it would become a state and not fragment and become part of Washington or Oregon Territories. I'm inclined to agree. We don't stand much of a chance making this district viable unless we can get a good wagon road for bringing in heavy machinery and developing some of the mines."

Like the O'Riley, Samuel thought.

Charles nodded. "How's the elevation? Does it get a lot of snow in the winter, or could someone farm it?"

"About the same as here, I expect. Not as high, but plenty of snow."

"Then it might not be any better than the Salmon River route."

"We have to do something, Charles, or there won't be a future here."

"I 'spect so," Charles said. "Any word on when the judge is supposed to arrive?"

"As far as anyone knows, he's still en route. Court is still scheduled for next week."

Samuel felt a jolt, thinking about facing Finney and Culler.

"In the meanwhile, I'll pack supplies for you, if you need, Scott," Samuel said.

His father shot him a look and Samuel shrugged. "Mr. Alexander says for me to call him Scott."

"Hell, Charles," Scott replied, "he's twice the man most of them around here are."

Charles nodded. "I won't argue."

Samuel left to find Chen. He was at his uncle's store.

"I'm going on a sales trip tomorrow. Want to come?"

Chen grinned. "Like old times, Sam. I meet you in morning."

That night, Samuel began breaking down the Sheepeater ore.

"I thought you had enough of swinging a hammer," Charles observed.

"I got to see what's in these rocks, Pa." He took another swing. There was something about breaking rocks and looking for gold that he couldn't resist.

The next morning, Charles packed his gear for McLane's placer. "Don't expect me back until the end of the week."

Samuel understood. "I'll try to get in a couple trips packing and selling."

"If something comes up and the judge gets here early, you'll know where to find me."

Samuel met up with Chen. He had packed Molly with the items Scott wanted delivered. He moved some of Chen's vegetables onto Molly.

"That will give you more room for riding."

Chen thanked him. They headed toward some of the Secesh placers.

"Maybe we find a new gold claim," Chen mentioned.

"I'll always be looking. That's for sure."

"Maybe you stay around if you find one."

Samuel wanted to tell him he had found one, but that it didn't matter.

After they returned and Samuel returned the unsold items to Scott, he visited with Chen and Sing Mann for a while, doing some writing with Chen.

"I think you're as good as anyone," Samuel remarked, after they had written for a while.

"You teach well, Sam. Thank you." He put away the papers. "So long, Sam. I go to Sang Yune's tonight for more vegetables."

"It's late."

"Old mule know the way now."

After Chen left, Samuel returned to his cabin and resumed pulverizing the Sheepeater ore. He figured he could wash it down and take what he found to Mr. Hinley and refine it. Maybe he would get an ounce.

Samuel dropped by Scott's in the early morning to pick up supplies for a delivery to Houston Creek. As usual he asked if there was any word on Williams.

"Nothing on Williams. I think he musta found something in Florence."

Samuel shook his head, disappointed. He still clung to hope for selling the mine before they left.

He rode out to McLane's placer and visited briefly with his father, relaying the word about Williams before continuing toward Houston Creek. Late afternoon he returned through McLane's placer.

"I'm going to be working through Sunday," Charles informed him. "As you know, Mr. McLane needs a watchman. You can keep me company if you want."

"I might do that unless I can do some more packing. I'm packing everything and anything I can right now for Scott."

"Good, maybe we'll have him paid off." Charles adjusted his hat. "Sheriff sent word out that the judge is here. He'll start the hearing for sure on Tuesday."

"Let's meet up Monday night, then," Samuel said.

"Monday night," Charles said. "Good luck with packing."

Reaching Warren's, Samuel noticed that the Chinese pack train was at the other end of town unloading. Chinese were milling about the street carrying items into the stores, including Sing Mann's. Samuel thought he caught sight of Chen.

He carried some remaining stock into Alexander's and placed it on the counter.

Scott greeted him. "That's all that's left?"

"Yep."

Scott seemed pleased as he began checking items in his ledger.

"I see the Chinese pack train is back," Samuel observed.

"One comes in now pert near every week." Scott appeared uninterested and kept making notes. "More and more Chinamen to outfit and feed, I guess." Scott peered at Samuel. "You're doing good, Sam."

Samuel didn't ask if they had finished paying their bill, but Scott surprised him when he tossed him a silver dollar.

"You could probably use some spending money," he said.

"I don't know what for," Samuel said. "You sell everything we need right here."

"I thought maybe if you head out to Burgdorf's you might want a swim and a meal."

"That mean you have some things for me to deliver out there?"

"More like I have something for you to pick up. Give Mr. Burgdorf this." Scott handed him a sealed envelope. "But I also want you to go up Grouse Creek and take this." He indicated a pile of goods. "See me in the morning for the fresh goods."

Samuel packed the items into Molly's packs and left Alexander's. He wondered if Chen would want to go. He noted that the Chinese had finished unpacking and were moving the mules out of the street. Sing Mann bowed politely when Samuel entered the store. Three other Chinese were present, having a rather animated discussion, but they quieted when they saw him enter. Chen was toward the rear and appeared to be packing for another sales trip. Samuel wondered why he had not said anything about it to him yet.

"You are going tomorrow, Chen. Where?"

He shrugged. "I still have to talk to Mann."

Mann and the other Chinese were watching. Chen glanced at them and then glanced uneasily at Samuel as if he wanted to say something more.

"Come out and look at what I got, Chen." Samuel motioned for him to leave the store. The others continued watching. Samuel walked to Molly's pack and pretended to be showing Chen something.

"I'm going over toward Burgdorf's. We can both go that direction."

"Okay," Chen said. "See you in morning. Now you go." He glanced back toward the store.

Samuel whispered, "What's going on?"

"They argue about when it is safe to take out gold."

"Is there a problem?"

"They see men who hold up the pack train last fall."

Dudgin and Smith. The thought rocked Samuel. It could not be Finney and Culler this time. They were in jail. "You need to tell the sheriff."

Chen gave a blank stare, and Samuel immediately realized that his comment made no sense. The Chinese would never involve the sheriff.

"Where did they see them?"

"Where you are going. Over to Burgdorf place."

Samuel shook his head. "I wouldn't worry, Chen."

"No, Chinese do not worry. This time, they take plenty of Chinese with pack string when it takes gold." He laughed.

"Tomorrow?"

Chen shrugged. "Don't know. No one knows."

Samuel was torn about telling his father. If it was Dudgin and Smith, they might try to stop the Chinese pack train but probably would not care about him or his father. Likely, they didn't know they were still here. Nevertheless, tomorrow he would ride out to see his father before heading toward Burgdorf's with Chen.

Chapter 44

SAMUEL WOKE BEFORE daylight in a sweat. He had figured out what was going on. He scrambled from his bed and quickly packed his bedroll. He grabbed what food he could and all the spare ammunition for the pistol. He wanted to travel light but took a few of Scott Alexander's items—tobacco, socks, gloves, and several lengths of rope.

After writing a note for his father, he stepped out. The morning was cool, and dew drenched the grass. He caught up Spooky. Molly grazed contentedly. *She should be all right,* he reasoned. Besides, his father would be back Monday night at the latest as they had agreed.

He rode through Washington and checked to see if Chen was at Sing Mann's. He knew he wouldn't be. Sing Mann tried to explain. "He go to sell."

"He was going to go with me."

Sing Mann shrugged and spoke rapidly in Cantonese, avoiding any English. Samuel figured he did not want to explain anything further.

"Thank you, Mann." He left, trotting Spooky back along the trail, intending to head toward Burgdorf's. Scott was not at his mercantile, but that didn't matter. Samuel didn't intend to make any deliveries. He hoped Scott would understand. The Chinese pack string was picketed in the meadow. Samuel prayed he wouldn't run into Quinton Dudgin and Ramey Smith, at least not until after he had found Chen.

About a mile out of Washington, he caught up to Chen. Chen tried to pull the mule off the trail, but Samuel spotted him.

"What's up, Chen?" Samuel asked. "You didn't wait for me."

Chen looked at him, dark eyes widening, a frightened look on his face. "You go back, Sam. You go back. I go to sell by myself."

Chen's mule was packed with a few vegetables but not the usual amount, and they appeared wilted.

"You aren't going to sell those miserable vegetables to anybody," Samuel said.

Chen stopped. "Yes, I am, Sam." He tried to smile. "These are very good vegetables."

"Then I'm going with you to see how you do it. I don't believe you."

"No. Don't go, Sam. Please."

Chen's desperate look unsettled Samuel.

"Look, Chen," Samuel whispered. "I wasn't born yesterday. I know you're packing the gold. You're taking it out, if not all of it, most of it."

Chen stared at him, eyes big. He started to shake his head. "Please, Sam—"

"Don't worry Chen. I ain't telling anyone. Besides, there's no one around *to* tell." Samuel glanced around, hoping he was still correct. The sun touched the tops of the far trees. "And I'm going with you. Don't know where, just yet, but I figure if you're taking it out, I'm going as well, and there ain't anything you can say about it."

The desperation in Chen's eyes softened. "We can't be seen, Sam. No one. Not even by friends. We have to go to Lewiston."

"Lewiston!" Samuel exclaimed and whistled softly. "That's gotta be a hundred sixty miles at least."

"Ten days," Chen nodded. "I have food. Do you?"

"Nah, I'll just eat some of those ratty vegetables, if you don't mind."

Chen appeared surprised. "Those are for sale." He tried to smile.

Samuel grinned. "Don't worry, I have some grub." He turned back toward the trail. "I can pack some of the *heavy vegetables,* if you want. We can make better time."

Chen shook his head. Samuel didn't press it.

They rode cautiously, both watching and listening for approaching horses or people. Despite their care, they came into sight of a lone rider on a sorrel horse off the side of the trail. The man saw them and waved.

Samuel approached slowly. "Let me do the talking."

"You always do," Chen replied quietly.

"Do not look, but there are two riders up in the trees." Samuel's heart began to race.

Chen fixed his eyes ahead.

Samuel recognized the small man. "It's Ben Morton." He noticed that he packed a rifle.

"I know," Chen replied. "He does not like Chinese."

"Howdy, Mr. Morton," Samuel called. "Everything okay?"

"Well now, what we got here?" exclaimed Morton, waving his arms. "I'll be. It's Samuel with a Chinaboy." He laughed. "What ya doin' with a Chinaboy, kid?"

"You know us, Mr. Morton. We're just taking things to peddle." Samuel was not aware if Morton knew that Chen and he peddled goods; nevertheless, he wanted to make certain the men listening from cover did. He felt clammy, his hands sweaty on his reins, knowing he could be dry-gulched in a moment. Already he believed that Dugin and Smith were the men, and they would recognize him. He braced, half expecting a bullet.

"With a Chinaboy? I knew it, kid. You and your pa are both Chinaman lovers."

From the corner of his eye, Samuel saw Chen stiffen.

"With all due respect, Mr. Morton, Chen saved my life. He's my friend."

Morton calmed and muttered something. "Well, you should know they have been stealing gold. I've got an injunction here to stop any gold shipments." He waved a piece of paper.

Samuel grew a little nervous and wondered if the paper had merit. "Sorry, no gold, Mr. Morton." He said it much more calmly than he thought he could. "Chen takes vegetables from his gardens on the South Fork and sells them. I deliver and sell goods from Alexander's Mercantile. The gold we get is earned fairly.

"What do you mean *stealing gold?*" Samuel asked. "I haven't heard about that. What I know is legal mining." He was thinking about Lance Baroon and the Slaughter Creek placers.

"You're wrong, kid. The Chinamen don't have *any* legal claims. You know the new mining law. I got an interpretation and I'm right. It's not their gold. I'm headin' in to see Sheriff Sinclair about it, and I'm tellin' everyone in the county to stop any shipments until we get what's legally ours."

Samuel's mind raced, wondering about what Morton was saying. "I can't argue with you at the moment. I got some wares to deliver."

"If'n I didn't know better, I'd say you were up to somethin', kid. Mighty early to be headin' out of Washington just to sell vegetables," Morton challenged, his eyes narrowing. "Where y'all headin'?"

Under normal circumstances, Samuel would not have answered such a demand. "We got to go to Miller's camp. I don't want to be gone longer than need be. I'm expecting a visit from Mr. Williams. You know him? He wants to look at my gold mine. Sure would be good to sell it. We get it sold, me and my pa are getting a bunch of money and heading out to Iowa." Samuel paused. Maybe if Morton knew several people expected him, they would not suspect what Chen and he carried.

"So, where're *you* heading, Mr. Morton? Back to Warren's? Kind of early to be out in this neck of woods with little reason to be here." Samuel could not help himself. Two could play this game.

Morton set his jaw. "A wise-mouthed kid, huh?"

"I said what we were up to. Just trying to be friendly."

Morton began to squirm. "I told you. I'm seeing Sheriff Sinclair. I heard that Hong King's pack string was delivered yesterday. I'm making sure the Chinamen don't try to ship out any gold."

Samuel hesitated. Maybe Morton had something.

"Hong King's pack string sure did come in. Chen and his uncle got all kinds of Chinese grub and supplies from China, didn't you, Chen?"

Chen seemed startled. "Good stuff, Sam."

"They should be heading back soon, but you know the pack strings, they're always coming and going. I just don't want to meet one on the narrow parts."

"Thanks, kid. Have a good trip." Morton's tone had softened.

Samuel knew he had given Morton what he was looking for.

Chen and he continued. Samuel had a nearly uncontrollable urge to spur Spooky into a trot down the trail. If it was Dudgin and Smith, the only reason he was still alive was that they intended to hit the Chinese pack train.

They rode until well out of earshot. Samuel glanced back. Where Morton had been was cut from his sight.

"He's bluffing," Samuel quickly said. "He has no legal right to stop any shipments. That's just his excuse for anyone on the trail he meets in case they hear about a pack train getting stopped."

"It won't matter, Sam," Chen said quietly. "You tell him too much."

"Look, I think I know who was hiding. I wanted them to think we were going to Miller's camp. When they learn the pack train doesn't have the gold, it won't take them long to figure out who does."

Chen seemed nervous. "Then they come after us."

"Trust me, Chen. We can beat them," Samuel said. "First, I need to see if I'm right. Whatever you do, you keep going. If you hear anyone, even think anyone is coming, get off the trail and hide."

"Sure, Sam." Chen was visibly shaken.

Samuel began a wide circle to where he would come out well above Morton. Nearing the spot, he tied Spooky and worked his way to a highpoint. Three horses with riders were working their way past just below him.

Dudgin and Smith! An icy chill swept over Samuel. So Morton was their new unsuspecting partner. He wanted to tell Morton about their other two partners—their dead partners.

Samuel noted Quinton Dudgin's skin appeared even more sickly yellow. The nick on his ear and scar across his check stood out sharply. His gray vest was tattered and, if possible, even greasier. His red hair was matted and caked, and a stubble beard covered his face.

Ramey Smith held his rifle across his pommel, revealing his two missing fingers. He wore the same long, black frock coat, despite the heat, and the same black hat pulled down, shielding his sunken eyes. Before, Smith had threatened Samuel with "unfinished business."

Samuel pulled back out of sight and hurried back to Chen, startling him when he burst from the brush. *So much for hearing someone and hiding,* thought Samuel.

"It's who I thought. It's Quinton Dudgin and Ramey Smith."

Chen's dark eyes widened. "The men who try to kill you."

"Somehow they've teamed up with Morton. Morton might even think he's got some legal right and he'll be able to convince Sheriff Sinclair to stop the pack train, but it won't matter. The minute Dudgin and Smith see the pack train, they won't wait for Morton to show any papers or fetch any sheriff. They'll hit it, planning on getting all the gold."

Chen stiffened. "We are in trouble, Sam."

"I expect they'll lie in wait for the pack train. I just hope nobody gets killed."

Chen spoke, voice shaky, "When they find no gold, they come for us, Sam."

"Most likely." Samuel touched the pistol that was shoved into his waistband. "We have to be really careful, Chen."

They passed the second summit and turned down Long Gulch to the Secesh River. Samuel turned downstream toward the trail to Miller's camp and Ruby Meadows.

"Wrong way, Sam," Chen said.

"I'm guessing they're following us by now. Probably they're watching us. If we don't head this way, they'll know for sure we have the gold."

Samuel scanned the horizon. A few clouds were building.

"Maybe we'll get a thunderstorm. We can double back on them."

They reached the Ruby placer, and the miners came to greet them.

"We got to make it look good," Samuel whispered. "Sell like you normally do."

Chen laid out his wares.

"Looks like we're on the bottom," one miner observed. "Pretty skimpy."

"No," Chen countered. "Good stuff. Lookee here. Good Chinee radish."

Curiously, Samuel realized that Chen talked more pidgin with these men than he did when around just him.

The men bought a few vegetables.

"How they doing down at the lower meadow?" Samuel asked.

One of the men, still selecting through some of the onions, muttered, "About the same as all of us."

"Heard they are opening up a trail from there all the way to Fort Boise. That the same trail?" Samuel nodded toward the lower placers.

"Yep, you'll see the new trail being cut through."

"Much obliged," Samuel said and headed the direction the man had pointed.

When they were out of earshot, Chen protested. "Wrong way, Sam. Really wrong way."

Samuel pulled up short. "You got to trust me on this, Chen," Samuel said. "I've been thinking. I figure Dudgin and Smith have probably got us figured out by now. Maybe they didn't even jump the pack train. At the very least they know who I am, and they want me dead."

Samuel sobered when he realized the truth of his words. No one would ever know what happened to him or Chen if Dudgin and Smith caught them here in the middle of nowhere.

"They're going to come after us, Chen. I know it. If I can get them to think we're headed down the new trail to Fort Boise, they might keep going. We're going to Lewiston. I know a trail that will bring us out at Shearers' ferry and make better time. Hardly anyone uses it anymore."

Chen quieted.

Samuel led the way. They sold a few items at the lower placers and again asked directions for the new trail. The trail cut down through thick timber down a steep slope. At the bottom, they crossed Summit Creek and climbed back up until they struck the Secesh trail. They turned upstream toward the summit.

"Where is trail?" Chen asked at length.

"Mr. Shearer said it intersects just past the summit."

Samuel worried that the trail might be hard to spot. In the early days, before the Chinese came up French Creek, it was the main trail. Now it was rarely used.

Topping the summit, Samuel could not help but pause. Jagged mountains of barren, tortured granite rose from dense timber on both sides of a narrow valley that snaked its way downward into dense timber. The thunderheads, which had been building, now towered behind the peaks, black and ominous. Lightning flashed from their bellies.

Somewhere below, the trail would emerge on the upper reaches of the Payette River, eventually reaching the shores of the big lake, a pristine, trout-filled blue jewel. Beyond, another hundred miles to the south, was Fort Boise.

The Elk Creek trail intersection was well marked.

"Don't turn up it, Chen," Samuel instructed. "Follow me."

He continued on the Payette River trail for a couple hundred yards.

"Now unload your vegetables so some can be seen. If Dudgin and Smith come this way, they'll for sure think we're heading out this way."

Chen started pulling out the vegetables, throwing them out alongside the trail.

Samuel helped. "Save some of the peas," he added. "We can eat them."

Satisfied with the decoy, Samuel said, "Now we ride." He continued down the trail with Chen following.

After a quarter of a mile, Samuel stepped off the trail and circled back until he intersected the Elk Creek trail a good distance west of its intersection.

"I don't want them to know we came this direction." He urged Spooky back onto the trail.

Chen replied. "I think you have a good plan, Sam. This is a good way to go."

The trail, not much more than a path, traversed a low ridge, winding through dense timber toward the northwest. The trees were blazed about fifteen feet up, marking the trail for winter travel. Shortly, it began gently descending toward a small stream and scattered marshes.

"Must be French Creek," Samuel pointed out. "Mr. Shearer said the trail came up out of Elk Creek and then dropped into French Creek."

The creek dropped into a steep, timber-choked ravine, and the trail began angling up until it broke out onto several marshy lakes and some thick, grassy meadows on a high bench. Several rugged peaks rose above the meadows to the east. A couple of elk got up and trotted off, snapping branches as they went.

Past the meadows, the trail suddenly pitched downward along a narrow ridge, descending through scattered ponderosa pines below a rocky outcrop and then angling straight down toward the creek. Dropping off the ridge, it entered a valley about fifty yards wide. French Creek tumbled through willows, around jagged rocks, and through talus as it dropped northward toward the Salmon River.

The trail ahead crawled back upward through the timber and reminded Samuel of the French Creek trail. It was just as steep. "Here must be where we climb back over the ridge into Elk Creek. We can keep going or stop here for the night. I'm guessing we won't find water when we start climbing."

Chen elected to camp.

The canyon walls masked the mountains toward the east except for a rocky finger that reached into the cobalt-blue sky, where it caught the last rays of the sun, reflecting an orange glow.

They moved well off the trail upstream and found a hidden alcove. Samuel built a small fire and heated some water for coffee. He ate dry meat and some of the fresh peas. "Told you I'd eat some of your ratty vegetables."

Chen smiled. He prepared his customary rice with a relish topping.

"Looks better than what I have," Samuel commented.

Chen began eating noisily, using his fingers to scoop the rice to his mouth.

"So how much gold do you figure we're carrying?" Samuel finally asked.

Chen stopped and shook his head. "I did not ask. All I know it is heavy. I have four bags."

"We'll make it, Chen," Samuel said.

"We have long way to go before we make it, Sam." Chen quieted.

"I can't believe they trusted you to carry all this out."

"No choice. Bandits would jump string."

"We'll make it," Samuel repeated. He rolled out his blankets. "Let's get some sleep. Be up early morning and get down to Shearers' before dark."

Chapter 45

SAMUEL WOKE CHEN at the first hint of light. He figured he had over twenty-five miles to cover this day, and not knowing the country, he wanted leeway in case of trouble. He had not heard any gunfire yesterday, but that didn't mean Dudgin and Smith had not jumped the pack train. He had to assume they were now on his trail, but with luck they were still heading toward Fort Boise.

They turned up the trail. *Exactly like French Creek,* Samuel thought. It traversed back and forth, clinging to a narrow ridge.

Chen seemed nervous, and Samuel remembered his first trip up French Creek. It occurred to Samuel that Chen may never have left Warren's or the South Fork since he had arrived three summers ago, and only recently did he ride the mule more than he walked. Riding an animal up or down a steep mountain trail was harrowing.

As they climbed, the day warmed, and clouds began building. Samuel figured they would have a good chance of a thunderstorm before evening. Yesterday it had been close.

He paused at one of the switchbacks. Barren slopes fell away on all sides and stretched above them until meeting the sky. "What do you think of the country, Chen?" Carefully, Samuel turned around. The height even made him a bit dizzy. Granite mountains, broken and fractured, spread in all directions as far as he could see. The nearest ridges across the canyon were carpeted with dense, almost black timber.

Chen did not look up but clung tightly to his mule. "I will walk now."

Samuel nudged Spooky onward. Once they started moving, he knew Chen would not dismount.

In another mile, the trail doubled back on itself, running due south. Finally, it swung west again and then veered north, where they crossed the ridge separating French Creek from Elk Creek. The trail descended into mixed conifers and aspens. A large meadow with a herd of elk near its fringe opened to the west.

Shortly, they emerged onto the canyon rim above Elk Creek. The trail appeared to dive off into nothingness. Samuel knew only by faith that somehow a trail would take them down into the canyon.

"You doing okay, Chen?" Chen had become silent and still clung tightly to his mule. Samuel knew it was worse heading down than climbing up. "Just hang on, Chen. That old mule of yours knows how to get down."

"You bet, Sam."

The clouds had continued to build until finally they filled the sky. Jagged bolts of lightning flashed through their black bellies; booming thunder raced after.

"Want to wait it out, Chen, or keep going?"

"We go."

Lightning lit up the hillside, followed instantaneously with ear-splitting thunder. Spooky shied, and Samuel had to grab ahold to keep from being unseated. Chen's mule was trying to turn and bolt.

"Hold him, Chen." Samuel raced back and caught and steadied the mule. "That was too close." He retraced his steps to a trickle of water and pulled under the protection of a grove of firs. The rain let loose. They huddled under the trees, feeling the wetness, smelling the fresh rain, and soon becoming chilled.

The rain increased in intensity. The trickle of water exploded into a raging torrent, forcing them to move uphill, where they huddled against some large tree trunks. The dense boughs shed most of the rain, protecting them. Below them and to the north, black clouds filled the canyon, punctuated with flashes of lightning and booming thunder.

An hour later, the storm passed, and the clouds lightened.

"It's getting late," Samuel said. "We best get a move on. I'd like to be down before dark."

Samuel could make out cliffs descending from the ridges across the Salmon to the north but could not yet see the river. Steeply falling ridges masked it. In the twilight, they at last reached the bottom. The trail ran north, following Elk Creek, straight toward the Salmon.

Cautiously, Samuel rode forward. He caught sight of a sawmill and stopped. "George Shearer built this mill."

Samuel pulled off the trail. They had seen no one since leaving the Ruby placer yesterday, and he didn't want to accidentally run into anyone now.

"The Shearers are my friends. They'll help us."

Chen shook his head. "No. They might be your friends. They might not be Chinese friends."

"I know them. They might ask me a lot of questions, but they'll help us."

"What about Morton with paper? He tell everyone the Chinese steal the gold."

Samuel hesitated. "The Shearers will trust me."

Chen appeared desperate. "I give my word. I tell no one; no one see me; no one help me. That was ohnee way to be safe."

Samuel realized Chen had already broken his promise by allowing him to help. "I understand, Chen, but how do we get across the river?"

"We swim river."

"We can't chance swimming it with the cargo you have."

"How we get across then, Sam?" Chen's dark eyes were frantic.

"Either we trust the Shearers or we take the ferryboat after dark."

"Not good, Sam," Chen protested. "They know someone go across. Ferry on wrong side when they wake up. They come after us."

"I know, Chen," Samuel replied. "Come on, we'll wait until night. We got to be less than a mile from the ferry."

They moved farther off the trail, picketed the stock, and ate a cold dinner. Samuel tried to rest. It had been a long day.

A tiny sliver of a waxing moon shone near midnight. The ferryboat bobbed against the landing, a black shadow, hardly visible. A canopy of glimmering stars spread above the canyon walls and reflected, sparkling, from the black water.

Samuel gulped as he listened to the rushing water. He wondered if he dared wait until some daylight, but he knew his pursuers would not.

By feel more than by sight, Samuel directed Chen to help him lower the ramp. They led Spooky and the mule onto the boat. Samuel noticed the water as usual swamping across the decking.

Chen pointed. "It sink, Sam," he whispered, frantically.

"No, Chen, it's decked."

Chen frowned.

"The two boats it rides on are covered over so they don't sink."

Chen still seemed upset.

"Trust me."

Carefully, Samuel angled the ferry into the current. It shuddered and began slowly moving out. The dim light from the Shearers' cabin grew smaller. The sliver of moon glinted from the rapidly moving water that gurgled about the bows of the two decked boats. Samuel had difficulty seeing how much to angle the ferry, and it slipped dangerously downstream. He adjusted the angle, and the current continued pushing them until they bumped into the landing.

In whispers, he had Chen tie him off. They let down the ramp, led the stock off, and then repositioned the ramp.

Samuel stripped off his clothes.

"What you do, Sam?" Chen stood dumfounded.

"I'm taking the ferry back," he said. "It's too dangerous to shinny across the wire. I'll swim back."

"In the dark?!" Chen exclaimed. "You drown, Sam. No."

Samuel laughed softly. "I can do it, Chen." He undid the line and jumped back onto the ferry, his heart in his throat. He didn't know if he could do it, but he was not going to leave the ferry on the other side. First, it was not right to the Shearers, and second, they would know someone had crossed—and, likely, their pursuers would also find out.

Carefully, Samuel guided the boat back. The sliver of moon drifted behind clouds, and darkness enveloped him like a cave. He listened to the water and tried to determine how much remained for him to cross. He now had no way of knowing the angle to keep the bow. He could see only the sparkle from a few stars. He prayed he would not drift downstream and possibly snap the wire. He angled the bow more. He drifted for longer than it seemed he should, but the light in Shearers' cabin slowly drew nearer. Suddenly the bow crunched hard into the landing, sending Samuel sprawling. The ferryboat was taut against the wire. Samuel leaped, hoping he would hit land and not water. He jammed his knee into his chest, knocking out his breath. He found the rope about the time the sliver of moonlight returned, tied the ferryboat, double-checked the knot, and waded back into the water, heart hammering. *If I get out of this alive,* he thought, *I'll pay a double toll when I get back.*

He waded in to over his waist, the current trying to knock him off his feet. Another step and his foot slipped off the slick cobbles. He dunked under and came up sputtering, swimming, and feeling the current taking him downstream. Desperately he fought not to panic. The river was many feet deep and powerful and carried him rapidly downstream. Clammy fear began to seep through him. He knew there was whitewater not far downstream. He kept his head up, scanning the pitch-black for the far bank.

It dawned on him to angle his body similar to the ferryboat, to let the current help him swim. The noise of pounding rapids increased, and now he saw the white spray caught in the moonlight leaping angrily below. Desperately he tried not to think of the rapids. He swam, keeping his angle, letting the current push him.

His feet hit rocks. He continued swimming, afraid to stand—afraid the current could pin his foot between some boulders—until he reached calm water. The dark shape of the bank loomed above him. He pulled himself onto the boulders and crawled from the river. The current had swept him well over a hundred yards downstream. Carefully he picked his way back toward the landing.

"That you, Sam?" Chen hissed.

"It is."

"You lucky, Sam. You very lucky." Chen handed him his clothes.

Samuel brushed the water off the best he could before dressing. "Not something I'd want to do again, Chen. Maybe during the day."

"I never want to do it, Sam. I can't swim."

"But we did it. We're across. If Dudgin and Smith come this way, the Shearers won't know we crossed. Morton can wave his paper all day at them, and they can't accidentally give us away."

They rode down the trail a distance. "We can spend the night in the cabin where my father and I stayed last winter. It's about four miles. Tomorrow, we'll go on. We shouldn't run into anyone now."

Chapter 46

BEFORE DAYLIGHT they left the cabin. Samuel rode ahead, scouted the trail for other riders, and then signaled for Chen to come up. In places this was impractical. The countryside was open with few places to hide.

The camp at Berg's bar was idle, abandoned until winter. They passed the mouth of the Little Salmon River and turned north.

"We're doing good, Chen. Now we go north to Lewiston," Samuel said, at last feeling some relief.

"I am glad." Chen smiled.

Nearing Groff's ferry, they entered a wash, dipping down off the level and then back up. When they did, Samuel spotted three riders coming off the ferry trail, heading toward them.

"The worst possible place, Chen." Frantically, he scanned for a place to hide, but the riders already hailed them. Samuel felt uneasy.

"What is wrong?" Chen demanded.

"Whoever these people are, they're bound to run into Dudgin and Smith. Morton is going to be asking about us and any Chinese shipments. They won't lie for us, and if Dudgin and Smith are close, we won't be able to outrun them."

Samuel waited for the three men. They exchanged greetings and talked for a moment. The men eyed Chen.

"He works for me," Samuel explained. The men relaxed a bit and nodded.

"Ain't never seen a Chinaman," one of the men said.

"Where you heading?" Samuel asked. He didn't say they were about to see a lot of Chinese.

"Headin' into Miller's camp. Know where that's at?"

"I've been there."

"Supposed to be some good placer. You ever do any minin', son?"

"Some." Samuel was short. He had no time for visiting.

"So where're y'all headin'?" One of the men finally asked.

"I do some packing and trading. I'm taking some things to Thomas Pollock. You should have passed his place on the way down the Little Salmon."

"We shore did. Nice fella."

"Yes, he is." Samuel had never met him. "Well, I best be off. Have a good trip."

They said farewell.

"Why you tell them that?" hissed Chen. "Really, really wrong way, Sam. We never get to Lewiston."

"I told you, if we're being followed, these men will be telling Morton everything there is to know about you. I'm sorry, but it's the only way I know of throwing them off our trail."

Samuel turned down toward the ferry. Chen had no option but to follow.

Reaching the landing, Samuel pulled his pistol and fired a shot. He didn't mind that anyone would hear. The men would figure he was crossing. Additionally, Samuel didn't want to chance waiting for the operator to notice them. That could take another hour.

When the ferryboat landed, Samuel didn't recognize the operator. Samuel introduced himself but not Chen.

"Howdy, Mr. Chambers, I'm Jason Weston. I just got hired on by Mr. Groff."

Samuel didn't ask about Jesse, the previous operator, and he was careful to pay with coin, thankful now for the money Scott had given him. He didn't want Weston believing he carried much gold.

Samuel noticed him eyeing Chen. "This Chinese works for me and my pa," he explained, sticking to the story he had told the three riders. "We're going up the Little Salmon, delivering some goods to Mr. Pollock."

Samuel felt unsettled with the hard look Weston gave Chen's packs as well as his.

"A feller by the name of Morton was by a couple days ago," he finally blurted. "Said to be on the lookout for some Chinese carrying out some stolen gold."

"I know Ben Morton." Samuel laughed. "You think we stole gold? You think I'm that stupid?" He reached into his saddlebag and pulled out the pair of new gloves. "See for yourself." He said it unkindly, but that seemed to placate the man.

"Sorry, Mr. Chambers, I didn't expect you'd know Mr. Pollock," he replied. "And it's not usual to see a white man and a Chinaman traveling together."

Samuel glanced at Chen and pretended to say something in Cantonese. It was gibberish. Chen bowed and replied something in Cantonese.

On the trail, Samuel apologized. "No offense, Chen. I had to think of something."

"That is okay. I tell him you a big lying foreign devil," Chen replied, grinning. "No offense."

Now on the south side of the Salmon, they backtracked to the confluence of the Little Salmon and turned up the trail. Samuel felt frustrated. He was uncertain how he would cross back to the Lewiston trail. He did not look forward to stealing Groff's ferry or going for another swim in the middle of the night.

They moved up the trail, but before moving out of sight, Samuel studied his back trail. Three riders were rounding the bend, heading in the direction of Groff's. His uneasy feeling had been right. He hissed to Chen. Luckily, they were already in dense cottonwoods and willows.

"It's them, all right," Samuel said. "For sure, they've got us figured out." Samuel's chest tightened. They had probably followed them over Elk Creek. They were better trackers than he had given them credit.

Chen was deathly silent.

"I figured they'd be onto us sooner or later. This works out good for us," Samuel said, trying to sound confident. "We'll say hello to Mr. Pollock and double back on them."

"They catch us, first, Sam."

"Nope," Samuel replied. "This trail is in thick brush and trees. I know it. Me and my pa came in this way." He clucked to Spooky, turning him back onto the trail. "Walk your mule, normal, Chen. If they see signs we're running, they'll know we spotted them. Right now they're about five miles behind us. They'll probably take the ferry, so I figure we got shy of an hour."

Desperately, Samuel wanted to run Spooky, but he held him in check. He hoped Pollock's ranch was near. They would not make it much farther before being spotted.

Finally, he smelled wood smoke and spotted the makings of a cabin in a clearing near an incoming stream. Rapid River he remembered it being called. No one was here last year; now a man worked on a fence.

Samuel introduced himself. "I'm guessing you're Mr. Pollock. You know Mr. Stromback."

The man greeted warmly, "I am, and indeed, I do know Jon Stromback." He leaned the ax against the fence and they shook hands. "How come you know Jon?"

"I worked for him a bit." Samuel noticed Pollock eyeing Chen.

"The Chinese is working for me and my pa, Mr. Pollock. My pa's back in Warren's wrapping up some work. He'll be along in a few days." Samuel did not care to be lying. "Might say we're doing like you've done. Mr. Stromback told us about a couple ranching spots up this way."

"Stromback is why I'm here," Pollock replied. "It would be good to have neighbors." He pointed upstream. "Several good areas on some tributaries coming in. Take your time and look them over good, then come on back and have some dinner."

"Much obliged," Samuel replied. "We'll need to pass on the dinner. I figure on going all the way to Salmon Meadows and look around up there as well." Samuel wanted to visit longer but knew his pursuers would be closing in.

"That is good land as well," Pollock said, "but you might have trouble with the Indians up that far."

"I've heard. Also heard there's a new route into Fort Boise through the meadows. You know about it?"

"There is," Pollock continued. "You continue through the meadows about eight miles past the hot springs and head east until you reach a little creek called Goose Creek. Packer John's cabin's near there. From there, it's about eight miles over the top into Payette Valley. The trail goes south through Payette Valley all the way to Fort Boise." Pollock eyed Samuel. "You ain't thinking of trying it? Got to be close to 150 miles."

"It's closer than going through Walla Walla," Samuel replied, having frequently heard the grumbling from the miners up in Warren's.

"True," Pollock replied. "I expect this will become the main route soon enough. Either this route, or drop over into the Weiser River and down."

"Thanks, Mr. Pollock." Samuel turned Spooky up the trail. "We'll try to drop by on our way back."

Samuel was thankful Pollock did not ask any further questions. He spurred Spooky and headed south up the Little Salmon. When they rounded the next corner, he cut into the river at a riffle and forded to the other side. Chen followed.

"They got to be close, Chen," Samuel whispered. "They might be talking to Pollock this very minute. Pray this works."

Samuel doubled back, leading the way along the opposite shore, keeping to the timber. He knew they would eventually run into cliffs and need to cross back before reaching them. At that point, he intended to hide and wait until night, and then he would attempt crossing the main Salmon. He had been thinking how to convince Chen to break the gold into two loads so they could swim the river. He did not intend to steal another ferry.

Samuel found what appeared to be a shallow area and eased Spooky into the Little Salmon to cross. The water came up deeper than he expected. The current pushed hard against them. He nudged Spooky onward. "You can do it, Spook." The animal surged forward, found footing, and climbed out, water streaming off him.

He glanced back at Chen. The mule was in trouble. It appeared to be swimming.

"Hang on to her, Chen," Samuel hollered.

The animal headed downstream. He prayed it would not roll like Molly had done in a similar spot the previous spring. It would likely lose its load. Samuel eased Spooky back toward the river, loosening his rope.

The mule wedged against a boulder, frantically thrashing as the water pinned her. Chen desperately held on.

"Here's a rope," Samuel hollered and tossed it. "Snub it on your saddle."

Chen ran it through the saddle grip and around himself. Samuel turned Spooky up the bank. The mule righted herself and, fighting, surged against the water. Samuel feared both Chen and the packs would be ripped loose. The animal lurched out of the water, found footing on the bank, and lunged to get up it. Then, she went down, her foreleg buckling, throwing Chen. Samuel felt sick. The animal struggled up, limping.

"Hold her, Chen," Samuel instructed. "Keep her steady."

He reached the mule and began stripping off the packs, taking off her load. Without thought, he strapped the packs onto Spooky, surprised at how heavy they actually were. An icy fear seized him. They would now have to walk. With luck, their pursuers were still riding upstream and had missed where they had turned off the trail to cross the river.

"We don't have much time, Chen," Samuel said. "We need to find a good place to hide until night."

Chen stared at him. "Mule is hurt. We are in big trouble." His dark eyes flashed.

Samuel tried to reassure him. "We can do it if we get a hiding place. If we can get back across the Salmon, maybe they won't figure we doubled back. Maybe they'll go all the way to Fort Boise." But Samuel doubted it. He knew it would not take long for the men to figure out that he had left the trail. Darkness was their only chance. He would have no choice but to repeat what he had done at Shearers' ferry.

"Mule can't carry me."

"No, we'll have to walk for now. Spooky can carry the packs."

Chen appeared frantic. "They catch us before night."

Samuel studied the sky. He figured they had two hours until dark. He remembered the Chinese stone hut on this side of the river, several miles downstream.

"Do you know any of the Chinese near here, Chen?"

Chen shook his head.

"There's a stone hut a few miles downstream where some Chinese have a placer. I've seen it. I think we can get to it. They have a raft."

"Might be wrong Chinese," Chen replied.

Samuel went numb. "What do you mean 'wrong Chinese'?"

"Wrong tong. They won't help."

Samuel recalled that the Chinese had factions that did not get along, but time was running out. "We have to chance it. If we can get there, we can use the raft to carry our gear across. I can swim Spooky. We'll leave your mule."

Samuel led Spooky well off the trail so their pursuers wouldn't see their prints and turned downstream. They were forced to climb above sheer rocks near Groff's ferry, following a thin game trail. Beyond, in the gathering darkness, Samuel studied the canyon. They would be trapped if they encountered more cliffs.

The mule struggled to follow, limping. It went down again. Samuel thought he might have to leave her.

Night fell. They continued until they spotted a light shining through the door of the stone hut. The distinctive odors of Chinese food and singsong voices drifted to them on the night air.

"You go, Chen," Samuel said. He pulled his pistol. Chen eyed it. "Just in case," he explained.

Chen departed and reached the hut. The door came open and a couple of Chinese came out, soon breaking into excited voices. Chen turned and motioned to Samuel. The men waited, silhouetted at the door.

"They okay, Sam," Chen said excitedly. "Kan Dick is here."

Kan Dick greeted Samuel joyously, and Chen interpreted. "He say thank you again."

Samuel knew Kan Dick. He was the Chinese man that Finney and Culler had roped last year and whom he had helped. Samuel bowed. "You are welcome."

Chen introduced the other men—Ahn Kee and Chow Lein.

Entering the hut, Samuel sat uncomfortably on his heels. The flimsy Chinese chairs were all in use. The hut was furnished similar to Sang Yune's but was slightly larger. A small table held an oil lamp. Clothing hung from pegs. Three sleeping pallets were against the sides of the room. He wondered if there was room enough for Chen. Samuel had already decided he would sleep outdoors away from the cabin.

Similar to Sang Yune's hut, the men also had a small stove outside near the door. A kettle of rice was being kept warm.

Chen chatted happily with the men. Ahn Kee brought Samuel a bowl of hot rice with a vegetable and fish relish garnishing it. The Chinese nodded at Samuel and then began eating and talking noisily, often gesturing at him. When finished, they put their bowls outside and prepared some tea.

Chen addressed Samuel. "They know we are carrying out gold."

Samuel felt queasy. Like Chen, he trusted no one. He had heard more than one story of Chinese turning on Chinese for gold or opium or gambling debts—of them hacking each other to pieces.

"They have seen men who stay across river and watch," Chen said. "These men know they have mined much gold. They think they wait until they cross river with gold and then steal it," Chen said simply. "Instead, they plan to take raft downriver to Lewiston."

Samuel almost dropped his tea. "The raft … downriver? That's impossible."

Chen shook his head. "No. Other Chinese do it."

"How do they get through the rapids? No raft will get through those rapids. It'll get busted up in the rocks."

"They stop for bad water. Use rope along shore and let raft through."

Samuel decided it made sense. He could also imagine that would be where the men would jump them. He wondered who they might be. *Dudgin and Smith?* He would have suspected Finney and Culler, but they were in jail. An icy realization washed Samuel. *No, they were probably free.* He had missed the hearing.

"So what's our plan? Leave Spooky and your mule here, float downriver to Lewiston, and walk back? It's still a hundred miles."

"Yes." Chen nodded.

RIVER RUN

Chapter 47

EARLY MORNING, just as light crept into the sky, the Chinese prepared a meal and began packing. Samuel took his gear to the raft and carefully lashed it on, knowing he might lose it in rough water. The raft consisted of several logs sandwiched between poles at opposite ends that had been deck-lashed to them. The Chinese had fashioned a rudder and lashed it to an upright pole, enabling it to swivel from side to side. A couple of other poles lay on deck for pushing the raft off rocks or poling it upstream.

Chen's gold had been secured in leather pouches inside burlap bags. Samuel took one of his blankets and split it, wrapping the bags yet again. He then securely lashed each to one of the logs. He had come this far; he was not about to lose the gold now. Similarly, Chow Lein lashed their gold to a log as well.

Chen climbed onto the raft and grabbed a pole, steadying the raft. Chow Lein stood ready to untie it. Samuel climbed back up the rocky cliff to get the last of their gear. He had left his pistol at the hut. He normally tucked it in his pants, but he didn't want it accidentally falling into the river while he was loading gear.

Ahn Kee and Kan Dick tossed a few pieces of perforated paper into a small stone cubicle next to the door to confuse the devil while they were absent, their last action before carrying their remaining gear to the raft.

Samuel headed back toward the raft, but paused on the edge of the bluff, taking in the grandeur of the river for a moment. The sun now touched the far mountains. The raft, a small square on the breathing water, bobbed quietly. He felt good. They would be in Lewiston in a few days.

Chen steadied the raft with his pole. Suddenly, he began shouting, frantically waving, pointing.

Samuel turned to see three riders coming down the rocky slope toward them, Quinton Dudgin in the lead. Ramey Smith pulled up and leveled his rifle. He saw the puff of smoke and heard the high-pitched whine of a bullet. The report reverberated from the canyon walls, shattering the morning silence.

Cold, icy fear flooded Samuel. He stood, terrified, rooted to the spot.

"It's that bastard, wet-nose kid," Smith cursed.

"Pull that raft in!" Morton hollered; he pulled his rifle and fired into the air.

Ahn Kee came running toward Samuel. Kan Dick hesitated near the hut.

Two rapid shots rang out. One bullet whined past. Kan Dick went down near the hut's door. He struggled up a moment and then went still. Samuel went sick inside. Desperately, he grabbed his pistol and returned two wild shots. Ahn Kee ducked down near Samuel.

He heard Morton. "We're after the gold, damn it, not the Chinamen."

Another shot rang out.

Morton yelled toward Samuel, "Stop those Chinamen, kid. They're stealin' our gold."

Samuel saw Smith aim his rifle and fire. The bullet whined past, and he scrambled for cover.

"Hey, kid, remember, me? I told you we had some settling to do." Smith fired again, the bullet kicking up dirt near Samuel. Smith was not aiming at *just* the Chinese.

Morton turned toward Smith, yelling something that Samuel couldn't make out.

Heart pounding, anger overwhelming him, Samuel ran toward the men and wedged himself behind a tree, cutting the distance. He carefully aimed at Smith and squeezed off a shot. The man spun away crazily, batting at his ear. Samuel thought he saw blood.

"Who's next?" Samuel hollered. "Come any closer, one of you is dead."

The men brought their horses to a halt, and Morton hollered down. "Don't be a fool, kid. That's our gold they're stealin'. Help us out, you won't be hurt."

"Is that what Dudgin told you, Morton?" Samuel hollered back. "You better ask him what happened to his partner from last fall when they robbed the Chinese pack train."

"Don't listen to the shirttail, Morton. He's just tryin' to scare ya," Dudgin shouted. "We didn't have nothing to do with any Chinaman train."

"Then ask him about a man named Bender," Samuel shouted. "I was there when they gunned him down. You'll be next, Morton. By God, I swear you'll be next."

"*You'll* be next, you bastard wet-nose," Smith yelled. A round went past Samuel's head. He squeezed himself harder against the tree. He saw Morton backing his sorrel up, turning, and galloping off.

Dugin cursed and yelled after him, "Lily-livered bastard." He fired at Morton. The man clawed at his shoulder and dropped his rifle. Morton continued riding from sight, slumped in his saddle. Dudgin turned and fired again at Samuel and then began reloading. Smith spurred his horse down the hillside.

Samuel stepped out. He could now see blood on the side of the man's face. *Good,* he thought. He took careful aim and fired. The horse staggered and went down, throwing Smith. It lunged back to its feet and, shaking its head, broke away, staggering up the hill. Smith scrambled to his feet, cursing, running toward Samuel, and flung himself behind a rock a few yards away.

Samuel saw him steady his rifle and the puff of white smoke. A bullet sprayed up dirt near his foot. Samuel heard Smith chamber another round and knew in moments he would be dead. The thought seemed strange, cold. He glanced to see Dudgin on foot working his way downward toward him.

Overwhelmed by anger, Samuel decided he would take at least one of the two men with him. He stepped out and aimed.

"You're dead, Chinaman lover," screamed Dudgin. He began firing at Samuel.

Ahn Kee scrambled toward Samuel, desperation in his eyes, shouting. His shout was cut short; his face went blank, and he pitched forward, crumpling a few feet from Samuel. One of Dudgin's rounds had found him.

Samuel glanced toward the river below. He saw Chow Lein wading into the water, pushing the raft out.

Ahn Kee continued crawling toward Samuel, pain flooding his face, eyes pleading. He quit crawling and gasped, mouth working, bleeding.

Samuel jumped up, put a bullet past Smith, and his last round past Dudgin. He jumped crazily down the bluff, almost tripping and tumbling, yelling toward the raft. "Get down!" Smith's rifle bullets buzzed past him.

He hit the water, diving, swimming for the raft. He lost his grip on his pistol, and it slipped into the depths. A slug plunged past him, kicking up a spray. In icy fear, he realized they would soon pick him off. Chen grabbed his arm and helped pull him onto the raft. Painfully slowly, the raft swung into the current.

Dudgin and Smith scrambled down the rocky bluff toward them, cursing. At the river's edge, they took up positions and began firing. Slowly, slowly, the raft slipped downstream, swinging out and away.

Samuel's heart wouldn't quit pounding. He watched upriver as the men faded to small dots. The two Chinese bodies lay where they had fallen. He shook until he got sick.

Chen's face was white. The raft drifted toward hanging up on the bank. Chow Lein ineffectively pulled on the sweep. Chen grabbed a pole and stabbed at the looming rocks. Samuel forced himself up and grabbed the rudder. Pushing against the current, he turned the bow back into deeper water. "I can handle it, Chen. You can set your pole down."

Shaking, Chen placed his pole on the deck and sat, Chow Lein next to him. Both seemed oblivious to the water that freely splashed up through the decking and washed across the logs soaking them. A few logs rode beneath the surface. Both men appeared terrified. "I can't swim, Sam," Chen whispered.

"You won't have to if we can make a few miles." Samuel tried to be reassuring. "Just the same, I reckon we should lighten up, in case we go in." He pulled his hat down firmly and then began unlacing his boots and pulled them off. He pulled off his shirt. "Tie these on, please," he instructed Chen. Both Chen and Lein removed their tunics as well.

He watched upstream as Dudgin and Smith headed back toward the ferry, riding double. Samuel figured they would soon steal another horse and again be on their trail, especially now that they carried even more gold.

Desperately, Samuel searched his memory for the placer camps, for where people who might help could be. But it was summer. No one would be working the bars until late fall or winter. They faced the river alone. The hopeless feeling he had nearly overwhelmed him.

Samuel tried to remember where the rapids were. All he could remember were the ones at Lucile Bar. Likely, Dudgin and Smith would know this as well and would be there waiting for them.

The current quickened and a line of spitting whitewater appeared below.

"Better hold on," Samuel cautioned. "Looks like rough water ahead."

Boulders crowded in from each side of the river with whitewater dancing around their edges. Samuel pulled against the rudder, sweeping the bow toward the glassy, black tongue of water toward the river's middle. He had spent enough time studying the river to know the water ran deeper in the glassy patch.

The raft dropped down into the trough and rose up on the descending swells below. Samuel felt the rush of the river and the raft yielding to its massive bulk. The river's power was deceptive. They slid through the swells into slower water that now curved slightly to the east.

After a short quiet stretch, they entered another quick section of water. The raft rose on the huge swells and fell down the other side. It bucked and strained. The logs shifted underneath the decking, turning freely. The ropes were loosening.

"Chen, you and Lein have to tighten those ropes," Samuel shouted, keeping his grip on the rudder, sweeping it back to force the raft left past the shoulder of a half-submerged boulder. Its shape rose black and menacing beneath the surface. Samuel braced for the collision, but surprisingly, they swept past.

Shaking, Samuel shouted, "There's more rope in my pack. Try to loop more over those logs."

They entered a section of quiet water. A cliff came down from the west edge, and the river swept back toward the east. A stream entered from the west, and a bouncing line of whitewater marked its boundary. Boulders littered the river. Samuel remembered studying these rapids from the trail. These were not good. Desperately, he swung the raft toward the west bank. He had no idea if they could walk the raft along that side from the shore, but he had no choice. He brought the raft into the bank directly above the bouncing, thundering water.

Whitewater rocketed down through chutes between the boulders, boulders as large as small cabins. The swells rose six or more feet at the foot of the chutes and tumbled back on themselves, foaming into white. A log trapped in a hole rolled over and over, rose up the swell, and then got hammered back down. Samuel had made the right choice. If trapped, the raft would have been torn apart.

With two ropes firmly anchored to bow and stern, Samuel eased the stern out until the current caught the raft and pushed it out toward the largest chute. Samuel wrapped the rope around himself, hoping he wouldn't be snatched into the river by the raft. He shouted at Chen. "See the angle? We got to keep this angle or the raft will get caught and be ripped apart."

Painstakingly they walked along the bank. Sheer rocks blocked their route, and they were forced to climb up above and around them. They kept the raft in the current. It rode through the turbulent whitewater, getting tossed and bucked.

The creek had brought in boulders that chopped up the water. Past its mouth, the rapids diminished into a series of explosive cockscombs dancing into each other until they quieted. At the far end, they brought the raft to shore, where they reboarded.

Samuel watched the far bank, but thankfully, he had not seen Dudgin and Smith.

"Maybe bandits don't follow," Chen observed. "They ohnee have one horse."

"Maybe." But Samuel figured they had probably already taken Morton's. Maybe he had more than nicked Smith. Maybe they *had* given up.

Samuel swung the raft back out into the current. The logs had shifted considerably. Chen and Lein worked to snug up the lines.

Samuel steered the raft to the river's center, and they swept downstream for a couple of miles, encountering only a few quick spots, but nothing difficult. The worst set of rapids above Lucile had to be near. He scanned the river ahead. It appeared as if it ran into descending cliffs. A dull roar began to fill his ears. This had to be the spot. They would have to land the raft again and line it through.

He peered back upriver for their pursuers and then shouted at Chen. "Maybe we should beach the raft and hide. Maybe we can fool them into thinking we already made it through."

Chen addressed Lein, vigorously talking. Lein shook his head.

"Lein say they will find us. They know this place."

Samuel glanced downriver and went numb as he spotted Dudgin and Smith, sitting their horses in the river shallows. "They already have." Both had their weapons aimed their direction. Smith rode Morton's sorrel, and Samuel guessed Morton was dead.

"Keep down," Samuel hissed. Blood pounded in his head and his mouth went dry.

"Bring the raft in, boy, and we'll let you go," Dudgin shouted. He aimed his pistol. "You don't, I'll kill ya."

Samuel knew Dudgin could see he had lost his own pistol. "If you do, you'll lose the gold," Samuel shouted back. The raft slipped toward Dudgin. Samuel tried to angle away, his hands grasping the rudder, sweaty.

"Don't be a fool, boy. Bring it in."

Chow Lein started to stand up, saying something.

Chen interpreted, "He say it is not worth dying. Too many dead." Desperation filled Chen's eyes. "I say okay."

Samuel felt defeated. Two men were already dead. He thought of his father. His father always said a man could start over, but not if he were dead.

He swung the raft toward the shore directly toward Dudgin, sweat stinging his eyes. Smith sat his horse a few yards downstream, his rifle held steady on Samuel. Without warning, he raised it and fired. Samuel flinched. He heard the bullet smack, and Lein slumped to the deck, bleeding profusely from a hole in his chest. Samuel went numb. Smith's bullet had been aimed for him.

"You bastards," he yelled. "Haven't you killed enough men? I said I was coming in. You can have the cursed gold."

Smith steadied his rifle. "I said we had some settling, wet-nose."

Dudgin threatened Smith with his pistol. "Damn it, Ramey. He's comin' in. I gave my word."

"Right." Smith laughed, but he lowered his rifle.

Samuel knew it was not over. Smith would kill him at the first chance given him.

Lein gasped, and bright red blood spread across the raft and into the water. His eyes were frantic. Samuel knew he had little chance.

Samuel whispered to Chen, carefully instructing him. Chen's eyes went wide.

"Smith is going to kill us anyway. You know that."

Slowly, Chen nodded.

"Chen is going to throw you a rope, Smith," Samuel said. "Pull us in."

Chen coiled the rope and tossed it squarely into Smith's face.

"What the—" Smith fumbled with his rifle, trying to get his hands free, trying to catch the rope.

"Pull us in, Smith," Samuel said coolly.

Smith pulled, bringing the bow toward him, swinging the stern toward the shore.

"Now!" Samuel hissed. He pulled the sweep from the water and swung it as hard as possible, striking Dudgin. Dudgin's horse bucked, and his pistol flew as he grabbed for his saddle. He missed, and clawing madly at the air, he helplessly tumbled backward into the water.

Chen jerked the rope, unseating Smith. Panic-stricken, the man smacked into the water, where he splashed frantically.

Samuel dipped the rudder, forcing with all his strength to spin the raft, sending the bow back into the current to be pulled back into the deeper water.

"Get down," Samuel cautioned. Moments later, a rifle bullet whined overhead. Another smacked the water.

Samuel crouched, keeping the bow upstream in the current, painfully slowly ferrying the raft out and away from the men. He intended to cross to the far bank and walk the raft through. The men's horses could not swim the river here.

He tried to convince himself they would not shoot him. If they did, the raft with the gold would be lost in the rapids. *I'll be dead,* Samuel thought strangely, *but they'll lose the gold.* He glanced at Chen. *Chen will be dead.* Chen held Lein, trying to stop the bleeding. An empty, hopeless feeling washed over Samuel. Lein was dying.

The raft slid sideways downstream. His hands slipped on the rudder. Samuel could not hold the angle. A frantic feeling filled him. The pounding waves below were sucking the raft into them.

"Hang on, Chen," Samuel shouted. "We gotta go through." The raft was backward, the rudder downstream. Frantically, Samuel began spinning it back around, trying to face the bow downstream.

He heard Chen pleading, "I can't swim, Sam."

"I can make it through, Chen." A terrible ache filled Samuel's chest. He was glad he had removed his boots.

The bow caught the chute and jerked downriver. Samuel pulled back on the rudder, straightening the raft. He was close to center. The trough below seethed in white foam, tumbling back on itself. Samuel prayed that the raft would not be trapped. It slid down the glassy green water into the trough. One side pitched up. Samuel lurched against the pole, losing his grip. Chen let go of Lein and grabbed on to the decking ropes. Suddenly the raft lurched in the opposite direction. A black, gaping hole opened beneath them. The raft hung momentarily on a rock, slid backward, and then bucked upward.

Samuel saw sky turning about him. Then he hit the water, its force pushing him under, downward, deeper. The world darkened. He twisted around, seeing light above him, feeling the weight of the water trapping him, pushing him deeper, the light above dimming and the bottom shadows reaching out toward him. Masses of silvery bubbles raced upward. He paddled after them, straining to hold his breath, fighting against the water pounding him back down. He broke the surface, gasping for air, and was immediately dunked again by the pounding waves. He tried to swim out. The power of the river spun him around and over, sending him tumbling, pushing him under. Suddenly, he was on top, gasping for air, struggling, swimming.

"Chen," he sputtered. "Chen." Frantically, he searched for Chen.

He saw Chen's bare torso and blue trousers; face down, motionless. Madly, Samuel swam for the form, caught Chen, and turned him over. The current swept them downstream. He battled to keep his feet down and his head up, cradling Chen between him and the surface. He rode the swells until the water slackened. Miraculously, he had slipped into a backwater.

He tried to stand and found he could. Pulling Chen to the bank, Samuel climbed out and dragged him onto the grass. Whitewater raced down the chute beyond.

Chen was not breathing. Samuel became frantic. "Don't die, Chen. Don't." He slapped him, not knowing what else to do. He rolled him over and hit him between his shoulder blades, then hit him again. Samuel found himself shaking. *This can't happen, God. This can't happen.* He shook him again.

Chen started moving, coughing. An incredible wave of relief washed over Samuel. He helped Chen sit. Chen coughed spasmodically and opened his eyes.

He yelled in Cantonese, swinging wildly with his fists.

"It's okay, Chen. It's me, Samuel."

Chen's eyes focused. "You not the devil?"

"You've called me that before." Samuel laughed. "Thank God you're alive."

Chen frantically looked around. "Lein is dead."

Samuel nodded.

"Gold is gone."

"I reckon." Samuel had felt the raft breaking up. He knew it had come apart. "I guess we can go home now."

Chen's eyes widened. "You go home. I go home, they kill me."

Samuel hesitated before replying. "Because you lost the gold?"

"I deserve it."

"They'll kill you because you lost the gold?" Samuel was incredulous.

"Three men never go home because of me."

Chapter 48

SAMUEL NOTICED for the first time that he had gashed his leg. Blood trickled down and across his foot. He scanned the far bank, looking for Dudgin and Smith. This end of the rapids was on an eastern bend of the river. Fortunately, cliffs blocked Dudgin and Smith from following the river.

The whitewater boomed and hissed toward the river's center and stretched below for several hundred yards. Samuel thought he saw some of the logs from the raft, shiny black, sliding through the rapids. The hole had trapped them, and they were just now being kicked out.

"We have to try to get out of here, Chen," Samuel said. "They'll know the gold was tied on. Some of it might still be."

Chen stared vacantly at him. "No, Sam. Gold is gone. I know."

Samuel studied the surrounding cliffs. "Either way, we got to go downstream a ways to cross. Doesn't look like we can go up." The riverbank dropped sheer into the seething water. They had crawled out of the river in a small alcove above a backwater formed by huge boulders.

"We also got to hide. Dudgin and Smith won't be able to hit us from across the river, but if they think we're dead, they won't be trying."

Samuel crawled up into the rocks and into a protected patch of brush. He feared going any farther in case Dudgin and Smith spotted them.

"They there," Chen whispered, pointing across the river.

Their pursuers had reached the river's edge and turned downstream, now walking. Samuel knew they were checking for their bodies or pieces of the raft. Frequently, they shielded their eyes and peered across the river toward them.

They waited a long while for the men to disappear before they resumed climbing the rocky face. Samuel realized that he would not go far without protecting his feet. He'd already cut and skinned them and stepped into a prickly pear, but rattlesnakes worried him the most.

They crossed the face and reached a bench above the river. The river swung away and curved, quiet and deep, opposite them along a sweeping bend.

Samuel spotted several of the logs from the raft. They had wedged themselves against the bank up into some driftwood and willows. They were still partially held together by the ropes—the ropes he had used to tie on the gear, he realized. Heart racing, he scrambled down, sliding into the water. The log he had tied the gold to was wedged underneath two others. Quickly he felt for the bags. *Four!* The other log and its gold were missing. Strangely, he realized the Chinese would no longer be needing it. He shook with disbelief. Frantically he gazed at the far bank, making certain he had not been seen.

Chen reached him, breathless.

"We're back in business, Chen," Samuel whispered hoarsely.

"But not other gold," Chen replied. He had noticed the missing log. Chen began to remove one of the bags.

"Wait, Chen," Samuel said. "Not yet. Dudgin and Smith are still out there looking for us. We got to get them off our trail. Neither of us are walking out of here, and we aren't walking far with this much weight."

Chen studied Samuel, fear creeping back into his eyes.

"We wait until night, Chen. We can hang on to a log and float the river with the gold."

Chen was frantic, shaking his head, eyes wild. "No, Sam. I die already. Not again."

"It will be okay, Chen. It's not that far to John Day's ranch. Maybe someone there will help us. I don't remember any bad rapids between here and there." Samuel knew if they could slip past Dudgin and Smith they could make it.

"Come, on, Chen. Give me a hand. We have to fool them." Samuel removed two of the bags of gold. "I double wrapped these. Dudgin and Smith won't know that." He took the two leather bags of gold out of the blanket and poured out the gold from one of the pouches into the blanket, except for about half an ounce. He ripped the bag, leaving the small amount of gold in a corner, and retied it to a different log. He ripped the straps from another bag, ripping them free from the top of the bag, and tied them to the log as well.

"It should look like the bags were ripped off," Samuel explained. "Give me one of the grub bags." He removed some of the food, leaving the remainder, and tied that bag onto the log as well. "Help me loop the rope around these two logs." He loosely bound the logs.

"What do you think, Chen?"

"It might work, Sam."

"It has to." He removed his trousers, slipped back into the river, and pushed the logs out toward the center to where they caught in the current. He figured they would carry downriver and lodge on the side where Dudgin and Smith searched.

Exhausted, Samuel pulled himself out of the river and returned to where Chen hid. Chen handed him some dried beef. "Thanks." Samuel ate hungrily and inspected his feet, bloody and raw from scrambling across the rocks and cactus.

"I wish you had tied my boots to the same log as the gold."

"Then we would not find anything."

"Probably not." Samuel took his trousers, ripped off the lower part of each pant leg, and wrapped them about his feet. He unraveled enough rope to tie them to his ankles.

"Should I make some?" Chen asked.

"Not unless you're going to walk." Samuel stood. "I'm going to climb that bluff"—he pointed—"and watch and see if Dudgin and Smith find the logs I released."

"Maybe I should go with you."

"No. Stay with the gold and watch our back trail. If someone is coming, whistle."

Samuel turned and hiked to where the ridge met the bench they were on. He began climbing, angling across the face to the edge to where he could see the river and yet remain hidden.

He watched both directions. The hillside was open with only small patches of buckbrush and an occasional pine. The day had grown hot, and he found it hard to breathe. A trickle of sweat ran down his face. He wished for his hat. Reaching the corner, he could see downriver about a mile. He recognized Lucile bar and more rapids. Of what he could see of the rapids, he thought he and Chen could ride through them.

He kept hidden in the spotty shade of some thorny buckbrush, its leaves thin and spindly, patiently watching. At last, he spotted Dudgin and Smith at the shore examining the logs he had released. They ripped the bags loose, examined them, and threw them down, cursing. Dudgin addressed the far bank, yelling, "You better be dead, Chambers. I'll find you and hang your Chinaman friend and slice you to pieces to feed the fish. You hear me if you're out there, boy." He kicked at the logs. Both men turned and walked to their horses and mounted up.

Samuel eased back, breathing hard, watching them ride away from the river. Then his heart fell. They split up. Dudgin headed downstream and Smith, upstream, still searching the riverbanks. They weren't finished.

He watched until both men disappeared from sight. Then he waited longer, hoping to see Dudgin return upstream. He did not. Now the day was long. Chen would wonder what had happened to him. He scrambled back down and began retracing his steps toward their hiding place. He met Chen coming his direction.

"I thought you find snake," Chen said, his look stony. "I come to find you."

"I saw Dudgin and Smith. They split up. Dudgin went downstream and Smith went up. I don't think Dudgin has his pistol anymore."

Samuel caught movement on the opposite shore. "Get down."

They both dropped into the weeds. Smith had returned. He came to some cottonwoods, dismounted, and climbed to the top of a rock. He scanned in their direction and then downstream.

"Nuts," Samuel breathed. "He's going to sit and watch."

Samuel studied his way back to their hiding place. It was too open. He figured if they could sneak to the river they could drop below Smith's sight and then work their way back upstream.

He whispered to Chen. They crawled on their bellies—snake height, Samuel realized, and shivered. When they reached the riverbank, they scrambled down between the boulders to the water's edge. Chen was farther downstream. His face blanched, and he began scrambling backward.

"Lein there."

Samuel's heart sank.

"He is in the water."

"We can't do anything, Chen. We can't let Smith spot us."

"We have to bury Lein. Devil will find him," Chen pleaded.

"Okay, Chen, but we have to wait until Smith moves on, or he'll see us."

"We got to bury Lein soon," Chen insisted. "Devil come."

Samuel looked around. He spotted a cut in the bank upstream that was blocked from Smith's view. "We can drag him up there."

Chen nodded.

They slipped down to the river's edge. Samuel saw Lein's bobbing body and felt sick. He did not expect to see it looking so pale. The hole in his chest resembled butchered white flesh, completely drained of blood.

Together they dragged Lein's body up the bank and into the cut, where they stacked rocks and driftwood on it until it was partially buried. Samuel pulled some brush over it, hoping it would not be recognizable from across the river.

Smith remained on the rock, alone, watching. Near dusk, he rose, caught up his horse, and headed downriver. Samuel realized that both he and Dudgin might still be looking for logs from the raft, hoping some of the gold was still tied on.

Samuel studied the river, flowing powerfully past, now black and frightening in the growing dark. It no longer seemed a good idea to float it in the night. In his mind, the rapids he had seen grew in size and intensity. He relived nearly being drowned, and he realized Chen must have been thinking the same terrible thoughts.

"We gotta go, Chen," Samuel finally choked. The stars were out. The moon would be rising soon. If Dudgin and Smith were watching the river, they might see them floating by. It was a risk Samuel had to take.

They tied their trousers to the log and began pushing it out, Samuel on one side and Chen on the other. Samuel could hear Chen's rapid, scared breathing. He wondered if Chen could also hear his.

Samuel waded out until the water reached his chest, feeling the current pushing against him. His feet slipped on the slick rocks on the river's bottom, and he kicked off from them. They were swimming; the log was riding the current.

All too soon, the sound of rapids downstream filled Samuel's senses. He could make out the spitting whitewater. It was little use trying to steer the log.

Samuel knew that just holding on to the log, the current would rip them loose of it. He wrapped a loop of rope about his wrist and choked up on it next to the log to get a tight grip.

"You better wrap the rope around your hand. It'll help you keep your grip." Chen did so, his breathing increasing.

"Now, grab my wrist with your other hand. I'll grab yours. With our wrists linked, we won't be as likely to come apart as if we were holding each other just by our fingers."

With his free hand, Samuel grabbed Chen's wrist and felt Chen's fingers dig into his own wrist. "Hang on, Chen," he called. "We're going through."

The water swept upward, hissing. They rose and came down, slapping the water, turning around and around, the waves kicking them back and forth and breaking over them. Samuel swallowed water and began choking. Each time he tried to get a breath of air, he took in water. He began panicking. He could not get air.

The log bucked upward, almost wrenching itself free from between them. Desperately, Samuel held on, feeling Chen's fingers dig deeper into his wrist.

They entered more fast water and slid downward through huge troughs and then descending swells until the river settled. Gasping and choking, Samuel coughed until he finally got air.

Nothing but blackness sprinkled with the specks of starlight spread before them. Samuel held on to Chen, barely able to make out his frightened features.

Samuel figured that they were through the rapids now, but he could hear the sound of rushing water increasing. It didn't make sense. *More rapids?* Samuel did not remember seeing these. *Where are they?* Frantically, he peered downriver, searching for the white cockscombs that would tell him how large and wide they were. He saw nothing, but the sound began to envelop them. Panic flooded him. It sounded like a waterfall. *There aren't any waterfalls,* he told himself. He felt the strength of the river pulling them. Whatever it was, it was sucking them in. His heart pounded madly.

"Paddle for shore, Chen." He released Chen's wrist and began paddling as strongly as possible, trying to angle the log away from the noise. They were dead center in the river. The deafening noise was directly in front of them. He saw the monster's black shape rising above him—*a huge rock.* They were headed directly into it. The water swept upward toward the massive hulk, half submerging it.

"Paddle," Samuel screamed. He didn't care if anyone heard him. "Paddle."

Too late. The power of the river gripped them. They rose quickly, the noise thundering in Samuel's ears. The water curved across the right side of the huge monster, revealing naked black rock on the left.

Their world dropped from under them. A black void opened, and they were falling, rocketing down into a trough of whitewater. Samuel lost his grip on the rope and found himself flying, and then he was submerged, being driven deep under the powerful wave behind the rock. He fought to hold his breath—looked for light, for the rise of silvery bubbles. He saw nothing but blackness. He felt his body being lifted, and he broke the surface, gasping for air. Chen frantically clawed at the water nearby. Samuel yelled, "Hang on!" He got a mouthful of water. The river swept them downstream, the noise quickly dissipated, and abruptly, the current slackened. They were in a deep pool. Moonlight glinted off the gliding water and the log. Samuel swam to it, grabbed it, and grabbed Chen, pulling him to the log. Chen seized it, coughing and sputtering.

"We made it, Chen," Samuel managed. They were in slack water. He kicked and swam for shore, towing the log. They found a soft, sandy beach and lay exhausted, trying to catch their breath.

"No more, Sam," Chen cried. "No more."

"We don't have to do any more, Chen. It's smooth the rest of the way."

They sat in the sand, shivering in the evening chill. John Day's was a short distance away.

"Come on, Chen," Samuel said, rising. "We can't walk there."

Reluctantly Chen reentered the water. They grabbed each other's wrist across the log again and kicked back out into the current. The river ran deep and quiet.

They drifted downstream, following the moonlight shimmering off the water. Magically, the light broke as they reached where the moon appeared to be standing, only to move farther downstream—it was like chasing a rainbow.

Samuel listened for any more rapids. He heard none. He saw the lights of John Day's ranch, but one light was not right. It was too near the river's edge. *A campfire.* Shadows moved across the fire.

"They're watching the river," Samuel whispered. He began kicking and pulling, turning the log toward the far shore.

"Come on, Chen, duck to this side."

Nervously, Chen moved around to Samuel's side of the log.

The current carried them closer toward the fire. The ranch lights were behind them, farther up the bench.

"We have no choice, Chen," Samuel whispered. "Duck down."

They both did, tilting their heads back, keeping low to the water. Samuel hoped Dudgin and Smith would not see the log slip past. He could hear them talking, but he could not make out what they said.

They slipped past the men on the shore and swung around the bend.

A heavy set of rapids remained before Slate Creek, where the river narrowed, but Samuel decided not to chance them. His body felt like lead. When he spotted the dancing cockscombs in the moonlight, he turned for the shore and paddled the log in. They hid it along the bank and crawled into the shrubs. Samuel felt chilled as the water from his body evaporated in the breeze. He was so exhausted that he found himself thinking that it didn't matter anymore. They could catch him. It was not worth the fight.

He got up. "Come on, Chen. We have to find a warmer spot."

They returned to near the river and found an area down out of the wind next to some boulders. Both he and Chen burrowed down into the sand with the sound of the river for company and slept for a short while.

Chapter 49

CHARLES RETURNED to the cabin late Monday afternoon, expecting to meet up with Samuel as agreed. He had had a good week working for McLane, mostly preparing the site for next season. He was surprised that Samuel was not around.

He noticed some tobacco and a pick—things Samuel would have likely taken on a selling trip. It didn't seem right, but a note said he *was* on a selling trip with Chen. The date was Saturday, and that concerned him. The two were never gone more than a couple of days.

He prepared a quick supper and took care of the stock. He realized Molly had not been cared for. An eerie feeling enveloped him. He checked the sluice for signs of any unwanted visitors. Nothing but Samuel's absence seemed out of the ordinary.

Tuesday morning, Samuel had still not returned. Charles saddled Buster and headed into Washington. He visited Mann's store, hoping that Mann understood English.

"You seen Samuel?"

"Not here."

"I can see he's not here. Have you seen him?" Charles asked, somewhat frustrated. "How about your nephew?"

"Not here." Mann shrugged and spoke at length in Cantonese.

Charles gave up and crossed the street to Hong King's saloon.

"Anyone here speak English?"

One of the Chinese came forward. "Engliss." He nodded.

"I am looking for the Chinese boy and my son, Samuel. You know Samuel?"

The man nodded. "Chen go to sell. Not with Samyew." He shook his head.

That made no sense to Charles. "I got a note from my son saying he was with the Chinese boy."

"Chen go to sell alone." The man shook his head more vigorously, but Charles had momentarily noticed a questioning look flash across the man's face.

"When did he leave?"

"Maybe three day ago, early."

Saturday, the date on the note, Charles realized. The Chinese knew Samuel often accompanied Chen, but apparently, they had not seen him. Chen had gone alone.

He headed to Alexander's Mercantile. Scott was busy sweeping in the back.

"You haven't seen Samuel around per chance, have you?"

Scott shook his head. "When I saw you come in, I figured to ask you the same thing. He picked up some stock for delivering to the camps last Friday, said he'd be in Saturday morning and pick up some fresh goods but never did." Scott put the broom aside. "You don't suppose he's in trouble?"

"He could be. Some of your goods are still at our cabin. This was there." He handed back the envelope marked for Frederick Burgdorf.

Scott took the envelope. His mouth tightened.

Charles glanced out the window. "When he was in, did he say anything out of the ordinary?"

"No, he was pleased with the selling he had been doing. I gave him an advance since he was heading to Burgdorf's. I figured he might want a bath and a plate of chow. He seemed excited about that." Scott went silent. "I should have gone out to check on him, Charles. I should have. That's not like Sam to not do as he says." He tapped the envelope against the counter.

Charles shook his head. "No, he knows when to get help. Something's up. Did he say anything when he left your place?"

"I know he headed out to see that Chinaman friend of his. The Chinese pack string had come in."

Charles raised his eyes.

"Hong King's," Scott explained. "I noticed that more than the usual number of Chinamen left with it."

"When'd it leave?" Charles began to suspect Samuel's absence was tied to the Chinese.

"I'm saying about midmorning Saturday. That'd have been when Samuel was supposed to be delivering things."

"You didn't happen to see if Samuel's friend went with it?"

"No, but he could have headed out earlier on his own selling trip. He's always doing that."

"That's what I'm thinking. Samuel left me a note saying he was going selling with the Chinese boy." Charles glanced toward Steamboat Summit. "Any idea if that pack train was carrying anything out of the ordinary?"

"Might have been." Scott leaned across the counter. "They have to take the gold out sometime. Might explain why the extra riders."

"I was thinking that." Charles feared what else he was thinking. "See any strangers around town recently ... like someone interested in jumping a string?" He knew Finney and Culler were still in jail, but he was thinking of Dudgin and Smith, two of the men who had held up the Chinese train last fall—the ones who had tried to kill Samuel.

"No, but I did hear word Ben Morton was talking about seeing a judge in Mount Idaho to get the Chinamen removed from his old claim under the new mining law. He didn't get any help from Attorney Poe."

"No, and he shouldn't have. He lost that claim because of his own fault."

"Well, he's been making noise about it again. Threatening he'd take some action, saying the Chinamen are stealing our gold—the same tirade as before, but now he seems more intent on convincing others." Scott straightened. "You don't suppose Morton'd be stupid enough to think he has the right to stop that pack train?"

Charles slowly shook his head. "Not on his own, but he might try to convince someone to help him." *And it might not be the best kind of help,* Charles thought. He began rounding up supplies—dried beef, dried fruit, some crackers. "And Morton just might be stupid enough to try to stop the boys to see what they're carrying. Samuel doesn't see eye to eye with Morton on account of the Chinamen. I'm guessing he'll do like I would and call Morton's bluff, but if Morton has any help out there and Samuel does that, he just might bite off more than he can handle."

Scott was silent for a moment. "I see what you're aiming at. Maybe you should get the sheriff."

"You tell him. I don't have time." Charles pointed at the cartridges on the shelf behind the counter. "Better give me a box."

Scott placed them on the counter. "You're going after Morton."

"I'm going after my son. If Morton gets in the way, I'll handle him if need be." Charles turned to leave. "Any word on Hong King's pack train? Any trouble?"

"Not that anyone's said. It would go out by way of the wire bridge to Florence," Scott said. "We'd know by now if it'd been jumped."

Not if it wasn't carrying the gold and Samuel is, Charles thought. "If I miss Samuel and he shows up here, tell him I'm on his trail … if I can figure out which one it is. I'll leave word at the Shearers' and at Slate Creek, if I get that far. Otherwise, tell him to get back to the cabin and stay put—or, better yet, stay with Ma Reynolds. I'll be back."

"You should ride with someone. Maybe one of McLane's hands."

"I'll be fine. They're probably coming back now." But Charles doubted it, and at any rate this was his responsibility. Besides, he could not think of anyone who might want to be helping a Chinese boy. "If you can, check on my mule a couple times. I'd be much obliged."

"Least I can do, Charles. Good luck."

Charles returned to the cabin and grabbed his bedroll. He wrote a note for Samuel in the event he returned first. He quickly checked the cabin again and headed back at a trot for the trail heading up Steamboat Creek, the route out. With each step, he became more certain of his thoughts. The boys were carrying the Chinese gold. He was not sure if they were headed to Fort Boise or to Lewiston. He recalled most of the Chinese were coming in from Lewiston, but the trail to Fort Boise was becoming more useable and more Chinese were conducting commerce there because of gold strikes in the Boise Basin.

He turned up the trail, scanning the earth and the surrounding country. If Dudgin and Smith had figured out that the boys carried the gold, Samuel could already be dead. But Charles did not sense that. He knew Samuel was resourceful and had probably realized that Dudgin and Smith were following him. If anyone could stay ahead of Dudgin and Smith, Samuel could.

Charles swallowed. He should have been around more and not left Samuel so much to his own. But it was for the family's good, he rationalized. He had done all he could to make enough money to take care of them—to get land, to start over. But no amount of gold was worth losing his son over.

The men working the first placer southwest of Warren's confirmed that the boys were together. They had not seen them return. They had full packs, and the Chinese kid had vegetables.

He pushed past Steamboat Summit and down into Long Gulch, not passing any other miners. He checked with one of the placers in Secesh Meadows. The boys had not stopped to try to sell anything, nor did anyone remember seeing them pass.

Charles reasoned that someone would have seen them pass unless the boys were trying to keep hidden or had taken another route.

He approached the trail junction to Miller's camp and paused, examining the hoofprints. He could not distinguish Spooky's and a mule's from any of the others. If Samuel thought he was being followed, he might head toward Miller's camp and attempt to throw his pursuers off and then double back. Something told Charles he had guessed right.

He reached the Ruby placer near dusk. He recognized a man whom he had worked with last season.

"Carl, you seen Samuel come through here?"

"I did. He was selling with that Chinaman kid he goes with."

"Thank God." Charles swung off Buster, letting the horse have water. "He didn't come back through by any chance?"

"No, and it was strange."

"About what?"

"The vegetables the Chinaman kid brung were about the worst he's ever had—like it was stuff he slapped together, but he pretended they was just fine, and your boy didn't have any customers here. Or anyways he didn't have anything they wanted. He always packs just what's needed." Carl paused to light his pipe, seemingly pleased to be taking a break. "And something else was strange."

Charles listened.

"Your boy wanted to know the route out toward the big lake and the Payette Valley. I told him the trail out that direction, past the other placers, would cut it." Carl pointed toward the timber. "They headed out that direction."

Charles wondered that maybe they *were* heading to Fort Boise, but if so, Samuel would not have asked for directions nor allowed himself to be seen.

"Then a few hours after they went through, three seedy characters came sneaking through. I seen a couple of 'em before. I wouldn't trust them as far as I could throw 'em. I was wonderin' if they weren't followin' your boy and that Chinaman kid."

Momentary dread gripped Charles. *Three men: Dudgin and Smith and Morton.* Morton had found his help. "Thanks, Carl," Charles said. "You've been a great help." He swung into his saddle. "You don't happen to remember if you heard any gunfire that direction?"

"Nah, nothin' close anyways." Carl tapped his pipe and reseated it. "'Course your boy coulda come back along the Secesh trail and not come back through here after visitin' those other placers. Don't know why he'd ask about the Boise trail, though."

Charles turned down the trail. "The men you said you thought were following him … did you notice if one of them was minus a couple fingers?"

"Nah, I couldn't see that far. Anyways, they didn't know I was up here."

"Thanks," Charles said. "I'm guessing they don't mean anything good by my boy—or the Chinese boy. I think they're the men I chased down into the Salmon River last fall—the ones that held up the Chinese pack train."

"I remember hearing about that," Carl replied. "Hope your boy's all right. Anything I can do to help?"

"If he comes back through, let him know the men following him are up to no good and to get back to Ma Reynolds's and wait for me. But I think he knows that. He tried to shake them by coming this way. I'll follow him until I either lose him or catch him." He clucked to Buster and turned for the trail.

Charles felt deeply troubled. The men were on Samuel's trail, probably aware that he was carrying the Chinese gold. He figured that Samuel would likely double back. He was not going to Fort Boise. Somehow, he had figured out that Dudgin and Smith were following him and had come this direction to shake them.

Charles continued past Ruby Meadows and headed west toward the trail intersection with the Secesh trail. Intersecting the trail, he searched for recent hoofprints. He noted several sets of fresh tracks that headed upstream. There was no way of knowing if they were just Samuel's or the three men who pursued him.

No tracks appeared to be returning. If Samuel had doubled back, Charles could not figure out how. Then it struck him. Samuel would go over the old Elk Creek trail. He laughed to himself. Dudgin and Smith would likely not know it even existed.

He spurred Buster upstream at a quick trot, crossed over the summit, and descended into the Payette drainage. Two sets of tracks were now clear—a horse and, most likely, a mule. He did not know for certain where the Elk Creek trail turned off—only what Shearer had said, that it was beyond the summit a short distance.

He pushed Buster, believing he had somehow missed the turnoff, almost turning back when he finally spotted it. He saw no fresh tracks turning down it but gambled that Samuel had hidden his tracks. He turned down the trail. After a couple hundred yards, he found the fresh prints. *Samuel.* He felt relieved.

Dudgin and Smith were not following. Charles reasoned that they had quit trying to outguess Samuel and had taken the French Creek trail, knowing that Samuel would eventually head up the Salmon River toward Lewiston and betting they would catch him. His son had been smart. He now had a large lead. If Samuel pushed hard, he might be able to keep ahead of them all the way to Lewiston.

Charles rode until he could no longer see the trail and was in danger of missing sign. He camped for the night and lay watching the night sky, thinking. None of the trip had turned out as he had hoped. He had been away from home far too long—over a year. He wondered how Elizabeth would look, and his nephew and nieces—how they would have grown.

He had been a fool for chasing O'Riley's gold—it had been nothing but a rainbow. He had not expected to get rich, but he had believed he would find it and be able to sell it for some good money. Samuel, more than he, had made something of it. He had never seen such determination in a kid—in a man. He smiled to himself, recalling how day after day Samuel headed into the mountains, searching for the ledge. He tried to remember if he had ever told him how proud he was of what he had accomplished. He could not remember. "God, get me back my son," he whispered. "Let him hear from me how proud of him I am. Get us both back to Iowa safely, and soon."

Chapter 50

THE COOL OF THE MORNING woke Samuel. Chen was sitting up, shivering. Hardly a hint of light showed. Stars still studded the western sky.

"Maybe it is okay to get help," Chen stated.

"Yes. This is Slate Creek." Samuel sat up. "I'll cross the river and walk to the ranch. You stay with the gold. Stay hidden. Don't take a chance on moving at all."

"You do the talking?" Chen kidded.

Samuel studied the far shore, making certain no one was around. He stuffed his foot wrappings into his trousers and tied them all around his neck. The rapids were directly downstream of him—too close for comfort. He walked upstream a short distance before wading in and then, swimming, allowing the current to help push him across.

On the far side, he checked if he could look back across and see where their log and the gold were hidden. It was still too dark. Even if a portion of the log was visible, unless someone knew where to look or what to look for, no one could see it.

He slipped into his trousers and wrapped his feet. He headed downstream, following the trail where it had partially been cut into the cliff. The cliff on the opposite shore came steeply into the water. The river piled against it, churning white for a couple hundred yards. He was thankful he was not trying to go farther on the river.

Some buildings came into his view, spread across the bench above the river. Samuel kept to the river and out of sight until he reached the creek. He turned up it, heading for the Strombacks' ranch.

No one seemed to be up. That was good. He worried about Roundup barking to greet him. He headed toward the bunkhouse and spotted Art walking toward the tack shed. He hissed. Art glanced in his direction, startled. Samuel held his finger to his lips.

Art stared at him. "What in tarnation? Is that really you, Samuel?"

Samuel nodded. He moved to the side of the building out of sight of the ranch house and beckoned to Art. About the same time, Roundup came around the corner all wiggly, recognizing Samuel. He whined but thankfully did not bark.

Art followed. "What in blazes is going on?"

"I need your help." Samuel explained what had happened. "I'm here to borrow a couple mounts from Mr. Stromback."

"And some clothes, I hope." Art looked him up and down. "You've been through some kind of hay mower, for sure. You look about like you did when Rex manhandled you."

"You heard I ran into him again?"

"Yep. You saved his hide. But you don't have nothin' to worry you about him anymore."

Samuel felt cold. "He dead?"

"Nope, nothing like that. He's left the country."

Samuel thought of Bonnie, and an emptiness filled him. He was also leaving the country—if he survived. At least Bonnie might now have a chance at finding someone better than Rex.

"He came back and told Mr. Stromback what happened up at Warren's. Stromback asked how you were. Then Rex told him how you pulled him out from under that tree. That was why he was moving on. He said you were a better man than he could ever be."

Samuel didn't say anything for a moment. "I think Rex could be a good man. You also said so. Just … " *He's so dumb,* Samuel thought. There was nothing else to say.

"Art, if it ain't too much, I'd not like Bonnie or the Strombacks to know I've been here."

"Kinda hard to have two missing horses not be noticed."

"Then let Mr. Stromback know after I've left, but ask him not to say anything. I don't think anyone would understand my going on to Lewiston with Chen."

"I can't understand it, either, but then you always were friends with those Chinamen. Just keep in mind that friendship just about got you killed. And you better plan on stopping on your return."

"I promise," Samuel said.

"I should go with you."

Samuel shook his head. "Been hard enough for me to come here and borrow stock. Chen wouldn't want it. Besides, I'm thinking we have nothing to worry about. Dudgin and Smith figure we're dead."

Art studied Samuel. "I'm guessing you won't listen to reason anyhow. Seems you're intent on seeing this through your own way."

Samuel nodded. "Thanks."

"Probably if you don't want to be spotted, you should head down to the creek. Give me a few minutes and I'll bring you a couple mounts."

Samuel returned to the creek and waited. After what seemed too long, Art came toward him, leading two horses.

Art threw him some clothes, including a hat. "The boots might be a bit big. Borrow these until you can get something proper. There's some for Chen as well." He handed Samuel another package. "Some grub for you. I had a little problem getting it, though. Mrs. Stromback was fixin' breakfast. She might be guessing something's up."

"Mighty obliged." Samuel began dressing, shoving the hat on first, thankful to have one again.

"I brought you the gray you rode when you were here working. The white mare is for Chen. She's gentle."

Samuel swung up onto the gray and thanked Art. "I should be back in about five days, if I got my distances figured correct and we don't run into any further problems."

"I'd keep my eyes peeled for Dudgin and Smith just in case."

"I reckon so."

"Got one more thing for you, Samuel." Art offered him his rifle and a cartridge belt. "Carry this in case of trouble."

"I-I can't," Samuel protested.

"You might be needin' it more than I will. This gives you a chance of evenin' things up if you do find more trouble, which you seem to have a knack for." He handed it up. "I just use it for varmints anyway. You just bring it back in one piece is all."

Samuel's eyes misted. "Mighty obliged, Art."

"Good. Now I best get back up to the ranch. I believe Mr. Stromback and I'll be heading upstream to see if we can't find some skunks. At least we can go bury the dead and round up Spooky. We'll send word to your father."

"Thank you kindly."

Samuel rode back toward the river. He still might be able to get back to Chen and be on the way before people noticed them.

Continuing upstream to where he had crossed, Samuel picketed the stock, stowed his new clothes and Art's rifle, and swam back to Chen. Samuel saw the relief on Chen's face change to concern as he surveyed his lack of clothing.

"No good?" Chen asked.

"Across the river," Samuel explained. He pointed toward the horses.

Chen shook his head. "You have horse? I see horse."

Samuel grinned. "Yes. They are on loan. I have a friend here."

"What if they take gold?"

Samuel understood Chen's lack of trust. "Not all white men are foreign devils." He could say nothing else. "Come on. We got one last swim and then we're done with this river."

Chen grinned broadly.

They climbed down to the river and loosened the log. Pushing it back into the water, they swam across. They quickly loaded the horses and were soon on the trail beyond Slate Creek.

"I think we'll be okay, Chen. I think Dudgin and Smith think we're dead."

They skirted White Bird, carefully concealing themselves. Samuel had no way of knowing how far Morton had spread the word. He knew there were many who did not care for the Chinese, and if someone thought they were carrying gold, especially stolen gold, they would make easy targets.

They climbed out of the Salmon River canyon and continued north along the rim before cutting west of Mount Idaho and veering northwest toward Lewiston. Samuel knew the Salmon River bent back on itself, flowing to the southwest until it emptied into the Snake. The trail cut north of the bend and angled toward the junction of the Clearwater with the Snake River and Lewiston.

This was high plains. Rolling windswept grasslands stretched in all directions, in places cut by deep draws. Only a small purple ridge marked the mountains along the Salmon River toward the southwest. This was also Nez Perce country, and Samuel kept watch for Nez Perce hunting parties. This was not a place to be caught in the open, either by men or by the weather.

Camas Prairie, he remembered. It was named for the camas bulbs the Indians dug for food. He recalled Mr. Hunt telling him of expressmen crossing the prairie who had to evade highwaymen intent on stealing the gold they carried, much as he was now doing.

Here the wind raced unabated. The thunderheads piled in the distance, lightning crackling from their black bellies. Birds were lifted in the wind, fighting to keep from being driven back to earth. Maybe someday this would all be ranches and farms, but not in Samuel's lifetime, he decided. Now it was empty, desolate, rolling hills and prairie.

"Hope we can reach the protection of a valley with trees before this hits," Samuel commented, pointing toward the approaching storm.

Chen hurried his white mare along.

A vast, deep basin opened before them. A few pines clung to the far side, edging several deep, shadowed draws. The trail traversed back and forth until it reached the bottom. They paused to water the horses from a rapidly flowing stream and then resumed following the trail, climbing back up onto the windswept prairie. The stream flowed northeast, which meant it emptied into the Clearwater River. Only a gentle rise to the west now separated them from the Snake River canyon.

The thunderstorm hit about the time they climbed out of the valley. They continued on, fighting the wind-driven rain until they reached another cutbank. They pulled to the leeside and rested, pulling their shirts over their heads, trying to protect themselves from the heavy, pelting rain.

When it eased, Samuel mounted and turned back toward the trail. "We can't get any wetter. Let's find a camping spot and try to dry out."

They continued along the trail until it dipped into another small valley. Cottonwoods rimmed the valley floor, where another stream felt its way eastward. They moved downstream until well out of sight of the trail.

Samuel chanced a fire. Most travelers would have stopped at the first of the rain. It was not likely they would be by at this time of evening. He set Art's rifle within easy reach. The rain had chilled the air. By dark, they had begun to dry out and warm some. They ate some of the food Art had given them and turned in for the night. Coyotes broke the stillness.

Early morning, Charles was again on the trail, climbing out of French Creek. As the sun climbed and the heat intensified, he topped out onto some lush meadows and small lakes. The two sets of prints remained strong, leading before him—a horse and a mule. The trail pitched steeply downward toward the Salmon. By midmorning, he passed the sawmill George Shearer had built, and shortly he reached Frederick Shearer's yard.

After an initial warm greeting, Frederick and Susan Shearer listened, concern etching their faces.

"No sign of Samuel or that Chinese boy," Frederick said. "We sure would have helped them some. Didn't see any men this way who were out of the ordinary. 'Course, this time of the year, if they weren't carrying much, they'd likely just swim the river. Are you sure Samuel wouldn't have gone across the wire bridge and up to Florence? That's the route the Chinese pack trains all take."

Charles shook his head. "He and the Chinese boy were spotted at Ruby, as were the three men following them. Samuel's tracks were as clear as day when I was coming down Elk Creek trail."

"Well, I guess the boys could have swum the river."

Charles did not think Samuel would chance swimming the river if they had a heavy load of gold. He guessed Samuel somehow borrowed the ferry, but he said nothing.

"I don't know why they wouldn't come fetch me," Frederick lamented. "I coulda sent George with 'em. I'd send him with you, 'cept he's up to Slate Creek for a few days."

"I'm guessing the Chinese boy would not allow it. The trip was not Samuel's idea. He's just helping."

"Yes, that may be. Those Chinamen sure are distrusting souls."

For good reason, Charles thought.

"You all come on in and get a quick bite afore you head out," Susan Shearer insisted.

"I'll trade out mounts for you, if you'd like, Charles. Don't know how far you gotta go before you find Samuel, but your horse will be awaitin' you when you get back."

"Much obliged," Charles said. "If Samuel shows up, keep him here, and that Chinese boy as well, until I can get here."

With a meal and a new horse, a fine sorrel, Charles headed out. He considered other routes Samuel might take. Shearer's suggestion that the Chinese would go through Florence had him thinking that Samuel might take one of the trails up that direction. It would not be much farther, and the old trail, similar to the Elk Creek trail coming down to Shearers' ferry, would be less traveled.

Charles checked the trail nearest the Shearers'. It showed little use. He rode downstream to the next trail, the one where they had jumped Finney and Culler last winter. He was less certain about the tracks. It seemed there had been recent use. On a hunch, he checked the cabin. Signs showed that someone had recently been there, and Charles knew that it was Samuel. He felt more confident that the boys had used the trail. They would especially do so if they were traveling during the day, which they almost had to do.

He hoped he could make it to Florence by dark and turned up, following the tracks, the sorrel horse laboring to carry him upward, climbing out of the Salmon River canyon. Similar to the French Creek trail, the Florence trail climbed over five thousand feet in elevation before leveling. The country spreading beyond, mountain upon mountain, and the canyons below, cut and tortured, became mesmerizing. Charles decided no man on earth would have ever entered this labyrinth of mountains and canyons had gold not been discovered.

He reached a summit where a ridge ran due north. A trail followed its crown, but Florence lay to the northeast. He studied the trail, but the tracks gave no clue. Each trail showed similar use. Possibly, the trail going north was just a miner's trail. He turned down the Florence trail. If Samuel had taken the spur trail, he would eventually come out at Slate Creek. At Florence, Charles could at least ask about the Chinese pack train.

He rode steadily and soon reached where the trail forked to the west and would continue past the Bullion Mine and drop down to the wire bridge. He stayed to the northeast and reached some played-out placers, and by evening, the town of Florence. The sight sobered him. Of the two gold camps, Warren's was clearly more vibrant. Here, several buildings were abandoned and deteriorating. The most robust businesses seemed to be the several saloons and obvious brothels that lined the main street. Charles decided that the town might show more commerce in the daylight.

The more numerous Chinese also caught his attention. They appeared to outnumber the whites nearly three to one, and their section of town seemed lively and booming.

He paused at one of the busiest saloons and talked with the owner. No one had seen the boys come through. Although Charles figured Samuel would keep from sight, a nagging feeling bothered him. If they had not come this direction and instead had followed the main river trail, their pursuers might have caught up to them. He tried to calm himself.

He asked around about anyone seeing Ben Morton and two other riders. He tried to describe Dudgin and Smith. No one had seen anyone matching the description, at least not recently. He asked about the Chinese pack train. It had come through three days ago. As far as anyone knew, it had not met with any trouble.

Charles felt uncomfortable with taking a hotel room and instead continued on the trail another mile toward Slate Creek before he camped. He dared not continue farther. The sorrel had done well, but it needed rest.

The night was quiet, except for the gurgle of the creek near which he camped. He heard coyotes yapping from somewhere up a nearby draw. Nearly always Samuel had been with him while he was camped along some trail. They had often wondered about the coyotes, how a couple seemed to sound like a dozen. Now he half expected Samuel to show up for coffee. He recalled last winter when they were going to Slate Creek for Christmas. Samuel should now be many miles north, perhaps even returning from Lewiston. Charles took solace in the thought. He should meet him on his return trip near Slate Creek—possibly tomorrow.

Chapter 51

EARLY MORNING, Samuel and Chen were on the trail again, moving rapidly along the shoulder of the divide. The trail continued to cut down into the draws and then climb back up to the broken plateaus. The prairie stretched on, empty, except for an occasional shrub or cottonwood.

Late afternoon, the trail cut downward along a broadly flowing stream and continued along its bottom.

"Must be getting close," Samuel observed. "This stream has to empty into the Clearwater. Lewiston will be a few miles downstream."

By evening, they had reached the Clearwater, a rapidly flowing river, crystal clear, reflecting its namesake.

They turned downriver and, just outside Lewiston, left the trail to camp. Chen told Samuel no one would be able to meet him until the next morning. Samuel worried all night that someone might discover them. The gold had grown heavier with each mile they grew closer to the town. He checked Art's rifle.

❧

Before daylight, Charles was back on the trail, intending to make up time. There was little sense in continuing to berate himself for guessing wrong. The sooner he reached Slate Creek, the sooner he would get some information. Surely, Samuel would have stopped there. He certainly would not pass up the chance to visit Bonnie. But then Charles recalled that the ranch hand, Rex, had taken an interest in Bonnie. His anger flared when he recalled the beating Samuel had taken. If Rex was at the ranch, it could be Charles would be the last man on earth Rex would see.

The trail soon dropped down alongside a creek, which Charles figured must be a tributary of Slate Creek. *Should be named crooked creek.* Hardly a section ran straight for fifty yards. It reminded him of the brush-choked and timber-filled creeks near Warren's. If men had not kept the trail clear, he wouldn't have made a single mile.

He could not keep his mind off Samuel, nor off the men pursuing him. Maybe they had not caught him. Samuel was good at watching his back trail and keeping an eye out for danger. Unaware, he found himself pushing the sorrel. This was a brutal trail. The animal was beginning to flag. Charles eased up. He had to reach Jon Stromback's ranch.

He tried to keep his head—tried to study the country and to watch for the men. Even though he believed they were on the main river trail, he could still be wrong. He caught himself hoping, almost believing, that Samuel was just ahead of him on this same trail, that around the next bend he would catch sight of him.

The creek began bearing west, dropping steeply in elevation as it drained toward the Salmon River. Charles thought he recognized the Salmon River gorge and peered ahead for signs of Stromback's ranch.

Late afternoon he reached the ranch, nearly exhausted from the ride.

Soon he sat at dinner with the Strombacks and Art, everyone talking at once, everyone sharing what they knew. Yesterday, Samuel had come up from the river to borrow a couple of horses and to get some clothing. Charles swallowed hard. He was two full days behind.

A couple of men from Slate Creek had gone upstream looking for Dudgin and Smith. Art and Jon went to the stone hut, but some Chinese had already taken care of matters. They brought Spooky and the mule back to the ranch. Seeing no sign of Dudgin and Smith or Morton, people figured they had left the country or just disappeared for a while, something they were becoming good at doing. Charles felt more optimistic that Samuel had made it.

He retired to the bunkhouse with Art.

"You got a fine son, Mr. Chambers," Art told him. "I don't know how you look on the Chinamen, but for Samuel to do what he's doing speaks a lot."

Charles wanted to disagree. The first thought he had when he began piecing things together was how foolish Samuel had been. Now he was uncertain what to think. All he knew was that Samuel was still out there.

At early light, Charles was on the trail, riding a bay horse that Stromback had loaned him. Lewiston was about ninety miles away. If his calculations were correct, and if Samuel hadn't taken another trail or been delayed, he should now be returning, maybe nearing halfway back. He might intercept him tomorrow. But he feared Samuel might have taken a cutoff or tried to avoid the trail, particularly if he believed he was still being pursued.

A few people had been about at White Bird, but none had seen the boys or any suspicious riders. White Bird would have been the most likely area for someone to spot them. Few people would cut across the Camas Prairie, and numerous trails crisscrossed it, making it easy for someone like Samuel who didn't want to be seen—to disappear. But for certain, Samuel would return to Warren's.

Charles climbed out of the Salmon River gorge. The slopes were largely barren and grassy with scattered brush. Elderberry and blackberry thickets choked the draws. Cottonwoods and mountain ash grew in the deeper, watered draws. Pines and firs lined the rim, at first as spotty clumps reaching into the bottoms of some of the north- and west-facing draws, now forming an unbroken forest reaching to the ridge tops. Much like the French Creek trail, the trail wound back and forth along the spine of a ridge, at first crossing empty, grassy slopes and then entering scattered clumps of pines.

Despite his nagging concern for Samuel, Charles paused to gaze back down toward the Salmon, a silver ribbon winking in the sun. *Beautiful country.* Soft morning light cast long shadows from the ridges and filled the side canyons with purple shadows. The pines were a deep, somber blue green. He scanned the ridges from the river upward toward the east. Wrinkled and folded fingers ran from shadowed draws and ascended into the light of the early morning.

All day Charles pushed steadily across the prairie, finally stopping at dusk. While he made some dinner, his thoughts returned to Samuel and the Chinese boy. "Chen." He said his name. He wondered about Samuel. True, Chen and his uncle had probably saved Samuel's life, but Charles recognized that the friendship that had grown between the two boys bridged a gap. Both were in a strange land, and both were trying to fit into a man's world but were not quite there. Samuel treated Chen as an equal. Charles realized that in this regard, Samuel was more a man than he was. Now he could only hope they were coming his direction, returning from Lewiston. He tried not to think the worst, that scum were possibly still pursuing them, desiring only revenge because Samuel had helped someone whom they did not find worthy of helping.

At morning light, Samuel and Chen rode into Lewiston. Samuel had no idea where he was heading, and Chen took the lead. As they rode, people turned to watch.

It was the largest city that Samuel had ever been in. The streets were choked with wagons and buggies. Shops of all kinds lined the streets. Several brick buildings rose two or more floors on either side of the street. There were hotels, saloons, mercantile stores, butchers, liveries, and blacksmith shops. There were even a couple of churches and a school. Samuel felt odd. This was the most civilization he had seen in his entire life.

Several docks ran into the Clearwater River and into the Snake. Huge boats, steam billowing from their stacks, moved on the water. Several were tethered, and men moved rapidly about them, loading or unloading cargo.

Samuel began noticing what seemed to be hundreds of Chinese. He realized he had entered a section of the city where everyone was Chinese. All the shops were Chinese, with brightly colored Chinese signs. The area was like a hundredfold version of Mann's store. Chen greeted several Chinese, asking questions but clearly showing caution. Finally, he entered a shop near one of the wharfs. Samuel waited outside with the horses. Several Chinese gathered around, making him feel increasingly uncomfortable. He guessed that they knew what he was packing. He kept Art's rifle at the ready. If they attacked him, at least one of them was going to die before he did.

At length, a couple of men emerged with Chen, and they removed the bags. Samuel felt an incredible relief. Sometime later, Chen returned, nodding. "All good, Sam." He grinned more than Samuel had ever seen.

Chen visited other shops. He loaded his and Samuel's horses with several bundles of goods.

"We sell back in Warren's," Chen explained.

Samuel was torn between leaving and staying longer. He loved the excitement of the city. He wanted to shop for clothes, despite the fact that he had no money. He wondered where Lilly might be—how surprised she would be to see him. He discarded the thought.

"We can go now," Chen told him.

"I wish I could stay and get a hot bath and new clothes," Samuel replied. But every minute he was away from his father, he was being eaten alive by not being able to let him know that he was okay.

They headed out of Lewiston, figuring on making as many miles as possible before night. Even Chen knew they would be an easy target because of the goods they carried. Only when darkness descended and they had traveled far back out onto the prairie did they stop to camp.

Chapter 52

EARLY MORNING, Samuel and Chen were on the trail again, pushing across the Camas Prairie toward the Salmon River.

"We're making good miles, Chen. Possibly we could make Slate Creek by tonight. Another three days after that and we'll be back at Warren's."

Chen smiled. "I will be happy."

They traveled quickly much of the day. The weather warmed. Grass rippled in waves across the prairie. The early-August heat had turned it to amber and gold. Once Samuel thought he saw a hunting party of Indians on the horizon, a mile or more distant. He could see the purple shadows of the Salmon River gorge growing wider and deeper. Shortly, they would be on the rim.

By late afternoon, the trail began winding down into a deep ravine. Nearing the bottom, they reached a dense thicket of cottonwoods lining a stream.

Samuel's thoughts were on reaching Slate Creek and Bonnie, and he failed to hear the brush snapping as Dudgin and Smith emerged from a brushy draw. Smith had his rifle aimed at Samuel's middle.

Clumsily, Samuel tried to bring up Art's rifle.

"Butt first. Hand it to me, boy." Dudgin snarled. "Buy this with the gold at Lewiston?"

Samuel knew he would be foolish to try anything. He handed the rifle over. Dudgin checked it and then aimed it back at Samuel.

"Figure this is a fair trade for my pistol at the bottom of the river. At least for now." Dudgin laughed. "Have a nice trip, boy?"

"Shy of you almost killing us and losing the gold ... other than that, you might say it was peachy." Samuel's heart was hammering. He remembered Dudgin's words. Frantically he tried to think of something. "How about you?"

"What the hell, Chambers," Dudgin spat. "That supposed to be funny? You didn't lose all the gold."

"Then how about you telling me where it's at so I can go get it?" Samuel pressed the issue.

"Figurin' by the amount of time you been disappeared, you already dropped it off in Lewiston."

"We been there but on other business." He patted the full pack. "I assure you, the gold's in the river."

"You're a lyin' bastard, shirttail," Smith spat. "We been all over this country. Been to Slate Creek. We woulda known. But I'm done wastin' my breath on ya."

Samuel saw hatred burning in the man's eyes.

Dudgin kept Art's rifle jammed in Samuel's ribs while Smith pulled Chen from the mare, driving him into the dirt and tying his hands behind his back.

"Your turn, shirttail," Smith snarled at him. "Or you can get down and make it easy on yourself."

Samuel briefly considered spurring the gray down the trail. He knew he could outrun these men, but he hesitated. They would kill Chen. He dismounted.

Smith trussed Samuel's arms up behind his back, pulling the rope hard, cutting into his wrists. Samuel winced, feeling the bite. He remembered the time before and immediately began struggling to loosen his bonds.

Dudgin ripped off the packs, tore them apart, and pulled out some of the supplies. He cursed and scattered the goods into the brush.

Smith searched Chen, finally pulling some papers from his boot. "What I thought." He opened them. Samuel could see the Chinese writing.

"So you lost the gold, shirttail?" He waved the papers in front of Samuel's nose. "I've seen these before. Chinese gold receipts."

Samuel eyed the papers. "Don't know about those. Never seen 'em."

"Ask your friend," Smith spat. His eyes narrowed. "You're going to wish you'd never climbed out of that river." He kicked Chen. Chen buckled to his knees. "Bastard, Chinaman. That gold belonged to us—to Americans—not to you, you yellow-skinned heathen."

Dudgin leaned into Samuel's face, his breath even worse than it was a year ago. "That was stolen gold. Morton had papers that proved it," he growled. "I warned you what would happen if you messed with them Chinamen, boy."

"Get them back onto their mounts, Ramey. We got some business to attend." Dudgin kept his rifle tight on Samuel.

Samuel frantically tried to think of something. "If you got business with me, I reckon it can be dealt with right here."

"Get movin'." Smith pulled his horse in behind Chen and Samuel, blocking their trail downstream.

Dudgin led out.

Samuel was becoming frantic. He glanced at Chen. Chen's eyes were desperate. Samuel tried to keep calm, tried to think of something. Nothing was coming to him. His throat was dry.

Suddenly he spurred the gray up the side of the trail, nearly unseating himself.

"What the hell, kid," Smith spat. "One more trick like that, and you're coyote bait."

Samuel knew he would soon be coyote bait just the same.

≈

At first light, Charles broke his small camp, and stood briefly studying the expanse of the windswept prairie before him. He swung into the saddle and headed northwest. He had decided if he did not find the boys by the end of the day, he would return to Warren's. This was a big country. They could be anywhere. *Maybe dead.* But Charles felt otherwise. In his mind's eye, he had seen them riding toward him for so long that it was not possible. *They're alive,* he told himself.

The vast Camas Prairie spread before him, its deep grasses rippling in the wind. White clouds were beginning to build in the heat of the day. If a man didn't want to be seen crossing this prairie, he wouldn't be, Charles told himself.

By midafternoon, the trail began winding down into a bowl, dropping into shadowed, tree-covered draws that descended back to the northeast toward the Clearwater. The Snake lay far to the west, its gorge hidden by low rolling hills.

He reached the bottom, studied the trail where it began ascending, and noticed a side canyon with a trickle of water emerging from it. Scuffed horse prints led into it. Alarm washed him. Other hoofprints told the story. He cursed to himself and frantically searched the area. He found some discarded Chinese silk lying behind some shrubs. It had to be Samuel and Chen. They would be packing some goods back to Warren's.

Pulling his rifle, he checked it and then spurred the bay up through the brush lining the broad gully.

No fresh tracks had emerged from the draw, only entered it. Throat dry, Charles pushed the bay forward. He could see a smattering of cottonwoods up ahead. The tracks were evenly spaced, indicating that the four horses he followed were not being pushed. The boys were being led up this draw, away from the main trail for only one reason, he believed.

Samuel and Chen were boxed in between Dudgin and Smith and had no choice but to follow up the creek until they had gone about a mile. Dudgin paused where a ragged cottonwood stood in the draw, its heavy limbs twisting upward. Smith began rigging a loop into the end of his rope, eyeing the limb.

A shock of icy cold flooded Samuel.

Smith casually tossed the rope over the limb.

"Chinaman first," Dudgin sneered. "You can watch what you did for your friend, boy."

"Now, wait a minute, Mr. Dudgin," Samuel pleaded. "He doesn't deserve this. He has a right to the gold. He's American born. Born in California."

Smith hesitated and then continued fixing the rope, placing it about Chen's neck. "He's still a yellow heathen. It warn't his gold anyhow. Even if he was just the mule, he knew what he was doin' by helping those yellow thieves." He tightened the rope.

Chen closed his eyes.

"Stop! If you want gold … I got gold," Samuel blurted. "I got a lot of gold."

Dudgin and Smith paused.

Dudgin eyed him. "I'm listenin', kid."

Samuel glanced at Chen. "The Chinese who were with us, Chen doesn't know … I found their gold still tied to a log."

Chen's face showed disbelief then anger. "How did—"

"Shut up, Chinaboy," Dudgin spat. "Keep talkin'."

"While you were scouting the bank, I found it." Samuel nodded toward Chen. "I buried it without him knowing. I can take you there."

Swallowing hard, Charles eased his horse along the creek, angling up the bank to where he could see ahead. Cutting across the bend of the creek along the bench, he came out to a point where he spotted the men and Samuel below. Chen sat astride a white mare with a rope about his neck. He was out of time. Quietly and quickly, Charles slipped from the bay and scrambled to where he lay prone. One man held a rifle—*Dudgin,* he figured. He was covering Samuel, forcing his son to watch Smith execute his friend. He did not know for certain if they planned to kill Samuel or not. Briefly, he considered calling out, but he thought of Chen. He would die. This was Samuel's friend—Chinese or not. He aimed past his son's head toward Dudgin and took and held his breath. He did not intend simply to wound the man.

≈

Samuel saw a black hole open in Dudgin's chest, accompanied by the report from a rifle. A red spray blew outward from it as Dudgin's rifle fired, slamming a round into the dirt. He pitched forward slowly, eyes fixed on Samuel, disbelieving. He hit with a thud and crumpled onto his side in the dirt, blood flowing from his mouth.

Smith cursed and hit Chen's horse. He jerked back on the rope, snapping Chen's head upward. Frantically, Samuel spurred Spooky forward, and lunged to block Chen's horse.

Another shot whined past, toward Smith.

Smith fell back, releasing the rope, throwing himself clear of his horse, grabbing for his rifle. He returned a wild shot. Cursing loudly, he chambered another round and lifted his rifle toward Samuel.

Chen's mare ducked its head, turned, and bolted, sending Chen crumpling into the dirt, where he lay still. A cry choked in Samuel's throat as Chen lay sprawled, unmoving. The rope must have snapped his neck. Samuel spurred the gray toward Smith, oblivious of the rifle being raised in his direction. Fear glazed the man's eyes as the gray charged into him. He raised his arms to ward off the animal, stumbling, falling backward. The gray clipped him, knocking him down, sending him spinning into the dirt. The horse whirled past.

"Ho, horse!" Samuel hollered. "Ho up!" With his knees, he tried to slow the animal, turn him, but was unable. He gritted his teeth, bracing himself for the bullet that he knew would find his back.

Two more shots rang out. A bullet buzzed past his ear. Desperately, he freed himself from the gray, somehow pulled his leg over, and managed to slip from the saddle, spilling to the ground and rolling onto his shoulder.

He turned to see Smith staggering a few yards away, blood soaking his shoulder. He had leveled his rifle directly at him and held it on him, wavering.

"Bastard, shirttail," he wheezed. "If I'm a dead man, you're coming with—"

His eyes widened, and Samuel heard the hammering hoof beats from an approaching horse. Smith turned and ran, catching and desperately swinging himself back up onto his horse. He kicked the animal viciously and turned it down the creek, heading downhill.

Samuel's father galloped hard toward him on a bay that he didn't recognize.

"He's getting away, Pa." Samuel shouted. He stared in disbelief as Smith rode down the draw toward the canyons beyond.

Charles pulled up, swung down, and put a boot into Dudgin, making certain he was dead. "He won't get far, I surmise. I think the bullet I put in him will stop him." He reached down toward Chen. Chen stirred, gasping, coughing.

Relief washed over Samuel. "Pa" was all he could say when next his father reached him. He began shaking uncontrollably.

"You okay, son?" His father pulled his knife and began cutting his ropes.

Samuel nodded. A burning flooded his eyes, and an incredible ache crushed his chest. He rubbed his wrists as his father went back and helped Chen to sit up.

"You okay, Chen?" Charles inquired.

Chen was stone silent. His eyes blazed with fright and relief. He nodded. Charles cut his bonds and examined the rope burn about his neck.

Samuel suddenly felt sick and stumbled into the shrubs to vomit. His chest felt like it was on fire. His eyes stung, watering. He picked himself up, stumbled to the creek, and splashed water onto himself. He shook his head, trying to clear it. He splashed more and then drank. Chen joined him, coughing, splashing himself with water as well. Finally, Samuel sat back and looked toward his father, who had gathered up the gear and horses.

"Y-you didn't give them much chance, Pa," Samuel stammered. "It may be terrible for me thinking this, but thank God you didn't."

"Not much choice when a snake has done its buzzing and is about to strike, son."

Samuel sat shaking, not wanting to move.

"I'm sorry you saw me kill that man, Samuel. In the war, it was different. I killed men who fought for what they believed in. Dudgin was scum, preying on the rest of us."

"I know, Pa." Samuel nodded. He turned toward Chen. "You know there was no more gold, don't you, Chen? The other gold was lost."

Chen smiled. "At first I thought there was, but you never a good liar."

"God, I wish there had been, Chen." Samuel began shaking again. "I really do."

"We did good, Sam. We got most of it." Chen was silent a moment. "Gold is not worth dying for, Sam. We should have let them have it. Kan Dick and others still be alive."

"I thought about doing that. You know they would have killed us anyway."

Chen nodded. "Probably you are right."

Charles led the stock toward the creek for water.

"We're gonna bury him, aren't we?" inquired Samuel. Although Dudgin and Smith had come to within a breath of murdering Chen and him, it didn't seem right to leave Dudgin lying in the sun. Already flies buzzed about his body. The blood had darkened to almost black. His eyes stared vacantly toward the sky.

"I reckon not. If the sheriff wants to come out here and bury the cuss, he can. I'll file a report when we get back," Charles said. "By the way, what happened to Morton?"

"Figure he's dead. That was Morton's horse that Smith was riding. I hit Smith's horse at the stone hut."

Charles nodded. "Can't say Morton will be much missed."

"Guess he let his hate override his senses," Samuel murmured.

Charles asked, "Think you two can ride?" He swung onto his horse. "Slate Creek is a long ways to go yet. Keep your eyes open. If Smith's still kicking, he won't hesitate to try to pick one of us off."

Samuel had the same thought. "It's not over, is it, Pa?"

"No, son, I'm afraid it's not, and if it's not Smith, it'll be Finney and Culler. We missed the hearing. I'm sure the sheriff has released them."

Samuel thought of them. "They'll keep coming for us until they're dead or we are, won't they?" Samuel almost choked on his words.

His father reached out and steadied him. "There will always be tough times ahead of us, son, but I don't intend for either of those things to happen."

Chapter 53

PAST NIGHTFALL they reached Jon Stromback's ranch.

Samuel could not remember such a fuss. Everyone talked at once. Mrs. Stromback was all over him. The children and Roundup were bouncing around. Only Bonnie seemed a little cool. Samuel knew he should have said something when he was through a few days ago.

Bonnie caught up to him for a moment before dinner.

"I'm sorry, Bonnie," he tried to explain. "As long as we were carrying that gold, we were tempting fate."

"You know Rex is gone," she said softly.

Samuel nodded.

"But you are going home to Iowa." A shadow crossed her face.

"I truly do want to see my ma and my sister and everybody, Bonnie, but my heart isn't in it." He said it quietly so his father could not hear. He had come into the room.

They sat at the Strombacks' large table, having some dinner. Chen remained outside despite Samuel's insistence that he come in. He had a plate of food while sitting on the porch.

Samuel tried to eat, but found himself falling asleep, the world spinning. His father and Stromback carried on a conversation.

"Maybe it would be best to hear all of the news in the morning," Mrs. Stromback observed.

Samuel joined Art at the bunkhouse. "Almost lost your rifle, Art." Samuel handed it to him. "Almost got to use it too. I sure do thank you."

Art nodded. "I'm glad it turned out the way it did."

Samuel invited Chen in, but Chen insisted on staying outside.

"Don't you think of running off on me," Samuel warned. "We go back together."

"I will be okay out here, Sam," Chen insisted. "We go back together. Maybe the ohnee way I stay alive." He bowed.

"He sure can stay in the tack shed, Samuel," Stromback insisted.

Samuel was asleep before Charles turned in.

In the morning, Samuel felt remarkably alive. He had slept so strongly, he remembered no dreams. He was thankful. Most everything lately had been a nightmare.

Breakfast was called. Chen joined him, and Samuel noticed that he stayed close. Chen struggled to eat anything. Mostly, he ate the eggs and cornbread.

Josef could not keep his eyes off Chen.

Mrs. Stromback poured some more strong coffee.

Samuel spent most of breakfast relating his journey. He felt a crushing ache as he tried recounting the Chinese murders. He could not help but see the concern in both Mrs. Stromback's and Bonnie's eyes. The disgust grew on Jon Stromback's and Art's faces. Josef took it all in like a fairytale. His two sisters were in the other room. Nevertheless, Samuel avoided some of the details.

"I should have sent Art with you, Charles, or gone myself," Stromback declared. "I regret that I didn't. I just figured those men had cleared out of the country. I should have known."

"You've done enough, Jon. You loaned us some good mounts. That's all I needed," he said. "But it's not over. Smith may have survived. I didn't want to take the chance of getting dry-gulched by a wounded man, so I let him go."

"Maybe Art and I'll take a journey downriver."

"I can't ask you to do that."

"I'd like to. Make sure the scum is gone."

Charles sat back. "And the two men we had locked up ... I'm assuming they had to be released. Samuel and I weren't around to testify, but I doubt it would have mattered. They go by Reuben Finney and Orwin Culler." Charles proceeded to describe them.

"Hell, you say, Charles," Jon roughly pushed at his plate. "I'll put out the word. They won't show their faces along *this* river."

"I'd be obliged," Charles replied. "Just the same, they're plenty good at keeping their heads down until they got you. Samuel and I will just have to keep a sharp eye. I don't 'spect they have any idea where we are at any rate."

Stromback turned to Samuel. "Here you be, lad, we found Spooky okay. He's ready to take you back to Warren's. We got a few pounds put back on him. Unfortunately, we had to put down Chen's mule. Sure am sorry," he addressed Chen.

Chen's eyes grew frantic. "Ohnee an old mule. Not much good."

Stromback shook his head. "She was too badly crippled and blowed by flies. Maggots everywhere." He took a swallow of coffee.

"We didn't have to bury any of the Chinamen, though. We got there, some other Chinamen were already there. We scared the living daylights out of them until they realized we were tryin' to help." He shook his head, slightly smiling. "They had already buried the dead one. The other one survived."

"Survived?" Samuel almost shouted. "Who?"

Chen's eyes grew big. He stared desperately at Stromback.

"Don't know who. The live Chinaman made it into the cabin. The dead one was near the bluff."

"Kan Dick's alive," Samuel breathed. It had to be Kan Dick. He was near the hut. "He's sort of a doctor, you know."

Chen seemed incredibly happy. "Kan Dick crawl into house."

Stromback raised his eyes. "Anyway, they've got him hid somewhere while he heals up."

Once more, Samuel and his father said good-bye to the Strombacks. Chen waited for them apart from the Stromback family.

"You're taking that white mare, Chen," Samuel explained. "Mr. Stromback is giving her to you."

Chen tried to protest.

"Here, Chen, you are in no position to refuse her," Stromback interjected. "You just take decent care of her, and remember she's not a mule. She likes to be ridden."

Chen bowed. "Thank you, but I will bring her back someday."

"Don't think I need to be shaking your hand, Samuel," Art confided. "For some reason, I expect somehow you'll be back."

Samuel knew better. He touched Bonnie's hand. "Maybe ... someday," he managed.

She peered intently at him, but he could see the pain in her eyes.

They kissed. Samuel didn't want to let her go. He no longer minded if others saw.

He swung into his saddle. She reached up and wedged a small cluster of the yellow roses under it. "For good luck, Samuel. You and your pa have a good trip."

Samuel felt slightly embarrassed with getting flowers from a girl, but no one seemed to notice. He turned Spooky and headed upriver.

Leaving Slate Creek, they made good time. Samuel studied the river more carefully than he had ever before. He noticed where he and Chen had lost hold on the log and almost laughed. A huge boulder sat in the middle of the river. Water piled high over its right shoulder. On either side were smooth chutes of water.

Samuel nodded to Chen, smiling. "The only boulder in the river, and that's where we went flying."

Chen did not smile. "Almost die, Sam."

Charles must have caught the gist of the conversation. "I wouldn't have made it through the first patch of fast water."

Samuel recognized the place where the logs they had sent downriver as decoys had been wedged. He could not bear to look for long at the Chinese stone hut. They paused again to catch the Shearers up on what had taken place. Charles again described Finney and Culler. The Shearers remembered seeing them on the trail last winter, or men who resembled them.

"They were the ones that robbed our sluice," Samuel explained.

The Shearers wanted to know why Samuel had not stopped for help. Samuel tried to explain and ended up nodding at Chen. The Shearers understood.

"Where'd you cross? I'd be afraid of losing that gold," Frederick asked.

Samuel explained how he had taken the ferryboat across, returned it, and swum the river.

"You want a job as a ferryman?" George asked half seriously. "Even I won't cross at night."

At Warren's, Charles turned himself in to Sheriff Sinclair for killing Dudgin. Sinclair quickly declared he would be found in self-defense.

"I'll need to get your statement and Samuel's. Sorry we had to turn those other two loose."

"Figured you would," Charles said. "We'll just need to keep on the watch."

"Judge told them they would be fools to show their faces around here again. Said maybe the next person taking a shot at them wouldn't be a kid needing more target practice." Sinclair nodded at Samuel. "The judge sure got a chuckle out of the jury, though. Especially when he said he wished you had a bit better aim. Everyone cheered."

Samuel did not reply.

"I've never seen two hotter men leavin' a courtroom. To be safe, I had a couple men escort them out of town and all the way to Groff's ferry. Last anyone saw of them was them crossing, at our expense."

"That might help somewhat," Charles said. "I left Dudgin's mount with Jon Stromback, in case you need it for evidence. Didn't figure the county needed to feed a horse. By the way, any word on Ben Morton?"

"Nope," Sinclair said. "Maybe he got the message and took off, although I'm thinking in his case it's more a bit of misguidance."

Samuel interjected, "I think he's dead. When he turned tail at the stone hut, Dudgin shot at him, and I saw him grab at his shoulder. Later on, Smith had his horse."

"That explains why Morton dropped his rifle," Sinclair said. "You want it?" He pulled a rifle from a rack. "One of the fellows that went to the hut found it. Thought I needed it for evidence. Reckon in this case, I never saw it." He thrust it into Samuel's hands. "Go practice." He winked.

Samuel did not like the idea of having someone else's rifle, but he decided that it replaced his father's pistol.

The Chinese received Chen with joy, especially his uncle. A flood of chattering broke out amid smiles and bows. Chen produced the papers and handed them to an elderly Chinese who glanced at them and then waved them over his head to the cheers of those gathered around. The older man studied Samuel while Chen chatted about the events. Their faces went quiet as Chen spoke, but they continued to glance from time to time at Samuel, until Samuel began to feel uncomfortable and felt his face going red.

The older Chinese gentleman approached Samuel and spoke at length to him.

"He say you are a good man, Samuel, and very brave," Chen interpreted. "You are always welcome to the Chinese. You will have a place of honor here."

Samuel felt embarrassed but warm inside. "Chen is a very brave man as well," Samuel managed. "Without him, your gold would have been lost. You must honor him as well."

Chen hesitated in interpreting. Some of the Chinese already understood.

"Tell them, Chen," Samuel insisted. "It was you who put your neck on the line for them. You were willing to go downriver." He smiled to himself, realizing that what he had said was literal.

Seemingly embarrassed, Chen repeated what Samuel had said.

Some of the Chinese added to what he said. They nodded gravely and each in turn, clasped Chen's shoulders and crisply bowed.

The older Chinese turned back toward Samuel, talking to him.

"You must come to celebrate with us now," Chen interpreted and motioned toward the communal dining hall.

Samuel declined. "This is for you, Chen. I need to get back to the cabin with my father. We still have a lot of work to do, but I will see you later."

Chen stopped smiling. Samuel realized he had inadvertently reminded him of his pending departure. His stony expression returned. He nodded and turned with the other Chinese toward the hall.

Charles and Samuel visited Alexander and returned the remaining stock. "If you're around a few days, you can still take a trip for me."

"How much do we still owe?" Charles asked.

"Can't find the ledger at the moment," Scott said. "Come back next summer, we'll see." He eyed Samuel.

Charles shook his head. "We don't need charity."

"None being offered," Scott said, appearing somewhat hurt. "I figure we're square enough."

Hinley could not quite figure out why no one had inquired about the O'Riley. "You certainly showed that the mine has great potential."

"What about Williams?" Charles asked.

"Aye. He did arrive a day or so after you must have left. He came in from Florence. He expressed some interest; however, he wished to talk to Samuel."

Samuel gulped. He had been gone for nearly two weeks.

"He did leave me a ten-dollar eagle and ask that you offer him first right of refusal. Seems he is heading south of the Secesh to examine some silver properties there. He indicates he shall be back through here in a week or two."

Charles muttered, "We aren't waiting around anymore. You know what we want, Ray. You settle it for us."

"Aye, I shall do that."

A feeling of finality sobered Samuel. All their work of over a year had come down to this. A meager gold placer and a quartz mine that no one would look at.

They visited with others, saying their farewells. Ma Reynolds was near tears and got right to the point. "We sure wanted to see you stay in these parts, Samuel. We was a hoping you'd meet that right gal and settle down. We need some new young'uns."

Samuel felt embarrassed. "Thank you. I'll miss you too."

It was true. He would. Families were not staying in Warren's. The easy placers were done. Life as a hardrock miner was nearly unbearable. The long hours of work certainly did not lend themselves to raising a family. He was not surprised to learn the Sauxe family had left and that the Osborns and the Manuels were planning on leaving. He felt a bit better when he learned the latter two families planned to homestead near Slate Creek.

Much later, Samuel wrote a long letter to his mother. He shared all that had happened and said they should be on the trail soon.

Homeward Bound

Chapter 54

THEY HELD ON TO a slight hope that some news would come through on the O'Riley. Charles settled up with people the best he could. Samuel didn't know all to whom they owed money. They had paid Faust. Maybe they still owed Ma Reynolds or Dr. Sears. He tried not to think about it.

Samuel visited Scott. A letter had arrived from his mother. He shook with anticipation of reading what she had to say but would wait for his father.

At the cabin, he finished powdering the ore remaining from the Sheepeater ledge and washed it down. The gold was surprisingly yellow. He felt the old excitement return as he gazed at its shiny brilliance. He poured some mercury into the pan and worked it into the fines, amalgamating the gold until he had a frothy mass. It was a surprising amount. In the morning, he would take it to Mr. Hinley.

Once more, he walked to the Sweet Mary. He studied the hillside. Had there been more water, the placer would have paid well. He was thankful for having done as well as he had. He was tempted to loosen the water into the box but for the first time decided against it. Someone else some other day could.

His father returned for dinner. They read the letter.

Samuel's mother had expected them back by this time and hoped they would not be reading the letter. If they were, the family was okay. They missed grandma. The crops were doing well. But the overall message was clear—come home.

"I just wrote Ma a letter," Samuel explained. "I said we were sorry for not being home, that it was my fault."

"I wrote one as well," Charles confided. "She should be getting them about a week before we get there."

There was not much for dinner, some remaining potatoes, some dried beef, a little corn mush. They would take the leftover mush with them.

Samuel handed his father some coffee. They sat quietly, both thinking about the past days.

"That was a damn fool thing you did, son," Charles said quietly.

Samuel glanced up, slightly taken aback.

"No man's life is worth any amount of gold. You even told me that once." He took a sip of coffee. "It was a damn fool thing—but honorable." He eyed Samuel. "You know, I'm not exactly in favor of those Chinese, never will be, but it was a good thing what you did for them, and I'm proud of you."

Samuel warmed to his father's praise, but he knew how lucky he was to be alive.

"You were a fool, and I've been a fool as well. I should have never taken Finney and Culler lightly last winter. I shouldn't have gone after them, and now that they've spent some time in jail waiting on us, I'm sure they aren't going to easily forget that."

"We're safe here, aren't we?" Samuel was no longer sure. "They were run out of the country, weren't they?"

"I'm guessing we're okay. I don't think they'd try to pull anything where they could be seen. But it only takes a clump of trees or a good rock outcrop, and you'd never see it coming. I didn't say this before, son, because it didn't make sense because Finney and Culler are lazy to the bone, but I think it was those two that hit us here as well."

"Here?" Samuel suddenly felt like he was being watched, being hunted.

"They started seeing gold, and they just kept digging."

"I don't like this feeling, Pa, that at any moment, we might be taking lead." He wondered if they were outside watching the cabin. He wished he had looked around more carefully when he had checked the Sweet Mary.

"We won't be after tonight. We're done. We got your ma and your sister to go back to and Uncle Jake and his family."

They packed what they could carry and stored items they would leave behind.

"Well, isn't this about the moment that you're supposed to tell me about finding a whole passel of gold while I was out and about?" Charles asked. "You did that last October."

"Nope, I didn't try. I figured it was someone else's turn."

Early morning, they rode into Warren's, leading Molly, heavily packed, heading out. They stopped by Hinley's. Samuel had brought the arrow.

Hinley was in the back, as usual, working on samples. He came out. "I surmise you are leaving?"

"We are. Any news?" Charles asked.

"No, sir, nothing new."

Charles's jaw tightened. "I still got a few loose ends I could use some help with."

"Would you like some coffee?" Hinley had already reached for the cups.

"Yes, thanks." They pulled up some stools.

"Since Williams didn't come through, do you want to buy out our quartz ledge? Maybe find a buyer after we've gone?"

"If you decide to let me in on the one you have not filed on, I should be interested, but not on the O'Riley." He eyed Samuel. "I respect your efforts, Samuel. You did everything right, but for an investment, it is still not possible for me." Hinley picked up some papers. "These are all placers and quartz ledges for sale. I am not purchasing claims, nor should I think I ever shall be. I shall have no trouble being your agent and attempt for a while to find you a buyer. However, I do not see many buyers these days."

Hinley sighed. "I have always had great hopes for Warren's camp. I still believe there is a future here; however of recent, I cannot say the prospects are as strong."

Samuel realized that this was the first time Hinley had ever expressed anything less than optimism. It distressed Samuel, and he sat quietly not knowing what to say before he remembered the Sheepeater gold. He handed Hinley the canister with the amalgam. "Here's the last of my gold, I didn't have time to retort it."

Hinley glanced into the canister. "I could show you a rough way for determining the content if you had time, but if not, I would guess you have about fifteen dollars' worth."

"That is more than fair by me," Samuel had figured three hundred pounds of Sheepeater ore could run between twelve and eighteen dollars.

"These will spend better where you are going." Hinley laid out three five-dollar gold pieces. "And these eagles are for your assistance for which I have never paid you." He tossed down two ten-dollar eagles.

Samuel shook his head. "I never expected any pay, Mr. Hinley. I learned far more than what I could have ever paid you." He slid the eagles back. "I'm mighty obliged, and I appreciate it, but I can't accept."

"Then look at it in this fashion," Hinley said. "I have always offered you a grubstake. The next ledge you find, you shall pay me back, plus five dollars. Is that fair?"

Samuel looked away a moment. "We're leaving, Mr. Hinley—for real. *Today*. I won't be doing any lookin' for any more gold—ever." He felt himself choke slightly as he said the words. Prospecting was in his blood. Given a choice of ranching or prospecting, he now knew what he would pick.

Hinley was quiet. "Samuel, I insist. Look at it as an investment in your future. You have struck me as a fine young man, and I should like to see you have a bright future."

Hinley's eyes told Samuel there was something else.

"Okay," Samuel said quietly. "We thank you kindly." He gathered up the coins. "One more favor, though?" Samuel asked, handing Hinley the Sheepeater arrow. "Hang this up where folks can see it."

Hinley frowned and took the arrow.

"I can't explain what I'm thinking. Just … if someone asks about it—no, if they recognize it—tell them about me. Write me a letter or something."

Hinley's brow deepened as he examined the arrow. "This is a Sheepeater arrow. You can decipher this by the three segments. This is a strange acquisition, Samuel. They roam quite a distance east of here."

"That's what I've been told."

Hinley studied it quietly. "Blazes, Samuel. That is where you discovered the rich ledge, is it not?"

Samuel had taken a chance and knew it. "Please promise me you won't tell anyone."

Hinley slowly shook his head. "Look, Samuel, I have shared with you a dozen times—I do the assays. That shall be what folks pay me for. I shall not be telling them about your ledge." Hinley balanced the arrow on a shelf where it was visible. "It is just as well. You are correct about that country. It would be nigh impossible to haul ore out of there."

They headed to Mann's store. Earlier Samuel had ordered a book from Scott to give to Chen. He hoped Chen would not be on the trail peddling vegetables. It would hurt not being able to give him the book and say good-bye.

The Chinese girl people called Polly stood outside Hong King's saloon. "Hello, Polly." Samuel waved. She quickly scurried inside.

"That's the girl I told you about, Pa."

"Looks strange, seeing a Chinese girl."

They stepped into Mann's store. Samuel was relieved to see both Chen and his uncle.

"I'm leaving, Chen. I came to say good-bye."

Chen glanced down. "I will miss you, Samuel."

Samuel noticed the careful pronunciation of his name.

"Don't worry about me. That Chinese girl is right across the street, maybe you can be friends with her now."

Chen grew flustered. "Not a joke, Samuel."

"I know. She's private property." Samuel softened. "Maybe more Chinese women will come. Maybe things are changing back in China."

"Maybe more women," Chen agreed. "But things are worse in China. More Chinese come to the land of the golden mountain. They don't go home."

"Then maybe you should plan on living in America."

"Why should Chen stay?" He gazed past Samuel, averting his eyes. "My friend goes," he said quietly.

Samuel swallowed hard. Chen had never suggested his personal feelings. They had shared a friendship, mostly because it had been necessary. They had never spoken of it. Samuel could almost not speak. "Things have a way, Chen. I have an obligation ... maybe someday ... I will see my friend again." He touched Chen's shoulder.

Chen's eyes brightened. "I will hope so, Samuel. We will sell vegetables. I will learn more about Ahmelicah."

Samuel pressed his finger to his lips, looked to see that his father could not hear. He felt bad about suggesting something which was untrue. He handed Chen the book. "You should have this. Practice."

Chen's eyes glowed more brightly. "Thank you, Samuel." He pressed it to his chest. It was a history of America.

Quickly Chen stepped away. He spoke to Sing Mann, who disappeared to the back of the store. They handed Samuel a dragon figurine.

"To keep with the snake," Chen said.

Samuel thanked them.

"We best be on our way, son," Charles said.

Mann shook his head. "Not go yet. He get vegebows."

Charles laughed. "We're good with what we have. Our old mule can't haul much else, anyhow."

"No, no," Mann insisted. "You take more good Chinese food."

Mann busied himself with wrapping a few items and bundling them up.

Chen came back in the company of a couple of elderly Chinese.

"We loaded some things for you on your mule," Chen explained, nearly out of breath.

Charles peered at him, questioningly. "Then we don't need any of this." He pointed at what Mann was wrapping.

"A littoh." Mann finished and handed the package to Samuel.

Chen said, "These men came to say thank you again, Samuel, and to say good-bye."

Samuel recognized them as the elders. He accepted their polite bows and was surprised when they returned his handshake. They chattered to him and his father.

"You are always welcome, they say. You and your father should come back. You have a place of honor with us."

Charles responded, "Tell them thank you, Chen. Tell them we are honored. If they want to come to Iowa, they are welcome with us. They can grow good crops in Iowa as well."

Chen interpreted and then shook his head. "No gold." The men laughed politely and bowed again.

Samuel swung into his saddle and steadied Spooky while he shook hands with Chen. "Good-bye. Find a big nugget so you can go home to China."

Chen tried to smile and walked with him a few steps down the street and then stood silently. He briefly waved.

Samuel tried to fix the image of his friend in his mind so he would never forget. A lump had risen in his throat, and his eyes misted.

Other people of Washington had come to the street. Samuel realized many people came and left Warren's camp. Rarely did anyone seem to notice. Today they did. They came and shook hands—wished them well. But the more steps he took away from Warren's, the more he realized, *I belong here, not in Iowa.*

They rode in silence, retracing their steps along the route out, stopping to say farewell at Fred Burgdorf's. Samuel had intended to go swimming in the hot springs, but now he only wanted to move on—to put miles between him and his memories. They had a cup of coffee and slice of pie. Samuel almost felt some of his spirits lift. He grew angry with himself. He was going home. He would finally see his mother, his sister, and Uncle Jake and his family.

They camped that night just beyond Burgdorf's. On another day, they might have stayed at Burgdorf's. Now they would be lucky to get back to Iowa with the small amount of money they had, and most of it was really supposed to be Samuel's, given to him by Mr. Hinley.

"It will be good to get back to your ma, don't you think, Samuel?" Charles had sensed what Samuel's silence meant.

"Yes, it will be good." Samuel tried to sound happy.

"Don't take it too hard, son," Charles continued. "We did our best. We make better farmers, anyhow. We'll get a crop going next summer; we'll be sitting pretty."

"I 'spect you're right, Pa." The thought of farming felt like stone to Samuel. He could not see himself a farmer any longer—*A rancher, maybe.* But that thought made things even worse. He found himself thinking of Bonnie.

He unrolled his blankets next to the fire and began pulling off his boots. "Think we'll be all right tonight, Pa, or do you think Finney and Culler might still be wanting our hides?"

"I was trying not to think of them." His father threw another branch on the fire and rose. "I'll sleep a bit over this way and keep watch awhile. That should be good enough."

Samuel suddenly felt very tired. He was physically and mentally exhausted. The two men could still very well be out there. He no longer cared, and he slept.

Chapter 55

THE MORNING LIGHT and twittering birds woke Samuel. He sat up, scared. He searched for his father. He was awake, stirring the fire, making coffee.

"I let you sleep, Samuel." He poured the coffee. "I thought you needed it."

"Thanks." He took the hot cup. "What about you?"

He shrugged. Samuel figured he had been awake all night.

His father threw some bacon into a skillet. "We'll plan on something more decent at the Shearers'," he explained when he saw Samuel watching.

They rode out, keeping alert, their rifles handy. They passed no one. Again, no one was at the freight landing. Samuel found it strange. He began wishing they would meet someone, someone they could talk to.

As they topped the Salmon gorge, Samuel paused to gaze at the mountains unfolding beyond and at the canyon shadows. He shivered at the sheer drop from the trail. He had been over it several times. He never grew comfortable.

They began working their way down the face and across the long traverses. Samuel remembered where he had encountered the pack train on their first trip in and shivered. He glanced over the edge to see if he could spot the mule carcass. It was still there.

"It'll be good to visit the Shearers again, don't you think, Pa?" Samuel wondered how he would be able to say good-bye to them as well.

Charles said, "Might spend the night there—"

A bird squawked and launched itself into the air from a pine near an outcrop.

"Get cover," Charles hissed. "They're here!"

Samuel felt Spooky shudder and stumble at the same time he heard the crack from the rifle. He saw the puff of smoke from the ridge above the draw as he flew from his saddle. *Spooky's hit!* Oddly, he remembered his father telling him if you wanted to stop a man, you stopped his horse.

Samuel hit hard, the air smashed from him. His rifle flew. Pain shot through his left shoulder. He tumbled, rolling downhill, slamming into the rocks, and a bright light exploded in his head.

Light slowly found its way into Samuel's senses. He woke, finding himself staring up at the blue sky, numb, trying to remember where he was and how long he had been out. He heard gunfire. Blood covered him. His shoulder was in agonizing pain. He tried to clear his senses. His head throbbed. Carefully, blood pounding in his temple, he turned to look toward the sound.

"Give it up, Chambers."

Samuel recognized Culler's voice.

"Your kid's dead. We got what we wanted. You can walk out of here alive."

Samuel checked himself to be sure he was not dead. He hurt like blazes. He figured he was alive, but barely. He tried to move. Painfully, he turned his body and looked downward. He was in a narrow ravine, far below the trail. Below him were sheer rocks. A few more feet and he would have tumbled to his death.

Samuel tried to move again. Dizziness wracked him. *Might as well be dead.*

An occasional shot sounded from above him. He tried to see his father. He could tell he was holed up in a cut. Samuel could see he had one of the men pinned down—*Finney,* he suspected. He turned his head to watch for Culler but couldn't see him. Then a puff of smoke showed on a knoll above his father, followed by the rifle crack. For the moment, his father was safe, and if Finney moved, his father could kill him. He saw movement on the ridge. His heart raced. Culler was trying to work his way to where he could get a clear shot.

His father fired toward Culler, causing him to duck, but it was a matter of time. One of them would eventually get into a clear position and kill his father. He could not keep them both occupied.

Frantically, Samuel wrestled himself up. They were no longer watching for him. He dragged himself through the weeds back upward toward the trail. He had to find his rifle. He saw Spooky's motionless form. He bit his lip, anger flooding him. He hauled himself upward. He figured that his shoulder was not broken, or he would not be able to move. It just hurt. His head throbbed worse.

He saw the glint of sunlight off his rifle. If Culler looked down his way, he would see him. Samuel had to risk it. He waited until his father fired again in Culler's direction, and he saw Culler duck. He lurched forward, grabbed his rifle, and dragged himself into the shrubs above the trail. He could no longer see his father or Finney. The occasional shouts and gunfire told him that his father was still alive.

Scrambling, every step wracking his body with pain, Samuel hauled himself up the slope. If he could get a bead on Culler, it would be over. He dragged himself toward the man. He didn't have the strength to crawl much higher. He gritted his teeth and lurched upward onto the knoll. Desperation flooded Samuel. Culler was still well out of sight, cut off by the descending knoll and rocks above him.

Culler hollered down again. "It's over, Chambers. Go now, you can live. I know you got a wife and daughter. Go home to them. Tell them how you got your son killed." He laughed and fired another round.

Samuel saw his father scramble backward, tripping. In a few more yards, Culler would have an unobstructed shot. *You bastard,* Samuel thought. *Come this side of the rocks so I got a shot at you.*

He brushed at the sweat in his eyes. His hand came away bloody. It was not sweat. He felt his heart hammering strangely, and a wave of dizziness swept him.

He pulled himself up farther; he could see Culler crouching, hiding. *Come on, Culler; come down where you can get a shot at my pa, you bastard. Where I can get you.*

But Samuel knew the moment Culler was in his sights, his father would be in Culler's. Hands sweaty, he checked the rifle, hoping it had not been damaged.

Culler moved, slid down below the rocks, and brought his rifle up.

Heart pounding, Samuel took careful aim, hearing Sheriff Sinclair's words—"a kid that needed more target practice." Shaking, he held his breath. He had no more time. He aimed at Culler, his full body in his sights. He squeezed the trigger, the same moment his foot slipped. The explosion rocked him, and his shot went wide.

"What the—" Culler whipped his rifle toward Samuel.

Frantically, Samuel chambered another round, bracing himself for the impact of a coming bullet. He ignored the overwhelming fear flooding him. He felt an inexplicable calm, and the buzz of a bullet burned past as he heard the rifle's report.

He had Culler in his sights, squeezed the trigger, heard the explosion, and felt the rifle butt slam his shoulder. Culler pitched forward, sliding downward and then tumbling, leaving a bloody trail staining the grass like a shot deer.

Other shots echoed from below. Samuel struggled up to see, fearing that Finney had jumped his father. Instead, Finney sat, slumped. His father kicked away the man's rifle. Samuel guessed Finney had run at his father the moment he had shot at Culler.

Painfully, Samuel sidestepped downward, trying to keep on his feet. He reached the trail and walked past Spooky, the animal's blood staining the earth.

Cocking his rifle, Samuel walked up to Finney. "You bastard," Samuel breathed. He raised the rifle. Finney was looking at him, eyes frantic, blood soaking the front of his shirt. He raised one arm in front of his face.

"Please—"

"Son—"

Finney was dead or soon would be, Samuel realized. He lowered his rifle and sagged down onto the trail, shaking, watching the man who wanted him dead. Fear flooded the man's eyes. *He's afraid of dying,* thought Samuel. Finney coughed. Clots of blood came up. He slumped over and then rolled, eyes staring upward. Samuel watched Finney's chest rise and fall. He began struggling; his chest wheezed up rapidly and then slowly relaxed. His eyes glazed, now sightless.

Charles kneeled next to Samuel and examined him. "How bad you busted up, son?"

"Bad, Pa," Samuel managed.

His father helped him lie back and got him some water. "Got yourself a nasty cut." He ripped cloth and bandaged Samuel's head. "Take it easy. It's a few miles to the Shearers'." He brought up Buster, hoisted Samuel up, and swung up behind him, holding him in the saddle.

Samuel could tell that his father was pushing Buster hard. He was worried. It might be the old horse's last trip.

He did not remember much, but he knew they had arrived at the Shearers' when he heard Mrs. Shearer's voice and he felt himself being lifted down.

Chapter 56

SAMUEL WOKE SHORTLY AFTER being carried into the Shearers' home. It all came to him, and he began shaking uncontrollably. Tears streamed from his eyes, but he made no sound. He remembered Spooky, his horse that brought him here and would have taken him home. He remembered his father trapped, unable to move, desperately defending himself, waiting for death. He remembered Culler in his sights and pulling the trigger. He remembered the man falling, tumbling, the red streak of blood in the grass. He had killed the man.

His father stood inside the doorway. Samuel didn't remember him coming in.

"You going to be okay, son?"

He tried to see him, his eyes blurry. "I killed a man, Pa."

"I'm sorry it had to be. For that, I will never forgive myself."

Samuel looked up, confused.

"You should not have had to go through that. You should have had a chance to grow up, you and your sister, on the farm, never having seen anything like this."

"But he's really dead."

"And you would have been, and so would have I, had you not killed him." His father sat, eyes tired looking. "The good Lord knows each man has to protect his own life and those of the people he loves. Sometimes it becomes necessary to kill a man. You did what had to be done."

Samuel knew he had been given no choice, but it gave him little solace. They were leaving, and still it had come to this.

After two days in bed, Samuel was up and near ready to go. His shoulder remained sore, but his loss of blood had been much worse.

It was not easy saying good-bye. Samuel noticed it was more difficult on his father. His father and George had been swapping stories for a good two days and were still at it. The two men had gone back, found Molly, and retrieved the gear. They buried Finney and Culler and had dragged Spooky into the ravine. This time, no one returned to Warren's, but instead, they sent word to the sheriff.

"We're heading out, Samuel. I figure they owe you at least two good horses for Spooky. And, if you want, another rifle."

Samuel didn't want the rifle. "Sell it to Mr. Shearer if he wants it, or someone else. We can use the money to get home on. Sell him one of the horses too." Samuel didn't want either Finney's or Culler's horse but needed one for returning to Iowa.

"You sure?" his father asked.

George had overheard. "I'll take the rifle." He dug in his pockets and handed an eagle to Charles. "And I think I'll swap Samuel a better mount than either of the two you brought in."

"That's too much," Charles replied. George shook his head.

Back on the trail, Samuel felt a strange sense of relief. For the first time in many months, he felt like he was no longer being hunted. He studied all the familiar sights: the cabin where he and his father had wintered, the narrows where Dudgin and Smith had first jumped them, the Indian hot springs, and Berg's bar, where they had met Hallelujah and Pete. But as they approached the junction of the Little Salmon and Groff's ferry, Samuel slowed up.

"You okay?" his father asked.

"Okay," he replied. "I just been thinking."

They crossed at Groff's. Jason Weston was still the operator, and he talked about Samuel's decoy trip up the trail. Samuel tried to forget. He just watched the deep green waters of the Salmon River sliding by. He wondered if it was the last time he would see this mighty river and the people who lived here. *The River of No Return,* he thought, ironically.

They rode back upstream toward the Little Salmon and about a half mile beyond before Samuel stopped. He could ride no farther.

His father sat his horse and turned, studying him.

"Pa—" he began.

His father raised his hand. "I've been waiting on *you,*" he said simply. "You best be on your way."

"Pa, I-I'm sorry." A terrible weight lifted.

"Don't be sorry, Samuel. You don't go now, she might be spoke for. Your ma will understand."

"I-I'll come see you someday. I sure will." Samuel managed.

His father nodded. "I reckon you will."

Samuel reached out to shake his father's hand. "Thanks, Pa."

"Samuel?"

He looked back at his father.

"Remember when I said this country don't much care how old you are whether or not you're a man?" his father addressed him quietly. "Well, I reckon that hasn't changed. The country still don't care. But I reckon what you've been through and what you've done these past few days, what people have seen from you, speaks pretty loud who you are."

Samuel felt warmth wash through him and, similarly, a deep sorrow. He was parting ways with his father, something he would never have imagined he could do. And he was parting ways with his family. He wondered when he would return to Iowa to see them, if ever. He knew in his heart Bonnie would have him. This canyon country was about to become his home. He would raise his own family here. A great ache welled within his throat, but a burning pride also welled within.

"I reckon I better be off" was all he could muster.

Chapter 57

WHEN CHARLES REACHED the spot above Thomas Pollock's, the one he had seen on the way into Warren's camp over a year ago, he paused. Carefully, he surveyed the valley. It was as he remembered, maybe better. It had good grass, good water, and protection from the wind. A wide bench above the river would make a fine cabin site. He laid out his claim markers.

The next couple of days he spent clearing the cabin site. He shot a doe for fresh meat for when Samuel returned. He guessed he would be back any day, but he could not help wonder if he would not.

He had the coffeepot on, boiling water, roasting some venison when he heard the horse approaching. He knew it was Samuel.

"Pa, is that you?"

Charles looked up to see his son grinning from ear to ear.

"I-it can't be, Pa," Samuel stammered. "How? I didn't figure on catching you until almost to Fort Boise." He swung down from his mount.

Charles stood and embraced his son. "Glad you could make it in time for dinner."

"What's up? What you still doing here?" Samuel's brow knotted.

"Tell me first—what'd she say?"

Samuel flopped down on the grass. "You know what she said, Pa."

"I reckon I do." He reached and shook his son's hand. "Congratulations. When's the big day?"

"We figure sometime next summer." Samuel beamed.

"Did you tell Bonnie that you're more a miner than a rancher?"

Samuel nodded. "She's good with that. Figures we can always visit the ranch and work there some in the winter."

"How about visiting this one?"

Samuel glanced around. *"This one?"*

"I figure we can pretty much have the cabin laid out and some of the logs cut before we should leave for Iowa."

"We're staying? I can't believe it, Pa," Samuel exclaimed. "I figured I'd ride on back to Iowa and say my farewells then come on back here. But I was real afraid I'd get to Iowa and not be able to come back—that I wouldn't be able to leave you and Ma."

"Reckon you won't have to worry about that part now."

"Figure we can make it back here by June, in time for my wedding?"

"Before that. Soon as the snow is gone over Council Summit."

Samuel pushed his fingers through his hair, eyes raised wide, biting his lip. "How we going to manage that?"

"I'm figuring on loading the stock onto that new railroad, whisking everyone out to Ogden, and taking the trail up from there. We'd get here several weeks earlier than we did last year."

Samuel frowned. "We can't afford that."

"You never checked those vegetables the Chinese sent with you."

Samuel searched for one of the Chinese packs, lifted it, and laughed. "Gotta be a couple extra pounds. It's gold, ain't it?"

"Yep. Guess the Chinese wanted you back as well." Charles poured a cup of coffee and handed it to Samuel.

They clinked their tin cups together and offered a silent salute toward Slate Creek and then toward Warren's. The sun still lit the highest peaks. The Salmon gorge was lost in purple shadows.

"We aren't in as much a hurry now, son. Ma knows we're coming. Might as well get some work done. As long as we get out of here before the first snow, we'll be good."

Samuel shook his head. He was home.